Love's

Celia tried to ignore Colin Campbell's manly presence, the pressure of his enveloping hand, but she couldn't. She could only feel her own quickening pulse as he leaned down toward her until his mouth was just a breath away.

She tried to smile. She wanted to make some sharp remark. To tell him where he fell short of courtesy's requirements, but his face was so close to hers and his sculpted lips were so attractive, so full, so inviting.

His one hand was pressing hers against her thigh, but suddenly he lifted her chin until she was looking into his eyes. The hunger she found there frightened her, yet somehow drew her on.

Responding to her soft moan, Colin pulled her to him until her lips touched his own.

"Kiss me," he commanded. . . .

The Thistle and the Rose

by

May McGoldrick

A TOPAZ BOOK

TOPAZ
Published by the Penguin Group
Penguin Books USA Inc., 375 Hudson Street,
New York, New York 10014, U.S.A.
Penguin Books Ltd, 27 Wrights Lane,
London W8 5TZ, England
Penguin Books Australia Ltd, Ringwood,
Victoria, Australia
Penguin Books Canada Ltd, 10 Alcorn Avenue,
Toronto, Ontario, Canada M4V 3B2
Penguin Books (N.Z.) Ltd, 182–190 Wairau Road,
Auckland 10, New Zealand

Penguin Books Ltd, Registered Offices:
Harmondsworth, Middlesex, England

First published by Topaz, an imprint of Dutton Signet,
a division of Penguin Books USA Inc.

First Printing, September, 1995
10 9 8 7 6 5 4 3 2

For Rosemary and George

Prologue

The fog and rain, mixed with the smoke of the English cannons, enshrouded the low fields at Flodden with a gray cover no man could see through, but James IV knew that his moment of destiny was at hand.

Rallying his Scottish troops with the war cry of his Stuart ancestors, the King wheeled his white stallion, swept the fifteen-foot spear from the hand of his page, and charged down the hill into the ranks of the English infantry.

For four hours the blood flowed onto the slippery hillsides, but the long Scottish spear was no match in close combat with the eight-foot English halberd, that grotesque crossbreed of spear and ax.

Before the gloom of day gave way to the darker gloom of night, ten thousand of Scotland's finest men lay dead in the muck, stripped of their armor and their dreams of a new Scotland. The northerners' camp followers—women, boys, clerics, and servants—were also dead and plundered, their throats cut by English border troops under the merciless Lord Danvers.

King James's son Alexander, the Archbishop of St. Andrew's; two bishops; two abbots; and twenty-six of Scotland's great earls and lords were hacked to death on that bloody day—Scotland's nobility annihilated in a single stroke.

And James lay naked with the rest, his red beard matted around the broken shaft of the arrow that had spilled the lifeblood of a king.

There would be no one left to protect the loved ones to the north; the warriors were virtually gone. And the English knew it.

To the victors belong the spoils.

The Thistle
and the
Rose

Chapter 1

The Devil of Danvers had brought hell to her door.

Celia knew from experience that the fire now raging in the rear sections of the oak and plaster manor house would soon engulf the entire structure. It was clear that the English marauders were trying to force the inhabitants of the late Caithness laird's new hall out the great oaken doors that had been barred in defense. This night raid was to be a bloody one.

Instead of wasting their powder blasting the entryway or wasting their time preparing a battering ram, the demons had piled hay from the nearby fields against the back of the building and laid their torches to it. This was a plan that Danvers had used all across Scotland— destruction of the great houses and slaughter of the innocents.

Celia peered through the notch in the upstairs shutter and saw the troop of horsemen waiting for the manor folk to begin pouring out. Some had dismounted, and the torches they carried flared as they raced to and from the man who clearly was directing the assault. Even from this distance Celia could see that he was a giant, and she could almost see his pig eyes sparkling with pleasure at this sight he had engineered.

Celia shuddered. She knew this man. Lord Danvers, the Scourge of Scotland.

But there was no time for these thoughts. Celia knew

he would slaughter the entire household. Since the King's destruction at Flodden Field, the man's name had struck terror into the hearts of mothers across Scotland.

He was the murderer of children.

But he would never get her little Kit, Celia vowed, not as long as she had life in her body. She turned to look at the wet nurse Ellen, who stood in the corner with the baby in her arms.

At that moment the wiry little priest scrambled into the bedroom, sword in hand. His face was smudged with soot.

"You're right," he shouted. "There are only a half dozen or so behind the house. The clooty-footed satan that's running these demons knows no one will be foolish enough to try going out through the fire."

"Then, by God, Father William, we will!" Celia shouted back. "Where is Edmund?"

The roar of the fire was deafening now, but the priest heard her.

"At the base of the stairwell," he shouted in her ear as she swept past him.

Celia took Kit from Ellen's arms and looked into her face. There was terror in her eyes, but Celia knew she would hold up.

"Ellen, take only the big satchel and stay in front of Father William. William Dunbar's not just a poet; he's a fighter, too." She half smiled and Ellen nodded. She would do as she was told.

Celia looked tenderly into the folds of the soft bunting that Kit was wrapped in. She felt a pain in her heart at the thought that anyone might hurt him, that he might not grow up to see the wonders this life has to offer. Celia held him close to her and smelled the good baby scent.

Looking into his face once again, Celia thought that Kit's gray eyes matched those of his father. He looked at her trustingly. She knew her little soldier would not even cry. The baby moved his mouth as if to coo, but Celia could not hear it. Father William tugged at her sleeve. They had to go now.

Down the stairs the small group ran. The smoke was thick below, and the pandemonium of terrified servants was at a fevered pitch. Some were fighting to unbar the great oaken doors, while others were fighting to keep the door closed.

Celia looked about her at the chaos of the scene. Earlier in the day, Caithness Hall had been the model of order and taste. It would never be that way again.

What a waste, she thought. What a crime.

The laird of Caithness Hall had died with his king, like so many others. She knew these people would not listen to her. She was, after all, half English. These people had no one to command them. This undefended manor house was like so many in Scotland; Celia knew the people of Caithness Hall were doomed.

Celia saw Edmund, her uncle, immediately, in spite of the chaos. The great warrior, long sword in hand, pushed his strong, middle-aged body through the crowd, and Celia pointed to the rear of the house. Edmund's eyes widened with surprise, but without hesitation he turned and pushed a path clear for his niece and her companions into the Great Hall.

The wall at the rear of the hall was a mass of flames. Celia could see by the extent of the flames above that the ceiling at the rear could fall at any moment. When Edmund shot a glance back at Celia, she pointed to the study door ahead and to the left.

Edmund led them along the left wall to the study door, kicked it in, and entered. The others followed through the falling embers. As Father William slipped through the door after the others, a huge crash could be heard from the Great Hall. This room was also ablaze, but the manor house was collapsing around them.

Celia handed the baby to Ellen and pulled a sword down from the wall by the fireplace.

She turned, coughing, and shouted to her uncle, "Unbar the shutter, Edmund. We go out here!"

Edmund could not help but smile with affection at this bonny lass who commanded like a general. Her black eyes flashed with anticipation of the battle that lay outside that window. He could see the frown of concentration that furrowed her brow; she was ready for anything that lay ahead. She was a fighter with brains. In the years he had been with her, since his sister died, Edmund had seen her grow in the company of her father's men—rough men, sailors and warriors. Edmund had taught her all he knew about fighting, and he'd seen several men pay dearly for misjudging the strength contained in that slender, feminine body. And her skills in combat were a secret no man would ever imagine in a woman.

As the old warrior pulled the bar from the window, the oak shutter swung inward with great force, and Edmund felt the rush of night air into the room. The marauding soldiers must have pulled open the outer shutter earlier, he thought. Edmund wondered why they hadn't smashed through with the halberds. Orders were to torch the place, most likely.

With the rush of air, the manuscripts in the study flamed up in a surge of heat. Edmund leapt through the window, with Celia close behind.

As Father William and Edmund helped Ellen and the baby through the fiery window casing, Celia saw that the stables beyond the formal garden were still in darkness. The raiders had not yet turned their attention to the Caithness livestock.

From the corner of her eye, Celia saw them. Five soldiers were running toward them. She could smell them coming before she even knew how many there were. She threw off the heavy cloak draped over her shoulders.

The light armor covering her upper body flashed in the light of the burning building.

As they came, she saw the wild gleam of blood lust in the eyes of the first one. He was holding a sword in his left hand. His eyes settled for a leering moment on the prize before him, but then his gaze swept past her to where Edmund was helping Ellen.

It was a fatal mistake. From her left side, Celia swung her sword at the helmeted head and struck the soldier below the ear. As he dropped to the ground beside her, she spun and swung the sword again at one of the two raiders that were now upon them.

The one on the left deflected her blow with his halberd, but Celia now was inside the lethal range of the weapon. Spinning again, she chopped the marauder's right leg at the knee, driving him into the other soldier as Edmund swept over them with upraised sword. With two quick strokes, the knight finished the fallen warriors as Celia turned to face their next adversary.

In an instant Edmund stood beside her, cloak in one hand. When the last two came close enough, the knight lunged with the quickness of a man half his age, engulfing with his thick cloak the spear and axehead of the halberd. Grabbing the shaft with his other hand, Edmund lifted the soldier holding on to it and slammed him into the burning wall of the house.

The last soldier paused in momentary amazement as the aging warrior, swinging the now freed weapon like a club, launched a blow at his head, sending him sprawling into the Promised Land.

Celia turned and motioned to Ellen and Father William. Together, they all ran toward the stables. Edmund stopped at the gate, and as Celia and the others entered the walled enclosure, two soldiers leapt in front of the group. The two grinned like idiots.

"Look!" said one. "Women and a priest!"

"And if I'm not mistaken," responded the other, "there's a baby in that one's arms."

"If it's a boy," said the first, "that'll mean extra reward for the little tike's carcass! Lord Danvers is promising extra for the boys, you know."

The second held out a hand to Ellen. "Give him up to me, you filthy Scot whore. He's bound to meet his Maker."

The soldier's hand dropped useless in the dirt, but he wouldn't have much time to miss it in this life.

Father William followed his short sword stroke with a thrust under the chin, lifting the soldier onto his toes before letting him sink lifeless to the ground.

"Don't be referring to the Maker in such casual terms, you mangy cur," he snapped at the slumping figure. He turned to see Celia pulling her blade from the dying body of the other soldier.

In a matter of minutes four horses galloped from the enclosure. Celia paused only for a moment at the gate while Edmund swung easily into his saddle. The sound of screams could be heard coming from the manor house. Celia looked back only once at the flames rising high above Caithness Hall.

As she rode into the darkness, Celia wondered where they would find safety. Where in Scotland could a baby boy be safe?

Chapter 2

The King has commanded this action, so it is my duty to obey. But I watch Lord Danvers, and I think he is mad. He sits on his black charger, watching the men set fire to the manor house. It is as he directed, and he watches with pleasure. But as the folk pour from the front of this place, this Caithness Hall, he is clearly looking for someone. We all know that he will pay bounties for any babies, alive or dead, that we bring to him, and some of the others are butchering innocent Scottish children now whenever they find them. Calmly, he smiles while the officers pay. But here, it is no baby he is looking for, and the screams of those he ... questions ...

No thoughts of this. I must obey ... I must obey ... the King's command.

Scotland's Western Isles; March, 1514

In the light of the full moon Kildalton Castle gleamed like a diamond over the Firth of Lorn. The wind was now whipping the western sea into a surging demon, and the waves crashed with a devil's rage against the rugged cliffs upon which the Campbell fortress perched.

No one could have expected the small sailing vessel that was scudding across the firth's surface. But it was, without question, being handled by a master.

At the small boat's helm, a huge man wearing light armor and a cloak shouted orders to the sailor who, crouched by the single mast, was busy shortening the sail. The third voyager, a warrior nearly the size of the helmsman, sat in the bow of the boat, holding his head in his hands. The sea spray on his armor glistened in the moonlight, but he was not a sailor; that was apparent. Low groans escaped from his handsome, full lips, and he kept running his long fingers through his golden red hair.

The giant's gaze swept from his seasick friend to the shining castle that was directly above them, and he pushed the tiller over with an ease that three men could not have accomplished. The seagoing warrior's long black hair streamed in the wind behind his massive shoulders, and the weathered look of his face could not belie the strength and agility of his muscular body.

For more than a month Colin Campbell had looked forward to this moment. For the first time in weeks his fierce scowl relaxed, and his gray eyes shone with a radiance that reflected the castle's moonlit gleam.

"Alec," Colin shouted to his golden-haired friend. "If you can muster the strength to turn your dainty head, you'll find a welcome sight."

Alec turned and looked in the direction that the boat was now traveling.

"Finally. Kildalton."

"That it is, Alec. Home to the Campbells."

Alec carefully worked his way past the sailor to his friend in the stern. It occurred to him that he was seeing a rare look on Colin's face. Why, Colin was nearly smiling.

Colin Campbell had certainly not been smiling at Torquil Macleod's gathering of the Highland chiefs at Dunvegan Castle. Colin had gone for his father, for he would soon follow the old man in his role as Campbell chieftain. And Colin had not been happy at what he'd heard.

None of the chiefs of the Highlands or the Western

Isles had been happy with the heavy hand of the Stuart king, James IV. But the squabbling and murderous feuding that Colin had seen start up immediately between the clans convinced him beyond doubt that the Scots would be ruled again by the English. Without a strong Stuart king to unite them against the English, they would continue to fight among themselves until they all fell to the tyranny of the butchers to the south.

Alec looked hard at that face. Colin's was a face of war, tan and scarred with steely gray eyes that froze men's blood in their veins. Colin's was a face that was fierce on a normal day, but when the great fighter was angry, it was a face to strike terror in the heart of an enemy. And when he had spoken for the Campbells in support of the Stuart successor as a lesser of two evils, the other chieftains' responses had brought a fierceness to that face that was truly chilling.

For only a few had understood his reasoning. Alec's clan, the Macphersons, had agreed with Colin. But they were not enough to outweigh the bluster and arrogance of the others who had combined for the moment to drown out the Campbell leader's voice. None of them would have faced this warrior alone in a confrontation— Colin's quickness to anger and the finality of his warlike temper were legendary—but together they could take the risk of opposing him.

Together and with a great deal of show, Colin and Alec had left the gathering with the plan of forging an alliance attractive to some of the fence-straddling chiefs, and to Lowland lairds as well. Colin just hoped the Stuarts would do something soon to help themselves. The rumors from court of power struggles were certainly unsettling.

But those thoughts could be put aside for a while. Colin was nearly home, and that made the giant warrior smile.

Suddenly Alec was aware that Colin was not steering

toward the small harbor village that lay dark and sleeping beside the fortress. Colin was heading directly toward
the surf-beaten cliffs beneath the castle walls. But there
was no pier, no beach. The cliffs were jagged out-
croppings of stone. Alec could see the waves breaking
over reefs that pushed up through the raging surf like
the heads and backs of so many sea serpents. Colin had
gone berserk, Alec decided. That's why he was smiling
so strangely.

The boat was fairly flying across the water. They were
now surrounded by crashing rollers and reefs that threatened to demolish the small boat before they even hit
the wall of rock. The distance between the boat and the
cliffs was closing at a truly breakneck pace. Alec clung
to the thick wooden side and murmured a prayer. Colin
had gone daft. Too many hits to the head.

Suddenly the boat dropped into the trough of a wave
and seemed to almost slide to the right. As it did, the
sailor pulled down the sail and heaved the short mast out
of its place, easing it quickly into the belly of the boat.

Alec watched the activity openmouthed, glancing back
at the smiling Colin still standing at the tiller, and then
shot a glance back at the cliff wall that was about to
crush them.

But the wall would not crush them—there was a low
and narrow break in that murderous cliff. He no sooner
saw the small cave opening than they were through it,
careening in the blackness through flat water and then
bumping up a gently sloping incline that slowed and
eventually brought the boat to rest.

Colin and Alec waited while the sailor struck a flint
to the torch that Colin held. The light flared, illuminating
the low-ceilinged cavern that stretched beneath the cliff
and castle.

Alec glared at his black-haired host. "You might have
told me we were going to try killing ourselves. I would
have prepared myself."

Colin laughed. "Oh, you mean you didn't know about the cave?" he said, knowing full well that the Macpherson heir hadn't any knowledge of it, in spite of his many visits.

Alec smiled in spite of himself. "That *is* quite an entry!"

Colin handed the torch to Alec and took some of the gear the sailor was unloading from the boat.

"Aye, I believe I've only wrecked one or two boats coming in at that speed."

"Three, m'lord," the sailor jokingly murmured under his breath to Alec. "I've still splinters in my buttocks from the last one that broke up."

"Those splinters are from you lounging too long on the kitchen bench, you lazy water rat." Colin laughed good-naturedly. "You go on up through the kitchen, now. In the morning get one of your boys to help you with the rest of the gear." It was good to be home.

Alec's handsome face looked thoughtful. "Now that I know about this entryway, it shouldn't be any trouble for me to come in here one night with fifty or sixty of my best men, and ..."

"Sure, Alec. And be sure to come in at high tide."

"High tide? Why?" Alec asked.

"Because then we'll fish your bones ... or, better yet, your war gear out of the water," Colin said wryly. "There's no trace of this cave at high tide."

"Then the fifty of us will sneak in at low tide, with these nice sharp Highland dirks," Alec continued, indicating the dagger at his belt, "and cut all your thr—"

"No fear of that," Colin interrupted with a smile. "Even if you were able to get through the entry, you'd wander through the caves that honeycomb this hill until your beard turns gray and your teeth fall out."

"All right." Alec yawned. "You win this one. What I need is a place to sleep after getting out of this wet gear."

"You'll sleep here in the guest room," Colin smirked, indicating the cave with a sweep of his hand. "All the bathwater you'll need."

"I'm glad you consider me a friend," Alec responded. "I'd hate to have to sleep in the dungeons."

"If you must be such a complainer, then we'll have to arrange that," Colin said with a gruff laugh. "Follow me."

Lighting a thick candle with the torch that he left for the sailor, Colin led his friend into the depths of the cave, through a labyrinth of passages, and then turned into an arched stone corridor. Alec followed until they reached a stone stairway. But Colin did not go up the stairway. Instead, the warrior stopped before the stairs and, with a threatening look, turned his back on the Macpherson, blocking Alec's view of what he was doing. Then he turned, gave Alec a wink, and pushed at a section of a stone side wall, which slid noiselessly open. The two men ducked through the opening and began the long, winding stair climb to the castle above. They passed through several levels of mazelike corridors. After traveling down a long passageway past several wooden stairways, Colin led Alec through another closed section of wall, then climbed a short set of steps with his friend at his heels.

At the top Alec could see a short corridor, and he followed Colin toward a wooden panel on the right. The wall angled in from there, squeezing the corridor from either side just beyond the panel. Alec realized they had come up between the stone walls of two rooms. The narrowed section of the passageway was simply the extra space needed for each room's fireplace. They had to be between two of the best bedrooms.

"This next panel's your regular dungeon cell," Colin joked. "If you recall, my dungeon is next door. Make yourself comfortable while I go drop my gear. I'm sure my father will want to greet you himself. He'll be glad to hear of your father's decision about backing the Stuarts."

Alec put his hand on Colin's arm and stopped him with a threatening look.

"All the times I've stayed in this room, and you never told me that there was a secret passageway in. I'll be sleeping with my dirk handy tonight."

"I never thought you wouldn't," Colin said, laughing. "I'll send a man up with some wood to light the fire."

"Send up a woman to light the fire," Alec joked.

"You can get your own wenches, Alec Macpherson! I'll not be getting them," Colin snorted as they stopped by the entry into Alec's room. "But, at any rate, you won't find any to suit you in this castle."

"Not if they've the face of a Campbell," Alec responded with an exaggerated shudder. "Oh, the nightmares that'd follow."

"Enough, you Highland horse thief. I'll be back in a little while . . . through the hallway door."

Colin slid a wooden latch and pushed the panel open. He could see the moonlight streaming across the stone floor, and, giving Alec a friendly shove into the room, pulled the panel shut.

He turned and continued down the corridor.

Celia didn't know what awakened her. When she opened her eyes, there was no noise other than the far-off sound of the wind and the waves from outside the small glazed window. It was still night, though the fire in the hearth had long been out. She peered out from the heavy cloth curtain that hung around the bed. The moonlight lit the room fairly well, and nothing was unusual or different.

She had barred the door to the hallway from inside. The only other door was the small one into Ellen and the baby's room. The hallway door to their room was barred as well, and Celia could see that the door between the rooms was closed. Perhaps she should leave the door ajar, she thought.

No, that was needless worrying. Of any castle in Scotland, Kildalton had to be one of the safest. Her mind was just playing tricks on her.

Celia's eyes began to close again, but in the next moment she sat upright when she heard a wooden latch slide. Soundlessly she drew her short sword from its place by the ornate headboard of the bed. Peering out again, she started at the sight of a tall warrior standing in front of one of the decorative wooden panels beside the great fireplace. Where had he come from? The wooden panel?

Still as a statue, she watched him for a moment look over at the bed, then begin to cross the room toward the baby's door. As he did, Celia watched him pull his long sword from its scabbard.

As his eyes adjusted to the darkness, Alec dropped his leather saddlebag to the floor and looked over at the great bed that awaited him in the shadows of the moonlit room. That bed was going to feel mighty good after the hard, wet journey from the Highlands and drafty old Dunvegan Castle. A good bed, a bedroom with a fireplace, and glazed windows—these Campbells spared no expense living the good life. It was practically sinful.

Ah, well, I can be as good a sinner as they, he thought, starting across the room to the wall pegs. I'll get out of this chain mail, hang these wet clothes on the pegs, and get ready for the short welcoming visit from Colin's father. Please, Lord, let it be short.

Pulling his sword from its scabbard, Alec glanced up at the pegboard beside the small door. Then the scream stopped him in his tracks.

Celia knew that because of his height, she'd need to cut him down, or knock him down, to get at his throat.

The chain mail would protect him from a straight thrust to the side of the chest.

When the intruder started for the small door, Celia erupted from the bed with a scream that could curdle a brave man's blood. It was a cry that a Welsh warrior in her father's service had taught her. Her uncle Edmund had laughed when he'd heard the lesson taking place, but he had told her that the Welsh had broken the nerve of many a hardened adversary with those war cries. It was the violent suddenness of it that went right to the bone.

Celia flew across the wooden floor with the speed of a striking snake. She swung her short sword at the knee closest to her. She'd drive into him with her shoulder whether she chopped the leg or not.

The white-shrouded ghost shrieked across the floor at him with a speed that he'd not thought possible. It was only instinct that made him swing his sword to deflect the flashing metal that he saw out of the corner of his eye arcing toward his knee. Then the "ghost" hit him with a shoulder that could hardly be called vaporous. As the breath was knocked from him, the giant warrior felt himself sailing backward.

With a crash, Alec landed on a three-legged wood chair that splintered into kindling. Before he could move a muscle, the ethereal figure was sitting on his chest, and the fallen warrior felt the point of a sword pushing meaningfully at the flesh beneath his chin.

But it was her eyes of black sapphire that pierced his will to resist.

Colin squeezed his great chest through the narrowed passageway between the fireplace walls and opened the panel into his room. Before he had the chance to close off the passage, though, that nightmarish shriek froze him. For a moment he thought that some unearthly, eldritch fiend was coming at him from the passageway, and he shook the thick candle from his hand and whipped out his sword.

The crash of metal and splintering wood that followed the scream came from the other side of the corridor.

Ducking back in and squeezing through the pitch-black passage, Colin easily found the wooden latch slide—he'd grown up playing in these passageways. Kicking the panel open, the giant leapt into the bedroom, sword first, ready for anything that he might find there.

The sight that greeted him stopped him dead.

It was a vision. There, in the moonlight, knelt an unearthly creature, a white-gowned angel who glowed in the darkened room.

With a toss of shoulder-length curls of auburn hair, black eyes flashed at him for the briefest of moments, shooting lightning bolts into Colin that seared the deepest recesses of his soul with a burning that he had never before experienced. Desire, fear, wonder, all merged and raced pell-mell through his body, wreaking havoc, leaving him gasping for breath.

Colin had been ready to do battle, but now his sword hung loosely at his side. The aura of beauty that surrounded this creature had dazzled him. One look had vanquished him.

The face of this angel was like no other human face Colin had ever seen. The perfection of the features: the eyes that made him burn, the high cheekbones that made him tremble, the lips that stirred in his loins a feeling more of lust than religious devotion.

Colin was indeed gripped with a fervor that quite nearly brought him to his knees. The warrior's eyes traveled from her face to her bare feet, and the journey was slow and thorough. The thin, white shift, modest though it was, could do little to hide the body within its luminescent weave. The perfect physical incarnation he was seeing was undoubtedly a product of the heavens, but what he was feeling was very much of this earth.

There, before him, lay the future chieftain of the Macpherson clan, with a short sword to his throat. Alec, too, was amazed by this thing of beauty about to spit his head on a sword. Resistance seems to be the last thing on his mind, Colin thought.

She was only half Alec's size and weight, and yet the two men were unable, or unwilling, to move.

Something made Celia hesitate. For perhaps the first time in her life, she didn't quite know what to do next. The giant who had seconds before burst through the wooden panel simply stood with the oddest look on his face, his sword at his side. The one at her mercy never even attempted to struggle; he, too, just looked at her.

As fierce as the one standing looked, these were the most noncombative pair of fighters Celia could imagine.

When she first reacted to the intruder, Celia had moved to protect the baby. No one was going to harm Kit. But now, looking at her captive and the warrior by the wall, she was at a loss. They certainly did not seem to be threatening her. And there was no indication that either one had any desire to go through the baby's door. No, they just gawked at her like a pair of oversized abbey schoolboys.

Why, the giant by the panel almost seemed entertained by what he was looking at. His amusement will cost this one his life, if he's not careful, Celia thought with annoyance.

Oh, how she hated when she was not taken seriously. She should slit this one's throat and get some respect.

Then Celia saw the look in his eyes change. He was looking at her, really looking at her. Suddenly she was very aware of the thinness of the gown she was wearing. The warrior's eyes seemed to look right through it as he surveyed every inch of her body. They paused with lustful intensity at her hips, breasts, and mouth as his gaze returned to her face.

This man was despicable.

But he was not going to get away with this.

Celia waited until his eyes met hers, and then she slowly looked him over from top to bottom with a look of sheer disgust. Her smirking conclusion would hopefully convey an attitude of absolute scorn. What a worthless piece of old meat, she wanted her careless look to say.

And it did.

Colin realized that this woman was actually appraising him. Him, the future chieftain of the Campbell clan. One of the most powerful warriors in the Western Isles . . . in all Scotland!

And she found him wanting!

Anger began to simmer in the veins of the giant. No woman had ever looked at him with such disdain. And in his very own castle! This was too much. How could he have let his guard down so?

And what was worse, he could see she knew that she'd rattled him.

But worst of all, Alec Macpherson was watching the whole thing! The amused look on his face! Oh, God!

Well, at least she doesn't have a sword to *my* throat, Colin thought. But this all had to stop. Lord help them all if anything should happen to Alec while he was visiting Kildalton Castle. There would be real hell to pay with the Highlanders. Colin had to speak to her.

With that, Colin unconsciously began to raise his sword and step toward the two on the floor before him. As he did, the woman raised her elbow, prepared to thrust her weapon into Colin's prone guest. She would kill Alec and be on her feet to face Colin before he reached her. The warrior stopped.

"Wait!" he commanded, though the word seemed to soften as he said it.

Celia shot a glance at Colin. His word rang with conciliation, yet his face showed fierce annoyance at the sound of his own voice. She had him, and it clearly irritated him that she did.

Her face showed the dominance she felt. That image of her, kneeling upon the chest of the vanquished foe, was a startling one for Colin.

Suddenly a pounding at the hallway door was accompanied by the sound of Lord Hugh Campbell's voice.

"Lady Celia, are you all right? Lady Celia!" he called. The old man's voice was quavering with concern.

"Aye, Lord Hugh, but I have two intruders," Celia shouted, keeping the giant in her peripheral vision while not taking her eye off the warrior beneath her. She was feeling a mixture of relief and pride at the moment's victory.

But why wasn't the one by the panel making his escape?

"Oh, my God!" she heard the old man roar, then shout down the hallway. "Runt, rouse Jean, Emmet, and Edmund, too, from the hall. Hurry, lad!"

"Father!" Colin called, silencing the ruckus in the hallway. "Father, it's Colin." His voice carried the steely edge of fury in it.

"Colin?" the old man returned.

"Aye. Colin. And Alec Macpherson, too. If he doesn't get murdered where he lies." Colin scowled at this she-devil with contempt in his eyes. Whoever or whatever this woman was, she had overstepped the bounds of a decent defense.

Celia yanked the sword point away from her captive's throat and, with a look of dismay at Colin, scampered across the room for her cloak, ruffled for a moment at the turn of events. She felt a sudden desire to be covered.

Colin watched with surprise this sudden display of timidity by the woman.

Still watching the woman who now appeared to be cowering on the other side of the room, Colin offered Alec a hand up, then strode to the door and unbarred it.

The door swung in, and Lord Hugh entered unceremoniously, dressed only in his nightshirt and holding a long sword in his hand. He was only slightly shorter than Colin, but as broad in the shoulders, and the scarred and weathered face of the old man told of a life of violence, care, and toil.

Behind him, his squire Runt carried a smoky torch and a short sword. Lord Hugh leaned his sword against Runt and embraced his son heartily.

"Colin," he said. "We weren't expecting you for another fortnight, at least! The usual pigheadedness in the Highlands, I suppose."

"Aye, Father. I had to leave, or kill someone." His last comment he directed toward the opposite side of the room, belatedly asserting his authority.

Colin walked over to Alec and clapped his great arm around the Macpherson's wide shoulders. "But Alec Macpherson's come to stay with us for a bit."

"Alec, my boy, it's so good to see you here again. It's like old times, you two boys ... ah, strong, grown men now ... together again. Maybe we'll teach you to swim and sail yet!" The old warrior smiled, greeting the young Macpherson with a crushing bear hug.

"Thank you, Lord Hugh," Alec said, returning the greeting. "My father sends his regards to you. I know he misses seeing you at the Highland gatherings."

"Thank him for me, lad. We've had many a good time together, he and I. And gotten into a bit of trouble, too, I'll warrant you."

The old man turned to Colin. "You lads must be dog-tired after that journey. Well, to bed, then; we'll talk in the morning. So you're putting him in this room, that's good ... *No!* My Lord, that's not good! Lady Celia! Where are you, lass?"

"Here, m'lord." Her voice was hardly more than a whisper.

Where Celia stood by the clothes pegs on the opposite side of the room, she had been partially blocked from the group of men by the heavily curtained bed. With the arrival of his son and the Macpherson heir, Lord Hugh had momentarily forgotten her, even if the two young men had not.

"Lady Celia," Lord Hugh began, moving quickly to her and taking her hand. "Lassie, these great baboons must've given you a terrible fright. Are you all right, dear?"

Colin could not believe what he was seeing. Hugh Campbell's ferocity was legendary in Scotland. In England, Hugh Campbell's name was rivaled only by the Black Douglas as the most fearsome of Scots. Mothers all along the Irish and English coasts invoked his name in the dark of the night to control their unruly brats. The Campbell wealth and fame had been bought with the blood of so many battles, so many raids. This man was war incarnate. For the past forty years, this had been a man to be feared.

And yet, here was this same man, reaching out with the gentleness of a lapdog. His voice, his look, the way he moved to this woman, all bespoke the manners of an abbey clerk.

And this woman. This woman who moments before had wielded a sword like a seasoned soldier. Who had upended and vanquished Alec Macpherson, an extremely capable fighter. This she-devil who had held even him, Colin Campbell, at bay . . . and then eyed him so scornfully.

And here she was, putting a limp and quivering hand into the laird's great paw. Here she was, looking into his father's eyes like some newborn fawn, fragile and vulnerable.

She had purposely changed from a lion to a lamb in the blink of an eye. The woman was a witch!

She was working her charms on his father, but they would not work on Colin Campbell. Not again.

Looking past his father's shoulder, Colin suddenly glimpsed a genuine look that he hadn't expected to see. Was it worry? Was it fear? Colin's view of women was that they were naturally fearful. God knows, in a land so torn by feuding clans and marauding Englishmen, women had good reason for fear. They needed strong men to protect them.

But that sudden flash of fear in *this* woman seemed extraordinary for some reason. Fear of what, he wondered.

But more important, who was she and what was she after, this woman? Why had she come to Kildalton?

"I'm fine, m'lord," she began sheepishly, suddenly feeling an uncontrollable urge to explain, to apologize. "I thought they were ... I didn't know who ... I know, perhaps, I ... If their lordships would see it to ..."

Celia was rattled. For some unaccountable reason she felt her face burn with embarrassment. It was good that the room was dark. The one torch that the squire held would not shed enough light to betray her flushed face.

Then, like a bolt from the blue, it occurred to her perhaps this giant warrior would persuade his father to throw her out. Where would she go next? She could see the glowering look of anger in his eyes now. Then, for a fleeting moment, she thought she sensed a change in those gray eyes. Concern, perhaps. Or sympathy. Whatever it was, the look passed quickly, replaced by the fierce scowl that she guessed could hide any soft feeling this warrior harbored.

"Calm yourself, my dear," Lord Hugh rumbled softly. "But you haven't really been introduced to these two ruffians, have you. Well, not tonight. Tomorrow will come soon enough to get acquainted."

"If you want to lodge your other guest here, m'lord, I'll just take a moment to move my things next door."

"Don't you worry, lass," the old man said gently, beginning to move toward the door. "We'll find another place for young Macpherson to be comfortable. You and the bairn will not be troubled here."

"Thank you, Lord Hugh. I really didn't want to cause your family hardship," she said, following the three men.

The old warrior's creased face warmed with a look of fatherly affection as he turned and took her hand again in his.

"Don't be concerned about our hardships. All Scotland's got hardships now, and you've had enough of your own. Good night, Lady Celia." The Campbell chieftain then turned on his heel and herded the rest from the room.

Colin threw this mystery woman a last irritated look as he left the room. His father was completely taken with her.

"Who *is* this woman, Father?" Colin exploded in the hallway.

One of Lord Hugh's shaggy eyebrows arched in surprise at his son's exclamation. He had never before asked *anything* about *any* woman of quality in his entire life.

"Fine-looking woman, isn't she," the chieftain remarked casually. "If I were your age ... well, perhaps a bit younger, I'd ..."

"Hang her looks, Father! Who is she? What's her business here?"

Colin is certainly worked up over her, Lord Hugh thought to himself. This is promising. The lad should have married ten years ago. We could have had a whole herd of little Campbells running wild in this castle by now.

Funny it should be this one that got his attention. If he's interested now, Hugh thought, wait till he finds out who she ... No, I'll not tell him. We'll just watch and maybe let things take their natural course ... for a wee bit, anyhow.

"Why, Lady Celia arrived with her uncle and her bairn a week ago. After that devil Danvers burned Edinburgh, he started burning every castle, manor house, and farm in the Lowlands, and they've been on the run ever since. The poor lass has been sick with worry about the wee one. Over a month they've been tracking through this miserable winter wet. The bairn has a terrible cough, Runt says."

"It's true, Lord Colin," the squire piped up from the rear. "The lady frets over the babe night and day. She's a wonderful, caring woman."

"Of course she would be," Colin snapped. "What mother wouldn't." Colin had known his own mother for only the first few years of his own life, but his vague memories were ones of tenderness and warmth.

"This woman was sick herself when they arrived," Lord Hugh added. "She never so much as gave herself a thought, though. The bairn, the wet nurse, even her uncle came first for her. She's a rare one, Colin."

"Well, she certainly made a quick recovery," Colin responded gruffly. "You can ask Alec about that."

Lord Hugh threw Alec a quizzical look, but the Macpherson feigned ignorance. He was not going to admit that this slender and sickly woman had knocked him to the ground.

"Aye, Lord Hugh, she moves with pretty fair speed for a sick woman. I didn't want to hurt her, of course, but . . ." Alec's voice trailed off as he searched for a new direction for this discussion. "Who is this Lady Celia, though, m'lord. You've not said."

"I haven't?" the Campbell chieftain exclaimed. "Surely when I introduced you all ... I didn't even do that properly, did I?"

"It's true, Lord Hugh," the trailing Runt chirped up. "You never made any proper introduction. You crabbed the entire meeting, you did."

"Quiet down, fish bait, or I'll ding you so hard, you'll wake up in Ireland," the old laird rumbled at his squire with a pretended show of anger. In truth, the Campbells had never been the kind of masters who beat those in their service, and because of this, the verbal exchanges sometimes bordered on insubordination. But Lord Hugh knew that he could count on every one of his retainers' loyalty and affection. He was looked on as a father to them all.

"Where was I," the chieftain continued. "Oh, yes. She's Celia ... er ... Lady Celia ... Caithness. Escaped when the cowardly English pig Danvers tried to burn them out. Her uncle Edmund and I have known each other for more than thirty years. The last we spent any length of time together was after that little brawl we started at Norham Castle, back in '98, I think it was. We were baiting—more than fighting—the English back then. A good fighter, he is. Maybe the best trainer of soldiers in Scotland, too."

"Then where's her husband to care for her?" Colin asked irritably. "Can't the Caithnesses protect their own wives?" He didn't know why this news upset him so, but he suddenly felt wrung out, as if someone had squeezed him out like a wet rag.

"Lord Caithness can't," Alec responded, cutting into the discussion. "He died with the King at Flodden."

The two Campbell men stopped and faced the Macpherson.

"You know her?" Colin snapped at his friend.

"Only about her, and that probably only thirdhand," Alec responded. "And I only knew Lord Caithness by sight, for he was closer to your age, wasn't he, Lord Hugh?"

"I never knew him myself, lad, him being a Lowlander, but I believe he *was* only ten years or so younger than I. If my memory serves me, I believe he sided with . . ."

"What do you know about her, Alec?" Colin interrupted, stopping his father midsentence, to which Lord Hugh took more amusement than offense.

"No more than mere gossip, Colin my friend," Alec teased with the most serious of expressions on his face, sensing the father's response from his surprised smile. "And I know you have no interest in hearing tales."

"No, indeed, lad," Lord Hugh cut in wryly before his son could respond. "The Campbells are not a bunch of old fishwives to stand about trading slanderous stories. No, indeed. But tell me, rather, about the business at the Highland tryst. There's serious talk for serious men."

Colin could not press Alec further at this point, but the matter was far from closed. As Colin turned his thoughts to the business of the meeting, Alec spoke up.

"Colin spoke clearly and to the point with the other Highland chiefs, m'lord," Alec said earnestly. "But your proposals were shouted down by Torquil Macleod and too many of the others. They're like a pack of greedy wolves, ready to tear apart what's left of Scotland, thinking they'll get a little piece. They'll all perish like the fools they are, with their petty bickering and their arrogance. But the Macphersons are with you."

"Good, lad. Your father's always shown wisdom in his dealings. We need to stand together against the English. The Stuart kings have never been great friends to us in the Highlands and the Western Isles, but they've always been a rallying point for us against the outsiders. And we'll be needing them now."

"My father thought that with spring nearly here, Colin and I could do a great deal to muster support among those chieftains who didn't go to Dunvegan, and maybe even among the Lowland lairds who survived this bloody winter."

"Aye, lad. Perhaps we'll be able to persuade Edmund to travel with you two. He's well known and respected among the Lowlanders. He's a man of honor, and he's trained enough of their fighters, I know."

"He'll be a real asset, at that," Colin commented in a surly tone. "He can start by giving Alec here a lesson or two."

"Sounds like there's a story here that I'd just love to be hearing," Lord Hugh said, yawning. "But I believe tomorrow will be soon enough to hear it. Why don't you put Alec in the Archbishop's room. He won't be arriving until right after Easter. Good night, lads. Good to have you safely home."

After Lord Hugh closed his own door, Runt curled up on his blankets in the alcove across from his door, and the two great warriors continued down to the room that Alec would be occupying during his stay.

"Well, Colin, if you don't think I'll run into any adventures trying to get into the Archbishop's bed ..." Alec quipped, half drawing his sword in mock defense.

"Not so quick," Colin said. "I want to know everything you know about Lady Caithness."

Colin's head was telling him that this Caithness woman was trouble; he had to learn more about her.

But as strange as this woman was, there was something even stranger about that rush of relief that he'd experienced, hearing that this perplexing woman was a widow.

She was beautiful, indeed. But Colin had known many beautiful women in his life, and none had ever gotten under his skin the way this one had: And so immediately! He was even more perplexed now. Something about this woman was affecting him. And this irritated him even more.

But he was not going to give in to these feelings. He had more discipline than that. And he was going to find out what this woman was doing here. Perhaps whatever Alec knew, or had heard, would give Colin a clue.

This woman is hiding something, the giant warrior thought, and I'm going to find out what it is.

Chapter 3

When they limped home after Flodden, we deserved to take something from them. That is the way of war. And the Scot king sought us out for battle. They say he was after dowry. That King Henry wasn't paying his sister's keep. What a price these Scots are paying now for the pettiness of kings.

He's bound to find out.

Celia replaced the heavy wooden bar on the door, then turned and leaned her back against it. She let out a sigh so loud that she startled herself. This was going to be so difficult.

Although the entire incident had occurred in just a few moments, Celia felt as if she had been through a night-long ordeal. The confused whirlwind of actions that had taken place suddenly took on a dreamlike quality in her mind. Standing alone in her dark room, she found herself wondering whether any of it had really happened. Aye, she could see the pieces of broken chair lying on the floor where Alec Macpherson had landed.

Of all the people in Scotland, she thought, it had to be a Macpherson.

An anxious look crossed her face as she surveyed the bedroom. If what she had experienced was real, then she had *not* just secured the only entry into the room. Her eyes lit on the panel beside the fireplace, and she walked quickly to it.

The moonlight still poured in the window, illuminating the room to some extent, but it was hardly light enough for her to see well. Running her fingers along the grooves in the woodwork revealed no latch or crevice that would allow her to pull the panel open. This was very clever workmanship, this secret passageway. She would need to examine this in the daylight. But for to-night, Celia would need a way to block this entrance. She knew that the two giants had entered from outside the castle. Others could possibly come in the same way.

As she peered into the darker recesses of the room, Celia suddenly shivered with the cold, pulling the heavy cloak more tightly about her. There were not a lot of choices for her.

The great wooden bed was like a mountainous island perched against the inner wall of the bedroom. From a foundation of wood, the high feather mattress beckoned to her with a promise of warmth and comfort. Like a great parapet, the heavy arras-draped canopy loomed over the bed, throwing its dark shadow over much of the rest of the room. Like a fortress against the troubles of her waking life, the bed offered at least the escape of sleep. But there would be no sleep for Celia until she could calm the fears that had been awakened by the intrusion of the two men.

Celia knew she could not change the past. The die was cast. There were very real and threatening things in this world, but she could only focus on the present. And for the present, this wooden panel must be blocked.

In the far corner of the room, beside the wall pegs, sat a huge oak chest, large enough for a grown woman to hide in. The chest, the only storage area in the room for clothing, contained only Celia's light armor. It's a good thing, Celia thought, as she began to drag the chest away from the wall. If this were any heavier, I wouldn't be able to move it alone.

Celia moved the awkward piece of furniture slowly,

trying as best as she could to create no sound that might draw the attention of her hosts. The dried reeds that covered the floor helped muffle the scraping sound. Finally, Celia succeeded in pushing the chest squarely in front of the panel.

It was only a temporary solution, Celia knew, and not a very good one, at that. If someone tried to come in through that panel again, they would certainly be able to push the chest away, but at least Celia would have enough time to react.

The exercise of moving the great chest did little to alleviate the numbing cold that was creeping up her body from her frozen feet. She could not afford to catch a chill now that she had recovered from their journey from the Lowlands. She needed to be ready at all times; there was still so much left to do.

There were times in her recent past, though, when Celia wondered how she could go on. Right now, the huge bed across the room looked like a warm and protective cocoon awaiting her.

But she needed to check on Kit first.

Moving quickly across the floor, Celia lightly tapped the prearranged signal on the door to the baby's room. She heard Ellen quietly unbar the door, and Celia slipped inside.

"Lady Celia, what was all the noise?" Ellen whispered, her eyes wide with concern.

"Lord Hugh's son . . . Colin . . . Lord Colin . . . arrived unexpectedly tonight and thought to put his friend in my room. We were *all* rather surprised, I expect."

"M'lady, I heard a god-awful scream, and furniture breaking, and voices. I . . ."

"It's all right now, Ellen," Celia said, putting an arm around her companion's shoulders. "Everyone has retired, and you do the same. But first I want to look at the baby. Has he been sleeping well tonight?" Celia looked tenderly into the heavy cradle.

Reaching in and smoothing the heavy wrapping that surrounded the child, Celia wanted to touch the baby's soft skin. Pick him up. Hold him close. She was still amazed at the sense of possessiveness, of protectiveness that overwhelmed her when she was near him. Celia had always heard stories of maternal instinct, but she never dreamed it would happen to her—not like this.

"He was a mite fretful for a short time, but he's been resting peaceful as can be most of the night. He's surely eating better than before," Ellen said softly, looking affectionately at the baby.

Celia thought of Ellen, losing her baby at birth, so soon after her husband's death. Although her own feelings were baffling to her, Celia could easily understand how Ellen's loss could have turned into loving Kit as her own.

They had been very concerned about Kit's health over the past few days, but yesterday the feverishness seemed to improve, although the coughing fits still continued. She and Ellen had certainly not gotten much rest since they had arrived at Kildalton Castle, and after tonight's unexpected activity, Celia wondered if she'd ever be able to close her eyes here.

Content that Kit was resting quietly, Celia scanned the room for possible secret entryways. This room, smaller than her own, had no panels beside the fireplace, and the plaster that covered the stone walls appeared smooth and solid. Not wanting to upset Ellen, Celia said nothing to her about the passageway.

Bidding her good night, Celia slipped back into her own room, listening while Ellen barred the door behind her.

Ellen had been eight months pregnant when she lost all those whom she cared for at Flodden—her husband, her father, and her only brother. They had all been wiped off the face of the earth in a single day. And then, only days later, when her own baby died at birth, her devastation had been complete. But Kit had brought Celia and Ellen together, and the grieving mother had found a purpose for going on, a reason for living.

What kind of a life had she found? Celia thought. A life of danger and uncertainty with consequences even more drastic than the ones she'd experienced before. Ellen, too, had made a decision, to give all that she had left—herself—and Celia knew that she owed her the best protection she could muster.

Retrieving her short sword from the wall by the clothes pegs, Celia climbed back into the bed and fastened the heavy curtains on both sides. Sinking into the depths of the feather bed, Celia doubted that the layers of heavy wool blankets that covered her could ever dispel the chill that permeated her body.

It seemed that she'd been cold since they left Caithness. Celia's thoughts wandered back to that wild night.

Escaping Lord Danvers and his men with just the clothes they were wearing, Celia and the others had ridden northward past Loch Lomand. The terrain had become rugged, and by the time dawn broke over a gray and drizzly morning, they were well into the Highlands.

Wet and cold, the weary travelers pushed past the looming peak of Ben Lomand, looking in vain for some shelter in which to rest. The high moors offered not even windbreak for them to huddle against.

"Edmund, we've got to get Kit out of this cold," Celia murmured as they rode.

"Aye, lass, and Father William looks like he could use a bit of warming, too," her uncle responded in a loud enough voice for Dunbar to hear.

"Don't you be worrying about me, you scar-faced infidel," Father William snapped back. "I'm doing just fine with this foul weather. And you might learn to appreciate it a bit more, yourself, considering where you'll be going when you're finished on this earth."

"If you're suggesting, priest, that my everlasting reward is to include a somewhat warmer climate, then at least I'll know where I am when I see your face."

"My face! I won't be going there, you booby. I'm a man of God."

"Maybe so. But I recall seeing a painting once of St. Michael driving Satan into the fiery pit, and that devil had your face, I'll swear."

"You're coming a mite close to blasphemy, you old scoundrel, and if you think I'll do anything to save your eternal soul . . ."

"Edmund! Father William! Must you two *always* fight with one another?" Celia rolled her eyes skyward.

She knew these two men respected and liked each other, though they were determined not to show it. Since the day they'd met, their banter had been a source of amusement for her—and for each other, she suspected.

Over the years, each had instilled a part of himself in Celia. She had acquired her physical training and prowess from Edmund, and her intellectual and spiritual discipline and insight from Father William's tutelage.

Though they were roughly the same age, they were very different types of men. Edmund, tall and stately, solid as an oak, was the very model of chivalry. He was directly descended from Robert the Bruce, and the quality of that lineage was embodied in the knight.

Over the years Edmund had taught her to value that lineage that was so much a part of her, as well. And Celia knew that it was the strength of that noble Scottish blood, passed on to her through her mother, that had helped her keep Kit safe.

Celia smiled to herself as she thought of this man whose ideas about proper behavior seemed so old-fashioned, so "by the book." That is, except where Celia herself was concerned. He had been more a force in her life than her own father had been, and he had given her a kind of education that allowed her to survive. Not exactly "by the book" childrearing, but the kind that developed an unconventional variety of skills he knew she would need in this world of men.

William Dunbar, small and wiry, was priest and poet, and as powerful with his tongue as Edmund was with his sword. His quick wit and fearless audacity had long made him a favorite at court. He, too, was not "by the book"—he wrote his own. When King James had licensed the printer Myllar and his partner Chepman to set up the first printing press in Scotland, Father William had put together one of the first books they had printed. And when the King wanted to insult a rival, Dunbar was the only man he called upon. The poet's acid tongue and whirlwind of rhetoric was deadly to an adversary's honor. In the world of the court, the wound of a word went deeper than the sword of any knight.

Always at the King's beck and call, Father William had continued to serve James faithfully. His only regret was that the King had never granted him the one thing he wanted most—a church of his own with God's people to serve and their children to teach.

But in spite of their differences, Edmund and Father William were both devoted to the Scottish national identity, an identity they all were in danger of losing now that the King was dead.

But they were all tired now, and needed to find food and shelter.

"A few hours farther on," Edmund said, turning back to Celia, "we'll come on the valley around Loch Arklet. There's shelter there, but we must be careful. The Gregor clan controls that area, and they'd sell their own mothers if they thought they'd profit by it. You'd better put on your best Gaelic accent."

"Would they go so far as to deal with the English?" Celia asked anxiously.

"They hate the English as much as they hate the

Stuarts," Edmund answered. "But they'd deal with Satan himself if it'd be in their interest."

As they began to descend into the valley, the craggy moors gave way to groves of huge oak trees. But the temperature was dropping, and the drizzle changed over to a thick, wet snow. Celia gathered the sleeping Kit closer to her within the protection of her cloak.

"It won't be long now," Edmund told the group.

"These folks offer lodging to travelers," he said soon after as they came to a halt before an old, thatch-roofed stone farmhouse. "If they're the same folk living here, they're honest enough."

As the weary travelers surveyed the shelter and its surroundings, the door opened and a shabby, angry-looking man stood slouching in the doorway, eyeing them warily.

"We need food and lodging for the night," Edmund called out.

"Aye . . . Can you pay?" he sneered.

"We can," Father William put in shortly. "And bring down God's blessing on you, as well."

"A king's shilling will do well enough, but we'll be glad of any other blessings that come with it," the man replied roughly, and turned back into the house.

As Celia and the others dismounted, the farmer reappeared at the door, driving an emaciated cow out into the falling snow.

"The shrew will show you where you can sleep," he said to the group, gesturing with his thumb at the door.

"And there's feed for the horses under the overhang at the back," he said to Edmund, continuing in that direction. As he walked he cast a sidelong look at the horses, covertly appraising them. "I can't promise your animals will still be here in the morning, though. There's all kinds that wander these parts at night."

Celia handed Kit to Ellen and went into the dark

farmhouse ahead of her, while Edmund and Father William went to care for the horses. Just inside the doorway, a thin woman, looking older than her husband, peered fearfully at them from the shadows. When she saw that Ellen carried a baby, however, she stepped into the light.

Celia and Ellen both caught their breath at the sight of the woman. One side of her face was swollen from a blow she had received very recently. Her other eye was blackened as well, perhaps from an earlier beating.

"Quality folks," she clucked with embarrassment, turning her face from the guests' concerned gazes. "And a baby, too. We can't have you sleeping on the same straw as that old cow. Let me just clear this corner out and put down some fresh straw."

"Thank you," Celia said, looking around at an interior devoid of any creature comforts but the fire that crackled in the huge open hearth and the large iron pot that hung simmering above it. "Let me help you."

Celia worked with the woman as she prepared their places and their supper. Seeing her battered spirit and condition, Celia's heart yearned to help this woman somehow in her troubles. But she knew there was nothing she could do . . . not now . . . not in the position she was in herself.

Then, during supper, as they all gathered in the cottage for the meal, the surly-faced husband grunted for his wife to pour him more ale. She scurried for the pitcher, but obviously not fast enough for his liking. For as she poured, his surly expression turned to a snarl as he knocked the cup away and leapt to his feet, raising his fist as the woman cowered in anticipation of the attack.

But the blow never fell. Edmund caught the man's wrist as he swung, lifting him back and away from his wife. Bending the husband's arm back, Edmund forced the man to his knees.

"We'll not put up with the abuse of any woman," Edmund growled.

"Not my arm," the husband pleaded. "Don't break my arm!"

Celia could hear the panic in the husband's voice. They all knew that a broken arm could mean not surviving through the winter, could mean that the spring planting would not be done. Her look traveled from the fear-stricken face of the husband to the anxious face of the wife.

"Swear you'll not strike her again, coward," the great knight ordered, bending the arm farther. "Swear!"

"I swear, m'lord," he whimpered. "I'll not strike her. By God, I swear."

"Just remember," Edmund threatened, releasing the trembling husband. "I travel this route often. I'll be back, and if I ever hear of you hurting her again, it will not be your arm that I break—it will be your neck!"

After supper Edmund decided that he would do best to stay outside under the overhang where he could watch their horses and put some distance between himself and the "host." Celia joined him in the raw Scottish dusk so that they might talk privately. The snow had turned back into a cold, gray rain.

"The Earl of Argyll will still be at the Highland chiefs' meeting at Dunvegan Castle on the Isle of Skye," Edmund said, settling down on an overturned bucket, his back to the wall of the house. "He may not get back to his winter castle before Easter, and I don't know that we'll find warm welcome there while he's away. He can't know what happened at Caithness Hall, and his servants won't be expecting us."

"But we can't just wander around the Highlands in this weather until he returns," Celia responded. "And I don't particularly like our host enough to stay here."

"I agree. In fact, if we stay here past the night, I may kill the bastard," Edmund stated with a frown. "These are very different folks than were here before. We need

to take our chances going to the Western Isles. The farther we get from those butchering English, the better off
we'll be. And besides, if need be, I've an old friend in
the Isles who lives about a half day's sail from Argyll's
winter castle, and he'll take us in for sure until Argyll
returns."

"Who is that?" Celia asked.

"Hugh Campbell, the most powerful chief in the Western Isles. A good man, but always too independent for
the King's liking. And I hear that his son Colin is as
good a—"

"Campbell!" Celia interrupted. "Before you and Father William and the husband came in from the horses,
I got an earful about the Campbells from Eustace, the
wife. You'd think they could both—father and son—
walk on water. This woman is from that clan, I gather,
because she never stopped talking about them—until the
moment her husband came through the door. It was the
only time she opened up, at all. I think she rues the
day she left her clan. But what were you saying about
the Campbells?"

"Well, from what I hear, the son is as good a man as
the father, and Lord Hugh is as fine as they come. Unlike some Scottish lairds, they care deeply about their
people. They say that for the Campbells, the people that
depend on them come before even the King."

"But that's not uncommon in these Highlands. Would
we be safe there?" Celia asked.

"While the King was being murdered at Flodden,
Colin Campbell was terrorizing that pompous Tudor
Henry and his English troops in France. I don't think
the English would even dream of bringing the battle to
Kildalton Castle. I hear it's got more guns now than
Edinburgh Castle itself!"

Celia knew that King James had sent some of his best
warriors to France when the English had invaded the

continent. But they had come back too late to join the King at Flodden.

"If we do go there, what could we tell them? Who will you say that I am?"

When they left Linlithgow, her benefactor Lord Huntly had insisted that Celia keep her identity a secret. There were many good reasons for it, and Huntly wanted her and Kit out of harm's way while he focused on reorganizing what was left of the Stuart court. Lord Huntly was the most powerful noble left at court, and he intended to see that Stuart rule would continue as the unifying force in Scotland. He had told them that if they found themselves in danger, they were to seek out the Earl of Argyll, who would shelter them until a more settled time.

They had thought they would be safe at Caithness Hall, and they had been—for nearly five months. With Lord Caithness dead and Lady Caithness with her family in England, Edmund's presence had been a welcome one at the manor hall. Edmund had been a close friend to Lord Caithness for many years, and his face was a connection with less troubled times. So they had become guests in a hall that housed many noble families uprooted in the turbulent days following Flodden. With so many widows in Scotland, her true identity had never been questioned. She was Edmund's niece, and that had been enough for the retainers left to manage the manor.

But Celia knew now that the devil Danvers would not stop until he had found them. She had been promised to the Englishman long ago. Celia was the daughter of John Muir and granddaughter of the Duke of York. It was not her rank or her money that he had originally desired that drove him on, but rather the hatred that he carried for her. She had wounded and rejected him. His honor had been injured.

Danvers had to be put off the track somehow.

"You could become Lady Caithness, Celia," Edmund suggested thoughtfully. "She has a bairn, as well."

"Won't they know the truth?" she asked uncomfortably. "Lady Caithness was quite well known at court."

"Most likely not," Edmund continued. "The Campbells were never ones for court society. I can tell you one thing, though, even if Lord Hugh guesses the truth, he would never confront us on an issue of honor."

Celia hoped that she would not have to deceive anyone, but most particularly those loyal friends of Edmund's.

Celia felt that the finest bed in the finest castle could not feel better than the couch of dried rushes that the woman had prepared for her on the fresh straw. She had drifted off with Kit and Ellen tucked comfortably in beside her, and Father William not far away.

She did not know how long she'd been sleeping when she was suddenly conscious of the movement near the open hearth.

The husband moved silently to the cottage door, unbarred it, and slipped away into the night. Not a moment had passed, however, when Celia saw the woman crossing the room to where the travelers lay. Eustace placed her hand on Celia's shoulder, but saw immediately that the young woman was already awake.

"You must go now!" she whispered urgently. "He's gone to get his filthy Gregor cronies. They'll murder you all for those horses of yours. They'd murder you for less, m'lady."

"You're putting yourself in danger," Celia said, on her feet and rousing the others. "What'll you tell him, Eustace, when they come back? We can't just leave you here."

"Aye, you can. He'll not hurt me. I'll just tell the blackguard that you heard him leave," she answered, following them to the door. "Don't you worry about me.

I may be married to this dirty Gregor lout, but I'm still a Campbell. I'll be fine."

"God bless you," Celia said, hugging her quickly as Edmund and Father William came around the corner with the horses.

Without another word, Celia vaulted onto her horse, took the baby from Ellen, and looked once more at the defiant woman standing in the farmhouse doorway.

Celia wheeled her horse and galloped with the others into the wet gloom of the Scottish night.

The Gregors gave up their chase when Celia and the others forded the narrow northernmost point of the loch and rode west. When dawn broke again, gray and wet, Edmund looked steadily at his young niece. Clearly, he'd been thinking about their next move.

"We should go to the Campbells, Celia. It's our best possible choice."

Celia agreed. Right now it seemed to be their only choice.

"Kildalton, it is then," she answered.

For the next ten days they traveled as well as they could, staying with farmers who, more often than not, had little to share in the way of food so late in the winter. Several times, they were able to stay at small abbeys and with religious communities that Father William knew of. Sometimes, reaching these places took the travelers nearly a day out of their way, but they knew that they would always find a warm lodging and a hot supper when they arrived, and that made the extra miles worthwhile.

Two days before they reached Oban, a fishing village that sits where the Firth of Lorn and the Firth of Mull meet, the baby became feverish. Celia knew that they needed to reach a place of refuge where Kit could be warm and dry. He had been a trooper through it all to this point, rarely ever crying, curious, it seemed, about the changing scenery. Now Kit cried incessantly, however, and his congested coughing began to unnerve Celia. Hugging the baby to her breast, she realized she had never felt so helpless in her life.

And then she, too, began to cough, and as her fever mounted, Celia felt herself weakening with every passing hour.

Celia insisted that they push ahead at a faster pace. She didn't know how long she could hold out.

There was no question by the time they reached Oban that they would not be able to press on to Argyll's castle. Celia listened through the buzzing haze of her fever as Edmund hired one of the fishermen to ferry them across the firth to the Isle of Mull and the Campbell stronghold, Kildalton Castle.

Father William was to continue on to the abbey by Argyll's castle for news of the Earl.

Celia had no clear memory of the trip over except the feel of the boat's rocking and plunging, sensations not unpleasant to a woman who had grown up sailing on her father's armed merchant vessels.

When the boat docked inside the protected harbor of the village that lay nestled beneath the high thick walls of Kildalton Castle, Celia was only vaguely aware of the voices that were all around her. She opened her eyes as she felt herself being lifted out of the boat by Edmund, and handed into the arms of another gray-haired man.

"Kit," she murmured. "Where's the baby?"

The man's great voice rumbled softly in response that the bairn was being cared for.

"Help Ellen ... please ... And Edmund, is Edmund here?"

"Aye, lassie," came the answer in deep fatherly tones, "you're all in my care now."

Lying comfortably in that great canopied bed, Celia

was grateful for the care she'd received at the hands of Hugh Campbell. These were not the people that were ridiculed, and feared, by those in the Lowlands. These were not the ugly, barbaric savages that they used in stories to scare children. These were kind, hospitable people who had provided Celia with the first sense of security she had felt in months.

Since she'd arrived, Celia had been benignly coerced by Lord Hugh and his servants to remain quietly in her room. Because of their care, she had quickly recovered. But even so, Celia had never been so confined in her entire life.

But now, Celia thought, perhaps the best thing I can do for the remainder of my time here is to stay as much out of sight—and away from Colin and his friend—as possible.

She was expecting Father William back any day with word about Argyll and her next move. What was keeping him?

Celia had not expected to even see Colin Campbell's ruggedly handsome face, and now she wished that she never had.

Colin's entry tonight certainly had had an unsettling effect on her plans. She had been forced to defend herself with skills possessed by few women. Celia had hoped to be the model of propriety during her stay at Kildalton, but tonight had shattered all that.

Colin Campbell does not fit into my plans, she thought.

"I know this Caithness woman is planning something, Alec," Colin said, pacing restlessly in front of his friend's fire. "I need you to tell me all you know about her."

"I'll tell you one thing," Alec said with a laugh, settling onto the one three-legged chair that adorned his bedroom. "This is not the Lady Caithness I would have expected to see."

"What do you mean by that?" Colin asked, shooting a hard look at his friend.

"For a lass as young as she seems to be, she's already acquired quite a reputation."

"She has no reputation that's reached Kildalton Castle," Colin exclaimed, surprised at the vehemence of his own voice. Colin turned and kicked at a log that threatened to roll out of the fireplace. Alec's room was warming up quickly now, and the light of the fire made Colin's giant shadow into a monstrous image on the far wall.

"Well, I'll tell you what I know, but we must be clear that this is only second- and thirdhand talk ... idle gossip coming from scurrilous, no good, parasitic court wags. In fact, you know them ... my brothers, John and Ambrose," Alec said, smiling.

Colin had to smile at that. Alec's brothers were both good men, far from Alec's facetious description. Before Flodden, they had both been constantly at court, representing the interests of the Macpherson clan. The three brothers had been with the King in the fight against the English, and although Ambrose had been badly injured, it was a miracle that all three had survived the debacle.

"She's a woman who was unhappy in marriage, plain and simple," Alec said. "Half English, half Scottish, and caught up in a bad marriage to old Lord Caithness."

"Did she choose to marry or no?" Colin asked, stopping in front of his friend, his feet spread, his hands on his kilted hips.

"Apparently, she didn't," Alec responded, surprised at the personal nature of Colin's question. This was so unlike him. "It was a marriage arranged by the King to settle a land dispute or some such business. But Caithness was old enough to be her grandfather, and the marriage had no chance from the start. According to Ambrose, she couldn't last at Caithness Hall even a year. And when she returned to court, the gossip really started."

Alec stretched his long legs out in front of him and yawned before continuing. Colin leaned his muscular arm on the stone mantel that spanned the fireplace and waited . . . but not patiently.

"They say that at court, she'd run around with anyone who caught her fancy. From what I hear, Caithness wasn't too sure about that bairn being his, either." Alec peered into his friend's face, interested in Colin's reaction to this bit of gossip, but Colin turned his face to the fire.

Colin looked into the flames before him. Something inside him didn't want to believe this old story.

"One thing I do know," Alec continued. "I saw him in the King's fight, and he may have been up there in years, but he was more than willing to do battle. He died in a swarm of bloody English foot soldiers, swinging his sword like the true warrior he was. For a Lowlander, that Caithness was a fighter."

"But obviously not much of a husband," Colin concluded. "Why didn't he just force her to stay put, and away from court?"

"From what I saw tonight," Alec remarked, feeling at his throat, trying to lighten the mood in the room, "that woman won't be forced to do anything she doesn't want to do."

Colin let his friend change the tone of the conversation. This was, after all, Alec he was talking to.

"Well, don't worry, Alec. I won't spread the word too far about you being bested by a woman half your size," Colin smirked. He was going to enjoy holding this over his friend's head for a long, long while.

"One thing my brothers didn't mention, though," Alec mused, "was how bonny a lass she is."

"Those brothers of yours have got court tastes now," Colin answered with mock disdain. "Those black eyes and auburn hair don't find their way into the love songs they hear at court. White skin and blue-gray eyes are all they think can be beautiful, more than likely."

"Truly said," Alec said, a wry smile creeping across his face. "But, you know, my friend, I'm a bit surprised that Colin Campbell would even notice this woman's eyes."

"You're daft," Colin replied, starting to pace again. "I didn't notice."

"No? Then why were you standing with your tongue hanging clear to the floor instead of living up to your reputation?"

"You didn't look any too anxious about being saved in there," Colin snorted, halting in front of Alec and giving him an accusing look.

"You know, my friend," Alec responded, smiling smugly back at him. "I wasn't. With those eyes looking so lovingly into mine, I could have lain there all night."

"Enough of this idle talk!" Colin snapped, walking across the room to the window. Sometimes Alec Macpherson could be quite annoying. "I still need to know why she's here."

"Why don't you believe what she told your father?" Alec asked, looking at the massive warrior curiously.

"Because it doesn't make sense. When the English burned Caithness Hall, any woman, especially this woman, would have gone straight back to court—not to the Highlands."

"That's probably true," Alec said thoughtfully. "From what I hear, every widow in Scotland is at court these days."

"Aye, all looking for husbands," Colin added.

"Well, then who is she after here?" Alec asked sardonically.

But Colin was not so sure. After all, he himself had not been expected back for another couple of weeks. She may have known that and come looking for another aging laird. Colin wondered bitterly if he had foiled her plan just by arriving early. His father clearly cared for this woman already. It must be Lord Hugh she was after, Colin concluded, and yet something in him didn't want to believe it. There had to be something else. The only thing to do was to stay close to her.

"I'll find out soon enough."

Chapter 4

We should be going home now. Instead, I hear we're moving farther north. We won't be leaving what remains of this fishing village soon enough to suit me, though. There is no one left here except us. We've murdered them all. Dragged them from their lofts and their root cellars and their sheepcotes and cut them down in their gardens. The others laugh now as they drag babies from the screaming mothers' arms. They all die when we find them, and Lord Danvers looks on with a smile.

No wonder they all flee from us when they can still run, the terror in their eyes. I've never in my life seen such destruction . . . such utterly senseless destruction.

Colin would not get too close to her the next day.

Celia was wide awake before dawn. Kit and Ellen were sleeping soundly, but Celia's night was finished. Restless, she paced the room like a lioness ready to hunt. She needed movement, fresh air, a good fight. Celia needed something to get her blood moving.

What little sleep she'd gotten had been riddled with dreams. Fires. Gray, windswept moors. Secret passages. And Colin Campbell.

Damn, what's wrong with me, she thought. She was acting like some starry-eyed girl. This isn't some French love poem. She was not a person to be affected by some handsome face. She'd seen many handsome faces in the courts she'd attended. His face was not so different from so many others—two eyes, a nose, a mouth. No, she was way past that stage in her life. Twenty years old. A grown woman.

And she had never thought of herself as beautiful or even attractive. No, she always had been practical. That was all that mattered. But last night when Colin had looked at her so appraisingly, she had felt demeaned. Her response had been unthinking—she'd wanted to strike back at him.

But lying awake during the night, Celia had seen that look again, in her mind, and striking back was not the response that permeated her being.

Celia had escaped from fire. She'd ridden through the harsh Highland winter. She'd blocked the secret passage. But Colin Campbell was a different kind of obstacle.

When the dawn broke clear and dry, Celia put on her travel clothes, the only outfit she had, looked in again on the sleeping Kit and Ellen, and quietly slipped out into the hallway.

This was the first time she'd been out of her quarters for fresh air since arriving. As Celia worked her way down the wide corridor, her eyes took in the magnificent architecture.

This part of the castle was clearly new. Celia had been impressed when she'd first awakened in a bright bedroom furnished with glazed windows and a fireplace. Even the new manor house at Caithness had only had glass in the top halves of the windows. The bottom halves, like the windows even in the King's castles at Stirling and in Edinburgh, had been shuttered with wood. But here, the windows were large and completely covered with a grillwork of leaded glass. What was most shocking, though, was that they swung open on hinges.

In this part of the castle the builders had used a style

she hadn't seen in Scotland before. The ceilings, even in the hallways, were higher, with arches that came to a point at the top, like some of the newer cathedrals in England. The effect was one of space. Why, the Campbells lived better than the King himself.

As she reached the wide stairway that led down into the Great Hall, she was startled by Runt's sudden emergence from an alcove farther down the hallway. Despite his name, Lord Hugh's squire was hardly a runt—the young man was not much shorter than his master. Ellen told Celia that she'd spoken with him in passing one day, and that he'd said he was called "Runt" because his elder brother, Emmet, was a giant—the size of Lord Colin.

Ellen had also heard that after losing their parents at a young age, the two brothers had been raised in Lord Hugh's household. While Emmet had attained the position of Lord Colin's top fighter, Runt was still training as Lord Hugh's squire.

"Lady Caithness! You're up and about today," he said, with obvious delight at the sight of the lady.

Suddenly Celia felt guilty, as if she'd been caught doing something she shouldn't have been doing.

"It's . . . it's time I got some air, Runt," she answered haltingly. "It certainly looks like a fine morning."

"Is that so, m'lady? If you'll let me, I'll wake up Lord Hugh. Or Lord Colin, perhaps. I know they'd want to show you around, now that you're feeling more yourself."

"*No!* Please don't, Runt," Celia answered quickly. "I'm not going far. I just want to go out into the courtyard for a few minutes. I'm not used to being cooped up for so long."

The last thing she needed was the company of Colin Campbell, the one man she was hoping to avoid.

"Then let me walk down with you, m'lady. I'll unbar the door for you."

This is far better than having to face that gruff master of mine first thing in the morning, Runt thought to himself. But even better would be meeting up with Ellen, that fair-haired, green-eyed beauty who's traveling with Lady Caithness.

"Thank you, Runt," she said as they moved together down the stone steps.

Walking across the Great Hall to the Entry Room, the two attracted the attention of several of the dozen or so dogs curled up in contented heaps throughout the room. Most simply raised their heads and peered disinterestedly at the pair, and then went back to sleep, but one, a gigantic black hound, lifted his massive body off the floor with a shake and trotted over.

This was undoubtedly the biggest dog Celia had ever seen in her life. Celia liked dogs, in general, but she knew that these dogs could be vicious defenders of a manor's property. So much for sneaking out for a quiet walk.

"That's Lord Colin's favorite dog, m'lady," Runt said, pulling at Celia's elbow instinctively. "Be careful of him. He's a vicious one with strangers. Away, Bear!"

Before he could move between Celia and the dog, though, Bear had moved in next to the woman and nosed her hand up onto his wide, square head. Celia couldn't help but smile as she petted the huge animal, scratching around his ears with both hands as the beast pushed against her waist with his head.

Celia laughed and braced herself with her feet to avoid being pushed over, as Runt stood openmouthed beside her.

"If this is one of the vicious ones," she teased, "I'd hate to see the lapdogs."

Runt, in one of the few speechless moments in his life, led Celia—and her new canine friend—past the gigantic oaken doors in the Entry Room to a small side door that the squire unbarred.

"I'll leave the door ajar, m'lady. The household will all be bustling in no time. The cooks have been working for hours already, I'm sure. Will you and Ellen ... er ... Mistress Ellen be joining the master for breakfast now? He likes to take it in the South Hall—I can show you where that is."

"No, Runt, thank you. I believe I'll stay to my room for meals a bit longer," Celia responded firmly. She wanted to make sure that her little walk would not compromise her plan.

"Aye, m'lady. But I must be telling you, Lord Hugh is looking forward to you joining him for meals. We don't get too many ladies such as yourself visiting Kildalton Castle."

"You mean Lord Colin doesn't entertain much?" Celia asked, working hard to keep the sarcasm out of her voice. She wondered where that question had even come from.

"Why, no m'lady! Lord Colin is far too busy fighting in France and raiding the English villages for such nonsense. Begging your pardon, m'lady. But we *have* heard tales about certain French ladies that were mighty interested in him."

Celia gave the appearance of ignoring the close scrutiny that Runt was giving her as he finished his last comment. There was definitely some matchmaking going on here, she noted with concern.

There was a tantalizing hint of spring in the courtyard air, and Celia enjoyed moving about with the huge dog beside her. Bear was positively playful, but Celia knew she could only stay out for a short time. She couldn't afford to run into anyone else.

Back inside, she had a difficult time persuading the animal to stay down the wide stairs, but eventually the dog allowed her to go up alone.

Once in her room, she was almost sorry she had gone

out. Having tasted the freedom of the open air, Celia now wanted more.

Celia did not appear at breakfast in the South Hall that Lord Hugh liked to use for his everyday meals. Albeit a warmer and brighter room, the South Hall was less roomy than the Great Hall, which the chieftain used for Legal Days and for occasions that warranted more pomp and pageantry. During the winter months, the smaller room was downright cozy.

When Colin strode into the room, the great black dog at his heels, Lord Hugh had only just seated himself at the long, slightly elevated table that crossed one end of the room. Colin greeted jovial groups that were seated at the long oak tables and benches stretching the length of the room on both sides. Servants were bustling about with trays of fish, great loaves of bread, and bowls of oat gruel, and all were vocal in their warm welcoming of the younger Campbell.

"Good morning, Father," Colin said, sitting beside the chieftain. "Looks like the fine weather is holding."

"Aye, lad. Before you walked in, I was just telling these rapscallions that on warm days like this, they should be building smaller fires in this room. They should be more careful with the AMOUNTS OF WOOD WE BURN." Hugh shouted the last words in the direction of Runt, who was eating at one of the lower tables with a group of fighters and ignoring the laird.

Colin sat beside his father, thinking how much he loved these morning meals, when a small, heavyset woman brought a broad trencher made of bread and heaped with a portion of fish appropriate for a warrior of Colin's size.

"Agnes." Colin smiled, rising and giving the woman an affectionate squeeze. "What are you doing delivering food yourself. There aren't enough things for you to do around here?"

"You think a woman doesn't have enough time to feed a fellow she's raised as her own?" Agnes had, indeed, raised Colin since the boy's mother had died of the plague when he was only five. When Colin's mother had come from France to marry Lord Hugh, Agnes had come as her companion, and for the past twenty-five years had run the household with a kindly but firm hand.

"I see none of the towers have fallen down since I left for Dunvegan," Colin commented conversationally, pulling her by the hand onto the bench beside him.

"No, Colin, we've been able to keep the old place running while you've been away, difficult as that may be for you to believe," Agnes said, giving him an ironic yet affectionate smile all at the same time.

"Not at all. But I see we've picked up a whole troupe of unexpected guests. Did you know that Alec Macpherson is in the Archbishop's room?"

"Aye, she knows," Runt piped in from his table. "She nearly ran up there herself when I told her he was there. Outrageous conduct for a woman her age, if you ask me."

"Mind your manners," Agnes snapped, glaring at Lord Hugh's wisecracking young squire. "Alec Macpherson has always been a delightful and mannerly guest in this house, unlike some who just loaf around and eat here."

"You can see nothing has changed since you were gone," Lord Hugh put in in between mouthfuls.

"Well, Agnes, I hope the other guests haven't been taking up too much of your time," Colin said in as casual a tone as he could muster.

"Oh, no, my boy," Agnes answered, "they've been no trouble at all. Lady Caithness is a quiet one and has stayed to herself . . . and the baby . . . since they arrived. I'm looking forward to speaking with her more."

Agnes leaned over and whispered in a voice loud enough for Colin's father to hear. "I even delivered a message from Lord Hugh to her yesterday saying that when she was feeling better, we'd look forward to her company at meals."

"Just being a good host," Hugh snorted.

"Well, considering she's a courtly lady, I don't imagine she'll be getting up for many breakfasts," Colin said sarcastically.

"As a matter of fact, my good Lord Colin," Runt responded, scuttering up to the dais and leaning both elbows on the table across from the warrior. "The 'courtly lady' that you imagine sleeping till noon was up and about before any of you had even stirred."

"What do you mean, 'up and about'? Up and about where?" Colin asked.

"Why, she was out in the courtyard for a bit of fresh air, but to tell the truth, I think she would have been happier to go beyond the castle walls."

"Well, that's good news. Maybe I'll wait for her to come down then and show her the village after breakfast," Hugh announced happily.

"I'll take her!" Colin exploded, attempting to recover a casual tone in his next words. "You don't need to bother yourself. I'll . . . I'll be going down into the village later to see how the new school construction is going."

"If you two bulls would stop fighting long enough for a woman to talk," Agnes broke in, "Lady Caithness has already eaten this morning, and she told the girl that she'd feel better taking her meals in her room for the next few days."

"If she's feeling better, then why the devil can't she come down to eat with us!" Lord Hugh grouched.

"Why can't she come down and . . . why is it that men can't see past the end of their own noses?" Agnes retorted, glaring into their perplexed faces. "The girl has nothing to wear besides the travel clothes she wore in

here. You think she's coming down in that? You two
don't have a clue about how a lady of quality thinks!"

Colin and his father exchanged that look that men
who know nothing often exchange.

"I don't know why I even bother telling you two anything. I'll take care of this." Agnes went out of the hall,
muttering to herself about men and their failings. She
was now a woman with a mission. But she also couldn't
help smiling to herself at Colin's obvious interest.

And Agnes was glad. Watching Lady Caithness deal
with her sick baby had given Agnes a warm first impression of the lady. And she had none of the demanding
habits of some other court ladies Agnes had known. The
lady was grateful for even the smallest things that were
done for her. Agnes liked her down-to-earth attitude. In
a way, Lady Caithness reminded her of Colin's own
mother. She wondered vaguely if Lord Hugh had seen
any similarity.

Going through the doorway into the Great Hall,
Agnes exchanged courtesies with Edmund, who was just
coming toward the South Hall from outside. She couldn't
help but blush at this man's presence. Even at his age,
he was an extremely handsome man and extremely polite. They don't make them like this anymore, she
thought to herself. But each morning since the visitors
arrived, the knight had walked down to the village pier.
He seems to be waiting for something, Agnes thought.

As Edmund walked into the South Hall, he thought
about how fine the improvements were that Lord Hugh
and his late wife had made. This room was a wonderful
place for the meals. As the sun rose higher in the sky,
the room warmed very comfortably, and the natural light
displayed the three huge, brightly colored tapestries that
hung above the two fireplaces at either end and on the
long wall across from the line of windows.

Lady Campbell had been French, Edmund remembered, a noble lady of ancient royal blood, and she had been a real civilizing influence in the life of Hugh Campbell. Edmund had been given what had been the master's bedroom in the old section of the castle, an honor befitting an old comrade at arms.

But he had been quite surprised at the amount of comfort that the new section provided. The sheer number of bedrooms was incredible. When he had been the Campbells' guest thirty years before, guests had all slept in the Great Hall, as was still the custom in most of the great castles to this day. But Edmund had really enjoyed the luxury of the great feather bed he'd been given.

Once the bairn's safety is assured, Edmund thought, *maybe it will be time to settle down and make some improvements to my own holding. Celia, as well, would really enjoy a project like that over the decadence of court life. But by then, with any luck, maybe she'll have projects of her own.*

Colin Campbell was everything Edmund had expected him to be—and more. His knowledge of modern warfare was impressive, but his strong opinions about the Stuart kings' role in Scotland's future surprised him. Traditionally the clan leaders in the West had taken every opportunity to oppose the Stuart kings. The Highlanders' independence was legendary. But this difference of loyalty to a unified Scotland certainly made Colin a standout among the Western and Highland leaders. Edmund wondered whether the Earl of Huntly knew of this ally in the Stuart cause.

As Edmund listened, he was pleased to see how much of the father had been passed on to the son.

For over an hour, Celia had been studying the panel that she was sure Colin and Alec had used to enter her room. After dragging the chest away from the wall, she had inspected every seam in the wooden panel, but to no avail.

The panel had been latched when she pushed the chest up against it, so Colin must have accomplished that when she'd crossed the room for her cloak. It must be very simple to do, she thought.

A knock at the door interrupted her search.

"It's Agnes," came the answer to Celia's response. "May I come in?"

Although Celia had only spoken with Agnes briefly in the few times she'd visited, Celia knew that this woman had been running the household for a long time. Each time they'd spoken, Agnes had been pleasant and hospitable.

But this time Agnes was not alone.

In fact, Celia was hardly prepared for the sight that awaited her. Agnes and an army of helpers appeared ready to lay siege to Celia's bedroom. Agnes, two burly men carrying a wooden tub, twelve boys carrying buckets of steaming water, and a legion of women carrying piles of carefully folded linens and clothing, jammed the hallway. Celia stepped back in surprise, and the invaders took full advantage, streaming into the bedchamber behind their assault commander.

The chaos that ensued was not the result of wartime pillaging, but rather peacetime furnishing.

Although Agnes was clearly in charge, it was only because her voice was pitched higher than anyone else's in the room.

"We've brought you a few things, dear," Agnes shouted, after searching through her rampaging army for her guest.

The bath was set up where the sun cast its beams by the fireplace, and the women laid out the linens and clothing on the huge bed. When those tasks were complete, Agnes unceremoniously dismissed her troops, closing the door firmly behind them. She turned and cast a firm yet affectionate eye on Celia.

Celia was nearly hidden behind the great oak bed.

Agnes walked to her and took hold of her guest's hands, coaxing Celia from her sanctuary to the middle of the room.

"Lady Caithness, it's time you felt at home here," Agnes said softly. She could sense a shadowy anxiety in this innocent-looking child.

"Please call me Celia," she responded with warmth. This display of motherly attention touched a tender chord in Celia.

"But what is all this?" she continued, nodding at the clothing laid out on the bed. Celia realized she had been clutching Agnes's hands, so she now gently released them.

"Don't you be concerned about that right now. First things first. Into the bath with you."

Agnes's tone left no room for discussion. And Celia had no intention of arguing.

The warm luxurious feel of the jasmine-scented water soothed away the aching tension that Celia had not even been aware of in her body. As the tightness melted away, she felt relaxed for the first time in ages.

While Agnes washed Celia's hair, the woman talked about her world at Kildalton Castle, but Celia found her attention drifting as the sleepless night began to take its toll.

Celia's mind drifted in an unexpected direction as she lay back in the warm water. Colin Campbell had been standing exactly here the night before. In her mind she felt his strong arms around her. Her smooth body rose ever so slightly to his caress, and her lips waited for the touch of his.

Suddenly Celia was conscious of the compliment that Agnes was giving her.

"You certainly don't have the body of a woman who's had a baby in the last year. You know, Lady Campbell was very much like that. After Colin was born, she was back to her regular size in no time at all, but she fed her own baby. That was not customary, of course, but Colin's mother had a mind of her own."

Celia desperately wanted to change the subject. Kit was seven months old now. She wondered what a woman's body *should* look like after seven months.

Celia looked over at the bed.

"Where did these things come from? I appreciate the thought, Agnes, but my travel clothes will meet my needs for the remainder of my stay here."

"You'll want to dress up a bit for dinner," Agnes coaxed. "Especially since this is Colin's first night back."

Recalling her momentary lapse into sensuality, Celia blushed at the thought of meeting Colin. But that was a fantasy, thought Celia, this is reality.

"If it's not a great inconvenience, I will continue taking my meals with Ellen and the baby here in my room, Agnes. I really won't be needing those things, but thank you," Celia said politely, not wanting to sound ungrateful in the wake of Agnes's kindness.

"But it is an inconvenience, my dear. If you don't begin joining us at least for dinner, *I'll* have to put up with Lord Hugh's sulking. It isn't very often we get such attractive company, you know."

"I know you're being a good hostess, but I'm sure that with Lord Hugh's son and Alec Macpherson here, there will be plenty of discussion at dinner."

"Aye. But without a young woman at the head table, think of how boring the conversation will be for me. Wars, battles, weapons, armies, and politics. How dreadful! And don't think your uncle improves things at all. He's as bad as the rest."

"I don't mean to be a nuisance about this, Agnes, but there is also Kit to consider. He is not completely well and ..."

"Nuisance? Nonsense!" Agnes said affectionately. "But I've already seen Ellen and the baby, and they can do very well without you for an hour or two a day. It'll do you good to get out of this room."

Celia could not think of another excuse, and she knew that Agnes would have an answer for anything she could come up with anyway. Agnes was a master strategist. Celia liked that.

Besides, Celia thought, I can keep dinner short and be back here in no time.

Agnes was awaiting an answer.

"Aye," Celia said, surrendering. "I'll join you for dinner."

"Fine, my dear," Agnes said cheerfully. She turned to the clothing on the bed like a general to his maps. "Then hop out of that tub. We've a great deal to do."

The battle was far from over.

The silver brocade dress with the square-cut neckline that Agnes laid out was far, far too revealing for Celia. She would dine in her travel outfit before wearing that dress in front of those men.

There were so many beautiful dresses. Agnes explained that all this clothing had once belonged to Lady Campbell. After her marriage to Lord Hugh, Lady Campbell's family in France had continued sending trunk after trunk full of the finest fashion accessories. Lady Campbell gave much away, as Agnes had after her death, but there were so many things that Agnes felt should be kept. Now she was very glad she had kept them.

They finally compromised on a burgundy-colored velvet gown.

The gown's thin fur trim at the round neckline accentuated Celia's auburn hair. And Celia liked the simple lines of the dress. It had a tight-fitting, long-waisted bodice, and a long skirt that flared at the hip and draped gracefully to the ground. The furred sleeves were wide and turned back to form a cuff. A loose belt encircled its low waistline and from it pendants of braided gold cording hung to the floor.

As daylight faded outside the window, Celia inspected the reflection in the long looking glass that Agnes's troops had brought in. The bold, confident eyes that sparkled. The full lips that seemed to dominate even the rich color of the gown. Celia saw in that mirrored face a beauty that was not her own. A beauty that was mocking her. The image that looked back at her belonged to someone else.

Lady Caithness had arrived at Kildalton Castle.

Chapter 5

I knew the two were getting as sick of this as I, but I never thought they would be so free with their opinions. So he guts them like animals. These are his own soldiers, good English soldiers... and Danvers hacks them up like meat. And we watch. We all just watch.

Kildalton Castle was too crowded for Colin's liking.

The crowd that filled the space between the long tables of the South Hall acted more like a group of rioters than an assembly of dinner guests. Colin's eyes traveled upward to the colorful tapestry above the fireplace at the far end of the hall. It was a depiction of a garden and lovers lost in the bloom of romantic love. The woman with the dark maroon dress held a white rose and seemed to look out across the room at him. Since childhood, Colin had always been affected by the tranquillity of that look.

On the dais, behind the head table, the giant warrior stood with his back to the small fire, his massive shoulders resting against the mantel, and his muscular arms crossed in front of him. The great black dog was stretched out at Colin's feet, Bear's huge head resting on his master's boot.

There were so many things left to do, Colin thought. These first days back were always so busy. On top of meeting with the Campbell clan's advising councilors regarding routine management issues, Colin had also needed to discuss with them the chieftains' meeting at Dunvegan. The day had been too far gone when those discussions ended for Colin to go into the village as he'd hoped.

For two years now Colin had been virtual chieftain of the Campbell clan, relieving his father of the grueling responsibilities that the position entailed. Hugh Campbell would retain the title of laird for as long as he lived, and that was just as Colin wanted it to be. Lord Hugh still sat at the head of the council, and his advice was actively sought and given, but Colin now made the decisions for the clan's future.

Not that his father was not capable or unwilling to make his presence felt. Colin smiled, thinking about the day's meeting when several of the members of the council had expressed their concerns over the potential vulnerability of the Campbell clan in standing alone against the other Highland clans. Their arguments had scarcely concluded when Lord Hugh stood up from the long table with a face that made no attempt to hide the wrath that was boiling up within him. Colin's ears still rang with the words of the angry chief.

"It it were up to some of you," Lord Hugh had begun, his voice rising in volume as he gave vent to his fury, "the Campbell clan would still be sailing in dugout canoes and living in stone huts with our oxen and our sheep! Where were you with this spineless counsel when Colin set off to Dunvegan. We all knew the risks of taking this position. But the risks of going along with the fools that Colin met with have greater consequences.

"Do you want your families dragged off or slaughtered by the English? Do you want to give up all the comforts and advances that we have achieved over the last forty years? Are you prepared to give up the freedom and independence that Scottish blood has bought?

"Have you forgotten what ten thousand of our brothers died for at Flodden, only seven months ago? Are you ready to trade their sacrifice for a future of fear and slavery?"

The silence of shamefaced assent that followed Lord Hugh's speech was now replaced in that hall by the carnival uproar of the dinner horde, and Colin knew that the councilors were convinced.

The younger Campbell looked around the room with pride. There, in front of the dais, his father stood with Alec, Edmund, and some of those same councilors, their conversation animated with gestures, as they tried to communicate over the ruckus that surrounded them. Colin could tell that his father was trying to convey some new idea that he'd had to the others.

The Campbell lairds had always been people of great vision, with far-reaching projects that changed and improved the lives of those around them.

Colin Campbell was no different.

As a child, Colin had been naturally drawn to the life of the warrior. Almost instinctively, he knew that his chief responsibility would be to protect the people who lived in the shadow of the Campbell name. And that suited the boy.

When Lord Hugh had taken Colin to St. Andrew's to complete his education, Colin's horizons as a leader had been broadened. All along the way the boy had seen people, ragged and thin, living in windowless turf huts, seemingly unable to help themselves to a better way of life. In the villages he had seen peasants who had been driven off their small farms by the lairds who were enclosing the land for sheep. All beggars now, joining the hungry fringe of war cripples and lepers. Colin was only fourteen years old, but mature enough to recognize widespread deprivation when he saw it. It seemed to him that the entire lower-class folk of Scotland were suffering.

Colin's eyes were opened to the realization that mere protection was not enough. The future Campbell laird had promised himself then that the people who depended on him would never know this kind of poverty and suffering. So he had set his mind to change things, to try new ways. If need be, he'd break the yoke of tradition and encourage the innovative, the untried ideas. Colin knew that for his people to thrive, it was change that was needed.

This was the source of Colin's vision.

Lost in his thoughts, Colin was the last person in the room to be aware of her presence. But when he looked up, he felt his chest tighten with a suddenness that shocked him.

Last night, in her room, his first reaction had been to a vision, a dream. He'd thought to himself, beauty such as this cannot exist in real flesh and blood. She stirred human desires in him, true. But she . . . she looked like a goddess.

But that was last night. Thinking more about her in the clear light of day, Colin had decided that it was the situation, the context, his fatigue, the surprise, that had made her appear to be more than what she really is. It was his weary mind playing tricks on his wearier body that had created the illusion.

But tonight . . .

This vision before his eyes was indeed very much of this earth. Lady Caithness was the most beautiful woman he had ever seen in his life.

He watched as her eyes roamed the room, resting momentarily on those who stood in hushed awe. And then her gaze embraced his own.

Her large, dark eyes were direct, captivating. For a

moment Colin felt himself getting lost in that gaze, falling in some airy space of unfathomable depth.

She stood there waiting and her eyes never left his. It was as though she were asking him something that he could not define. This questioning look was meant for him; he knew that.

Suddenly he realized that she had not yet entered the hall. Could it be that she was waiting for a sign from him? An invitation from him? This, Colin had not expected.

Slowly, imperceptibly to all but Lady Caithness, Colin straightened from the mantel and nodded once to the woman before him.

Celia had needed to find Colin first.

Oh, yes, she was certain that by now he would have heard of Lady Caithness's reputation. Celia was sorry that she'd agreed to assume her identity. Of all people, Lady Caithness, the free-spirited Lady Caithness. Although she had never met his friend, Alec Macpherson, Celia knew of the Macpherson brothers. Alec was sure to have heard the stories from them. He was sure to have told Colin.

Stepping down the great staircase, wearing his mother's dress, Celia knew that she could not avoid seeing him, speaking with him, probably even sitting beside him. And something inside her wanted to make a separate peace with Colin Campbell.

Celia wanted to make sure that Colin did not mistake her intentions. She was certainly not in search of a husband. Not him. Not his father.

And Colin could easily come to that conclusion, she was certain of that. It was only logical. And the future Campbell lord was probably being chased by every available woman in Scotland . . . and then some.

As she'd reached the foot of the great staircase, she

asked herself why she cared at all what Colin Campbell thought of her personally. She'd be leaving soon enough.

But stopping at the doorway of the South Hall, Celia's eyes found his immediately in that crowded hall. He might have been the only man standing there, because he was the only thing she could see.

Colin Campbell was a beautiful sight, and Celia was having difficulty remembering how to breathe. Her reaction to this warrior was inexplicable. She couldn't stop staring at him.

All she knew at this moment was that she did care.

As if they were the only two people in the room, Celia understood when Colin nodded to her. She stepped into the hall.

Lord Hugh was hardly gentle as he bulled his way through the guests to reach her. She'd made her appearance; he was not going to let her get away.

Suddenly as he broke through the crowd, the full effect of this woman hit him. Like a hot iron spike in his heart, something about Lady Caithness reminded him of the woman he had lost twenty-five years earlier. The woman he had never stopped loving. The woman he would never replace.

The kind of woman he had been hoping his son would also find.

"Lady Caithness! Come in, come in, my dear," Hugh boomed, taking her by the hand and leading her into the hall. "I am so happy that you've joined us tonight. And Runt tells me that last night I completely ruined any chance of introducing you properly to my son and his friend. Please give an ignorant old boor a chance to do it properly."

"Lord Hugh, the only thing that happened last night was that you rescued us all—especially me—from a very awkward moment," Celia responded, smiling. She was genuinely touched by this gentle man's show of affection. "But I would certainly like to meet your family properly."

"That's just fine," the laird said, scanning the room in search of Colin.

Colin slowly worked his way through the crowd that surrounded Lady Caithness. Like the queen bee, he thought with annoyance. Her buzzing drones are already falling into formation.

By the time Colin was able to get through the throng, Alec Macpherson was speaking with Lord Hugh and Lady Caithness. Edmund hovered nearby, finishing an argument with one of Hugh's men.

As Colin approached, he noticed his huge black dog had reached the group before him. Disgusted, he watched as the dog pushed his massive head up under her hand. As the woman continued to converse, she began to scratch his ears. Colin scowled at his dog, and Bear eyed his master with what almost looked like a grin on his face. Traitor.

"Lord Hugh," Alec was saying with a wink at Celia, "Lady Caithness has a unique way of driving home her points."

Colin noticed her color rise at the comment.

"I didn't know you two had a chance to even speak to one another last night," Hugh said, looking perplexed.

"Aye, that we did," Alec responded, rubbing his throat and smiling slyly in Celia's direction. "Lady Caithness's arguments are short, but extremely pointed."

"You should know," Colin teased, coming up behind Celia. The woman in front of him did not turn immediately, and Colin could smell the fresh feminine scent emanating from her uncovered auburn tresses. The top of her head barely reached his chin, and her hair hung in loose ringlets to her shoulders. He had to restrain a sudden urge to slip his hands around the beauty's waist, to pull her into him, to feel her body contours against his own. This is ridiculous, Colin thought, I have to get control of myself.

"Colin," his father said, his grave and formal tone undercut by the twinkle in his eye. "Let me introduce you to Lady Caithness."

"Welcome to ..." Colin stumbled in his attempt to finish the sentence, for as she turned and their eyes met, Colin's world stood still. Her look was so steady, so open, so incredibly beautiful. Colin felt that he was looking directly into her soul—pure, strong, gorgeous. What had been so powerfully attractive at a distance just moments before was literally stunning face-to-face.

But he was quick to recover when she lowered her gaze.

"Welcome to Kildalton Castle, Lady Caithness," he continued with as much smoothness as he could muster. Focusing on her full lips, Colin wondered whether she knew what was going through his mind. "I hope your stay has been pleasant and comfortable so far."

"It's been quite pleasant, thank you, m'lord," Celia said, not trusting herself to look him in the face. She had recognized the look of desire in his piercing gray eyes—she didn't want him to see the same in hers. Not now.

How could this be the woman who led a life of such scandal? Colin thought, wanting to look into her eyes again. Something in Colin wanted this woman to be that wild creature of impulse. He had seen something of the wildness the night before, but there was no hint now of that decadence he had expected.

"Colin," Hugh said, attempting to sound sincere. "If you'll keep Lady Caithness's company a bit, I have to show something to Alec and Edmund right now."

All Colin could do was nod his head, before his father practically dragged Alec away by the elbow. Colin was quite amused by the pained look in Alec's eyes. Colin also noticed the affectionate squeeze that Edmund gave Celia's elbow before following Hugh and Alec.

Honestly, Colin was thankful for his father's action. And he didn't really care why his father wanted to leave them alone like that. Colin just knew that he wanted her to himself for a few minutes. If you could call being left in a room with dozens of people "alone."

But Colin wanted to know more of this woman. Maybe even provoke her into revealing something of the truth about herself. Eyeing the silky skin above the dress's round furred neckline, he thought about maybe getting her to show him . . . well . . . more than what meets the eye. Colin definitely had two things on his mind, and he unconsciously shook his head to clear it.

No, what he was really looking forward to was getting her riled up, getting under her skin, though the thought didn't escape him that he wouldn't mind getting on her skin, as well.

How did her witty peacocks at court do it? he thought, growing angry at the idea. After all, that's the kind of men she's accustomed to.

"Lady Caithness, we have beautiful summers in the Western Isles. From what Edmund has told us of your journey, you would have done well to wait until warmer weather before coming to Kildalton," Colin said, trying to keep the sarcasm from creeping into his voice.

"I'll be sure to tell Lord Danvers your opinion the next time I run into him," Celia said, flashing angry eyes at him. She knew full well that Edmund had explained Danvers's burning of the Caithness holding. If this is the game we are going to play, she thought to herself, then two can play it.

"Oh, do you run into him often?" Colin asked with an air of amused superiority. He saw the flush of emotion cross her face. How easy it was to get to her.

"More than I care to remember," Celia responded

directly. "How about you, or do you go out of your way to avoid him?"

Colin flushed red with irritation, taken aback by her remark. He knew what she was implying. No, he hadn't been with the King at Flodden, but he wasn't running around at court, either. He had been doing his duty, as his king had commanded. He . . .

"Did I say something to displease you, Lord Colin? Your frown hints at some displeasure."

She had turned the tables on him. He had the most remarkable urge to strangle this imp before him. She was not even trying to hide her amusement at his discomfort. She was smiling openly at him, and Colin could not help himself. Strangle? No. Seduce? Well, that's worth giving more thought to. She was so damned attractive. And his smile back was genuine. She was certainly more quick-witted than he'd given her credit for.

"Displeasure? No, m'lady," Colin answered, putting on his fiercest scowl. "I was just taking a moment to recover from your highly unwarranted attack. I do feel more sympathy for my friend Alec, however, now that I've been put in that position myself."

"I do hope that you are only jesting, m'lord," Celia said, with real sincerity in her voice. "My response was only in self-defense. You were the one charging me with jeopardizing the life of a child simply to visit your holding during a bad time of the year.

"In addition, sir," Celia continued in a more conciliatory tone, "from what I'd heard of your courage and intelligence, I was fairly certain that you would not be skewered so easily by my admittedly cutting comment."

Colin looked at her with amusement. She had just scolded him for his sarcastic remarks, and then given him a compliment in the next breath. This was one remarkable woman. Colin could see that he had to start all over again, but this time more carefully . . . for his own sake!

"Are you always so quick to draw?" Colin asked with smiling eyes. He clasped his hands behind his back, leaning slightly forward in a confidential attitude. "Do you always kill first, then try to ask questions later? Don't you sometimes find that difficult?"

"Not at all," Celia responded, smiling broadly. As he leaned toward her, she felt the power of his manly presence. His nearness was strangely exciting. She felt her heart pounding in her chest. "However, I do have to admit that I am finding myself responding strangely when you're about."

"Oh, do you, m'lady?" Colin said, lowering his voice seductively, leaning even closer to her.

"You know I don't mean it that way, m'lord." Celia couldn't stop her blush from spreading. His lips were so close to her ear now that she could feel his warm breath on her skin. She lowered her head, making an attempt to rearrange the folds in her gown. As she did, Bear lifted his muzzle to her hand. Celia caressed the beast's huge head. He was deliberately misinterpreting her words.

"I would still very much like to hear about this response of yours," Colin continued in a low teasing tone. He was truly enjoying this flirtation. But, to be completely truthful, he was quite pleasantly surprised—no, amazed—that he could actually make Lady Caithness blush. By God, she looked positively flustered.

Celia continued to stroke the dog's head, and Colin reached down as well, and as he did, their fingers entwined for the briefest of moments. But in that split second, a crackling shock of passion radiated through their bodies.

But it was only for a moment, though, for Celia withdrew her hand with the quickness of lightning.

"Wh-what I mean is . . ." Celia faltered, then stopped, bittersweet at the sight of Lord Hugh and the others approaching them.

"There you are, my dear," Hugh said, taking Celia's arm in his. "I won't have Colin hiding you away on me."

"But . . . but, m'lord, neither of us has moved an inch!" Celia stammered, unable to regain her balance with these two men.

"Too bad," boomed the laird. "Colin, I thought I brought you up better."

"Father," Colin responded, thoroughly enjoying this, "the night is still young!"

Celia's composure was now almost completely shattered. The apple has clearly not fallen too far from the tree in this family, she thought. And Edmund had thought she'd be safe here. Even he was enjoying this embarrassment.

"Well, Lady Caithness, if you haven't been talking about anything interesting, then I assume my son has been boring you with talk of the changes he is making in the village."

Celia was delighted at the change in topic, even if she hadn't the slightest idea what Lord Hugh was talking about.

"No, m'lord. Lord Colin hasn't had a chance to tell me about your village."

"I'll put you to sleep over it at dinner," Colin interjected, smiling.

"I'm not so easily put to sleep, sir," Celia snapped, immediately sorry she'd said that as she looked at Colin's one raised eyebrow.

"I've been known to rise to the occasion before, Lady Caithness," Colin replied, holding in his laughter. The other men were chuckling, less successful in their restraint.

"Now that I think of it, sleeping might be a preferable position than the one I've gotten myself into here." Celia glowered at the tall half circle of men before her.

"I'm an open-minded host," Lord Hugh said with

comic gravity, "but I won't have you two sleeping together on my dinner table."

Celia couldn't believe her ears. These men were too much.

Colin stood watching Lord Hugh lead her to dinner. As his father placed her in a seat between them, Colin thought that he might actually enjoy Lady Caithness's visit at Kildalton. Never in his many travels to Europe's great courts had he been so charmed as he'd been already this evening. Lady Caithness seemed so natural, so impulsive, so different from other court ladies he'd known.

Even though the gadabout Lady Caithness was far from what he wanted in a wife, this woman was definitely attractive and witty enough for a short-term relationship. In fact, he might even look forward to being her spring fancy. Aye, just a short-term thing, he thought to himself. Short term.

Celia was really going to enjoy this short visit at Kildalton Castle.

The moon was just rising over the water outside her window, and the soft rays illuminated Celia's room with a shade of blue. Celia sat snugly in her great bed, her knees hugged to her chest, listening to the sounds of the sea. Occasionally, as she sat dreamily recalling the events of the evening, muffled sounds of the after-dinner revelry would reach her ears.

A Weavers' Guild had come into the castle to perform a play for Lord Hugh's household and his guests—some religious play in keeping with the season. Celia had wanted to stay, but she couldn't trust herself in that room any longer.

Dinner had been wonderful. Colin's attentions to her even better.

He had been a true courtier, anticipating her needs,

serving her at table, keeping up a witty conversation that often seemed to have double meanings. He was definitely flirting with her, and Celia had enjoyed every minute of it. To her own dismay, she had even found herself returning it at times.

Something was very different here at Kildalton Castle. If some man had spoken to her at the Queen's table the way Colin had at dinner, Celia was sure she would have dumped a goblet of ale on him and left the room. She'd always been very sensitive about the way men treated her in public. But she felt different about this situation, somehow.

It had been more than just flirting. Colin's attentions to her had awakened feelings that she'd never known even existed. For the first time in her life, she felt herself desired as a woman, a complete woman.

Celia had even enjoyed watching Colin's humorous act of possessiveness. She smiled, thinking of how Alec Macpherson and Lord Hugh had tried to get into their conversation.

Lord Hugh had been seated in his customary chair, the only one in the hall. She and Alec had been seated on the benches on either side of him, and Colin had sat down beside her.

Celia had been polite, speaking with Lord Hugh and Alec when the conversation warranted it. But at one point Colin stood up and asked if they could exchange places for a moment while he spoke with his father. She did not hesitate to comply, believing the seriousness of his tone.

Celia had been shocked when, after she had moved, Colin sat down in her place and turned his huge back to his father and Alec, effectively shutting them out of any contact with her for the remainder of the meal. Her last view of them was Lord Hugh's astonished face disappearing behind Colin's shoulder.

But there had been serious talk as well, talk that had interested Celia.

When Colin had spoken of the village and his dreams of modernization, he had spoken to her as a real person, and Celia had glimpsed another side of him that she hadn't anticipated. And he'd 'seemed surprised by the questions she'd asked and the genuine interest that she'd shown.

Celia had traveled all over Europe with her father, and even gone to the Far East as a child, and she'd seen a world that was rapidly changing, and those changes fascinated her.

There were many facets of this man's personality, and so far Celia liked every one of them.

In fact, there was enchantment in some of their moments together.

She half closed her eyes, thinking of the moment when she'd held her goblet up to be filled. Colin had taken the pitcher himself and placed his huge hand over hers as he'd filled the cup. Celia shivered as she recalled the heat that had coursed through her body at that moment. It might have been her imagination, but she had felt his fingers caress the back of her hand.

Perhaps she had imagined the lingering touch of a knee, the caress of an elbow, but each time it occurred, Celia's breathing had shortened and her pulse quickened.

But it didn't matter if it was her imagination or not. Sitting alone in her dark, empty bed, Celia listened for the sounds of the hall and was very aware now of the chill in her room. She was opening doors that she was not ready to step through. That's why she'd had to excuse herself. That's why she'd had to return to her room.

That's why she had to get away from Colin Campbell.

Chapter 6

We've spent two days around this old farmhouse, and Danvers has nearly filled the huge pit that we dug in the field. The troops are now making excursions into the countryside, and the people they lead back are dragged into the farmhouse and tortured. The word is that he is asking them all the same question. It's a woman. A lady we are searching for.

And then we throw dirt on what's left of their bodies.

Sweat glistened on Colin's bare skin as the first rays of the sun came over the castle's outer curtain wall.

Again and again he hammered the straw-covered post with the great two-handed Highland sword. Spinning and slashing, backing and charging, parrying and thrusting, the warrior pushed his fatiguing body through the painful training that made him so fearsome an opponent. His muscular frame ran with sweat until he completed a regimen that would kill an ordinary man. In fact, it had. Many.

Only two of his ten handpicked fighters remained outside in the training area, inspecting the new German swords that had just been received from France. The other eight, among them Runt's older brother, Emmet, had been exhausted by the fierce workout their master had put them through. But they were now en route to the castle's great kitchen to harass the cooks for their breakfasts. Each would now spend a greater part of the day training his own troops, and with similar intensity. This discipline made the Campbell fighters the most feared and respected of all Highland soldiers.

Alec appeared, yawning and stretching in the brisk morning air. Eyeing his friend as Colin picked up the towel that lay near a neat line of weapons, the Macpherson heir sauntered to the arms and picked out a short, vicious-looking sword that had two shorter, parallel blades commencing at the hilt.

"Were you making all that racket out here for the past quarter hour or so?" Alec asked nonchalantly.

"Quarter hour!" Colin exploded. "Try two, you lazy, shiftless, poor excuse for a fighter."

"Two hours!" Alec continued with mock surprise. "Imagine that! Then I guess this is . . ."

Dropping the sword at Colin's feet as he spoke the last words, Alec leapt onto his friend's back as Colin reached down for the weapon. The two giants rolled away in the dust, with Alec gripping the slightly larger Colin around the chest, pinning the massive arms to his sides.

As they rolled, Colin was able to get to one knee, and with a mighty heave of his muscular arms broke Alec's viselike grip, reached over his shoulder, and threw his friend into the dust in front of him.

Before Alec could even react, Colin was on him like a cat, sitting on his chest.

"You cheated," Alec gasped. "I wasn't warmed up."

"You've been using that excuse for more than twenty years, Macpherson." Colin grinned.

Colin stood and offered Alec a hand up.

"I thought you were going to train with us this morning," Colin asked. "God knows, you need it."

The two men watching nearby had been listening to this kind of exchange for as long as they'd served under Lord Campbell, and knew that, after Colin, Alec Macpherson was probably the strongest warrior in the Highlands.

"I was going to come down and play with you gorillas," Alec responded, "but I'm on holiday."

"When are you not on holiday, you fragile little marmoset?" Colin growled.

"I wonder if this sour disposition might have something to do with being dismissed by a certain Lady Caithness last night."

"Dismissed? I've never been dismissed by any woman," Colin replied, becoming genuinely irritated now. "The woman has a bairn to look after."

"Bairn?" Alec laughed, moving a safe distance away. "Everyone saw that you weren't able to hold this woman's attention through dinner."

"Hmmph," Colin scowled, not wanting to let Alec know just how much he really had been disappointed at the sudden retreat of Lady Caithness. Last night he'd caught her looking at him. She was attracted to him, no question about it. It was in her eyes, her manner. But then, unaccountably, she had run.

"Well, because of your rudeness at dinner last night, I had ample opportunity to talk to Edmund about his niece." Alec smiled, realizing he now had Colin's full attention.

"I wonder," he continued, "if she'd be interested in teaching me to sail today. Spring has really come early this year. You wouldn't mind if we used one of your small boats, would you?"

"If there were a chance of just you drowning yourself, I wouldn't mind at all," Colin answered. "But it's the lady's safety I'm concerned about. What would this woman know about sailing?"

"As Edmund tells it, she was sailing before she was walking."

"This is sounding better and better. She'll really be impressed when you throw up on her."

"As a matter of fact, Lord Campbell, sailor extraordinaire, her uncle says she even has a remedy for seasickness that she learned in the Far East."

"Far East? Hmm, this woman has a considerable range of experiences," Colin mused, thinking back over the very intelligent questions she'd asked over dinner about the village and his plans. "What else did you find out about her?"

"I'll tell you what," Alec responded. "Tonight at dinner I'll sit next to Lady Caithness. That way you and Edmund can talk about her all night."

"I don't think so. But thanks for volunteering."

"Well, then, how about volunteering one of your boats for the day?"

"Alec," Colin responded, pausing a moment, giving the request the grave consideration it deserved. "Only because you're my oldest friend, my clan's ally, and my guest, I have to say . . . *no!*"

There is no way in hell, Colin thought, that I'm going to let these two out on a boat without me. Whether she would go or not was hardly the question. After all, Alec has good looks and a charming way with women, and she apparently has her own reputation in that area. If anyone's going sailing with her, it's going to be me.

A few minutes later the two warriors entered the South Hall still arguing over the loan of the boat.

At the table Lord Hugh and Agnes were engaged in their own argument—over the appropriateness of hunting during the period before Easter. This was an annual discussion and one that Agnes always lost, but not without making her position clearly known.

"I'm telling you, Hugh Campbell, it's wasteful to hunt meat during the one short period of the year when you can't eat it."

"Agnes, every year you tell me this, and every year you preserve the meat."

"We have enough meat to feed the entire Western Isles for a year," Agnes responded stubbornly.

"Then, I'm telling you, woman, we're going for the sport, for the exercise. Not that I need it, but the horses do. We're not going to slaughter every red deer and partridge on the island, you know."

Agnes was unconvinced. Every year when the winter weather broke on the coast, Lord Hugh would plan his infamous hunt. Every year the dogs would get more meat than they were worth. There were skins taken and meat smoked, but there was no need for it. Period.

"Besides," Hugh continued with a sparkle in his eyes. "Lady Caithness is sure to join in, given the amount of hunting that the King liked to do at court. This would be a great opportunity for her to get to know our island. To get to know our family a wee bit better ..."

Agnes's objection vanished immediately, for at that exact moment Colin came up from behind and put his arms around her. Aye, this year's hunting might produce something valuable, after all. Colin and Celia certainly looked enchanted with each other last night. Perhaps an opportunity to spend a full day together would move things along even quicker.

"Agnes," Colin put in, smiling down at her. "Fighting that same battle again this year?"

"No, dear!" Agnes replied. "I think hunting is a wonderful idea this year. The weather is most agreeable, and the ground has dried out remarkably in the past week. Oh, no. We're discussing how soon you can all go."

Hugh's eyes nearly popped out of his head as he listened.

"When would be a good day for you, Colin? We need to go soon, while everyone is being so agreeable," Hugh said, recovering quickly.

"I still have a few things to do," Colin said. "How about next week?"

"That's settled, then," Hugh stated emphatically, rubbing his hands briskly together. "Then, Alec, you and I have a lot of work to do. We're just finishing up getting two new Welsh falcons ready out in the mews. They came in with the shipment from France a few weeks back, and they look like beautiful birds."

"Wonderful," Alec said happily. "I believe I enjoy watching those birds move better than the kill itself. I'd be happy to help out for the next few days . . . especially since I won't be doing any sailing." As he said the last words, Alec sent a wry look Colin's way.

Alec was well known for his abilities with falcons. Hugh knew that a tercel trained by Alec was often better than the finest Welsh falcon. Besides, Hugh thought, smiling at his own cleverness, it would be good to keep Alec busy.

"Good. And I'll tell Edmund and Lady Caithness when they get back from the village," the laird said.

"Village?" Colin said, surprised. "What are they doing in the village?"

"Sir Edmund has been going there every morning since they arrived," Agnes replied. "But I've no idea why he goes."

"I do," Lord Hugh added. "He's waiting for a priest who was traveling with them. He needed to go up to the abbey near Argyll's castle for some reason. Edmund says that when he returns, which should be any day now, they'll be on their way."

"No! We have to convince them to stay until Easter," Agnes said with dismay. "There's no reason for them to be on the road during Lent."

We need more time, Agnes thought.

We *do* need to keep them here, Lord Hugh thought. We need more time.

What's her hurry? Colin thought. Why should she be pressed for time?

"Aye, two more weeks here would certainly be good

for her baby," Agnes continued. "And going through the Highlands, they'll still be facing some bad weather."

Even though Colin was quite irritated at the thought of Lady Caithness running off, he couldn't help but smile at Agnes's contradictory use of the spring weather in her arguments.

"Well," Lord Hugh said. "We should be able to convince her to stay till Easter ... for the bairn's sake, anyway."

"Colin," Agnes said sweetly, turning the discussion, but only slightly. "Have you seen her son yet? He is the most handsome little tiger. He was out with her this morning, in fact, poking at your dog's eyes and pulling his ears. I've never seen Bear so docile and patient. They say dogs are very good judges of character."

Colin and the rest burst out laughing at Agnes's innocent expression. To be any less subtle in her matchmaking, she'd need to hit him over the head with a stick. And this was so different for Agnes, who in the past had found reasons to disapprove of any potential match for him.

"Did Lady Caithness take this marvelous bairn with her to the village?" Colin asked, smiling.

"No," Agnes replied. "Ellen has the baby in their rooms."

"I believe that Edmund was going to show her the village," his father added. "Something you said last night caught her interest."

"Oh, Colin," Agnes said. "You should be showing her your projects."

"Definitely," Alec added with a smirk. "In fact, if you get going right now, Agnes will pack your breakfast."

"Alec Macpherson!" Agnes scolded. "I'm sure I don't know what you're taking about."

As the words were leaving her mouth, Agnes had Colin by the arm, turned him toward the door, and shoved him on his way.

Colin smiled at the roar of laughter that followed him out of the hall.

Agnes did, indeed, have oat bannock cakes, smoked salmon, and a jug of ale ready for him when he left the castle.

By the time Colin and his dog completed the short walk to the village, the sun was well up in the sky, and the good weather had brought the inhabitants out into the open air. Winters were wet, windswept, and bitterly cold in the Isles, and when the opportunity presented itself, his people came out of their stone houses *en masse.*

As he walked down the slope of the stone-paved main street, Colin thought with pride that there were only a handful of towns outside of Edinburgh that had even the main street paved. Colin, in laying out the new plan for the town two years earlier, had insisted that even the narrow side streets be paved and sloped to accommodate waste and water drainage. As a result, the village would be even cleaner than the capital. That is, if Edinburgh ever rises out of the charred timber and ash that the English left behind.

Colin wondered if she'd noticed.

Working his way to the sheltered harbor at the foot of the thoroughfare, Colin was repeatedly stopped by the townsfolk that he encountered. All knew him, and none felt any hesitation in approaching him and sharing their personal news, though some kept one eye warily on the huge black dog at his side.

At the bottom of the long hill, the main street inter-sected a front street forming a Marketcross by the water. To the left, docks jutted out into the harbor. To the right, a church stood, and beyond it, a sandy beach stretched out along the other side of the harbor. This protected strand bordered the rocky point of land that rose up to bluffs on the firth side.

Inquiring after Celia and her uncle, Colin directed his steps toward the docks. Approaching the area deserted by the fleet of small fishing boats that were also taking advantage of the good weather, Colin spotted Edmund in conversation with the captain of one of the three larger, heavily armed trading vessels that were moored in the harbor.

Colin's eyes traveled the dock as he realized that Lady Caithness was not with her uncle. That's curious, he thought with some disappointment.

But she had not returned to the castle ...

Before he could address the knight, Colin noticed that Bear had left his side. Turning his head with alarm, he saw the great beast galloping down the beach toward a group of children huddled in the sand at the water's edge. He was a ferocious hunter, but this was not normal behavior. Fearing the worst, Colin sprinted after the hound.

As the animal reached the children, Colin saw the group scatter. Bear pounced, knocking down one who had been crouching in the middle. Colin shouted as he ran, watching in horror as the dog swarmed over its prey.

The children were shrieking, and the growls of the hunting dog pierced Colin's heart. This would be a killing, for sure. The dog was too strong, too vicious. It looked like a young girl under the dog's massive body. The shock of the attack would wound the entire village. Why had he brought the dog along? But Bear had never attacked a child before. He was a hunting dog, and he only attacked on command.

Colin was nearly to them. But he knew he would be too late to save the child. Too late.

Suddenly something was wrong. No, what was this going on in front of him? Penetrating his brain was the sound of laughter, children's shrieks of laughter. As he reached the group, Colin slowly began to comprehend the scene before him.

As he stumbled to a halt, the dumbfounded rescuer watched the victim grab Bear by the ears and roll him onto his back in the sand.

Colin stopped dead in his tracks as Lady Caithness bounced up, laughing and holding the dog's muzzle in her two hands. Colin knew it was time to get a new dog. His fierce hound had become a lady's pet.

Colin stood and watched, his heart pounding in his chest. His first reaction was an overwhelming desire to wring someone's neck, and Bear was not his first choice. He clenched and unclenched his fists, trying to regain his composure, but he could still feel the heat in his face.

Then, gradually, as he looked at her, his anger was replaced with something else.

The sight before him took his newly recovered breath away. Even though she now saw the fiercely frowning warrior, the lady could not stop her unabashed laughter. She was not a product of some court. She was a product of nature. Of the wind. The sand. The sea.

Truly, she was a mess.

And a devastating natural beauty. Not some primped and practiced courtly mannequin. Colin thought that he'd never seen a more desirable woman in his life. He wanted her.

"I think your dog likes me," Celia said, looking innocently in Colin's direction, trying to quiet the still playful animal. Colin stood directly in front of her with the dog between them.

He actually looks worried, she thought. Angry, but worried, too. And definitely surprised.

Celia liked that. Colin didn't even seem winded from his long sprint down the beach. His beautiful, thick black hair had fallen across his forehead from the run. She had a wild impulse to reach over, to touch it, to push it gently back in place.

He looked absolutely magnificent. She realized that this was the first time she'd seen him in the clear light of day. Hardly disappointing. Quite to the contrary. He was by far the most handsome creature she had ever seen. The features of his face had the same clean, chiseled look as the wind-carved bluffs that distinguished this rugged coastline. His gray eyes were the most beautiful shade. The lashes long and black.

Unexpectedly, Celia felt a giddy lightness in her head as she looked into his eyes. She felt . . . no . . . she wished she could just stand there and stare into them, be lost in them for an eon.

This giant with the gorgeous gray eyes made her feel like a silly, adolescent girl.

"Well, there's no accounting for taste," Colin responded, teasingly and obviously inspecting her up and down. "Although, I have to admit, this latest court fashion is . . . most becoming."

Oh, God, I must look like hell, she thought. And I've probably been gawking like an idiot.

Celia began to brush off her clothes, frowning as darkly as she could.

"We're not at court, m'lord," Celia retorted, not raising her head to address him.

Colin reached over and gently lifted her chin, gazing into her eyes.

"Lady Caithness, isn't it time you called me by name?" Colin allowed a moment to pass before removing his hand from her soft, warm skin.

"Very well . . . Lord Campbell," Celia said, reaching a hand into her tangled curls to shake the sand out. Retaining her composure was becoming more difficult by the minute.

"Then, as lord, I command you to stand still," he said,

turning her around and gently working his fingers through her auburn ringlets.

Colin could see the goose bumps rising on the skin of her slender neck, and he felt himself responding physically to the silky feel of her hair.

"And, as lord, I could command that you accompany me on a tour of the village." Colin knew that he needed to sound facetious, or she would become angry. Already, he knew that this was not a woman who would take orders well. And this was not the moment to drive her away.

There was hardly any sand in her shiny locks, but Colin was in no hurry to stop. He wanted to bury his face in the tangled mass and run his lips along the skin beneath her ear.

"Command, Lord Campbell?" Celia whispered, amazed at the freezing fire that was coursing through her veins.

Colin brushed his fingers lightly across the skin of her neck, gently sweeping the hair back from where it fell to her shoulders. He felt her shudder at the touch. He wanted to do more.

"Would a request be better . . . Celia?" he asked gently, turning her by the shoulders until she faced him.

"Right now, Colin, it's all the same."

The two stood looking into each other's eyes as time stood still.

Then, abruptly, Celia stepped back, putting both hands to her flushed cheeks. Colin saw panic replace the passion that had welded their gaze for the eternity of a moment.

Colin feared that she would run.

Frantically she searched in the sand around her for her shoes. Finding one, she jammed it on her foot. Unable to locate the other, Celia suddenly felt a wave of helpless vulnerability wash over her. How could this man have this effect on her? She wanted to cry, and fighting the tears added to the confusion. Where *did* the damned shoe go?

"Is this what you're looking for, Celia?" Colin asked gently, taking the shoe out of the dog's soft mouth.

Celia looked at the shoe in Colin's hand. Glancing around, she saw that the children's attention had already returned to their playing. Colin handed her the shoe and followed Bear as the dog joined in the children's play.

Something had just happened. What? Celia thought. How could she want to run and *need* to stay ... all at once?

Looking at his broad back as he bent over a little girl, examining a shell the tot held up to him in her tiny hand, Celia felt once again an exhilarating rush begin in her face and race through her chest and middle, finishing in her back with a sensation that made her shiver. What was happening to her?

Colin straightened up and called to Bear. As the dog loped over to him, the warrior turned and walked back along the beach, shielding his eyes against the sun as he gazed toward the docks and Edmund.

Celia watched Colin pass without a word. His look was so passive, so expressionless. It was as if nothing had happened. Nothing.

My imagination, Celia thought. Wishful thinking is more like it. To think that this handsome man, this hero, this laird as wealthy as the King himself, could possibly be interested in me. Wishful thinking is right.

And what am I? I'm a fugitive. A woman with no home. No money. No land. No real title to offer. A woman with a child. A lost soul on the run.

I'm not even what I seem to be. I'm a woman with no identity. Lady Caithness, she thought bitterly, I can't even be that.

I'm an impostor.

Here I am, using these good people. Taking the refuge they freely offer, and giving nothing in return ... not even the truth. Edmund had been right. They had opened their home to us, taking us in with not even a question asked. Relying on our honor. Our honor.

But I can't tell them. They have a right to know, but I can't tell them. I can't.

Celia waved good-bye to the children and stalked deliberately down the beach. As she breathed in the crisp salt air, Celia felt the guilt wash into a stronger emotion. Anger grew more insistent with every step she took. She was angry with him for his show of affection. Angry with herself for her vulnerability to his attention. Who was he interested in, her or Lady Caithness? Who was he running from?

Her eyes followed him as they made their way down the beach. At one point she thought Bear was going to run back to her, but Colin must have given a clear command, because the dog returned quickly to his side.

I'm not even good enough company for his dog, she thought angrily.

By the time she reached the place where Colin and Edmund stood in conversation, Celia had worked herself up to a full fury.

She was angry at the world, angry at Colin, angry at herself.

"Celia," Edmund said cheerfully. "We will be privileged to take part in one of the grand spectacles of the Western Isles next week."

"I pass," she responded quickly, shrugging her shoulders nonchalantly.

"What do you mean, 'pass'?" Colin blurted out, surprised. "You don't even know what it is yet."

"All right, what is it?" Celia asked in a resigned tone.

"The annual Easter hunt," Edmund announced importantly.

"An Easter egg hunt?" Celia responded wryly, turning

to Colin. "I thought that was only a French tradition. What kind of eggs will you hunt, m'lord?"

"We're hunting red deer," Colin said in a disgusted tone, "and any bird we can find."

"I don't think deer lay eggs, m'lord," she responded innocently.

"We're not hunting eggs!" Colin exploded. "And the French be damned!"

"I really don't think you should be cursing the only allies we have in Europe, m'lord, just because red deer don't lay eggs."

Speechless, Colin just stared at Celia, certain the woman had either lost her senses or was trying to make him crazy.

As Edmund laughed behind him, Colin realized that he was being had again.

"I know you're only jesting with me, Lady Caithness," Colin said through clenched teeth, trying to recover. "But I'm sure you will enjoy the hunt. Our game forests are far superior to those you've been hunting with your court friends."

"I'm certain they are, Lord Colin. I still pass."

"Why?" Colin asked, totally perplexed. "Edmund's told me that you are an accomplished archer, and I've seen you with a sword."

"Aye, but I find it stupid for grown men and women to race around forests and fields, in all types of weather, riding down and inflicting mortal wounds on defenseless little animals."

No wonder Agnes likes her, Colin thought. He'd been hearing Agnes argue this every year from the moment he picked up his first bow.

"Then how in God's name did you become so proficient with hunting weapons?" Colin asked, becoming exasperated.

"It's very simple, Lord Colin," Celia answered, with a

smile at Edmund. "By riding down and inflicting mortal wounds on defenseless Highland lairds."

With that, Celia turned her back on Colin and looked at the village.

"Are you going to show us the village, m'lord?" she asked sweetly.

Totally baffled by this woman, Colin led the two visitors into the village.

Soon, however, Colin's composure returned as he turned his attention to the growing town. Telling them of the changes that had been occurring, Colin swelled with pride at the recent efforts.

Two years earlier Colin had begun a revitalization of the town, convinced that if Scotland was to thrive in Europe in these changing times, they must develop new ways of doing things, develop new industries to employ its growing numbers of people.

Moving past the low stone warehouses that would soon be filled with wool, Colin excitedly led them to another long, low building.

"This is something they don't have as yet anywhere else in Scotland," Colin said proudly, ushering them through the stout oak door.

Before her, Celia saw an amazing sight. The shuttles of ten looms were busily click-clacking away, and rolls of wool cloth were stacked nearby, ready for storage and shipment. Workers bustled back and forth carrying spools of spun wool and the rolls of finished cloth.

Colin towered alongside her as Celia returned the smiles of the master weavers who sat basking in the glow of Lord Colin's approval. She reached over and touched the wool; it was fine quality material, undyed, but clearly the product of skilled workmanship and the very good wool.

"This wool has the feel of Spanish Segovian!" she said in a shocked tone, looking up into his smiling, gray eyes.

Celia was extremely surprised to find what seemed to be the finest of the wools that Europe was producing here in the Western Isles. The finest wool available came from Spain and the top Spanish wool came from the hills surrounding Segovia, and she knew all about the various qualities of wool in Europe from her experience on her father's merchant ships. Scotland's wool was far inferior to this. "This can't be Scottish! But how could you get it now?"

"This *is* Scottish wool," Colin replied, surprised but very impressed at Celia's knowledge of the commodity.

"It can't be. This has none of the tar one finds on Scottish wool," Celia said in disbelief. Scottish wools were unpopular owing to the tar frequently smeared on the sheep as a protection against the weather.

"But I'm telling you it is, Celia," Colin said, taking hold of her hand for a moment. "This wool came from Campbell lands."

"You're telling us that you are producing quality wool on *your* lands, and making quality cloth in *your* village? This is incredible!" Celia exclaimed excitedly, pressing his hand as she spoke.

Colin grinned, pleased with the response. Without releasing her hand, he turned to go back out the door.

"Aren't you going to show us the rest of the cloth works?" Celia asked, stopping him with a tug of her hand.

Colin turned with surprise at her tone.

"Of course, if you're interested."

"I am! I've never had a chance to see the inside of one of these places." Celia's face was lit with anticipation. Edmund's, however, was not.

"If you two will excuse me, I told Lord Hugh that I'd continue helping him with the new falcons. They're beautiful birds." Hunting was a lot more interesting to this knight than commerce.

Hiding her disappointment, Celia let go of Colin's

hand, saying, "I'll walk with you, Edmund. It's time I got back to Kit and Ellen."

"No, Celia," Edmund said with a gentle note in his voice. "I'll check in on Ellen and the bairn. It's such a beautiful day, perhaps I'll take them both down to watch the hawking."

"I should go with you, Edmund," Celia protested.

"Enjoy the day," the knight said coaxingly. Celia had never shown such interest in a young man before. This would be good for her. "Think, lass, you might not get an opportunity like this again. That is, if Colin doesn't mind seeing you back to the castle later."

"Of course! I don't get many opportunities to show off what we're doing here," Colin responded, taking Celia once again by the hand.

Once Edmund left, Colin introduced Celia to the lead weaver in the building. As they walked through, Colin showed her the various types of cloth they were producing. The ten draw-looms, with a weaver seated and a draw boy working beside each one, were a constant blur of motion. Celia was impressed that Colin knew each worker by name.

Colin was ready to lead her out a door on the other side of the building, when he realized that Celia was no longer with him. Colin leaned with his broad back to the door, watching as Celia made her way back through the room, stopping at each loom and complimenting the websters on the weaves and their obvious mastery of the craft. She has a way with people, Colin thought.

Their eyes met for a moment across the room, and her delight was evident.

Entering the next building in front of Colin, Celia found a room full of spinners. The women were chatting and singing as they entered, but quieted somewhat when they saw Colin. Giggles and whispering could be heard instead, and Celia thought to herself that obviously she was not the only one affected by this man. She also noticed the appraising looks directed her way.

In the center of the room, an imposing middle-aged woman was frowning at her from where she sat. There was more than a hint of possessiveness in her look, Celia thought. She glanced back at the handsome laird and could understand the feeling.

But I don't need any more enemies, Celia thought. Not her, not any of these women. I have to make peace with these people. She walked toward the woman and stood beside her, watching as she skillfully, smoothly, spun the puffy shreds of wool into fine yarn.

"Your work is beautiful," Celia said sincerely.

"Thank you, m'lady," the woman responded politely. "But it's simple work, really."

"Could you show me how?" Celia looked into the woman's surprised eyes.

"You, m'lady?" The tittering around her made Celia very self-conscious, but she wanted to see this through.

"Aye. If you've the patience."

"Sit, m'lady," the older woman said, standing and glancing up at the laird for approval.

Colin watched as Celia took her seat at the wheel. The other women stared in silence as their fellow worker explained the process to Celia. Celia started, working slowly, hesitatingly, but in spite of her caution, or perhaps because of it, the work began to tangle within a few seconds. With an explosion of voices, the other women leapt from their places, flooding the giggling Celia with instructions and advice.

It occurred to Colin as he watched that even *he* could have done better at the spinning than Celia was doing. Then he realized that she knew exactly what she was doing. In one stroke Celia had moved inside their circle. Everyone was enjoying herself, Celia most of all.

It took Colin a while to extract her from her newfound friends. As he led Celia out of the building, he could still see the flush of excitement in her face. He watched as her expression suddenly grew serious.

"You never said how you've managed to produce wool of this quality," she asked, stopping and giving him a direct, questioning look.

"Aye," he said, faking a hard look at her. "And how do I know you won't be selling our secrets to the enemy?"

"You're not going to let me fall into enemy hands, now, are you?" Celia asked, a pretense of fear showing on her face.

"Let?" Colin repeated mischievously. "No, lass, I might turn you over to them."

Celia made her look so pathetically pitiful that Colin couldn't keep up the play. He smiled outright.

"All right, I'll tell you," he said, growing serious. "We've been enclosing the land for sheep grazing as some of the larger barons are doing in England, but we're not throwing the farm folk off to become beggars. These people that you see working here are those that were struggling on the small farms. We've taught them the crafts. Here, they can earn a better life for themselves."

"For themselves, or for the Campbells?" Celia asked, tossing her head in sudden defiance. How was this life better for those workers? Was it just another way to make the lairds richer?

"The Campbell lairds have been accumulating wealth for centuries," Colin flashed defensively. "If it was just wealth we were after, we wouldn't be spending money and bringing in outside tradesmen to build a school, to improve the village, to house these folk, and to teach them new trades. Our village has attracted some of the finest craftsmen in all Scotland."

"You're doing all that?" she asked in a conciliatory tone. "That is not the way I've ever seen land owners behave. The custom seems to be to bleed the people of everything they have."

Colin knew that what he was doing here was, in a way, revolutionary. And Celia was right about bleeding the people. But he was surprised to hear a court lady voice such concern for those beneath her.

"Aye, we're doing all those things—except the bleeding part," Colin responded, lightening the exchange. "In fact, we still operate the spinning school, which I may have to enroll you in."

"You think there is hope for me?"

"Absolutely." He smiled. "If you're planning on staying awhile."

"I might like that," Celia returned. "But you *still* haven't told me why your wool is so fine."

"The trick was getting the folk that have been left to tend the sheep to stop greasing the animals with the tar. There's no need, now, because we've built shelters—sheepcotes—to keep the livestock in during the coldest weather. Then, we use Spanish shearing techniques and sort the finest wool out for our own weavers to use."

Taking hold of her hand, he pointed to the third building.

"That building is where we do the sorting, washing, and carding for the spinners, but that's off-limits to you . . . for today, at least. You've disrupted the works enough already," he stated with an exaggerated frown. "Besides, I've other things I want to show you, as well."

"You said you're building a school," Celia anticipated, "is that what you want to show me?"

"Maybe," Colin continued, patting the satchel strapped to his waist and whistling to his dog. "But first, you have to share this food Agnes packed for me. And I know a good spot."

Still holding Celia's hand, Colin led her up past the warehouses and the docks until the paved road ended.

*   *   *

Celia felt happy and alive, as she nearly ran to keep pace with the tall man's strides.

They followed a stony path up the hill that overlooked the village and the harbor. As they neared the top, Celia could see that only the castle was higher, and its view dominated the entire area. From here, she could see the building that was going on in the village. On the far side of the Marketcross, behind the church, there was considerable activity around a partially built structure of timber and stone.

"Is that the school?" she asked eagerly, letting go of his hand and pointing across the rooftops.

Colin could see in Celia the same thrill that he felt each time he looked at the ongoing changes in the village. He was surprised and touched by this woman's humane interest. This was no pretense. And Colin was finding himself attracted to her even more. If only he knew more about her.

"Aye, it is. You seem to be very interested in that school." Colin took Celia's arm, and they continued over the crest of the hill as they talked. Bear began to wander, his nose to the ground, through the low, windswept grasses. Occasionally he lifted his head, looking back as if to check on his master.

"I am. Will the school be for all the children in the village?" Celia asked this tentatively, almost afraid that his answer would ruin her developing image of him.

"Aye, all the children will attend," he responded matter-of-factly.

"The girls as well?"

"Aye, the girls as well."

"That's quite progressive," Celia said, knowing that education for women was a rarity—even in the privileged classes.

Colin stopped and turned her toward him. He knew he had to explain.

"My mother read to me as a child," he said softly.

"Agnes reads and writes, as do all the women in the household. The Campbells don't hold with those who believe that education damns a woman's soul. We believe it makes her more valuable."

Celia was amazed. She'd never heard such things from a man of Colin's stature before. She herself had learned many things growing up, matters of the arts of war, of sailing, of commerce and finance, of the mechanics of things, but not reading.

"I wish I'd had that opportunity as a child. I never learned until I arrived at court. My friend Father William was the one who taught me."

No sooner had the words left Celia's lips than Colin shook his hand free of her arm and picked up his pace. His parting glance looked angry to her, but what reason had she given him for such a response? She had felt drawn by everything about this man. Now, on the heels of her admission, his unexplained anger cut her like the slashing tear of a Highland dirk.

Colin reached an outcropping of stone and threw down the satchel containing their lunch at the base of the rock and stormed a few paces off.

"Those must have been happy days at court," Colin snapped, turning to face her.

Celia paused for a moment at the realization that Lady Caithness's reputation was the cause of his anger. If only she could tell him the truth.

"No, I hated court," Celia said softly. She fought the tears that were beginning to well up in her eyes. "The happier days went before."

"Before?" Colin was confused. He saw the hurt look in her face. He changed his tone, asking more soothingly, "Where were you before?"

Celia paused before answering. "Everywhere and nowhere. I lived with my father and Edmund."

"What does that mean, 'everywhere and nowhere'?" Colin pressed, fighting successfully to keep the irritation out of his voice. He was genuinely interested but he hated riddles.

"I grew up on my father's ships. He was a merchant and he took me everywhere."

"That was a dangerous way to raise a child."

"He knew it was dangerous, but he couldn't bear to have me be away from him. I was all he had left." Celia unconsciously unfastened her cloak, spread it on the ground before the boulder, and sat looking out at the blue of the sea. Across the water Celia saw islands that were a bluer shade than either sea or sky. She had always felt so safe beside her father out on those treacherous waters.

"What about your mother, the rest of your family?" Colin crouched beside her on the cloak, watching the expression of her profile. This was the first glimpse of her past that she had shared with him. So openly. So honestly.

"My mother died when I was very young. Edmund has been the only other family I've known. My father's English family never accepted his marriage to a Scottish woman. They never acknowledged me at all."

"Clearly, that was their loss. But it must have been difficult for you." Colin's hatred of English arrogance flared at the thought of any child being made to feel unwanted, particularly this one.

"Aye, because I never really knew a home," Celia said pensively, but then her expression brightened. "But growing up aboard ship was a magical experience. Exotic lands with people of every color, speaking languages I could almost understand. Waking up to the sound of the sea and the motion of the ship. The smells of the ports and the cargoes that we carried. Hiding in the holds among bales of Spanish wool and spices from the East."

Colin smiled tentatively at the image of the little girl playing happily while dangers lurked over every horizon.

"How long did you live on his ships?"

"My father died of a fever when I was fourteen. That's when everything changed." Celia shook off her reverie, realizing that she had already said too much. She couldn't let Colin Campbell—or anyone—get close to her right now. She reached down and opened the satchel.

"How so?" he asked, trying to quell her sudden flurry of activity by laying his hand over her long slender hands. Her nervous fingers fluttered like a bird under his for a moment and then lay still. Celia looked directly into his eyes.

"I'm not saying another word about myself until you feed me, Lord Campbell." Celia tried to ignore his manly presence, the pressure of his enveloping hand, but she couldn't. She could feel her own quickening pulse.

"If we're going back to that Lord Campbell form of address, then I'll just have to start giving commands again. And I won't let you off so easy . . . this time." Colin leaned down until his mouth was just a breath away from hers.

She tried to smile. She wanted to make some sharp remark. To tell him where he fell far short of courtesy's requirements, but his face was so close to hers now, his finely sculpted lips so attractive. She wondered if those lips tasted as wonderful as they looked. They were so full, so inviting.

His one hand was pressing hers against her thigh, but suddenly his other reached to her chin, lifting it until she looked into his eyes. The hunger that she found there frightened her, yet somehow drew her on.

Colin looked into Celia's direct gaze. For a moment— he didn't know how long—he was mesmerized, lost in the dark depths of her black eyes. Moving his hand slightly, he brushed her soft lips with his thumb, smiling at the tremor that she visibly experienced. She closed her eyes momentarily. Sliding his hand across her cheek, Colin brushed back the silky ringlets that hung teasingly against her face. Running his fingers through her hair, he traced a course around her petite ear and stroked the velvety skin beneath it.

Responding to the soft moan that he felt rather than heard, Colin reached his hand around her neck and pulled her upturned lips to his own.

"Kiss me," he commanded softly, his voice as gentle as the warming sunlight.

Celia's good intentions were overwhelmed the moment his soft hands traveled across the skin of her face and neck. She wanted to brush her lips across his, to feel his warm, strong body pressed against her own. She wanted to be so close to him that there could be no breath between them. Colin's lips awaited hers.

Celia's lips touched his lightly, chastely. Then her hands came up to feel the chiseled features of his eyes, his cheekbones, the strong, clean cut of his jaw. Bringing her hands together like a sculptor shaping a masterpiece, Celia's thumbs caressed his full lips.

She fought the urge to taste those lips, to reveal the fire that was raging within her, to feel herself melt into him.

But she knew she had to stop now, or there would be no stopping.

She stopped.

"There you are, m'lord, I've done as you commanded. Now feed me."

In one quick, outward snap of her arm, Celia dislodged his hand from her neck, placed her hands firmly against his chest, and shoved the leaning laird back on his haunches.

On her feet the next instant, Celia stepped back a safe distance and looked playfully at the surprised warrior. He looked so comical, his legs stretched out in front of him, his face openly perplexed. But she knew that he was just an instant away from being very, very dangerous.

"You are teasing me, you imp," he growled. Her speed and sureness in disengaging herself were impressive to the giant. But as he looked at her, he knew that they would someday bring great pleasure to each other. He'd seen that look of passion in her eyes. She desired him as much as he wanted her.

"No, m'lord," Celia said. "But you promised me lunch, and a promise is a promise."

At that moment Colin moved deftly to his knees, and as he did, Celia took another two steps back, smiling.

"I'm giving you fair warning, I'm a *very* fast runner." Truly, it was not Colin that she was afraid of. He was being as chivalrous as one could imagine. Celia was afraid of her own reactions, of her own desire—not to run away, but to run to him—to give herself fully to this man. Never in her life had she felt that way.

Colin laughed and sat back onto the cloak.

"All right. Lunch. A promise is a promise. I only hope you don't choke on it, m'lady." Colin began to pull the food from the satchel.

Smiling, Celia moved back to the edge of the cloak and knelt down, keeping her eye on him. Colin broke up an oat bannock cake, handing her a small piece and placing the rest on the cloak.

As Celia ate the cake, Colin continued to empty the satchel, removing the stopper from the jug of ale and placing the bottle just off the cloak, but within Celia's reach. Breaking off another piece of the cake, Colin tossed a portion to Bear, who had just wandered back from his exploring.

"Aren't you going to eat, Colin?" Celia asked, reaching for the small jug.

Colin's head was turned toward the dog when Celia reached for the ale. But with the speed of lightning, his hand shot out, taking her wrist in a viselike grip. In an instant Celia found herself on her back, her wrists pinned to the ground, and the huge warrior leaning over her. He is faster than a man his size has a right to be, she thought.

Suddenly she laughed out loud at the ridiculousness of such a thought at this moment, and her laugh brought a look of pleasure to Colin's face.

"Well, did you get enough to eat, my speedy runner?" Colin asked with a wry look.

"I think being so full slowed me down," she responded, "but perhaps we're only as fast as we want to be." As the words left her mouth, Celia regretted saying them. As much as she wanted him to kiss her, she knew that she couldn't let it go far beyond that. The consequences were too serious. But she *did* want to feel his lips against hers once more.

Looking into her eyes, Colin saw that spark of desire glowing like an ember in a midnight fire. He knew that it only matched his own. Releasing her wrists, Colin slowly lowered himself beside her outstretched body. She could roll away from him, run if she wanted to, but he knew she wouldn't.

Propping himself on one elbow, he cradled the side of her face gently with his other hand.

"You are so beautiful," he murmured, smiling at the blush that spread immediately from her face to her neck, disappearing under the collar of her dress. Celia returned his smile with the look of an angel. She looked so innocent.

And yet, as Colin studied her, he thought of all the metaphors of courtly love that she must have heard in her life. But still, she blushed at his simple words.

"Never in my life," he continued, "have I . . ."

"Please don't," she interrupted in a whisper, silencing him with a single finger pressed to his lips.

Colin watched her lift her head from the cloak, and as she did, his lips descended to meet hers.

At first, their lips tentatively brushed against the other's, creating a sensation of shock waves that shuddered through their bodies. Colin was surprised that such a harmless act could trigger such a response in him. There was a simplicity, an honesty, an openness in the act—and in the resulting pleasure—that he had not expected.

Colin did not want the magic of this moment to pass. He pressed his lips to hers again, as a sense of urgency began to seize him. He wanted to kiss her deeply, to taste her, to delve into the mysteries of this woman.

The pressure of his lips increased, and Celia's head sank against the cloak. Colin ran his tongue lightly across her lip.

Celia's startled hands flew up, one clutching at his back and shoulder, the other gripping the back of his neck. Again his tongue darted across her full, sweet lips, seeking access. He moved his hand to her chin, lightly pressing downward. Her lips parted, and again his mouth descended upon hers, his tongue thrusting into the luscious opening—sampling, tasting, learning the texture of her soft mouth.

Her tongue responded to his, tentatively at first. She had never experienced the kind of heat that was coursing through her veins. A raw desire was growing within her. What restraint she had in her was quickly slipping away. Her tongue became as bold as his, searching and rubbing against his in an exploration of discovery. She loved the taste of him, the scent of him, the pressure of his body against hers.

Colin lifted his face from hers and looked once into her eyes. The clouds of passion that he saw there answered his unspoken question. Gently burying his face in her neck, he took her earlobe between his teeth and lips. His warm breath surged in her ear, bringing renewed shudders from her slender frame. Her smell was so fresh, so sweet, so warm and inviting. He traced a line with the tip of his tongue from her neck, along her jawline, to her waiting lips as he reclaimed her mouth hungrily.

Colin felt his own discipline crumble as passion ripped through him. He wanted to touch her completely, to feel her, to be inside her. Colin's hand ran the length of her side, rising under her elbow and gently caressing her full, soft breast. Her body responded to his touch, arching against his hand instinctively.

But even as her body was melting into his, as her mouth yielded up its soft mysteries to his searching tongue, as her hands traced the muscular lines of his shoulders, of his back, something within Celia was alerting her to the line they were about to cross, a line that threatened the security of all who depended on her.

Within her, a new life was awakening, a life she desired with all of her being, but a life that she also was fearful of embracing.

Colin's impulse was to unfasten—no, to rip away—the clothes that kept them apart, to crush her skin, her breasts, her thighs beneath his own. Colin wanted to make love to her wildly, without reserve, to enjoy her mounting passions, her crowning ecstasy.

But something in her resisted his impulse. He sensed this. It was almost a resistance that was growing in spite of her own surging desires.

Colin paused, looking into her eyes for a sign that would let him sweep away her doubts, her fears, her past. Regardless of what was, Colin wanted this woman to want him now.

Looking deep into the black sapphires of her eyes, he saw a look that told him . . .

Bear's fierce growls had Colin on his feet in an instant, and Celia leapt up beside him. The dog's attention was directed to the crest of the hill overlooking the village. In a moment they could both hear the cries that had alerted the animal.

"LORD COLIN! LORD COLIN!" the man shouted, running breathlessly into sight. His relief was evident when he saw the laird, but his pace never slackened until he panted up to them.

"Lord Colin," he gasped out, looking only at his master. "You must come ... to the castle ... Runt's been hurt ... your guests ... attacked ..."

"What guests?" Celia interrupted, her face going white.

It couldn't be, she screamed inwardly. It can't be.

"Your son, m'lady ... the bairn!"

Chapter 7

These days I wander about in a fog, as if I were lost in some endless maze.

The countryside is now completely deserted. There are no animals. We have slaughtered them all. There are no people. Those who escaped us have fled to the north. Those who did not will have no need of their livestock. They dream in another world.

But who is this woman that is the cause of this nightmare of destruction? Who is this woman and child that we follow?

"Oh, God, what have I done!"

"They didn't get to the bairn, m'lady," the servant continued. "Runt and your uncle stopped them. They're all back in the castle . . ."

"How badly is Runt hurt?" Colin demanded, taking Celia by the arm, restraining her. She was edging away from him, pulling hard against his grip, ready to bolt. Colin knew that there would be no holding her back if he let go of her now. He had to somehow keep control until they knew more.

"I don't know, m'lord. They took him right in."

"Take the dog. Go back through the village and get the priest," Colin commanded, pulling Celia toward the cliffs behind them. "This way, Celia. It's faster."

Without any more explanation, Colin swept up the

cloak and, gripping Celia's hand, began to run along the bluff toward the castle.

Celia ran beside him, and the fifty questions shrieking incoherently in her brain shrank in an instant to one guilty thought ... she hadn't been there! The knot that had formed in her throat upon hearing the serving man's words sank into her chest—clenching, squeezing her heart with fingers of white-hot steel.

Why wasn't I there? she moaned inwardly. *If only I'd been there. Aye, if I'd been there ... What would have been different? No, think straight,* she told herself. *Nothing would have been different. The baby is safe. Thank God they didn't harm him. But what about now? Now that they've found us. Damn them!*

Poor Runt. Hurt doing what I was supposed to do. Please, God, don't let him be hurt badly. Damn them!

But he won't be the last. They knew we're here, and they'll be back. Colin and his people don't know how devious a foe Danvers can be. And this has to be his work, she thought.

And I can't tell them what I know.

And where is Father William? she thought. *I've got to get a message to him. We can't stay here.*

Celia and Colin were now an arrow shot away from the castle's thick outer curtain wall. Celia knew they still would need to go nearly halfway around the great fortress to enter. Suddenly Colin slowed and moved to the edge of the cliff, working his way through some birch scrubs. Following him, Celia looked down the precipice to the surf crashing on the rocks far below.

Colin jumped.

Celia screamed.

Dropping to her hands and knees, she peered wildly over the edge. There, perched on a narrow ledge nearly a lance-length beneath the apex of the cliff, Colin stood looking up at her.

"Jump," he said.

Celia eyed the space in which she needed to land, and without a moment's hesitation dropped to his waiting arms on the ledge.

Colin had been ready to coax Celia into lowering herself gradually to where he could reach up and minimize the drop. *I should have known,* he thought. *The woman is fearless, and as lithe as a cat.*

But steadying her slender body, Colin sensed her agitation. He wanted to comfort her, to apologize to her somehow, but this was no time for it. He had a feeling that she probably wouldn't have stood for it anyway.

Keeping a firm hold on her hand, Colin led Celia a few feet along the ledge, then dropped to his knees and crawled through a low cave opening in the face of the cliff. Celia followed him into the darkness.

She was still on her knees when Colin struck a flint to a torch, lighting up the narrow cave. As Celia got quickly to her feet, her eyes adjusted, and she saw that the cave forked immediately beyond where Colin was standing.

These tunnels must lead to the castle, she thought. *Colin wouldn't have taken me this way otherwise.* As they had gotten closer, as she had felt her heart pump with the exertion of the run, Celia had felt a sense of— what was it? calm? trust?—confidence that all would be well? *Perhaps,* she thought, *but how safe is a castle with open caves for tunnels.* Before he could turn down the right-hand tunnel, the one that would lead in the direction of the castle, Celia put her hand on the warrior's arm.

"Is this how you got into my room . . . the night you arrived home?"

"Aye, through the caves and passages that lead under the castle."

"You mean anyone could come through them?" Celia knew what the answer was, but she needed to hear Colin say it.

"No, Celia. Only the most trusted members of the household know about them, and even those people know only the way into the kitchens."

Colin understood why she was asking this. He knew he was responsible for their safety while they were guests in his home. What was worse, Celia had come to Kildalton seeking protection for herself . . . for her bairn. "I will not allow anyone else to harm you for as long as you stay at Kildalton Castle. I don't know what happened today, but I promise you, it won't happen again."

Even in the darkness of the cave, Celia could sense the intensity of his voice, his expression. She felt her heart warm at Colin's concern and at his promise. If she could only tell him the truth. Celia could see he was holding himself accountable for the attack.

Celia slipped her arms around his waist, hugging him fiercely and quickly releasing him.

"I know that, Colin."

Colin peered in the semidarkness at Celia. He was so surprised and moved by her simple show of affection that he hardly knew how to respond to it. For the first time since they'd met, Colin felt that she was displaying some kind of trust in him. He was not going to let this slip away. Turning, he moved rapidly down the passageway, with Celia on his heels.

As Celia followed Colin, she noted that the cave walls quickly gave way to hand-hewn tunnels. In a few short minutes the tunnel split into three passages that had walls made of stone blocks, then split into three more that looked exactly the same. Suddenly Colin stopped and pushed at a section of wall, revealing—to Celia's amazement—a low opening into which the warrior ducked.

Celia followed and found herself standing in a corner of the castle's great kitchen, shielded from the vast work area by a huge stone baking oven.

A group of the kitchen workers stood huddled by a doorway that Colin and Celia crossed to. When the giant warrior was spotted, a babble of voices erupted, but the two passed quickly through into the South Hall.

At the far end of the hall, a crowd gathered around one of the long tables.

"What the devil happened?" Colin boomed, drawing the attention of startled faces in his and Celia's direction. Inside the opening circle of warriors, Celia could see Ellen sitting beside Runt and holding the baby tight to her breast. Lord Hugh, Alec, and Edmund stood beside them, and Agnes had her helpers scurrying back and forth with bandages. Runt's shoulder was wrapped, but still obviously bleeding. His face was pale, but he showed no other signs of the pain Celia knew he must be feeling.

Celia went directly to Ellen, who stood and embraced her mistress. It was obvious that Ellen was greatly relieved to see her. Celia gently received the sleeping Kit.

"They never touched him, m'lady," Ellen whispered. Celia nodded, holding the baby tightly to her, as an overwhelming sense of relief washed over her. She glanced at the tired, grim-faced Edmund, who tried to smile at her. His look told her that they needed to talk.

"Colin," Lord Hugh responded. "I'm glad you're here."

"How could this happen?" Colin asked angrily, leaning over Runt and gently pulling away the dressing. The weapon had pierced the right side of Runt's chest, below the shoulder blade. From the narrow length of the wound, Colin figured Runt had been stabbed with a dirk or a short sword. But whatever it was, the weapon had been thrust straight through, missing the vital organs.

Aye, Runt should live if Agnes can get the wound to heal cleanly, Colin thought.

"The bastards were waiting for them," Hugh said bitterly.

"Who were they, Father? Where did this happen?"

"We were walking back from watching the master work the new falcons, Lord Colin," Runt answered. Celia thought his voice sounded strong. "There were four of them hidden in the tall wood glade by the path to the mews. A lot of the staff went down to watch, so there were a number of our folk around."

Runt paused, clearly amazed at the assailants' boldness, and Lord Hugh took over.

"Ellen and the bairn were walking back with Edmund and this young warrior, here, when this pack of wolves sneaked up from behind."

"Sir Edmund killed one right off," Runt went on. "While he was fighting a second one, the other two went right after Ellen and Kit."

He turned his head to Celia. "They aimed to hurt the bairn, m'lady . . . I'm sure of it. They were looking right past me at him. If I'd been armed with more than my dagger, we'd have killed them all, though."

Celia felt her blood boil. Aye, she would have enjoyed killing the would-be assassins herself.

"Easy does it, Runt," Agnes commanded gently, replacing a blood-soaked dressing with a clean one. "You'll not stop bleeding, if you don't sit still."

"Runt took the sword in the shoulder and still managed to knock the two clear of Ellen," Hugh said proudly. "Edmund finished off all but one, who ran across the moor."

"Did you get him?" Colin growled menacingly. "I'd like to . . . talk . . . to him."

"No, they had a boat and a crew waiting for them," Hugh finished in frustration. "There was no time to get a boat out after them. They'd planned the whole thing out, including their escape."

"Who were these cowards?" Colin asked, glancing fiercely about. "Were they English?"

"They wore kilts," Runt answered. "But no plaid, and no sign of any clan."

"They were not English, nor Lowlanders," Edmund said with finality. "Their weapons and the way they fought were definitely Highlander." Edmund had spent most of his life training fighters. These men relied on strength over speed and were more willing to take a blow than avoid it. These were Highlander traits. They may have sold their souls to the devil himself, but they still owed their fighting style to the land that spawned them.

"I want to see them," Colin demanded. "Where are the bodies? I want to know where these gutless dogs came from."

Celia looked at the warrior before her. Despite his fierce anger and hard expression, Colin was in total control, and she could see his fighters already heading back toward the kitchens. She knew that he would do what was necessary to protect those who depended on him, but she also knew that she could not endanger these people any longer.

"If you'll excuse us," Celia interjected quietly, not wanting to interfere, "we'll be going up now."

Celia handed the baby back to Ellen and, leaning over Runt, kissed him on the forehead.

"You did a great thing today," she whispered. "More than you know. Thank you."

Runt nodded, and his eyes quickly found Ellen's.

Celia took Kit back from Ellen and turned to leave the hall. As she did, she was startled to feel Colin's huge hand on her arm. Celia stopped and looked at him towering above her, surprised at the openness of his action.

"I'll look in on you later," Colin said, his eyes warm with affection, engaging hers. "I haven't even had a chance to meet this little fellow yet." Colin's gaze dropped to the sleeping child in Celia's arms for a moment. A strange stirring occurred in the giant as he looked into the innocent face, snuggled so peacefully in the mother's arms.

The hush that fell over the room penetrated their momentary isolation. Colin was the first to recover, and his face darkened with seriousness as he continued. "Also, for the time being, I don't want you going outside the castle unescorted."

"That won't be necessary. I can . . ."

"Celia, no arguments," Colin commanded, his fierce scowl leaving little room for discussion.

Celia paused, then nodded in agreement, and moments later left the hall with Edmund and Ellen trailing behind.

When they reached the upstairs, Ellen took the sleeping baby into her room. Edmund stood by one of the windows of Celia's room, waiting for Celia to close the adjoining door.

"We have to leave, Edmund," Celia said, pacing her room with the energy of a caged tiger. "We can't stay here now."

"I know lass. But if we leave right now, we could be playing into their hands . . . whoever they are. That could be exactly what they want."

"Are you certain they weren't Danvers's men, Edmund?" Celia asked.

"No, Celia, they weren't," he answered. "They were definitely Highland fighters."

"Then we have more enemies than we thought. Who would have put them up to it?" Celia asked. "Do you think it could be the Queen?"

Edmund's brow furrowed. "Highlanders working for the Queen? It would truly have to serve their interests immensely for them to deal with her."

"She could reward them well," Celia said. "And she's still the Queen, even if she is the English king's sister. Until the coronation, she's still a power to be reckoned with."

"Aye, but we're talking about killing, here. And she

wouldn't go so far, even with her English blood." Edmund was certain of that.

"Then who's left?" Celia's frustration was growing.

"I don't know," her uncle responded. "Although I wish we could somehow communicate with the Earl of Huntly about this. I know he wasn't expecting this. He'd only considered the English as a threat to us. I know he thought the Western Highlands would be far enough away. But he *must* be nearly finished with his business at court."

"Why can't we just go to Argyll ... now?" Celia blurted out. In her head she knew that leaving Kildalton Castle right now was probably not the best of plans. But with so many things pulling at her, Celia simply could not sit still. She was not built for waiting. "Edmund, I'm worried for these people. I want Kit to be safe, but I don't want to see anyone else hurt. These people are building something good here, and I'd hate to see the plots and the destruction that are following us ruin innocent lives."

"That's another reason I wish we could contact Huntly," Edmund said. "If he'd known where Colin Campbell stands and what he's doing here, he would have chosen him to help us rather than Argyll. Not that I have doubts about Argyll, but Colin is a driver. He would have been involved at every stage. And he would have taken a personal interest in Huntly's plans—they're the same type of man. Colin sees his successes here as a model for the rest of Scotland.

"And these people are not isolated from Scotland's turmoil," Edmund continued. "The Campbells see clearly what is going on around them, but their vision extends beyond that. They'll protect the present, and prosper by it, but they also plan for the future. They are true survivors. What happened at Caithness Hall will not happen here. Colin will not allow it."

"But unless Huntly agrees," Celia said with resignation, "we can't confide in them, can we?"

"No, we can't," Edmund agreed. It was the Earl of Huntly's game they were playing. It was his call to make. "We must continue as planned. We will know Huntly's plans when he arrives there just after Easter. But we need to be at Argyll for that."

"But what can be holding up Father William?" Celia asked impatiently.

"I don't know, lass," the knight said gravely. "I do think it's time we sent a message to him. As far as we know, he's still at the abbey by Argyll's castle. I suspect he is just waiting for Argyll to get back, and that's why we haven't heard anything. Argyll should have heard about the attack on Caithness Hall by now. He'll be looking for us to arrive. It's just a matter of time."

"So we just wait?"

"No, I'll send the message today. We'll know in a day or two what is detaining Dunbar. We'll stay that long, at least."

Celia watched in solitude as the sky above the white-capped sea grew gray. Standing by the window, she could feel the spring chill once again descend upon the castle. The rain would begin again soon, she thought, raw and sharp and penetrating.

In spite of all that she and Edmund had talked about, in spite of all common sense, in spite of all impending danger, Celia wanted to stay. In her heart of hearts, there was nothing she wanted more. What had been occurring since Colin's arrival was so incredibly new to her, so wonderfully surprising, that Celia still hadn't even had time to sort it out.

And now, she almost didn't want to. More than anything else, she was afraid to.

I have Kit to focus on, Celia thought. There's nothing else that I can put before that. Even Colin Campbell.

Colin Campbell.

Oh, God, why now? Celia thought. Why did they have to meet this way? Why right now? Six years at court, never once feeling at home. Never once even tempted to care for someone. Never once in control of her destiny. A destiny controlled by others. Enforced by kings.

The inevitable impossibility of their situation settled upon her, damp and cold and painful.

By the time darkness fell, the cold rain had begun in earnest.

Despite the wet chill without and her own gloom within, Celia chose a soft, white cotton dress. She wanted to feel comfortable and at home. Just a pretense, she knew, but Celia wanted to somehow dispel, or at least ignore, the heavy gray shadow that loomed above her.

When a man carrying turf and wood and one of the serving women had come in to light the fire, Celia had suddenly felt self-conscious of the low-cut front of the dress. But they came and went without any indication of impropriety in her attire, and Kit had then easily captured her attention.

A short time later, sitting on the great bed with Kit, Celia was laughing out loud at the baby's antics. She had never imagined how much fun a seven-month-old could be. Kit had just finished pulling himself up to a rather wobbly standing position, a fist full of Celia's hair in each hand, and had now begun to jump up and down with the bubbling, joyous laughter only an infant can make.

Celia loved these moments. It was at times like this that she felt so connected with Kit. Lady Caithness be damned, it was at times like this that she felt she could be a real mother.

Ellen had gone downstairs to get dinner for them both. Celia had suggested going to the kitchens herself, but Ellen had jumped at the chance of going. When

Celia had slyly mentioned that perhaps Ellen could check on Runt's condition while she was downstairs, the blush that had arisen in Ellen's fair skin had confirmed her suspicions.

Celia had sensed the attraction between the two. She was glad, for she knew Runt would take care of Ellen. But more important, Celia had seen a new liveliness in Ellen that she hadn't seen before. And the security that the Campbells could offer was what Ellen needed in her life.

But Celia knew her too well. Ellen would never back out on their plans now. Once they were safe at Argyll, though, she could talk Ellen into returning to Runt. That was the least she could do for her. When the time was right, Celia decided, she would speak to Colin about it.

Kit had been mouthing Celia's face, planting the sloppiest of kisses, and was now using her chin as a teething toy, when the knock at the door forced her to break off the play. Putting the baby on her hip, and laughing as she attempted to wipe off her wet face, Celia opened the door for Ellen.

"I think you're right about weaning Kit," she said, pulling open the door as Kit grabbed at the neckline of her dress front. "He's definitely st—"

The huge figure leaning in the doorway was not Ellen. Behind Colin, one of the kitchen workers stood with a platter of food. Celia's questioning eyes traveled from the food back to Colin's relaxed stance and up to his handsome face. Damn it, he was doing it to her again. The way he looked at her made her heart race. His wild mane of thick black hair, his clean-shaven bronze face, the shimmering gleam of his gray eyes, the broad muscular frame that strained at the confines of his clothing . . .

"I never did feed you properly, this afternoon," Colin said wryly.

It was good that he had prepared that line in advance. Eyeing the beauty before him, Colin's mind emptied of every thought but one. How could a dress so innocently plain, so stylistically simple, be so sensually provocative, so exquisitely commanding on this woman standing in the open doorway.

"Where's Ellen?" Celia said pointedly, shaking the giant out of his silent reverie.

"Are you going to let us in, or should we eat out here in the hallway?" Colin said, recovering quickly.

Without waiting for an answer, Colin stepped across the threshold and put out both hands to the baby. Kit paused for only the briefest of moments, then dived forward into the warrior's outstretched arms. Celia was so stunned at the response that she hadn't time to restrain the move gracefully. She released the baby's legs, and Colin brought him snugly to his chest.

The warrior moved to the newly replaced chair before the fire and sat down, bouncing the delighted Kit on his knee. Colin was as stunned as Celia at the bairn's open acceptance of him—happily stunned.

"Jean," Colin said without looking up from the child. "Put the food on the bed and bring the good chair and a bench from my room."

Celia just stood there watching Colin and the babbling Kit as Jean did as he was told. A moment later, after spreading the food on the bench, Jean left the room, closing the door behind him.

"So, they are going to stop feeding you, hmmm, my little man?" Colin asked, briefly casting his eye on Celia's low-cut dress. "Don't tell me you bit something you weren't supposed to bite? Let me tell you something, man to man. Women are so sensitive about the silliest things . . ."

"Give me that child, Colin Campbell," Celia said, marching in his direction. "I'm not going to stand by while you corrupt this child with your ridiculous male . . ."

But Colin was up from his chair in a flash, the quick movement drawing squeals of laughter from the baby.

"This might be my only chance to corrupt anybody," Colin retorted, shielding the child with his body from Celia.

"Colin, you give that baby to me right now," Celia demanded. "You are scaring him."

Colin held the red-haired, gray-eyed, laughing baby high in the air, then lowered him, muzzling Kit's little button nose with his own. Kit reached up and tried to grab the giant's twinkling gray eyes. "Aye, he is a timid little thing. Just like his mother."

Hearing that, Celia snatched Kit out of Colin's hands and held the squirming infant tight to her breast.

"Colin, I asked you where Ellen is? What are you doing here?"

Colin ignored the questions and began to serve up portions of the dinner from the platter. "Come and sit down and I'll feed you. You haven't eaten much today, have you?"

"If my memory serves me, sir," Celia responded, moving closer to him. "*You* are not to be trusted."

"Celia ... Celia ..." Colin protested comically, his face projecting the most pathetic anguish. "You cut me deeply. Besides, what have you got to worry about. Your little warrior there will protect you."

"I want you to know, Lord Colin, Kit comes from a very distinguished line of warriors," Celia said, giving her attention to the squirming bundle in her arms.

"As distinguished as a quarter-blood English Lowlander can get," Colin cracked, adding directly to the baby, "No offense, little fellow."

"You may bend your knee to him yet, you pompous, piratical peacock."

"Celia," Colin said, taking hold of her shoulders and pushing her gently into the chair. "Sit."

Before Celia could shift Kit into position where she'd have a free hand to eat with, Colin began to feed her.

"Colin Campbell, I'm not a baby that needs to be fed," she said, her mouth full.

"It seems to me that you're going to need both hands free." He grinned, nodding toward the baby who was busily, and successfully, undoing the laces that held the bodice of her dress together. "Not that I mind, particularly."

"Kit!" Celia scolded, wrestling with the determined infant.

"Can I help you?" Colin asked innocently, enjoying her losing battle.

"Aye, you can," she answered. "It's about time you did something productive."

As she held Kit at arm's length, Colin reached around the child and took hold of the laces himself.

"COLIN CAMPBELL!" she shouted, clutching the baby defensively to her chest and slapping *his* busily successful hands away. "You're worse than he is!"

Colin laughed heartily, and Celia could not keep herself from joining in, though hurriedly tightening the undone laces.

It flashed through Colin's mind that he loved this sense of companionship. He had come up to Celia's room to talk to her about the attack that morning and about the abbey by Argyll's castle. But that whole business now seemed somewhat less important. Never had Colin Campbell been one to put his own pleasure before business, but never had he enjoyed being with a woman as much as he did Celia. There was a freshness about her responses to his attentions ... almost a naïveté.

"I knew it wouldn't be safe to eat with you," Celia scolded, pretending to be angry. "Give me that spoon."

Snatching it from his hand, Celia gave it to Kit, who immediately jammed the utensil into his mouth and contentedly gnawed away at it.

"I really would like to know how you bribed Ellen into letting you bring up the dinner."

"It wasn't difficult, really," Colin answered. "She's down feeding Runt, who had full use of his hands until he saw Ellen appear. I don't know that she's speeding his recovery along."

"Ellen seems to be growing very fond of Runt. She was pretty anxious to check on him tonight. Is he any better?"

"With Ellen's beautiful face attending to him, he'll probably take forever to heal."

Celia's glare of feigned jealousy in Colin's direction caught him up short.

"Not that I think she's beautiful, mind you," Colin said. "She's Runt's type."

Celia touched Kit's soft hair with her chin. She was never one to bring attention to herself, but she simply had to ask.

"Really. And what's your type?" Celia whispered—thinking, hoping, knowing.

Colin's eyes traveled lingeringly from her auburn ringlets to the silky skin of her neck and shoulders. He gazed at the perfect symmetry of her slightly exposed, softly rounded breasts, at the slender taper of the waist, at the womanly fullness of her hips. His eyes engaged hers with an earnestness that silenced any complaint that she might have uttered, and when he answered, his voice was husky with feeling.

"You are."

Celia now realized that while undergoing Colin's searchingly tender gaze, she had stopped breathing.

Colin glided to her chair with the grace of a ship under sail. Dropping to one knee beside her, he slid one arm around the baby nestled in Celia's lap and used the other to gather her in.

There was no hesitation once their lips met. Since their encounter earlier in the day, each had been haunted by doubts about the reality of what they had felt, of what they had experienced. But what each of them was feeling now went beyond the physical attraction of the morning. And they both knew it.

Wrapped in the warm fire glow of the evening, Celia drew Colin even farther into her embrace. As Colin's lips pressed against hers, his simple touch inflamed her. His strength surrounded her, infused her with a soft, tender ache. As Colin's grip grew tighter, his head angled deeply, and Celia felt his full lips open over hers. The luxurious warmth of his mouth conveyed tenderness, care, and, above all, a passion that could not be hidden away, ignored, or denied. Celia had no intention of denying that . . . something . . . which promised to consume them. No, she wanted to bury herself in him, lose herself within the solid goodness of him. Celia knew, deep inside, that in the end, she would be powerless in the face of their flaming passion.

Colin felt her lips open, admitting him to the velvet richness of her depths. He wanted to embrace her, protect her, have her. The sweetness of her thrilled him, tortured him with an agony that he knew would grow more exquisite with every moment.

But Colin knew that this was not the right moment for the feelings that threatened to unhinge their innermost desires. Their thoughts were in unison, for as they broke off the kiss, each smiled down at the bairn who was so contentedly watching the activity above him.

As Celia smiled down at Kit, her mind and body were in a state of turmoil. She could still feel Colin's strong hand against her back. Her lips still tingled from the pressure of their kiss. Her body ached at the very core of her being, crying out for more of his touch, his warm strength, for fulfillment of the longing that was growing within her.

But in her mind, a war was being waged in which reason was being blinded, in which the very presence of this man was enough to drive out common sense and control. When she looked at him, Celia felt her soul expand. Fed by the senses, something else within her was gaining strength, overwhelming her.

Gazing down at the child, Celia shuddered with confusion. What her heart was drawing her on to feel and to do, she knew was contradicted by other loyalties—by other promises.

Colin looked up at Celia's face, willing her eyes up to meet his. As their gazes met, Colin saw emotion welling up in her. Her look inflamed a desire to reveal himself to her, to let her know the depth of feeling that traveled clear to his soul, the feeling that touched her and all who were dear to her, as well.

Colin tried to express this by drawing her to him again. He brushed his lips lightly against hers, then leaned down and kissed the soft, red hair of the child on her lap.

Raising his head, Colin thought to gently kiss the mother's full, tender lips once more before standing away, before putting an end to this sweet torment. He wanted Celia, but he knew that this was not the moment. He tenderly moved his lips to her warm face for one last, soft touch, but the scent of her skin ignited the passion within him. Suddenly the agony was too great to restrain. He claimed her mouth once more, devouring her so completely with a new possessiveness that rocked him. Then Colin pulled away from their embrace and stood up.

"I'm having a rather difficult time, Celia," Colin explained quickly, backing toward the fireplace, "keeping my hands off you."

Celia simply looked down at Kit, but Colin could see the blush come to her cheeks.

"But I'm looking forward to continuing this . . . discussion . . . soon," Colin finished, stumbling against the great oak chest. He turned with a smile. "Been redecorating, Celia?"

"Aye . . . right after you and Alec arrived . . . I moved

it there," Celia answered, still feeling a bit dazed by
their moment's embrace, but also a bit embarrassed
about Colin noticing the relocated piece of furniture. "I
know it won't stop anybody, but I wanted to have a little
warning if any stranger tried to use it. I still don't know
where that panel leads, or even how to open it."

"If you'll trust us enough to let me move it away, I'll
show you how it works."

Responding to Celia's nod, Colin easily pushed the
chest clear across the room to the opposite wall. If she
uses this chest to block that entrance again, he thought,
I'll chop it into firewood myself. Coming back with a
smile on his face, he motioned Celia toward the
fireplace.

Celia stood, cradling the baby on her hip, and moved
to the fireplace. Colin was reaching one hand into the
left side of the open hearth. Bending her head, she saw
his fingers easily locate a nearly invisible gap between
two of the stones. He slid a thin piece of wood out
slightly until the nearby panel popped open. Colin took
a thick candle from the mantelpiece and lit it in the fire.
Celia followed him to the panel, which Colin pulled
open and stepped through.

Her face lit with anticipation, Celia walked through
the opening and looked down the dusty, narrow passageway. On her left, Celia could just make out a set of steps
leading down into darkness.

"Those steps eventually lead down to the same passages we came in earlier, but there are a number of
doorways that are inaccessible to anyone who doesn't
know the secret."

"Who knows the secret?" Celia asked.

"My father, Agnes, and I are the only ones who know
how to get up to this passageway. These entries are not
used, so you can be assured that no one will be coming
up those steps. You really are quite safe."

Celia turned around and tried to look past Colin's

massive body. She could see the wall of her fireplace jutting into the narrow corridor. There was what she assumed to be another fireplace jutting in from the other side.

"What's beyond the fireplaces? Can someone go out into the hallway from here?"

"No," Colin responded, leading her past the fireplaces.

"Then where did you come from the first night?"

"From my room."

"Your room! Where is that?" she asked suspiciously.

"Through this panel." He grinned, sliding back the wooden latch and pushing open the panel into his room. "We conduct late night tours."

Celia peered hesitantly into the warm glow of the warrior's room. The rich tapestries on the walls and the comfortable furniture did nothing to lessen the masculine atmosphere of the chamber. The character of the room was surprising, just like its inhabitant. Her eyes traveled to the huge bed, its dark curtains drawn back.

"Is this tour open to all visitors to Kildalton Castle, m'lord?" she asked sarcastically.

"No," Colin responded devilishly. "Just you."

"Such a cozy arrangement. What was it that you said about my safety, just now?" Celia asked, smiling before turning her back on his handsome face. "I think I'll be moving the chest back over."

Colin stopped her before she could reenter her room. "I won't come into your bed until you invite me," he said, gazing steadily into her eyes. "But if you want to come to me, you won't find any chest blocking my door."

It would be only natural for him to assume that she would go to him—for him to assume that, after all, Lady Caithness had done this many times before, Celia thought.

Celia looked up into his face, but as much as she

wanted to tell him everything about herself, to reveal all the truths that she held so tightly inside, truths that threatened to strangle her, she knew that there was no answer she could give him. Silence could be her only response.

She turned and carried the baby back into her room.

When she entered her bedroom again, Kit began to cry. "Are you getting hungry, my little man?" she said, trying to turn her attention from her own agitation. "I think we'll just change your wrappings and get you ready for when Ellen comes back."

Celia crossed to Ellen's room and got the dry change of clothes for him. Carrying Kit back, she laid him on her bed, noticing that the panel was still open and that Colin had not reentered the room. It would be better not to think about him right now. It would be better not to think at all. She busied herself stripping the wet things off the baby and cleaning him. When the child was free of the wrappings, he babbled with delight and pulled himself up to a standing position, holding Celia's fingers.

"Why would anyone want to hurt your bairn?"

Celia started at the sound of Colin's voice, in spite of the gentleness of his tone. Looking up, she saw he was standing with his back to the fireplace, and the panel to the passageway had been closed.

"Danvers has a bounty on every baby boy in the Lowlands."

"A bounty?" Colin said with a mixture of surprise and disgust. "What reason would he have for doing that?"

"I can't say," Celia responded, looking intensely at the child and avoiding Colin's searching look. "I only heard it from two of Danvers's men when we were escaping from Caithness Hall."

"Well, we're not in the Lowlands, and those weren't Danvers's men," Colin said sharply, sensing that Celia was not telling everything she knew. He had come to know the directness with which Celia communicated, and the way she was now avoiding his eyes, the visible tenseness in her body, told him that she was not being completely forthright.

"Well, you tell me who they are, then," Celia snapped, her temper flaring momentarily.

Like two bulls butting heads, the two stubbornly refused to reveal anything they knew. Protectiveness restrained Celia; her sense of duty forbade her to speak. Colin's stubbornness was a direct response to hers.

"I can't say," Colin said, echoing Celia's own evasive words.

"Well, I'll find out on my own . . . and soon enough."

"From whom? Your friend at the abbey by Argyll's castle?"

"What do you know about Father William?" she said, startled by his question.

"Who is this Father William? And what is he doing there?" Colin was going to find out what the connection was between Celia and the abbey.

When Colin had gone to look at the bodies of the dead attackers, his village priest had accompanied him. The priest had immediately recognized the third body they examined—he had been one of the soldiers in the brigade that protected the abbey. And the only link between the abbey and the attack on Celia's bairn was this priest.

"He's my confessor and my friend. He is an educator and a priest." Celia's voice expressed her rising anxiety. "Why? Have you heard something? Has something happened to him?"

"How would I know? But why *should* something have happened to him? He's a miserable court priest. Why should somebody be after him?" Colin said in a biting tone.

"I don't know, but your nastiness is uncalled for," Celia exclaimed with feeling. "Aside from Edmund, Father William was the only real friend I had for the six long years I spent in that empty court. He taught me mathematics, philosophy, history, Latin, and even Greek—things that are forbidden for women. He's as much my family as Edmund is."

Glaring across the room at her, Colin understood that Celia was not going to tell him anything she didn't want him to know. She seemed genuinely concerned about this priest. And now she was blatantly ignoring him, having turned her attention completely to her child.

Colin stalked to the window and looked through it into the blackness outside. The sleeting rain was beating against the panes of glass in wind-driven gusts. As he listened to the icy rain and thought over all that had been occurring, he came to realize that he very well might have been wrong in his original assumptions about her. After all, she must have experienced real horrors confronting Danvers's soldiers, knowing that her child was merely a prize of war. The hardships of her escape were nothing, he knew, to the pain she had endured this morning hearing that Kit had been attacked.

Aye, she was holding things back. But in her own mind at least, she had good reason for it. It definitely seemed as though Edmund and this priest *were* all Celia had; there didn't seem to be anyone else. But what about the husband's family? Why weren't they helping her . . . and their own Caithness heir? Perhaps that was it, Colin thought, grasping at straws. Perhaps they had something to do with the attack today.

Whatever was behind it, everything Celia held dear was at stake. But to help her, he had to convince her that she could trust him. And interrogating her this way, he thought, was definitely not the way to do it.

Celia was now sitting on the bed, letting the bairn chew on the knuckles of her hand. She was deep in thought, but looked up with troubled eyes when Colin approached her.

"Celia," he said, searching for the right words. "I want you to know that if I'm angry, it's because I'm frustrated trying to understand the reason for the attack today. It's my responsibility to protect my people and my guests, and an assault like the one that took place today simply doesn't happen here. My family has worked very hard to make this place strong, and by making it strong, we have made it safe. No one attacks Kildalton, even in such a cowardly fashion as those animals did today. *No one* attacks people who have taken shelter here."

"Colin," she said, looking directly into his eyes. "I honestly do not know who those men were today."

"I believe you," he said, sitting beside her and taking her hand. "But I also think you're not telling me some things ... perhaps to protect the ones you love. I can respect that. But I want to somehow earn your trust ... so that I can help to protect you *and* them."

Celia looked at him with gratitude for his attempt at understanding, and affection for his caring support. Before she could open her mouth to answer him, though, Celia heard Ellen open the door into her own room.

Colin stood immediately and moved to the fireplace.

Ellen knocked softly at the half-open door and, at Celia's response, entered the room, casting an embarrassed look at her mistress. She knew that she'd been gone a longer time than she'd anticipated, but Celia's reassuring smile comforted her concerns.

"Shall I take the bairn, m'lady?" Ellen asked in a hushed voice, very aware of the laird's presence.

"Aye, Ellen," Celia responded, handing the freshly changed baby to her. "He's all cleaned up and ready for you. How is Runt?"

Ellen's fair-skinned face flushed bright scarlet. "He's ... he's doing better, m'lady."

Celia stood and put her arm warmly around Ellen, walking her toward the door. "You make sure that Runt gets the care he needs."

After Ellen disappeared with Kit into her room, Celia made a point of leaving the door half open. Crossing to the fireplace, she didn't have to look at Colin to know that his eyes were following her. She felt his presence dominating the room, dominating her attention. But she didn't want to pick up that discussion where they had left off. She just could not tell him more than he already knew—it was as simple as that.

She just wanted to look at him as she knew he sometimes looked at her. She wanted to look at him and memorize every detail of him: the way his hair lay tossed back on his shoulders, the way his searching eyes always sought out hers, the way his face could not help but display his every mood, the way he would stand with his arms folded across his broad chest, leaning deep in thought before the fireplace. But she realized that this vision was already branded in her memory. It was emblazoned there in colors to last a lifetime . . . for a lifetime of lifetimes.

Nonetheless, he was there before her now, and she simply had to look at him. Now . . . while she still had time.

Celia's gaze washed over him.

"If you're going to look at me that way," Colin whispered, smiling. "You'd better go close that door." He certainly liked the way she went about changing the subject.

Celia blushed at her indiscretion, but shook her head, smiling at his suggestion.

"Then I'll go close it," he said, straightening up as if to follow through on his threat.

"No, Colin. If you do, I'll just open that door right up again."

"That will be very difficult after I nail the damn thing shut."

"Colin, don't you dare!" Celia said, moving between Colin and the door.

"My house," the young laird said, stepping closer to her.

"My doors," he continued, taking another step closer.

"My nails," he said in a low voice, moving ever closer.

"My rules," Colin whispered, encircling her with his arms and holding her tightly to him.

"Really," Celia said, trying to sound as maternal as she could, knowing that she had brought this sweet torture on herself. "Kit acts more maturely than you do, sometimes."

"He doesn't have to do outrageous things to get close to you," Colin said, burying his face in the curls covering her neck. "Clearly, I do."

Celia shuddered, feeling his lips on her neck, taking her earlobe between his teeth and lips, suckling gently.

"Clearly, you are a poor, neglected, little thing." Celia smiled, firmly pushing him away and turning him toward the door. She had to stop this now, before her defenses completely crumbled. "But it's time you went on your way."

Colin hung his head dramatically as he released her and headed for the door. As he reached it, however, he turned and gave her a sly look. "You have to promise to come and tuck me in later."

"Out!" she said with a smile, pushing him into the corridor and shutting the door with a sigh.

In Colin's dream Kildalton was under attack. The long cannons perched on the crenellated walls were pounding away at the English ships at sea. Celia, dressed in white, was seated among red roses in a garden located oddly in the South Hall. The English wanted her, but she held a thistle flower protectively in her arms. As the English cannon fire began to reach the castle, Celia held out the thistle flower to Colin. The sounds of the cannons grew louder and louder. Colin reached out for Celia, but the floors had become slippery, thick with mud. His hands reached out, but all he could grasp was the flower. And then Celia was gone, leaving Colin with the thistle. Where she had been, there was only a rose—a white rose.

The smoke in the hall was growing thicker; the huge guns were now booming in his ears. Over and over the pounding continued ...

Colin awakened to his soldier's persistent knocking. Leaping from his bed with his cloak around him, the warrior pulled open the door. Outside his window, only the first gray shades of morning were apparent.

"M'lord, we need you down at the harbor Marketcross."

"What's wrong?" Colin snapped, moving back into his room, quickly wrapping his kilt around him and belting on his sword.

"Two fishing boats full of mainland folk have come into the harbor. They're asking for protection, and they say there's more coming."

"Protection from whom?"

"They say the English. They've got women, children, and wounded. But that's not all."

"What else?" Colin asked sharply.

"They seem to think the English are coming this way."

"The hell they are." Colin hurled himself past the soldier and down the steps into the gloom of the Great Hall. Shouting orders to the gathered fighters and emerging servants, Colin swept out of the castle and into the swirling predawn mists.

Throughout the night, the heavy wind-driven rains had pelted Celia's windows, but when she awoke, it seemed that the storm had moved inside the castle walls. Sounds of shouting and turmoil were coming from the Great Hall. Celia threw on her clothes and ran down the hallway to the top of the stairs. She froze.

The hall was a sea of human motion. Soldiers and servants were bringing in injured men and women. The sound of frightened, crying children filled the air, punctuated by Lord Hugh's commands.

Spotting Agnes, Celia hurried down the steps, working her way through the crowd toward her. As she passed the wounded, Celia could see and smell the gashes and the burns that covered great portions of many of the victims. She shuddered involuntarily, and a cold sweat broke out on her body. She knew only too well the signs. She knew the devil who had caused this suffering. Had he arrived so soon in the west? Was he already here at her door?

"Celia, are you all right, child?" Agnes asked, placing a hand gently on Celia's arm. She had seen the young woman pale at the sight of the burned peasants. Agnes knew that Celia had been through this before, and her heart went out to her.

"Who are these people?" Celia asked, regaining her composure and focusing on the sights before her.

"Mainlanders from areas to the south of our land. Mostly peasant folk." Agnes decided not to trouble her with the sketchy details that were beginning to emerge.

"Who did this, Agnes?"

"We don't know, darling. Colin, Alec, and your uncle are down at the harbor right now. These folks say that there are more boats coming."

As Celia's eyes roamed the room, she could see that many of these people needed immediate attention. Agnes's helpers were circulating in the room, but there were more injured than they could handle by themselves.

"How can I help?"

Agnes looked into Celia's face. The clear, steady gaze assured her that the young woman was back in form.

Agnes handed her a bundle of clean dressings and watched as Celia went to work.

Over the next four hours, Agnes saw Celia take control of the activities around her. Large bowls of hot water were continually being brought in from the kitchen as they moved quickly among the injured, cleaning wounds and stitching deep cuts with long needles and white thread. Those with burns were carefully stripped of their charred clothing. Agnes watched Celia gently apply the salves that she had been given. She almost seemed to absorb the pain, sharing in the suffering of the folk she tended—those she worked with seemed to gain strength from her very touch. Working in harmony with their helpers, Celia and Agnes brought some comfort to those whose lives had just been torn apart.

Weary, Celia wiped the blood of the last wounded farmer from her hands and sat for a moment with the group of children huddled together by the doors to the Entry Room. These young ones will be the long-term casualties, Celia thought. No parents, no home, no hope for a future. A nightmare that could last a lifetime.

Alec Macpherson entered the Great Hall and, as he crossed to Lord Hugh, looked around him at the groups of suffering people who had come to the Campbells for refuge. As those in the Highlands trusted his own father, these common folk on the coast trusted Colin's. Like the Macpherson's Benmore Castle, Kildalton would always be a refuge for those in need. This was one tradition, this tradition of trust, that he and Colin would definitely preserve.

Celia stood and hurried toward Alec and Lord Hugh, hoping to learn something about the situation. She reached them just as Agnes did, listening to Alec's news.

"Some of the boats Colin sent out are just returning

from the mainland. He asked me to tell you that there's no force following these people. Whatever the English are doing, they're staying to the south. But your soldiers at Oban are on the alert."

"Good. Are there any more injured coming in?" Lord Hugh asked.

"No. When I came up, though, there was one small boat with a few who are not injured. And there is a priest with them . . ."

A priest! Celia thought, her mind running ahead of the information that Alec was conveying. A priest!

"Lord Hugh, I'd like to go down there," Celia said as Alec finished speaking. She had to find out if the priest was William Dunbar.

"Colin wants some blankets and food sent down to the church for this last group," Alec responded. "I'm going back to see if there's anything new, so I can take you down if you like."

Celia nodded and ran quickly to her room. Checking on Ellen and Kit, she informed Ellen of the events and returned to the Great Hall with her heavy cloak thrown around her shoulders.

Without another word the two left for the harbor.

As they hurried along the stone road that wound down to the village, Celia was aware of the fatigue that was clouding her mind. Alec, trying to lighten the silent mood that hung over them like the gray drizzly day, searched for a topic that they could converse upon.

"It always impresses me that these sailors can keep their bearings on sunless days like this," Alec said as the harbor came into view beyond the village they had just entered.

"They have to . . . it's their living," Celia responded, peering unsuccessfully through the mists toward the jetties at the base of the stone-paved road.

"Your uncle tells me that you've done quite a bit of sailing in your lifetime."

"Aye," Celia answered, only half attending to what Alec was saying.

"In fact, he says that you are an excellent sailor."

"My uncle likes to boast about me," Celia answered, feeling a bit embarrassed by Edmund's avuncular affection. "I pretty much grew up on the water."

"My whole family has been involved with boats," Alec said, smiling. Actually, his family had made a fortune raiding merchant ships like the ones Celia grew up on. "But my stomach was never suited to the work."

"Oh?" Celia really didn't want to trade confessions with Alec Macpherson. Her mind was too preoccupied with the flood of danger spilling northward, and its impact. Once again so close. Once again on her trail. Following them.

But Alec was not one to let a beautiful woman off the hook so easily. He knew from watching them together that Colin was really taken by Celia, and he would respect that. However, this was just innocent conversation. "Did you sail much at court?"

"Not much," Celia responded shortly, surprised at her own abruptness. He is just being friendly, she thought. I suppose I shouldn't be rude.

"That's understandable," Alec said with a devilish glint in his eye. "There are gentler, more appropriate pursuits for ladies of the court."

"Actually, Lord Alec," Celia snapped. "I did get a chance to navigate the *Queen's* boat in the sailing race during the anniversary celebration last summer."

Alec had been at court for the King and Queen's tenth wedding anniversary celebration last August, but the festivities included a great deal of hunting, an activity that drew Alec's attention more than any other. The King's entourage had carried the celebration from Linlithgow to Stirling for the hunting, and to Edinburgh for the remainder of the festivities—including sailing races. Alec, though, had stayed at Stirling to hunt with the King for an extra week while the celebration moved on ahead of them.

"You must have sailed quite a bit, then, preparing."

Celia could see that Alec was in some way impressed.

"We did sail often during the summer, but not as much as I would have liked," Celia responded. "But there was a great deal going on."

"I should say so," Alec said. "And a great deal since." It was still so hard to believe the amount of changes that Scotland had undergone in the past seven months. And like so many, this woman, too, had undergone so many changes in seven short months. Seven months, Alec thought suddenly.

"You know, Lady Caithness, my family speaks highly of you," Alec said, watching her expression. "I meant to tell you earlier . . . I'm sorry that I was not in Scotland when you visited Ambrose at our home in Benmore Castle, but my parents truly enjoyed your stay."

"I . . . er . . . I enjoyed meeting them, too." Celia darted a look at Alec. Just my luck, she thought. Lady Caithness and the Macphersons. Time to change the subject. "Did you say you don't care to sail, m'lord?"

"I'm a bit prone to seasickness," Alec said roughly, his attention now turning to the village harbor that lay directly ahead.

There was something that annoyed Celia about the abrupt change in his tone. However, following Alec's look, Celia saw Colin standing with a group of men where the beach and jetty met. The beach that had been empty the day before was now lined for some distance with shallow-bottomed fishing boats. Celia spotted Edmund near two fishermen who were just pulling a boat up onto the beach. As they passed across the Marketcross area, she saw scattered groups of refugees huddled around sputtering turf fires. People were moving about from group to group, and Alec roughly took hold of Celia's arm as they weaved their way through the open square.

Seeing Edmund alone, she knew that Father William had not been among the arrivals. She had known that her uncle would have sent word if Dunbar had arrived, but certain now, Celia felt a mixed sense of relief and disappointment.

Colin saw her. Alec was leading Celia past a group of peasants. The warrior separated himself from the others and walked quickly to them.

"You two out for a stroll?" Colin snapped, looking at Alec's hand on Celia's arm.

"Hardly," Celia responded shortly. "I came down to see Edmund."

Colin watched as Alec dropped her arm, his friend's grim face reflecting the sound of Celia's abrupt tone.

"Well, I'll take you to him," Colin said gruffly, trying to take her arm as Alec had. But Celia shook loose from his light grip.

"That won't be necessary," Celia said. "I can see him."

Annoyed at her treatment by the two giants, Celia moved quickly ahead of them toward her uncle. She wasn't going to stand for either Alec's moody questioning or Colin's accusing looks. She had enough problems of her own to deal with.

A tug on her cloak spun Celia around.

"Thank the Lord. They didn't catch you, m'lady."

Celia took a moment to recognize the woman.

"Eustace!" she gasped, surprised at the sight of her. Celia embraced the woman warmly. "No, your husband and his relatives gave up the chase soon enough."

"I didn't mean that lowlife, horse-thieving brute . . . m'lady," the woman said bitterly.

"You know this woman?" Colin asked Celia as he and Alec came up on either side of her.

"Aye. This woman defied her Gregor husband to save us from having our throats cut as we slept." Celia grasped the woman's hands in both of hers. "She risked her life for us. She's a brave soul."

"And I'm not a Gregor, m'lord," Eustace said emphatically. "I'm of your clan."

"What happened to your husband?" Colin asked.

"I think he ran off into the hills when the English soldiers came looking for this lady here." Eustace looked from Celia's shocked face to those of the two giants who flanked the lady.

"How do you know that the soldiers were looking for her?" Edmund broke in. He had seen Celia be approached by the woman and, recognizing her from their journey, had crossed the stone square to them.

"I heard the soldiers, m'lord," Eustace said, curtsying to the knight. She would never forget him or his kindness for as long as she lived. "They were using the cottage for their evil business. I was hiding in the root cellar after my husband left me, and I could hear the English scum torturing answers out of the local crofters. The screams were horrible, m'lord. I never heard the like."

Eustace shuddered at the memory. "They were looking for your lady here, m'lord."

"How do you know they were looking for this lady?" Colin asked roughly. He was about ready to shake some answers out of this woman himself, but what she had been through must have been truly dreadful.

"For two days, I heard him, the leader, say the same thing over and over. A dark-haired lady with a bairn, a fair-haired nursemaid, a tall knight, and a priest. He even knew your name, m'lady."

"What name did they say?" Alec asked accusingly, looking from Celia's blanched expression to Edmund's hardened face.

Eustace looked carefully into Celia's eyes before responding cautiously.

"Why, Lady ... Celia," Eustace answered. "They were looking for Lady Celia."

"I'm glad no harm came to you," Celia said, looking gratefully at the woman. "Do you have a place to stay?"

"Aye, m'lady. My sister will take me in. She lives here ... just outside the village."

"I'll stop and see you then, before we leave."

"LEAVE?" Colin's barely restrained voice resounded over the stone paving.

Celia turned and looked steadily at Colin, speaking to her uncle without once taking her eyes from the warrior's fierce face.

"Edmund, please take me back to the castle."

"Celia, we need to talk," Colin said, his voice steeled with authority.

"We'll talk later," Celia said, turning from him.

Colin grabbed her elbow, demanding her attention. "We *will* talk later." Turning to two of his fighters, Colin directed the men to accompany Celia and Edmund as far as the castle gates.

Celia turned and strode off, leaving the men in her wake.

Colin watched her disappear into the crowd. Then, turning gently to Eustace, the warrior invited her to come up to the castle after she'd settled in.

As the woman withdrew, Colin looked into his friend's scowling face. Alec was obviously angry, but Colin hadn't any idea what had triggered his anger. He wondered if Alec had learned something new from Edmund that Colin didn't know.

"What's bothering you?" Colin asked, looking intensely into Alec's eyes.

Alec shifted his eyes away from Colin, looking out at

the ships anchored in the harbor and at the fishing boats lying beached on the sand.

"I've found out something that you might care to know," he said, turning his gaze back to Colin. "She's *not* Lady Caithness."

Chapter 8

You'll be home for Easter, the messenger from the south tells us on the sly. King's orders ... we'll all be home for Easter. But that was yesterday. Today, the messenger is gone. Today, Danvers gives his command ... we are moving north. Today, tomorrow, the next day ... we go where he commands.

"Aye," Colin replied coolly. "I know that."

"What?" Alec asked, dumbfounded. "How long have you known that?"

"For the past half hour."

Colin and Alec walked down to the fishing boats lying heeled over in the sand. Colin leaned back heavily against one of them and looked out into the gray murk beyond the harbor mouth.

"How did you find out?" the Macpherson heir asked.

"The priest who had just come in when you went up to the castle recognized Edmund," Colin explained. "He was from a village on Caithness land. From the way the priest talked, Edmund *is* a legend in the Lowlands. And the priest knows the real Lady Caithness. He says she's in England with her bairn."

"Then who is Celia?" Alec asked.

"He says that in the days following Flodden, Edmund arrived at Caithness Hall with a group, including his niece, a Lady Celia. Everyone knew she was nobility from the moment they arrived. The priest was driven toward the coast ahead of the English army, so he didn't know what happened to them. But later on, when he was traveling with the other refugees, he heard that the English were looking for a woman with her description, as this woman Eustace just said. That's all he could tell me, though."

"So that's what the English are after," Alec thought out loud.

"I've known something wasn't right from the beginning," Colin continued. "I just didn't know what it was. In fact, I still don't. But how did you find out about her?"

Alec explained the lie he had used to test Celia during their conversation walking to the harbor. He had known full well that Lady Caithness had never visited Ambrose and his family, and Celia had been so different from the image that his brothers had conveyed.

"But I had tested her only when she gave me reason to suspect something else," Alec said, looking at his pensive friend.

"What else?" Colin queried, expecting the worst.

"I think that bairn might not be her own."

"What?" It was Colin's turn to be dumbfounded. "What makes you think that?"

"She told me she was sailing in the King's anniversary celebration races last summer."

"So what?" Colin could see no relevance in Alec's comment.

"Agnes told me the bairn is seven months old."

Colin looked at his friend blankly.

"Seven months old?" Alec grinned, watching Colin work through the calculations in his mind. "I'm no expert on women's conditions around the time of childbirth, but I have a hard time believing she could have been sailing last summer. Maybe she did sail in those races ... or maybe she didn't have a bairn at all."

As Colin absorbed the import of Alec's information,

he felt a wave of hope. When he'd first heard that Celia was not whom she claimed to be, a vague fear had washed over him. If Caithness was not her husband, then who was? The thought of her having a living husband had chilled him to the bone. In his heart he felt that together they could work out any difficulty ... except that.

Colin's mood, when Celia and Alec had arrived at the harbor, had been anything but cordial. He had wanted to take Edmund aside and question him about the priest's statements, but he had held himself back. Colin had wanted to ask Celia directly. He still wanted to.

But now there was a glimmer of hope in the cloud of confusion Colin was experiencing. If Kit was not her baby, then maybe ...

"Who do you think she is?" Colin asked.

"I think you should just go up there and ask her."

"No, she came to us for help. If I confront her with this, she'll run," Colin said, knowing deep in his heart that this was the last thing he wanted to happen. He cared for her so much already.

"How about Edmund?"

"If I were to question that knight's honor, then I'd have to be prepared to fight him," Colin responded quietly. "I'm not ready to kill an old friend of my father's."

"Well, then, what do we know for sure about them?" Alec threw out, his mind trying to recollect and sort what he knew.

"Honestly, we know very little," Colin responded. "And in the conversations I've had with my father, he's been strangely evasive about them. The only things I really know are that Edmund was a part of the King's entourage, that the English followed Celia and the bairn clear across the Lowlands, and that there are Highlanders willing to kill her ... or the bairn."

That was enough for Alec to like her, to want her to

be protected, but he sensed that he needed to reason clearly right now ... for Colin's sake, as well.

"But we don't know the reason for any of this, do we?" Alec asked. "Why is she running? Who is she? Is the bairn hers? Or if not, whose is it?"

"God knows," Colin answered. "With all the nobles that died at Flodden, Kit could be the child of any one of a thousand different lairds."

"Then why are the English chasing her?" Alec went on.

"And what is her friend, this Father William, doing up at the abbey by Argyll's castle," Colin added thoughtfully.

"It seems to me," Alec concluded, "that this woman— whoever she is—is trouble you'd be better off without. If she's not going to be honest with you, then why not just let her run?"

"That's not an option I want to give her right now."

"Why not?" Alec asked. "You have enough to worry about right now, getting the clans to rally behind the Crown Prince."

"That's true," Colin said. "In fact, I got word this morning that Argyll has returned to his winter castle, and I want to talk to him about where he stands ... and soon."

"So we'll be going up there?"

"Aye, tomorrow or the next day," Colin answered. "And while we're there, we'll find out about the abbey soldier involved with the attack."

"And what are you going to do about Celia?"

"I'll make sure she stays here until we get back." Colin would use information about her priest friend as enticement for her to remain until he and Alec returned. "If she runs from here with the English after her, more people will get hurt. If we have to fight Danvers and his English butchers, let it be right here."

But inwardly, Colin's feelings were different from

those he was willing to express to Alec. There was too much about this woman that appealed to Colin, that attracted him. He was sure that beneath the cloud of circumstance, beneath the veneer of false identity, Celia could be the woman he'd been searching for his whole life. He simply could not let her walk out of his life right now.

Celia and Edmund moved quickly ahead of the two trailing soldiers on the paved road. As they walked, Celia focused her eyes downward on the shiny wetness of the round paving stones, but she was thinking only of Colin's fierce glare, a look that had frozen her blood in her veins.

Moving up the hill toward the end of the village, she felt a tearing sensation in her chest, a suffocating closeness that encompassed her like a cloud. Celia felt something akin to grief, to the mournful sense of loss that accompanies the death of a loved one. She felt that she had somehow lost a dream of happiness. A dream to love and to be loved. A dream that Celia knew had never really been a possibility, but was a longed-for dream nonetheless.

"Argyll is back," Edmund said in a low voice, casting his eyes backward to make sure the soldiers were out of earshot.

"You heard from Father William?" she asked, painfully aware that the time had come for them to leave.

"I received a note from Dunbar, but I haven't opened it yet," he replied. "The fisherman that I paid to take the message to the abbey brought back word that the Earl had just arrived."

"Read the letter to me, Edmund," Celia said resignedly. She was holding back her tears, now. Already there existed in Celia a clear sense of just how painful that parting from this place, from these people . . , from Colin . . . would be.

Edmund broke the wax seal that held the folded parchment closed. They continued to walk as his eyes perused the scrawling hand of the priest.

"Just like Dunbar," Edmund said ironically. "We ask for a straight answer, and he sends us a poem:

> "Walking solitary, you alone,
> Seeing nothing but sticks and stone;
> Out of your painful purgatory
> To bring you to the bliss and glory
> Of Argyll's place, a merry town,
> We here convey this joyful sound.

Well, at least, he's clear about the message. We'll leave for Argyll in the morning."

"No, Edmund," Celia said, taking the paper out of her uncle's hand. "Something's wrong. He's warning us to stay away."

"How do you read that?" Edmund asked, looking perplexed.

"William Dunbar is a master of the ironic," Celia answered with a slight smile. "When we exchanged messages at court that we didn't want understood by others, we wrote them in verse."

"So?" This was not getting any clearer for Edmund.

"We both knew that if we received a *poem* from the other, then the message was really the exact *opposite* of what was written. It was a kind of code we had, and he's doing it now."

"Then what does he mean?"

"Look at the lines," she said, pointing at the message. " 'Walking solitary, you alone.' He knows I'm not alone. 'Nothing but sticks and stone . . .' He heard Eustace talk about Kildalton Castle as a paradise. As far as 'this joyful sound,' when did you ever hear Father William sound joyful?"

"I'll buy that," Edmund joked.

"The real message is that Argyll's place must not be too 'merry,' and he doesn't want us to be there." Celia thought over the message in her head. Something wasn't quite right. If Father William thought that the Argyll part of the plan was no good, then why hadn't he simply come to Kildalton? There was something he was not sure of. She wished she were there to see for herself.

"Then we wait." Edmund shrugged. "Maybe now that Argyll's returned, whatever has been bothering Dunbar will be resolved."

"Maybe. But what about the things that Eustace said in front of Colin?" Celia wondered.

"Don't fear the Campbells, Celia. We have to trust Dunbar's judgment about going to Argyll right now. Until he sends us word, this is still the safest place for Kit."

Fear Colin Campbell? Celia thought as they passed through the drawbridge of the castle's thick curtain wall. Never. Celia knew that she would pour her body and soul into his hands if she could. If she only could.

After spending an hour with Kit and Ellen, Celia returned to the Great Hall. There were no new arrivals, but many of the injured were still in distress. Children were running here and there among the groups of wounded peasants, and the sounds of dogs and children lightened the air of suffering in the room.

Celia went from group to group, checking the wounds and the burns, talking to those who felt up to it, cheering those who could be cheered, comforting those who could be comforted.

It was in the midst of this that she saw him. Colin, still wearing his heavy leather cloak, was standing with his father, talking to him. She could see his eyes were roaming the room, she saw them fix upon her. She had just sat down to change the dressing on a young man's shoulder. Celia tried to focus on the shoulder wound, a gash that had been stitched so neatly. The wound was clean, she thought.

But it was no use. Colin's eyes were piercing her to the core of her existence. She felt her eyes drawn irresistibly to him. He had turned his head and was saying something to Lord Hugh. As she watched, his face was that of a statue, his eyes were ice as his gaze returned to her.

She could not stand Colin's glare any longer, so she lowered her eyes and devoted her attention to the patient before her. But she couldn't help wonder whether she had been the subject of the discussion between father and son. She dreaded the talk that Colin had warned her about. Oh, how she hated the lies. And how she hated, more than anything else, the scornful way Colin had looked at her at the harbor.

How he must hate her now. Now that he knew that she was bringing their enemies to his door. Now that he knew that she was the one being sought after. Now that the blood of innocent Highlanders was being spilled because of her. How he must despise her.

Celia nodded at the young man as she finished her work on his shoulder. Standing, she looked up at the spot she'd seen Colin standing last, but there was no sight of him. She let out a weary sigh, relieved that the anticipated discussion might be put off.

Celia backed up slightly to make room for an elderly woman who was trying to pass.

Celia backed into a human wall. Startled, she knew who it was before he even spoke.

"I want to talk to you now."

Celia could tell from his tone that he was not going to be put off.

She turned around and looked at him questioningly, hoping against hope to see some hint of softness, some hint of gentleness. Celia was hoping . . . But his expression was hard, revealing nothing. He took hold of her hand, expecting her to follow. She held back.

"Where are you taking me?" Celia asked, delaying the inevitable.

"A place where we can talk . . . privately," Colin said, facing her. "I believe there are a few things that you and I need to discuss."

Without another word exchanged, Colin led Celia from the Great Hall into a narrow arched corridor in the older section of the castle. Celia had not been on this side before, although she knew that Edmund's room was somewhere above her on the second level. The corridor intersected other corridors, and there were a number of solid oak doors along the passage.

When Celia had returned from the village, she had noted two soldiers stationed in the upstairs hallway that led to her bedroom. Now, in this older section of the castle, they passed several more guards, stopping before one who was standing before one of the entryways. The soldier stood aside for Colin, who pushed open the heavy wooden door, and Celia followed him into the dark chamber.

She knew before she even stepped through the door that this room was the Campbells' library. The odor of vellum and old parchment swept out into the corridor like escaping spirits. But these were not spirits antagonistic to Celia. She loved this smell. It was the smell of knowledge, of wisdom.

Celia knew it was also the smell of money. The guard posted at the door was protecting some of the Campbells' most valuable possessions. Only the wealthiest of the nobility in Scotland could own books, though many of them up to the present had chosen to forgo what they saw as the "luxury" of a library. That's what the wealthy, old monasteries were for. But since James IV put into law that the sons of the lairds had to learn to read, the value of books was increasing rapidly.

Colin moved through the library and lifted the wooden bar on another oak door. Pulling it open, he ushered Celia out into the misty twilight of the Scottish dusk.

She found herself standing on a broad stone terrace, and the sight before her was breathtaking. A garden, or rather what had once been one, stretched out in front of her, and beyond the wall at the far end, the line of cliffs and crashing surf of the firth curved away into the mists.

Two stone stairways flanked the terrace, and the high wall of the South Hall to Celia's right bordered the west side of the garden. To her left, a high stone wall provided privacy from the rest of the castle's outbuildings and training grounds. The garden itself, large enough to exercise a troop of mounted horsemen in, had been broken up into four sections by four tunnels of latticed wood, radiating from a raised stone pool in the very center. The symmetry of the design was exquisite.

But if the design was superlative, the overgrown garden beds themselves were not. Her eyes took in the trellised tunnels, the wild tangle of climbing roses that covered them. Celia looked at the areas of lawn where the precisely knotted designs of low hedge or herbs had grown into an unruly mélange of brush and sticks. The low walls, too, that formed bench seats around several sides of each of the sections had once been planted with grasses or close-growing herbs. But now, huge tufts of weeds sprouted at intervals along the walls—last season's growth spilling from the seats in a brown cascade.

There was, however, one aspect of the garden that appeared to have matured in spite of going unheeded. In each of the four corners of the garden, there was a large cherry tree. The trees were all approximately the same size, and as Celia went to the top of one of the stairways leading from the terrace, she could see that the fuzz-covered buds on the branches were preparing to open. Reaching out to one that was overhanging the stairway, Celia could almost feel the life within the small bud, growing steadily, pushing at the season, preparing to burst into a renewed cycle of life.

Of all the things Celia had missed growing up on her father's ships, she most regretted not having a place to grow things. She had always dreamed of a cool green place where friends could meet amid the reds, and blues, and yellows of the spring and summer flowers. A protected place where she could take refuge when she was sad, and hurt, and confused. A place of solitude strangely devoid of loneliness.

Celia loved this place. She never had any idea that Kildalton Castle had such a garden, and she wondered why it had been so ignored.

Abruptly she turned to Colin, wondering why he had brought her here. Why now, when his anger seemed to be all that was left of the few precious moments they had shared. The giant warrior was standing by the low stone wall at the edge of the terrace, looking out at the untended garden. Turning to her, his eyes showed none of the coldness that Celia had seen in the Great Hall.

"I'm going away for a day or two," Colin said simply. "I want you to stay here until I come back."

"Stay? Why?" she questioned. At first perplexed by his request, Celia suddenly felt all the doubts, guilt, and sorrows that she'd been keeping pent in inside her gush up, flooding her conscious mind with overwhelming emotions. "Why? Haven't I done enough? Haven't I caused enough trouble and suffering for you and your people? Your Great Hall is filled with innocent people who are hurt and homeless simply because I passed near their homes. Don't you know that the same could happen here?"

Celia's head dropped to her chest. Two tears rolled off her cheeks to the stone slabs at her feet. A chill swept over her as she stood alone, not wanting to look at him. She hugged her arms around her and turned toward the tree as she spoke.

"Don't you hate me? For what I am? For what I've done?"

Removing his cloak, Colin moved to Celia's side and wrapped it around her. Pulling her to him, the young warrior enclosed her in his arms, laid her head against his chest, pressed his lips against her hair.

"Hate you? You really don't understand, do you?" Colin whispered, softly rubbing his chin on the top of her head.

Celia braced her arms against his chest, pushing back slightly until her eyes met his.

Colin looked down into her velvety eyes. They were glistening from the tears that had welled up in them.

"Celia, I care for you deeply. I want you and Kit to be safe," he began. "Look around you. This garden is so much like the Campbell lands ... so much like Scotland itself. It's a place where life must begin again, where new starts can ... no ... must be made."

Colin released her from his embrace and, taking her by the hand, sat her beside him on the low wall at the edge of the terrace. As they sat, he clasped her hand firmly in his, resting them in her lap.

"And I want us to spend time here, the two of us," he continued. "Getting to know each other. I want to know everything about you, and not just the glimpses you've allowed me now and then. And I want you to know me as well. You don't know me; that's why you don't trust me. But if you stay, you will know me. You will trust me."

Celia sat quietly, her exterior hardly betraying the tumult of emotions within. This was all she had ever dreamed of, more than she had ever hoped. She had never even imagined that the overwhelming happiness that was surging within her could also hurt so terribly. The tears began to flow freely as she answered him.

"Colin, I want all these things, as well. My life was an empty shell until I met you. These past days have filled something in me. They have given me something that I will cherish my whole life."

Celia paused and, pulling her hand from his, stood up and backed away from him. She turned slightly and looked out beyond the garden at the mist-enshrouded sea.

"But I can't," she continued. "I won't make a promise that I can't hope to keep. I care for you too much to be the cause of even greater sorrows that are sure to follow ... when it's all over."

"Over? Why over?" he asked. Something in Colin hardened at her words. "Celia, is there someone else?"

"Aye," she said, stumbling over her answer. "And no."

The muscles of Colin's jaw contracted in anger and frustration. Celia saw the hurt and anger flash across his face. His hands clenched into fists as he stood, turning away from her.

"I'm telling you the truth," she said quickly, laying her hand on his arm. "If you really want to know me, then you'll listen now. But you have to promise me that what I tell you will be enough. Please promise me that you'll ask no questions."

Colin turned back to her, looking steadily into her eyes. Aye, he was angry ... and disappointed, too. But looking at her, Colin saw the pained look in those black eyes. She spoke of telling the truth, but should he believe her? A voice inside was telling him that this was not pretense. She was as upset as he was. And Colin knew he must hear what she had to say. There was so much he wanted to know about her. He nodded solemnly. "I promise you."

Celia took a deep breath and sat on the wall again. Colin placed one foot on the wall beside her and leaned one elbow on his knee. His gaze wandered from Celia to the garden behind her, finally coming to rest on the tree beside the terrace steps.

"When I was very young, arrangements were made for me to marry. But it was to someone I've always hated and despised, now more than ever. These plans were made after my father died ... I was only fourteen at the time and a ward of the court, and I had no say in the matter. At that time it was only because of Edmund that I was able to postpone the marriage. He would not even agree to a formal betrothal. But I knew the time would come that not even my uncle could stop it from happening. When that time came nearer, I ran."

Celia paused—tired of the pretense, tired of being someone else, tired of hiding from what she wanted most.

"I ran away from court, in part, to escape that marriage, to escape a fate that is to me worse than death, but it is a fate that I know I cannot escape in this life."

Celia's eyes surveyed the stone slabs before her. The area beneath the tree branch appeared spotted and stained. They were dark stains ... like drops of blood. If there was one thing she was afraid of, it was the lie she was about to reveal.

"And, I'm not who you think I am. Perhaps you were taken with that someone else. But I'm telling you now, I'm not Lady Caithness. That was just a ruse to disguise us. The real Lady Caithness is in England."

Celia raised her eyes to Colin's face. His gaze shifted to meet hers. She was trusting him, and Colin knew it. It was a trust he would not betray. He felt a glow of affection, of appreciation for the honesty that Celia was exhibiting, even though she was telling him something he had already discovered. In Colin's mind, this trust elevated the feelings between them to a more precious level.

"Colin, I've known my fate for a long time, and because of it, I've avoided knowing—or caring for—any-

one. That is, until now. You've changed all that ...
you've made it impossible. But that is all I can tell you
right now. All you can know. So please let it be ... as
you promised ..."

Like a bolt of lightning, the thrill of her words charged
Colin's spirit. She cared for him, as he cared for her.
Mutually, exclusively, sincerely. They *would* make this
relationship a possibility. He knew it now.

With a single sweep, Colin lifted her up from where
she sat, crushing her body to his. His mouth found hers,
and their lips bruised each other with a passion so different from anything they had shared before. It felt to Celia
as if their souls had entwined as their bodies were seeking to. All the insecurities that had been following her,
tormenting her, evaporated into the garden's misty air.
She felt his tongue searching the warm recesses of her
own, and she responded with a desire to envelop him,
to take him in as far as he could reach.

Colin's passion seemed to explode, but there was
nothing in Celia that even thought to hold back. The
untried passions that she had so carefully disciplined for
so long erupted. Indeed, Celia was as frantic as he, her
fingers gripping his hair, compelling him to kiss her. She
wanted more of him. There was a fire building within
her body, traveling through her veins, sensualizing her
being. She never had known this urgency before, and
nothing mattered now but to touch, to feel, to taste. She
could not get enough of him.

Colin felt an inferno raging in his loins. The unbridled
passion of Celia's response was pushing him to the very
limits of his control. He knew that in the span of a moment, he would take her where they stood, regardless of
the consequences.

But a thought was pushing through the white-hot sensations that were engulfing his conscious mind. The
thought began as a cold blue spot, and steadily grew,

forcing itself through the blinding flames of his lust and his desire for her.

This would be their only lover's embrace. She was giving herself to him for this one moment of passion. For this one moment only, he realized.

Abruptly Colin ended the kiss.

Entwining his fingers in her dark locks, he pulled her head gently back, his lips still only a breath away from hers. Looking into her passion-clouded eyes, he forced himself to say the words he knew he must.

"Celia, this moment will not be enough for me. Tell me that there will be more, that this is just the beginning."

Tears welled in her eyes, and her ragged breathing gave way to a soft whisper as she responded from her very soul.

"Colin, my future is not my own. It hasn't been for a long time."

"Celia, I will not let you go. It cannot be your destiny to wed someone you do not love."

These were words that, for so long, Celia had not even allowed herself to dream of. But now, hearing them come from Colin, the only person in this world who seemed able to awaken in her the feelings, the sensations . . . the love . . . that she thought would never be hers to have or to give . . .

Was this only a dream? If this be a dream, she never wanted it to end.

But the way he held her, the way he touched her, the way he spoke to her . . . these things were not dreams. His touch and his words radiated through her. And she believed him. For the first time, Celia saw a glimpse of herself as a woman with a future. A future!

And what would that future hold? Love, she thought. As her parents loved. A sharing of dreams. Through hardships and joys. And only one man had ever made her think this way. This man.

But first, there were battles that needed to be fought.

"Colin, it's more than that . . ." She stumbled for the words.

"Then tell me, make me understand." Colin released her from his embrace, gently taking hold of her hands.

Celia's brow furrowed for a moment as she searched for a way to warn him about the path that she was traveling. A path that could soon lead to Argyll's castle . . . a path that could lead anywhere.

"I have a responsibility that I have sworn to fulfill. And until the moment comes when I have done so, my life and the choices of my life do not belong to me."

Colin wondered whether the responsibility she spoke of was Kit. But he wanted to make her understand that he would help her.

"All I'm asking is for you to remain here for a few days . . . until I get back from seeing the Earl of Argyll . . . then I will aid you in whatever way I can. Together, we can be . . ."

"Argyll . . . you're going to see Argyll?" This is what Celia needed. To get to Argyll herself. To find out why Father William was hesitating. To complete this leg of her journey.

"Aye, I just received word that he's returned to his winter lodging," Colin replied. "I will find out for you about your priest friend, if you like."

"I want to go with you," she said, stepping away from him.

"Where . . . to the abbey?"

"Aye, to see Father William."

"Why do you need to go yourself?" Colin asked pointedly. "Why can't I see him for you?"

"Because I need to see him myself," Celia responded, pausing. "Colin, you promised to ask me no questions. I'm holding you to that promise. All I can tell you is that I need to go with you."

"No, I won't take you," he answered flatly. He assumed that Celia knew nothing more about the attackers' identities than she had said, that she had no idea of any connection between the attackers and the abbey where Father William was staying. But in their discussion in the Great Hall, his father had expressed reservations about the Earl of Argyll's allegiance. Forty years of navigating the treacherous waters of Scottish politics had given him insights that Colin knew it would be foolish to overlook. And if Lord Hugh was correct, then the trip could possibly be dangerous. If there was one thing that Colin knew, it was that he didn't want to put Celia in any more danger.

"Colin, you just said you would help me," Celia said, her anger flaring. "Then take me with you."

"I can't," he responded. "There could be dangers on this trip that I don't want to expose you to."

"Don't try to tell me that a short trip like this could be more dangerous than what I've already been through," Celia said shortly. But she knew that to convince him to take her, she had to soften her tone. "Besides, I'll be traveling with you."

"Celia, this is the Western Highlands. People here have a different view of women than they do in the Lowlands. There are dangers here that you have never faced. Whatever you need done there, I'll do for you."

"You can't," she replied softly. "I won't hinder you, either. I can take care of myself. I grew up on ships that no pirates even dared to attack. Among men whose view of women would make attitudes out here pale by comparison. But I have things that I need to be doing."

Colin had sensed Celia's strong-willed nature, and he could see that she was determined. He knew he would do better to try another tack, if he wanted to persuade her amicably.

"Celia, what about Kit? What will you do about him?"

Celia hated the thought of leaving the bairn after what

had happened, but she had to speak with Father William. Edmund would protect Kit while she was gone; she was certain of that.

With the English pressing ever closer, Celia felt time was running short, and she needed to learn the reason for Father William's hesitation. With Argyll back, Celia also hoped that going there would expedite their next move.

"He'll be fine here with Ellen and Edmund. You said we'll only be gone a day or two."

"Before we had this conversation, you didn't even know I was going to see Argyll. I don't understand this sudden urge. Were you planning to go yourself?"

"Colin," she responded, quietly moving to him and taking his huge hand in hers. "I simply can't tell you the business that I've sworn to complete. A few moments ago you said that this garden is like Scotland. It's true. To enjoy the fruits of the garden, there is work that must be accomplished. Trust me."

"The way you are trusting me?" Colin looked Celia squarely in the eye. She was expecting more of him than she seemed willing to give. How could he be sure that the course she was taking was the best for all of them?

"I do trust you, Colin Campbell. You know more about me than I was permitted to tell anyone. What you know now, I have told you because I believe in you. And what I am doing now, you would also be doing."

Colin turned and looked out at the two trees at the far end of the garden. He knew all four of these cherry trees would be flowering soon, as they had every spring since his mother planted them so long ago.

What curious terms she uses, he thought: "permitted" and "sworn to complete" are such odd terms. Who's behind all this, anyway? What is this business about that she was sworn to complete? There were so many questions running through his mind. Perhaps one way to get some of the answers was to take her to Argyll's winter lodging.

Aye, he would take her, but he would protect her, as well. If Argyll were somehow connected with that attack, Colin was not going to allow her to be an easy target. He would take more precautions than he had initially planned. But that was, perhaps, the wisest course, anyway.

"Celia," he asked, looking at her seriously, "will the Earl of Argyll recognize you?"

Celia gave him a puzzled look, unsure of his question.

"Has he ever seen you? Would he know who you are by sight?"

"No. Not if I were alone. But why are you asking this?" Celia knew that Colin had decided to take her.

"It would not be wise for you to travel to Argyll's castle as Lady Caithness. We need to find some other name for you."

"I can do better than that," Celia said with a smile. She had a solution. "I have, more times than I can count, disguised myself as a boy."

"You, a boy?" Colin grinned. This was the most outrageous thing he'd heard yet. She was so beautiful. How could she possibly hide the soft skin, the stunning auburn hair, the sensuous mouth ... "I don't think so. Perhaps the men in the Lowlands are blind, but out here a beautiful woman is ..."

"I'm telling you, Colin, I am a very convincing boy." Celia thought of all the times she had effectively freed herself of the restraints of womanhood in the guise of a lad.

"You have too beautiful a shape for a boy, Celia." He smiled, stepping back and eyeing her appraisingly. "Even under my cloak."

"You'll see," she responded matter-of-factly. "Clothes cover a great deal."

"That may be a good thing in some cases," he answered wryly. "But some things are better not covered."

Celia flushed crimson at his suggestive response. "Perhaps I'm one who is better covered."

Colin grinned broadly. "Then perhaps I'm the man to cover you."

Celia stamped one foot at his incorrigibility. He was hopeless. "For some reason, I don't think we're talking about the same thing."

"I think we are," he replied innocently. "Aren't we talking about your body?"

"We are *not* talking about my body," Celia scolded. "We're talking about disguising me."

"Too bad," Colin sighed. "Such an uplifting topic."

Celia considered doing bodily harm, but she didn't trust herself to get too close right now. Instead, she manufactured her fiercest glare, a look she could not sustain as her own amusement bubbled to the surface.

Colin burst out laughing at her poor attempt at intimidation.

"We'll have to come up with something better," he said, shaking his head with a smile. "No one will be fooled."

"If I can fool Alec," she suggested brightly, "would you agree to take me as your squire?"

"Squire? You won't fool Alec," he said, laughing. "Alec has a sixth sense where women are concerned. He'll ferret you out in a moment."

"If you don't alert him, I will fool him," she stated. "Will you train in the morning?"

"Aye, before sunrise."

"Good. I'll be there." Celia realized that it was nearly dark now. She hadn't even been aware of the descending twilight.

"I'm not going to leave you and Alec Macpherson alone," he said, suddenly serious again.

"You won't have to," she said confidently. "But I

have a great deal to do to get ready. So when you see your new squire Jack in the morning, don't give me away."

Celia turned toward the door leading back through the library. She stopped after a step and turned back to Colin, removing the cloak from her shoulders and handing it to him.

"By the way, Colin. Thank you for bringing me out here. I love your garden."

Colin took the cloak from her hand, holding her slender fingers in his grasp for a moment.

"I'm glad, Celia. We'll be spending a great deal of time here."

Celia smiled and moved toward the door again. She stopped once more at the sound of Colin's voice.

"One question before you go," he said. "But you don't have to answer if you don't want to."

She stood quietly, her face obscured by the darkness and the distance.

"What is your name?"

She paused before answering.

"Celia Muir," she whispered. And then she was gone.

Muir, Colin thought in amazement. She's John Muir's daughter.

Chapter 9

Why does he take us farther north? As we move up into the Highlands, there is less and less of value for our scavengers to take. What we find is ravaged more viciously than ever before. And every day we are farther from England.

I begin to think we no longer serve any king.

The dawn was breaking clear by the time Colin was able to drag Alec into the open training area he used with his select group of warriors. His eyes scanned the scene of ten fighters practicing with various weapons, the squires and pages scurrying to and fro in response to the shouted commands of the fighters.

Colin surveyed the half-naked bodies of the warriors, sweating from their exertion despite the biting dawn cold. His eye was drawn to the flashing arcs of the long swords and the knives, the slashing cuts of the halberds and the glaives. This is a very bad idea, he thought, suddenly aware of the dangers he was exposing Celia to here in the training yard.

Colin couldn't believe he hadn't objected to this plan last night in the garden. He had been so surprised by and caught up in her idea that the possible consequences had not even entered his mind. He circulated among the fighters and the working boys, trying to pick her out to put a stop to it, but she was nowhere to be found. He thought with relief that perhaps she'd decided against going through with such foolishness.

Colin hadn't been able to go to sleep for a long time, thinking about Celia Muir.

Celia Muir, daughter of John Muir, the notorious pirate and scion of the noble York family. Such a strange world. Colin had never met Muir himself, but he knew that Hugh and Alec's father had met him once, when they had divided the Irish Sea between them. Although Muir had been given a license by the English king to harry French ships while carrying on his own thriving mercantile trade, it was well known that he often crossed the fine line between privateering and open piracy. But Celia's father had always honored his agreements with Hugh Campbell and Alexander Macpherson, men whose activities so closely mirrored his own.

No wonder Celia had felt so powerless in determining her own future. After her father's death, the Tudor king must have cast a greedy eye on the enormous wealth and the fleet of ships rivaling his own. Celia's fortune had been usurped, and her future had become the plaything of kings. What had she said? A "ward of the court." It was the English court. But she was in Scotland now. And more important, she was here.

Colin was, in a very satisfying way, thrilled that she had confided her identity to him. Knowing who she was only served to increase his affection for her. She might have lost everything, but she had a legacy of wit and courage.

And her inner qualities were matched by her physical beauty. Since that first night, Colin had not gone a moment without an image of her in his mind.

Alec went to the rows of weapons and picked out a broad sword that he swung about him a few times. As he did, a squire ran to him with a pair of heavy leather gloves. Colin watched as the lad took the sword from Alec and stepped back, watching as the Macpherson heir stripped quickly to his waist, exposing his massive shoulders and rippling muscles. As Colin strode quickly to them, he could see Alec and the boy exchanging good-natured banter.

"Wait a moment," Colin shouted, running the last few steps and grasping the squire by the elbow. The broad sword fell to the ground as the boy whipped around to face the master. "This has gone far en . . ."

The startled look on the boy's face was matched by Alec's. The two looked at Colin as if he'd lost his mind. Colin knew the lad, and abruptly dropped his elbow as if he'd been burned. He searched for something to say in explanation, but immediately gave up.

"Are you just going to stand around all day?" he snapped at the two of them, turning on his heel and striding away. She must have given it up, he thought.

Colin watched the workouts of his men, joining them when he felt inclined. Alec worked very hard, keeping several of the boys running for new weapons and drinks, crossing swords from time to time with one or another.

After the exercises, the fighters began to drift back toward their quarters before breakfast, and soon Alec and Colin were alone, with just a few of the boys who were busy returning the weaponry to its place.

Alec finished his regimen with an impressive flourish of swordplay, handing the steel war implement and the gloves to a boy before walking to where Colin stood waiting.

"You're not your usual happy-go-lucky self today." Alec laughed, slapping his friend on the shoulder. "Lady Celia stand you up again last night? Her absence at dinner was rather conspicuous."

"Don't you worry about me and Lady . . ." Colin began as they started for the door.

"Excuse me, m'lord," a squire called, running up with Alec's shirt in his hand.

Alec turned and took the shirt, pulling it in one motion over his head. Colin stood impatiently, turning his thoughts to what Celia could call herself during the trip to Argyll's castle, and wondering as well what excuse he would give to Argyll for having a woman along. In truth, there were lots of places Colin wanted to take her, but Argyll's ruins was not one of them. But there was no denying it now. He'd given his word to her. Unless, he thought happily, she had changed her mind and come to her senses.

"Thanks, laddie," Alec said. "You did well. What'd you say your name is?"

"It's Jack, m'lord," the squire said, turning quickly to trot off.

Colin's arm shot out, and he collared Jack, grabbing the squire by the back of the shirt and pulling him back. "Oh, no you don't," he shouted.

"What's wrong with you today?" Alec exploded, shocked at Colin's abrupt actions.

Colin looked into the dirty face of the "squire." The old hat covered Celia's hair. Her clothes were filthy, well worn, and covered any hint of femininity in her figure. But the eyes were unmistakable.

"Did you enjoy yourself?" he asked, glaring accusingly at her. Colin was angry at Celia and at himself, thinking of the danger she had been exposed to during his men's workout. One step in a wrong direction and she could have been seriously hurt.

"Really, Colin, the lad worked hard for me," Alec said in defense. Something is wrong, he thought. He never treats young squires like this. He's always positive and encouraging with them. Poor kid is probably terrified. "He's strong and smart. He'll be a good fighter one day."

"Thank you, m'lord," the "squire" returned saucily. "So will you be."

Alec turned a dumbfounded glance toward the "squire" he had just praised. He didn't look scared. He was actually mocking him, daring him with his bold black eyes. "Why, you little . . ."

Alec stopped short as Colin's laughter erupted, echoing off the castle walls. Still laughing, Colin protectively pulled the squire behind his back. But the wisecracking youngster immediately worked himself back to the front, still daring him. Alec looked from one face to the other. Everyone seemed to be losing their minds today.

"Alec," Colin said, putting aside his worries of a few moments earlier. "We've both been had, this morning. I think you'd better take a closer look at my new squire Jack."

Alec peered at Jack suspiciously. He looked like all the others. Young and eager. But with an attitude problem that would bring him some trouble if he didn't curb it.

"Alec, this is Celia," Colin said finally, smiling at Alec's perplexed look. "Let's get something to eat. We'll be leaving for Argyll's castle with the midday tide."

Celia smiled brilliantly at Alec as she passed him.

"Some sixth sense!" She chuckled proudly.

"You're getting too old, Macpherson," Colin needled. "You're losing your touch."

"I knew it was Celia all the time," Alec protested lamely as the other two grinned back at him. How did I ever miss those eyes and that smile, he thought. "I did. I knew it."

But Colin was convinced. They were all going to Argyll.

Colin had sent out a small boat at midnight to let Argyll know he'd be arriving around nightfall. And when Colin arrived with Alec, Celia, and a troop of fifty men, the dismal gray day was just decaying into dark over the Earl's rain-soaked countryside.

Alec had been ill a number of times on the short journey, even though the steadily falling rain had kept the water fairly smooth and the wind steady. Celia had kept his company and promised him that she would try to help him on the trip back with a remedy she had learned in the Orient. She'd explained that the remedy must be applied before the seasickness occurs. Alec had simply looked at her wretchedly before leaning over the side of the boat again.

As they sailed into the harbor, Celia was very aware of the difference between the Campbells' village and Argyll's. Even taking into account the miserable state of the weather and the dreariness of the hour, the filthy, run-down group of huts reeked of absolute squalor and poverty. Huddled around the stony strand that ringed the small harbor, the thatched turf hovels all displayed the evidence of the fishing trade that was barely supporting them. Before each house, a small boat lay idle on the pebble beach, with nets in various stages of disrepair spread around them.

The dripping, threadbare group of villagers who gathered at the beach stood and gawked as Colin and his entourage landed. Celia, standing behind Colin with the other squires, looked into these thin, haggard faces, into the vacant stares of the skinny, ragged waifs that huddled about them, and she knew that she wasn't going to like the man who spent five months of every year in the old-fashioned castle overlooking the harbor.

Wading up the slippery mud path that led to the castle, Celia considered the situation she was facing. She didn't need to like the Earl of Argyll. It had to be enough for her that the Earl of Huntly had sent her to him. But before she did anything, before she revealed herself to Argyll, Celia was determined to see Father William and learn the reason behind his message. Sur-

veying the barren countryside around her, she could not
see the abbey, and decided finally that it must be in a
direct line behind Argyll's small castle. She was wondering about the possibility of getting to the abbey tonight
when Colin broke into her thoughts.

"You will stay close to me," he said quietly. "Tomorrow we'll see that you get to the abbey."

Celia nodded to him and continued to trudge up the
short hill to the drawbridge spanning the filthy pit that
surrounded the castle walls.

Inside the curtain wall of the old fortress, Celia saw
that the main building of the holding was not much big-
ger than Kildalton's stables, though its two wide square
towers gave it a substantial, formidable appearance. A
set of portable wooden steps led from the courtyard to
the elevated main doorway into the building. Celia
thought that this was a man who was either too cheap
to spend his wealth on his holding or too insecure about
defending it.

At the top of the steps, a gaunt, large-framed man
stood looking down at the approaching contingent. His
wide shoulders were covered with furs that flapped
loosely about his wasted body like rags on a scarecrow.
To Celia's thinking, the smile that he directed toward
them looked more like a grimace.

So finally I meet Kit's uncle, she thought.

"Welcome to my home, Lord Campbell and Lord
Macpherson. Come in, come in."

Argyll's voice had an odd quality to it that Celia took
a moment to consider. It was the voice of a big man,
but there was a hollowness to it that made her think he
was sick. Certainly his appearance substantiated that.
But there was something more in it. A certain waver . . .

Fear, she thought. Argyll is afraid of something. Of
Colin perhaps. Or Alec. She couldn't be sure. But she
knew that he was afraid.

Celia's eyes sought out the faces surrounding her.

Colin and Alec were like strangers to her. Their faces were hard as steel, and their voices, in response to his greeting, were formal and polite, but hardly friendly.

Celia and a number of the entourage followed the warriors into Argyll's hall. It was a high-ceilinged affair with a great cooking fire burning in the center of the room. The benches that ringed the smoky hall were crowded with soldiers and servants. Women who appeared to be there for the primary purpose of entertainment were circulating and laughing at soldiers' outrageous comments. They seemed to be teasing the men, moving from lap to drunken lap.

As the Campbell contingent entered with Argyll at the lead, some of the warriors stood, and the noise lessened somewhat, but for the most part, the carousing continued unabated. Only the women seemed to take real interest in the newcomers, and Celia watched with annoyance as several moved toward Colin like bees to honey.

Runt's brother, Emmet, who was in charge of Colin's select fighters, stood beside Celia. Colin had entrusted him with the true identity of his squire Jack, giving him the task of shadowing her and shielding her from any difficulties. He had spoken with her on the ship, and Celia had been impressed with his devotion to Colin and the Campbell family.

Celia realized, as the revelers gravitated toward the newcomers, that between Emmet and Colin and Alec, she was completely encircled. They were taking no chances with her. She could barely see Colin's action in waving away the wenches, but their quick alteration in course was evidence of his effectiveness in dismissing them.

Argyll was shouting at servants to clear places at the head table for Colin and Alec, and those knights who were sitting at the table gave up their places grudgingly. Colin took hold of the Earl's arm and spoke into his ear, whereupon Argyll gestured for one of his stewards.

"Oswald, before they eat, our guests want to be taken to the rooms that were prepared. And see that a bowl of fresh water is put in each of their rooms." The Earl gave Colin a wry look. "Although I hope you've not become one of those court fops who bathes more than twice a year."

Colin's lack of mirth was hardly lost on Argyll, who turned quickly and moved to his place at the table.

"Emmet ... Jack ..." Colin said, turning to his people. "You come with Alec and me. I want half of you to stay on this side of the hall. The rest of you try to avoid getting the pox from these wenches."

Oswald, a rat-faced, greasy-looking little man, led them up a winding stone stairwell into one of the two squat towers that rose above the castle's main building. At the top of the first flight of stairs, two doors opened off a damp, narrow landing.

"Lord Macpherson," Oswald whined, pointing to one of the doors. "And Lord Campbell, in here."

The steward pushed open the two doors and turned unceremoniously to retreat down the stairwell.

"Steward," Colin commanded. "Have the water brought up now. And send up a heating brazier for each room, as well."

Celia watched Oswald avert his eyes from Colin's fierce glare, and with a furtive "Aye, m'lord" disappear down the steps.

"Emmet, I want you on this landing for now. I'll send one of your men up." Colin turned and looked into the room.

As Colin began to step through the door, Alec took Celia's arm, winking at her. "Jack, my good squire," he said, loud enough to stop Colin in his tracks. "I'll be needing you to help me with my armor."

Colin glared at him over Celia's smiling head. "If you need any help with your gear, Macpherson, I'll come in and help you."

Taking her other arm, Colin detached Alec's hand from her elbow and pulled her into the room.

"Emmet," he said, taking one of the torches from the landing wall. "You're here to guard my squire from *any* intruders—including the one next door."

Colin closed the door behind him and moved across the room, placing the torch in a sconce on the wall by the curtained bed.

Celia watched in silence as the warrior investigated every inch of the small room. The only furniture in the room was the bed, and the narrow archer's slit in the wall served for a window. The opening was covered with a piece of skin that flapped about in the chilly breeze.

The wood floor was covered with rushes, but nowhere were the rushes thick enough to hide a trapdoor. Nonetheless, Celia watched him inspecting the floorboards, peering under the bed and out the window, then running his fingers over the internal stone walls, obviously searching for another entrance. This was a lesson in itself.

Once he'd completed his search, he turned around and placed his dripping cloak and satchel on one of the pegs near the bed.

Based on what she'd seen already, she could almost understand Father William's hesitation over having Kit brought out here any sooner than necessary. The castle and its surroundings were filthy, but more importantly, the obvious lack of discipline that the Earl of Argyll allowed made Celia wonder if he could even protect himself . . . never mind Kit. It was hard to believe that this man was married at one time to so noble a lady as Kit's aunt.

Celia had not known her; she had left the court for the west and her marriage to Argyll long before Celia had arrived in Scotland. But although she had been illegitimate by birth, she was still of the noblest blood of the realm and had brought wealth and honor to Argyll's household.

"I can see there is no love lost between you and the Earl," Celia said, remembering Colin's shortness with Argyll.

"I don't trust him," Colin said, removing his light armor. "And neither should you."

Colin had known the man all his life and never liked him. But Argyll was kin to the King, and had been James IV's strong arm in the west early in his reign. While the Campbells had kept their distance from the court, Argyll had actively traveled the avenues of power. When the Highlanders had openly rebelled against the Stuarts years earlier, Argyll had been the royal force in the west, while the Earl of Huntly had taken James's battle to the Northwest Highlands.

For years now, Argyll had been living off the rewards of that loyalty, draining the lands of their value, living a life of personal luxury, never building for the future. By contrast, Huntly had used his power and prestige to build a better, more unified Scotland.

Right now Huntly was working to secure the future for the young King James V. That was what the Campbells and the Macphersons and a few other powerful clans wanted as well. That is why Colin had come to Argyll's winter castle. He wanted the Earl's written commitment that he had not forgotten his allegiance.

"We're going back down to the hall, aren't we?" she asked. Celia was eager to get another look at the Earl himself. She realized that, so far, her judgment of him had been based solely on the condition of his keep and the village, but that was not quite fair. It was only until Huntly finished the negotiations that she and Kit would have to stay with Argyll. But Celia knew that she would not come here until she at least felt safe.

"I am," Colin answered. "But you're not. If one of those wenches were to get close to you, you'd be discovered in a moment. And who knows what would happen then."

"But . . ."

"No buts, Celia," he continued in a commanding tone. "We'll get you to your priest friend tomorrow. But until then, you stay put."

Colin was not going to lose sight of her in that crowded hall downstairs. But it was even more than her safety that he was concerned about right now. He knew that never on her father's ships, nor in court, would she have witnessed the type of sordid entertainment that Argyll would probably be providing.

"Well, now I know what Emmet is really out there for," she responded stubbornly. "To keep me locked up here."

Celia knew that Colin had a point about the possibility of being discovered down there. She had fooled many men with her disguise, time and time again, but with women, she hadn't had much experience. But how else could she get close enough to the Earl to make a judgment of her own?

"Not to keep you locked up, but to keep you from harm as much as I can," Colin replied, moving over and standing in front of her, his hands resting on her shoulders. His gaze locked on hers. He knew full well that he had to convince Celia to stay put in this room. Emmet would be no match for her, if she didn't agree.

"Celia," Colin continued. "You've asked me to do things and to make promises without letting me know your reasons. But still, I have gone along with them because I trust your judgment, and because I think of you as an intelligent, reasonable person who would not endanger anybody's life, including your own. Now, I am asking *you* to make a promise. You have to trust my judgment on this—going down there is a very bad idea."

Celia knew that everything Colin said was true. From the beginning, he had been so generous, so trusting, so caring. He had accepted her for the person she was inside, and for what he could see, not for the woman he'd heard about. That was all a part of why she loved him so much. Love? she thought in amazement. Love.

"Celia, are you listening to me?"

"Aye ... you ... were saying."

"Promise me," Colin said as he gently shook her shoulders. He had to get her attention.

"Promise you what?" Celia said, gradually recovering from her own admission. As if she could ever recover from that admission. She looked into those beautiful gray eyes. She could feel his strong grip on her shoulders, his fingers burning her flesh through the layers of clothing. She wished he would hold her in his embrace right now ... kiss her right now ...

"Promise me you'll stay here in this room," he said. "Promise me you won't try to leave or do anything foolish."

Celia nodded slowly. She wanted to promise him that she would stay with him always.

"Promise me," he said, bringing his face closer to hers. "Say it."

"I promise," Celia whispered.

Colin's mouth came down on hers. The kiss was hard, unyielding, warm, and it ended all too quickly. But Colin let go of her shoulders slowly, looking affectionately at those beautiful eyes and the smudged, dirty face. Smiling, he turned and left the room.

Alec was standing with Emmet, waiting for Colin, leaning against the door to his room in the hall. When Colin appeared, Alec and Emmet both chuckled at the sight of his face.

"You two have a problem?" Colin growled.

"We don't have a problem," Alec said good-naturedly. "But we don't kiss our squires. Actually, that's a side of you I didn't know anything about."

Colin realized that some of Celia's muddy disguise

must have come off on his face. He ran his fingers over his face trying to wipe off the smudges. Laughing, Emmet and Alec both pointed out in exaggerated terms the incriminating evidence.

The woman bringing the bowl of water up the stairs was greeted at the landing by the sight of two giants trying to wipe the third one's face. Before she could even react to this, the water was taken away from her by one of them, and she was sent on her way with directions to bring more.

Celia, not knowing what else to do, began to arrange Colin's armor on the floor beside the bed. Hearing a light knock, she turned to see the door of the chamber open. Immediately reaching for the sword at her belt, she spotted a young woman carrying in the big bowl of water. The girl gave Celia a quick appraising glance, followed immediately with a half smile as she placed the water in a corner of the room. Without another word, she turned and left, leaving the door open.

From where she stood, Celia could see Emmet standing outside the door. Just a moment later the girl returned, carrying a hot brazier, which she placed next to the water after kicking the door shut with her foot. Celia just stood there, waiting for the girl to leave the room, but she didn't. She just crouched there, busying herself with the turf fuel of the brazier, glancing in Celia's direction now and then.

She was taking forever. Celia was getting very tired of the servant's slowness and scrutiny when finally the girl stood up to face Celia and asked, "Should I stay, or come back later?"

"Stay?" Celia asked, feeling exasperated. "What for?"

The girl gave Celia a raised eyebrow, followed by a flirtatious look. She moved closer to the bed and began to pull up her dirty smock.

"We have time before your master comes up. Unless

maybe you never done this before?" The girl stopped, eyeing her prey with amusement. "Have you?"

"Of course, I have," Celia stumbled, now understanding completely Colin's concerns.

"No, I could tell you haven't. But you can try me first, before your master does."

"Try you?" Celia snapped. "You think Colin Campbell's going to try you?" She would take his eyes out first, before letting him pull something like this around her.

"Why? You think I am not good enough for your master?" the girl asked saucily.

"That's it," Celia said. "Actually, there is nobody in this castle that is good enough for Lord Colin Campbell."

"That might be true right now, but not for long," the girl said, bragging.

Celia knew from her days in court that the best pieces of information always came about during conversations like this one.

"Sure, talk is cheap," Celia said, taunting her. "Your earl never could get any lady of quality up here, not like the ones *my* master is used to."

"He could, too. In fact, he's done it. Any day now we are expecting a quality *noble* lady to arrive "

"Arrive where?" Celia asked, looking around her. She laughed to herself at the thought that she was the "noble lady" this young woman was speaking of. "In the middle of this dump? This place is so dirty and worn out that no quality lady would stay here."

"Aye, here. And the word in the kitchen is that the lady will stay, too. My earl is going to have her marry him."

"He ... can't!" This was more than Celia had expected to hear. Her initial dislike of Argyll had just been substantiated. But could Father William have known this?

"He can, too. Word has it that this lady has a lot of money, so the Earl is going to force her to marry him before anybody finds out. With all her money coming here, this place will look better than where you came from, laddie."

Celia felt a knot growing in her throat, ready to suffocate her. But she had to get rid of the girl first.

"Get out of here, you scurvy daughter of a leprous harbor wench," Celia said, half drawing her sword from its sheath. "My master won't need you or any other like you."

The girl turned and fled the room in surprise at the suddenness of the squire's violent response.

Celia leaned heavily against the stone wall of the tower room before allowing her body to sag to the floor. This whole time her only concern had been to get Kit to safety. But she had never expected that what would be freedom for Kit would be a lifelong imprisonment for her. Getting Kit to Argyll and then waiting for Huntly had been the plan. But she knew Huntly would never be a party to anything like this.

Celia's back straightened where she sat. For all she knew, Argyll had drained the wealth and the lifeblood from one woman already—Celia was not about to become his second victim.

Before the door was completely open, Celia had rolled out of the big bed, fully awake, her sword in hand. Melting into the dark shadows created by the partially drawn curtain of the bed and the flickering light of the brazier, Celia tried to focus on the huge shape coming through the door. She knew who it was before he even closed the door.

"Er ... Jack ... it's Colin," he whispered into the darkness. "Don't cut my throat before my eyes adjust to this light."

Celia smiled and stepped from the shadows.

Colin's heart skipped a beat. Even in the dim light of the brazier's flames, Celia was exquisite. She had rid herself of the boy's clothing that had revealed nothing of her femininity. Instead, she now was wearing his own shirt as a nightshift. He had never seen anything as homely as his own shirt transformed so completely with such exotic, alluring power.

She had washed off the dirt that had hidden the beauty of her face, and her eyes sparkled like black diamonds.

"What are you doing here?" Celia whispered, surprised that he had come back to her room.

"That's not my kind of party down there. But damn it, why did you have to wash up?" he growled. Colin had thought that he might be able to control his desires if she looked like Jack, but this was going to be pure torture.

"Wash up? Don't be ridiculous. I was filthy. Besides, I asked you what you're doing here? In this room?" she said. "I thought you were going to share Alec's room tonight."

"I would much prefer sleeping with you than with Alec," Colin joked as he moved away from the door and walked toward the bed. "Not to mention that Argyll walked us up here. It would have been very difficult to explain why my squire should get his own room while Alec and I shared a bunk."

"But . . . this . . . we . . . is not proper at all," she said, feeling shy, uncertain, and not a little bit self-conscious. The reality of the moment struck her with tremendous force. The day before Celia had been nearly willing to give herself completely to him. But now, with the sounds of some frenetic orgy wafting up the stairway, she was not at all ready to explore pleasures that she longed for, but which also frightened her. She gathered Colin's shirt tighter in front, but then released it, realizing that in pulling the shirt closer, her figure was more clearly defined.

"And I want my shirt back," he said, moving to the opposite side of the bed from her.

Before she could even think of a response, he shouted in a stage whisper, "NOW!"

"You can't have it," she shouted back in the same stage whisper. "I found it in your satchel. I was hoping to find some food, but this is what I found instead."

"Too bad," he said, removing his sword. "That means if there was food in there, you wouldn't be wearing anything."

She scowled at him threateningly across the bed.

"Colin, you don't mean to sleep here in the same bed as I am. Do you?"

"Of course I do," he responded. "You won't see any at Kildalton Castle, but Highland ticks are roughly the size of small dogs, and they'll suck every drop of blood out of a human body."

Colin looked dramatically about him before continuing. "This scum bucket is probably infested with them."

Before Colin was even done with his mild exaggerations, Celia had joined in the pretense, jumping into the middle of the bed with her bare feet tucked under, peering at the dark floor around the bed, her sword still in hand.

"Move over," Colin ordered. "And get rid of that sword—you won't be needing it tonight."

She squirmed to the opposite side of the bed and leaned the short sword against it. As she did, Celia continued to watch his every move.

Colin sat on the edge of the bed with his back to her and removed his boots. Without standing he pulled his shirt over his head.

Celia looked wide-eyed at his broad, magnificent back, his contoured muscles, at the jagged scar that ran from the outside of his right shoulder to the center of his back . . .

"Stop looking at me like that, or I'll . . ." he said threateningly.

Celia flushed with embarrassment at being discovered.

"I wasn't looking at you," she said hurriedly. But at the same time, her hand went out to touch his back. With her fingers, she lightly traced the scar from shoulder to backbone. "How did you get this?"

Colin sat bolt upright as her fingers sent shock waves of intense pleasure through his frame.

"Our . . . host," Colin said through clenched teeth.

"Argyll?" Celia asked. "How?"

"Every year, the clans gather for games . . . to compete," Colin replied. "When I was fourteen, I wrestled for the first time as a man. Argyll was in his prime then. I beat him, but afterward, he attacked me with his sword, claiming that in my boasting, I'd offended his honor."

"Did you?" she asked, feeling again the wide band of white that could have meant his death.

Colin half turned. "Of course I did. I was fourteen."

He gazed at her, his desire growing with every moment that her fingers lingered on his skin. Her face was so pensive as she looked at the old injury. The V-shaped neckline of the shirt hung away from her body as she leaned forward on the bed, and what Colin could not see in the darkness of the room was enhanced by his own vivid imagination.

But he did catch sight of a large, circular medallion hanging from a chain. In the dim light, all he could make out of the medallion was a triangle of black stones, one larger than the other two. But it was not Celia's jewelry that interested Colin.

As he turned completely to face her, Celia's hand snapped back as if she'd been burned. She moved quickly back to her side of the bed, folding her hands in her lap and lowering her eyes.

"Celia," Colin said in a husky voice. "I don't want you to stop touching me. But more than anything else right now, I want to hold you, to kiss you, to feel the softness of your skin, to discover a part of you that I long for. I want to make love to you."

Celia felt herself stop breathing. A sensation of intense heat raced through her, set her ablaze. Colin's words alone were making her body flame with desire. But she was unsure of the surge of feelings that were taking over her physical being—these were feelings as yet unfamiliar. Her life had been so ... self-contained ... for so long.

And the place where they were kept pushing itself back into her consciousness. The Earl of Argyll's seedy winter lodging was not the place where she wanted to make love to Colin Campbell for the first time.

She just sat there at a loss for words. She didn't know how to make him understand. She wanted him, but not now, not here. And suddenly her worries about this place and about Argyll's plan for her paled in comparison to the apprehension she felt right now about the act of making love.

Colin looked at her, perched like an angel on the bed, her hands a deathgrip in her lap, her cheeks flushed crimson, her eyes trying not to meet his. She looked scared, uncertain—but of what? Of him? At this moment she seemed so innocent, so unready, so virginal. She had been at court for six years, but Colin had a growing sense that he might be the first man she'd ever known. But as much as he wanted her, as much as his desires were boiling to the surface at even the sight of her, he wanted her to understand that he would never force her to do anything that she wasn't ready for. With time and patience on his part, Colin knew, she would want him as much as he wanted her. And he wanted her, not just for tonight, not for a short while. He wanted her for eternity.

"Celia, I will not take advantage of you, of this situation we are in," Colin said soothingly. "We will have other times and other places together."

Her eyes shot up to meet his. He could see the look of gratitude in them. She was not ready. And he would wait.

"But you're going to have to be more helpful," he said with a half smile.

"What do you want me to do?" Celia asked solicitously.

"Get under the covers," Colin ordered.

She moved under the blanket in one swift movement, pulling it all the way to her chin.

"Stay on your side of the bed," he continued. "Don't touch me. Don't look at me. Don't even think about me. Do you understand?"

She nodded with a slow grin, turning her back to him as he continued to undress.

"Trust me, you'll pay for this," he said, smiling, pulling the blanket back to get under it.

The cold breezes of the spring morning brushed across Colin's naked shoulder where the blanket had slipped down. Still more asleep than awake, he snuggled closer to the warm back that had fit itself to the contours of his abdomen.

He was not entirely conscious of the leg that was lying between his own, nor of his own arms that had encircled her body. Celia's head lay on his arm, and her back was pressed snugly against his chest. The shirt that she wore had ridden up, and the skin of her legs lay warmly against the skin of his.

Colin's hand was resting on her full, round breast, and when he moved, Celia responded to his tightening embrace by pushing her body even tighter against his.

As she did, Colin's hand brushed lightly across the

sensitive areola of her breast, and her nipple hardened in response.

Colin came fully awake as he felt Celia react to his unconscious touch. They had gravitated toward each other with a natural magnetism during the night, and he had not even been aware of it.

In her dream Celia was adrift in a golden sea. The boat was filled with flowers of every color, saturating the air with an aroma that intoxicated her. She lay on a bed of gold, and the blue sky above was unmarked by any cloud. She felt the warm, gentle breeze rippling through the thin linen that covered her body. Suddenly she was aware of a man beside her—holding her, touching her.

She felt herself being drawn into him. While one hand held her close, his other softly stroked the skin of her face, her neck. As his touch spread, Celia felt herself extend to his hand. She felt the smooth linen move against the skin of her breasts. Her nipples rose to the fingertips that circled the sensitive spot, driving waves of pleasure deep into her body.

By now, Colin was fully aroused as Celia's warm body pressed ever tighter against his own. Her scent mingled with the fresh breeze coming in the narrow window opening, and Colin was somewhat overwhelmed with the mixed feelings of tenderness and desire that he was experiencing for this woman lying so contentedly in his arms.

His hand continued to explore her breasts, cupping the fullness of one, and traveling to the other, gently squeezing with a pressure that caused her to breathe in sharply. He pushed aside the heavy gold medallion and chain.

Into Celia's dream vision came seabirds, wheeling high above—wild, flashing specks of white in the brilliant blue of the day sky. His hand left her breasts and moved down across her belly to her hip, where the linen of her shift ended. He lifted the light fabric, and his fingers slid upward again across her smooth skin to her breasts. Shivers gave way to shudders as she felt him gently massage and pinch the erect nipples.

Celia was now awake and deliciously conscious of the warm closeness of him behind her, around her, enveloping her. She had awakened to the magic that his hands were working on her. She felt no fear, only desire and intense anticipation as his lips found the soft angle of her neck. His lips were hot against her skin, and Celia rolled her head along his biceps to give him better access. Her skin seemed to rise in response as he placed hot kisses along the smoothness of her neck. His teeth and lips were gentle as he took her earlobe, suckling lightly.

With a gasp a single word escaped her lips, "Colin . . ."

Colin lifted his face slightly to take in her beauty.

"I'm here, love," he whispered.

With those simple words that came so naturally to Colin's lips, Celia's spirit was lifted into a new world. Lying there in Colin's arms, she felt safe, cared for, desired.

Colin wanted to make love to Celia now, to share with her pleasures that he sensed she'd never before experienced. He wanted to release the passion that he knew she had within her.

Celia turned slightly in his arms, facing him, opening herself even more to his tender touch. Their lips met in the frenzied white heat of desire for each other, frantically devouring each other, tasting each other with insatiable tongues that danced and probed, rubbed and met within the soft recesses of her mouth.

Colin could hear the sound, originating in his own head, the low roaring that he knew would build and eventually block out all other sounds. But as it grew, a sign of his own surging passion, he wanted to bring Celia with him to those heights of ecstasy that he knew lay ahead. Trying to focus on her, a task that would require all the discipline he could summon, Colin turned his head slightly, moving his lips to her chin, tracing hot tracks with his lips and tongue down the front of her neck deep into the V of the shirt's neckline, then into the valley between her breasts.

Lifting one breast with his strong, tender hand, Colin's lips tantalized her by suckling her nipple through the thin linen of the shirt, causing Celia to moan as her back arched to the sensation.

Tremors shook Celia's body as his hand left her breast and moved down her belly to the small triangle of soft hair at the junction of her thighs. Instinctively, her hips rose to his pressure, her legs scissoring open slowly as his fingers lightly explored the sensitive nub and the folds beneath it, already moist with desire. Flashes of red and white were now streaking through her vision, and Celia could feel her breath shortening as her body began to pulsate to a rhythm she had never known ... and always known.

Celia found herself fighting back a sense of urgency that was sweeping through her. Desperately she wanted to feel his skin beneath her fingertips, to hold his body close to her, to make him feel the things that she was feeling. She turned to face him completely as Colin lifted his mouth again to hers. His hand moved over her hip to the firm, round flesh of her backside, pulling her firmly against the erect presence of his manhood.

Celia gasped at the feel of the throbbing hardness against the skin of her thighs. It was like nothing she had ever felt against her body before.

"You slept with nothing on," she exclaimed, thrilling at the sensations that were flooding through her. She moved her fingers across the contours of his powerfully muscled chest.

Colin paused as her words penetrated the whirring roar that was filling his head. He moved one leg over her, keeping her on her side and pressed against him as he reluctantly pulled back his head. He looked into Celia's angelic face, at her expression of mild shock, of wonder, of curiosity. He wanted to prolong this moment if he could, to savor it.

"Mmm . . . do you like it?" he growled, his hand and leg tightening her against him.

She was a bit overwhelmed by the pulsating organ pressed against her belly so intimately. She nodded tentatively.

"I do, Colin . . ." she whispered, hesitating before she continued. "But I'm frightened, too."

"Why?" he asked vacantly, caressing the silky skin of her lower back.

"Because I've never done this before," she answered, her eyes fixed on his mouth.

"I knew you were a virgin," he said. Full of mischief, his eyes drew her gaze to him.

"What do you mean?" she asked seriously, raising both hands to his chest. "What ever made you think that?"

"Because you've had plenty of opportunities to ravish me, but you haven't . . . yet."

Celia shoved Colin over on his back, and he let her, pulling his leg back from its position over her thigh. She rolled onto him and, putting her weight directly on him, propped herself up on his chest with her elbows. Her necklace dangled from her neck, and the medallion lay on his skin.

"Ravish *you*?" she exclaimed, smiling down on him. "Is *that* what you're accustomed to?"

"If you're the one doing the ravishing, I could easily get used to it."

"You aren't answering my question," Celia said, taking his face in both her hands, sliding her body up his torso to kiss his lips. As she did, her hip ground softly against his arousal, and a groan was his only answer. Her mouth descended on his, and she kissed him lightly, nibbling at his full lips, her tongue darting out to tease him, to tantalize.

"You're playing with fire, woman," he said, his voice ragged with passion.

She smiled down at him, continuing her amorous play. She knew what was coming, and for the first time in her life, she sought it out.

She was driving Colin insane, and he loved it. But he was also rapidly losing control. The roar in his head was blocking out all other sounds. Her auburn hair hung loosely around their faces. His fingers moved over the skin of her back, over the smooth rise of her buttocks, to the toned flesh of her thighs. Her hips moved as he touched her, as she kissed him. He wanted to be inside her ... now ... deep inside her.

With a shrug of his massive frame, Colin rolled her onto her back, covering her completely with his body. Taking hold of her hands, he pulled them above her head, pinning them there. He gazed down at her, his eyes filled with desire.

Celia heard the voices on the landing outside the door and turned her head toward the noise. Colin seemed oblivious to the disturbance outside.

"Colin!" she whispered urgently. "Colin! Listen!"

Colin's eyes cleared instantly as the voices penetrated. Emmet's voice was the loudest, and although he did not sound threatened, he was obviously trying to alert his master to the presence of intruders. Colin released Celia's hands and reached across the bed for his sword. Pulling back, he felt Celia, freed of his weight, propelling herself to the top of the bed. Glancing at her, he realized that she already had her short sword in her hand.

They listened to the voices a moment and heard Alec's join in.

"It's that damned Argyll," Colin muttered, relaxing his guard. "He was all too agreeable in our discussions last night, and here he is bright and early with a scribe from the abbey, no doubt. He's awfully eager to get rid of us, for some reason."

Celia edged off the bed. If she could help it, she would not let her identity be discovered.

Colin reached over, grasping her wrist and pulling her back toward the bed. "I want you, Celia."

"We can't, Colin. Argyll ..." she whispered, looking worriedly at the door.

"The hell with Argyll!" he said, smiling at her concern.

"But the door!" she insisted. "There's no bar on the door!"

"I know, love," he answered, caressing her cheek. "But our moment *will* come."

Turning to the door, Colin shouted roughly, "I'll be only a moment." Celia listened as the voices subsided on the landing.

Releasing her, Colin reached down for his sword belt. As he straightened up, he saw Celia's back as she stripped the shirt over her head. Her soft curves, the milky skin, the beautiful legs that seemed to go on forever. Colin paused momentarily in rapt admiration as Celia quickly dressed in the squire's clothes that she'd worn the day before.

Colin threw on his clothes and buckled on his sheathed sword. Moving around the bed to her, he drew her to him as she was pulling on the oversized hat that covered so much of her beauty.

"We'll be home tonight," he said softly, drawing her lips to his. "But for today, you stay close to Emmet. I'll get you to the abbey when I've finished this business with Argyll."

Celia nodded, lifting her mouth to his again.

In Argyll's Great Hall there was no sign of the previous night's revels. Celia had followed Emmet down the stone stairwell a few moments after Colin and was sitting among the Campbell fighters, finishing the morning meal. A middle-aged cleric, dressed in a brown woolen gown edged in fur, sat at the dais table with Colin, Alec, and Argyll, silently listening to the increasingly hostile discussion and nervously fingering the beads looped through the silk cord at his waste. Argyll must have sent for the Abbot himself, Celia thought. Watching the faces of the men, she could see Colin's cool, fiercely controlled look as he continued to make demands of the Earl. Argyll himself was growing more and more agitated, until, abruptly, he stood angrily at his place, looking around at the large number of people watching the leaders attentively.

Leaning over the table, Argyll said something in a low voice and turned on his heel, striding toward the stone stairwell on the opposite side of the hall. The Abbot followed immediately, but Colin spoke into Alec's ear before following. Alec walked directly to Celia and Emmet and leaned down between them.

"We're going up to Argyll's chambers to write up and sign the documents," Alec said seriously, gesturing toward the doorway through which Argyll had disappeared. "Keep an eye on things, Emmet."

Alec turned as if giving an order to the "squire" sitting beside Emmet. "You look mighty pretty today, Jack," he whispered in a voice that was barely audible. "Without all that dirt on your face."

Celia barely held back the urge to put her hand to her face. She'd forgotten to cover her features with dirt, finishing the disguise. She lowered her gaze, and as Alec walked across the hall, Celia pulled her hat even lower over her eyes.

"Argyll must be a bit miffed by the punitive conditions that Lord Colin wants written into this agreement," Emmet said in a low voice.

"Punitive?" Celia asked. I can think of some particularly appropriate punishments for the Earl of Argyll

right about now, she thought. Forcing me to marry him
. . . I'll kill him first.

"Payment that will be exacted if Argyll doesn't live
up to his bargain," Emmet answered.

"What bargain is that, Emmet?" Celia asked, suddenly very curious about this deal between Colin and
Argyll.

"About backing the Stuarts' crown prince, m'lady . . .
uh . . . Jack," Emmet stumbled.

A sense of relief rushed through Celia's body. She
should have figured that by now. After seeing, hearing,
experiencing what Colin Campbell was all about, she
should have known that Colin didn't need a request
from anyone to do what was right for Scotland. Colin,
protecting, backing the Stuart prince, she thought happily. But Colin had said that Argyll was not to be
trusted. What did he think Argyll's position would be?

"Colin is trying to drum up Argyll's support?" Celia
asked. "I thought Argyll was devoted to the Stuart
cause. After all, he is related to the Crown."

"Was . . . he *was* related when his poor wife was
alive," Emmet said as his eyes surveyed the room. "You
have a Lowlander's view of Argyll. He has them all
fooled down there. We see him as he is out here."

"Please, Emmet, tell me." She was deeply interested
to hear what Runt's brother had to say. "What is it that
you know about him out here?"

"I know that nobody out here would spit on him if
he were on fire. You talked about devotion. The Earl of
Argyll is only devoted to himself . . . nobody else. He
has no loyalties, no honor. When he does anything at
all, he only does it in a wolf pack. He has no guts of his
own. When he was at Dunvegan Castle with the other
clan chiefs, he sided with those against Lord Colin—but
quietly, as I hear it. Last night, though, he didn't even
give as much as an argument. I tell you he is not trusted

in the Highlands, and with good reason. Even his own people dislike him."

"Then how could he count on his people? I mean in times of danger . . . for protection?"

"He buys them," he said, looking around at the filth in the hall. "Not all of them, but enough, I suppose. Still, it costs a lot of gold to buy that kind of loyalty. You knew he married rich once before. He had to . . . his crofters won't work the farms the way they should. Knowing him, he'll do it again . . . marrying rich, I mean. I already feel sorry for the poor woman."

It won't be me, Celia thought. If he got his hands on her, he'd never believe anything she told him. She shuddered to think what would happen once Argyll found out her fortune was all tied up in the Tudor king's promise to marry her to that English murderer. She wondered how long she'd live under the thumb of a man like Argyll. And that murderous English devil, she thought. Where was he now? Would he ever leave off his pursuit of her and Kit? A concern to her, but not her most immediate worry. Argyll's loyalty was the question. Could he be so clever as to fool even Huntly?

Suddenly Celia had the sense that eyes were upon her. Looking up from under her hat, she saw a man at a table across the room staring at her. Their gazes locked for a moment before he turned away, but not before Celia noticed a spark of recognition in the man's eyes. Celia flushed with a momentary fear that her disguise had failed, but this emotion quickly gave way to the feeling that she too had a recollection of seeing that man somewhere before. His clothes were those of a Highlander; his face was bearded and ferretlike. There was nothing that she could see that would make him distinctive, but she still felt she'd seen him before.

Celia snapped her head around at a commotion behind her. A large group of Argyll's men had converged around someone.

"You'll come with us, priest," rasped a harsh voice.

"For what reason do you lay your hands on a man of God?" responded a voice that Celia recognized immediately.

Her hand went to Emmet's elbow. "Emmet, you've got to stop them."

Emmet looked down at her questioningly.

"That voice . . . it's my friend Father William," she whispered urgently. "He's the one I came here to see."

Emmet stood and took a step toward the group. The benches beside Celia cleared of Campbell fighters.

. "What do you want with this priest?" Emmet demanded in a loud voice.

The soldiers turned toward the Campbell warrior and his men.

"It's no business of yours," the raspy voice answered, separating himself from the group that was now moving toward the door. He was a large, burly, porcine man with a cropped head and a pox-scarred face.

Emmet gestured with one hand toward the door, and a dozen of his men quickly cut off the group's path to the exit. Emmet had made sure that several groups of his fighters had been sitting at strategic positions throughout the hall. If push came to shove, they could take control of the room in moments.

"I'm making it my business," he said, his eyes surveying the potential opponents in the room. With the exception of the group in front of him, all the other Argyll men in the hall were still sitting and watching with some unconcerned amusement. It looked like they couldn't care less about what the outcome might be.

"He's needed at the abbey," the leader of Argyll's soldiers spat out. His specific orders were to take the priest before he reached the Campbell men. The nosy rat has been spying all along, he thought. It was too bad that they hadn't discovered this until today. They could have put a sword in his back and avoided this confrontation.

"Aren't there enough priests at the abbey?" Emmet responded.

In spite of the early hour, this man has exhausted his wit for the day, Celia thought, watching the leader search for some answer to the question.

"I want to see this priest," Emmet said, striding into the group.

The group parted almost involuntarily, and Emmet came face-to-face with a wiry little priest, whose hands were being held by two soldiers. The fierce spark in the cleric's eyes was defiant and unbridled. He was dressed as a priest, but Emmet judged that the energy radiating from the small frame was that of a fighter.

As Emmet looked at the men holding him, he recognized one of them immediately. "I never thought I'd see you again," Emmet began grimly, looking fiercely into the face of the man he had followed after the attack on their guests and his brother.

"I . . . I don't know what you are talking about," the man said. "I never seen you in my life."

"Well, I'm happy to tell you that there is not much left of that life," the warrior responded threateningly. "And when we're through with you, you're going to wish you were as dead as the three friends you left at Kildalton."

As the man backed away from Emmet, the tall warrior reached in and grabbed the priest by his cloak, pulling him from the circle of soldiers before they could react.

Dunbar and Emmet were backing toward Celia and the other Campbell men now. From the corner of her eye, she saw a servant slip out through a door at the rear of the hall. This could turn into a fatal trap for all of us, Celia thought. Eyeing the doorway through which Colin and Alec had gone, she knew the time would be short to warn them.

Celia backed quickly across the room, ignored by Argyll's people, who were now watching the confrontation with keen interest. She could hear Emmet's voice responding to the pox-faced leader's harsh shouts as she ducked into the stairwell that led up to Argyll's chambers.

Out of the corner of his eye, Emmet saw Celia slip around the table and head across the room. Guessing her intention, he immediately motioned one of his fighters after her. Colin didn't want her left unattended for even a moment.

Dunbar, as well, saw Celia disappear through the doorway leading to Argyll's tower chambers. *She doesn't know how dangerous it is for her here,* he thought as he bolted after her.

The hammering on the door jolted the three lairds, but only the Abbot and his clerk leapt from the table where they all sat. Argyll gestured, and the clerk opened the door.

"Father William . . ." the young cleric stammered before being pushed aside by the wiry Dunbar. Colin's fighter followed him through the door with his sword drawn.

"Where's Celia?" Dunbar shouted at the lairds. His eyes scanned the plush, wood-paneled chamber. Celia was nowhere in sight.

Colin and Alec bolted from their benches. It took only one look at the priest's face for Colin to know something was very wrong.

"What makes you think she would be here?" Colin replied, his heart skipping beats. He looked at his fighter for some explanation.

"What's the meaning of this intru—" Argyll bellowed before Colin's man had a chance to explain.

"What have you done with her?" the priest snapped at the Earl, drawing a short sword from beneath his robe.

"No, William . . ." shouted the Abbot, backing away from the table.

This is Father William, Colin thought in a flash, and Celia is in danger.

"She was in the hall," Colin shouted, pushing past the priest.

"We followed her up here, m'lord, and there was no other door for her to go into," Colin's fighter exclaimed, running out onto the landing after Colin. Dunbar and Alec followed on their heels.

Colin could see that a door closed off the stairs leading to the top of the tower, and that it was barred on the outside. He yanked the bar from the door, and Alec pulled it open.

"I'll check the tower," Alec said, his sword in hand, disappearing up the dark steps with the fighter behind him.

At that moment Emmet charged up to the landing, and Colin turned to face him.

"Did Celia come back down?" Colin shouted at his man, a hint of fear in his voice.

"Nobody's come down, m'lord," Emmet returned. "She came up after you!"

Colin's eyes swept around the landing, fearing what he couldn't see. Alec returned from the upper portion of the tower, shaking his head.

Oh, my God, Colin thought wildly. They've got her.

Chapter 10

The word is going around the camp that we have allies to the north. They say it's a powerful chieftain. I don't know. I only know that these wild hills loom up around us, and hellish weather breaks over us out of nowhere.

If we have friends to the north, it is only because they do not know us. And what kind of people can they be?

The winding stone stairwell was dark.

Entering from the hall, Celia's eyes took a moment to adjust in the dimness, but she vaulted the steps without pausing. If Argyll's servant raised the alarm with his fighters, they could be cut off in the hall, and Celia knew that Colin should know that. Who knew what Argyll would do if he was given the opportunity, especially considering the fact that one of the men who attacked Kit and Ellen had been discovered in his own hall.

The stairwell had a musty, damp, dead smell that made Celia think that this tower must be older than the one where she and Colin had slept. Something is not right, she thought as she reached the landing. Why wouldn't Argyll put his chambers in the newer tower? What was special about this one?

The small landing leading from the stairwell was dark, with a torch on a wall near the door ahead. There were large, ugly, matching tapestries hanging on the walls to either side of Celia as she started for the door.

The blow from the butt of the sword came from behind, and she never saw it coming.

Celia staggered, dazed from the shock, and the man's arm encircled her neck, dragging her roughly toward the wall.

Struggling to clear the brilliant fog in her head, Celia felt the tapestry being swept aside and brushing her face as she was pulled behind it. Vaguely aware of the sound of a door opening, Celia found herself dumped in a pile on a dusty wood floor.

The room was spinning, but Celia forced herself up and at the figure who was quickly trying to bar the door. She lurched into her assailant and spun off, landing hard against the stone wall a few feet away, causing him to drop the bar and turn fiercely toward her. The ferret-faced man whom she'd seen in the hall grabbed her by the throat with an iron grip, pinning her to the wall, ripping her hat from her head.

"If it weren't for the fact that Lord Danvers is quite anxious for his bride, Lady Muir," the rough voice hissed into her ear, his English accent distinct and unpleasant. "I'd cut your pretty throat right here."

In a horrifying moment Celia realized where she'd seen this animal. And she knew he was Danvers's man.

Ferret Face jerked her roughly away from the wall and back again, slamming her head against the stone. The bright flashes of light in Celia's head blinded her for a few seconds, searing pain shooting through her brain.

"But you'll do as *I* say, you slut," he whispered fiercely in her ear. "Because when Lord Danvers is done using you . . . you'll be mine!"

The man's disgusting closeness was suffocating Celia. Turning her roughly, he dragged her across the small room, his viselike hand still squeezing her windpipe closed. Celia was aware of her knees buckling as she tried to get her legs under her.

If only she had reached Colin. He doesn't even know that Argyll is harboring the enemy here. Are there more of them? she thought. Hiding in the darkened corners . . . waiting? She desperately thought of Colin, only next door, the people down in the Great Hall, and Dunbar. How long would it take them to realize that she was missing? She knew they would never leave without her. And Colin would turn this place inside out and find her. She just had to hold up.

Ferret Face's grip loosened slightly as they reached the far wall, and air rushed into Celia's lungs. Then the sound of a wooden panel being opened wrought in her the horrifying realization that Argyll had stayed in this old tower because it had its own secret passageway.

Fear swept over her with the certainty that if this animal got her through this opening, Colin would never find her. This would be the end.

But she couldn't let it happen. No, not now. Not without a fight. Not now that she had come so close to the possibility of freedom from Danvers's malicious plans. She had to fight back. A surge of adrenaline pumped through her, and Celia slammed her head backward into the face of her captor. His hand released her neck involuntarily, and Celia dropped to the floor and rolled away, feeling desperately for her sword. Her head was pounding with the reverberation of the head butt she had delivered, and she felt as though she were watching herself from somewhere far away. As if in a bad dream, she saw herself trying to control the arms and hands that seemed to lack all coordination, that resisted her will to draw her weapon against the attacker.

Through the haze before her, Celia saw Ferret Face lunge toward her, his sword raised, and his mouth and nose gushing blood. She felt herself pushing backward away from the oncoming assailant when the dark room burst open at the seams.

Colin's sword tore through Ferret Face's neck and collarbone before he could even react to the sight of the onrushing warrior. The force of the blow drove the Englishman back to the far wall where he sat heavily against the panel, convulsing in his final moments of life.

The room was suddenly crowded with men, but Celia saw only Colin beside her as she lay back on the floor.

"Celia ... thank God ..." Colin said soothingly, reaching for and caressing her face. In the darkness of the room he couldn't make out the extent of her injuries. But he could see the small pool of blood beginning beneath her head.

Celia's hand reached up and gripped his as it cradled her face. The strength of her fingers entwining his own gave him the hope, the sign that he was looking for.

"When they told me you were missing, I ..."

"Argyll ... traitor ... Danvers," Celia murmured, interrupting him, feeling herself beginning to drift. She had to warn him.

"Emmet," Colin shouted over his shoulder. "Get Argyll."

Colin looked down again at Celia. Now, from the light of the torch just brought in, he could see the lump developing on the right side of her head, behind the ear. Her eyes were trying to focus, but the eyelids continued to flutter over the black orbs. Colin rolled her head slightly, looking for the source of the oozing blood, and found the wound at the back of her head.

Argyll is going to pay for this, he thought, his rage building within him.

Dunbar crouched beside him, looking at her injuries, and Colin leapt to his feet.

"She should survive," said the priest, looking up at Colin. "She's had worse than this."

Colin turned to the door as Emmet rushed in, the young fighter behind him.

"He's gone," Emmet exclaimed.

"What about the Abbot?" Colin demanded.

"Dead. And the clerk, too," Emmet replied. "He murdered them on his way out."

"How could he get out?" Colin spat at the young fighter. "You were on the landing."

"He didn't come out to the landing, m'lord," the fighter answered.

Colin heard Celia murmur again and crouched beside her.

"She said 'Passage' and tried to point over there," Dunbar told him, gesturing toward the panel that the dead attacker lay against.

Colin strode to the panel and shoved the body aside. Stepping back, he kicked the panel forcefully, splintering the wood and revealing the dark opening beyond. Putting his head through, he could see a ladder leading down into the black hole of a tunnel. Argyll's chamber is on the other side of this wall, he thought. He must have gone out this way.

"Alec," he said, turning to his friend. "I need you to stay with Celia."

Alec nodded, and Colin faced his fighters. "Emmet, secure the hall and send out for the rest of the men," he commanded. "I'm going after Argyll."

Taking the torch, Colin plunged through the opening and scrambled down the ladder. At the bottom, his torchlight showed a long, wet, low-arched tunnel. Sword in hand, he splashed through the tunnel to a narrow wooden panel that swung outward at his push. Colin found himself crouching in a plain, stone-sided box of a room. Pushing the stone walls proved fruitless, but the stone slab that served as a ceiling slid easily to one side. Hopping up and out, Colin found himself standing in a crypt, beside a plain stone tomb. He slid the top of the tomb closed again.

"Rest in peace," he muttered to himself.

As Colin started for the short flight of steps, something glinted in the corner of the crypt behind the largest of the stone tombs, something metal reflecting the light of his torch. The warrior moved quickly to the corner and stopped in amazement. The steel that had caught his eye was a weapon that was protruding from beneath a number of woolen tarps. Colin whipped off one of the tarps. Hundreds of new English halberds lay in piles behind the tomb. Their evil-looking heads of ax, spear, and pike gleamed menacingly in the torchlight.

English halberds in Argyll's castle.

The abrupt thundering of horses' hooves outside shook the subterranean vault. Colin turned and ran for the steps, which led up into an empty chapel. The warrior yanked open the oak door that led outside, sprinting into the courtyard and the clouds of dust that hid the quick exit of Argyll and a large group of his men.

Shouting to his own fighters who were now pouring out of the main building, Colin dashed toward the stables, only to find them empty. His face a portrait of fury, the Campbell leader walked back outside, frustrated for the moment but undaunted.

"We'll get that bastard yet," he muttered to himself, walking through the group of fighters who had followed him to the stable.

"The main building's secure, m'lord," Emmet said, trotting up to Colin. "We have a couple dozen of Argyll's men. Those left behind have no desire to fight."

"What about the gate and towers?"

"We took those just as Argyll and the rest rode through," the fighter said. "We couldn't get the gate closed in time."

"I want the village and the abbey secured as well," Colin told him. "We're taking everything the traitor has here. What about the other fighters that followed us up the coast last night?"

"I sent out word," Emmet said. "They should be here within the hour."

Colin had indeed taken precautions on Lord Hugh's advice. A force of his troops had been ordered to follow the coast road from Oban the night before, and to wait within striking range of the village.

"Too late to catch Argyll," Colin muttered bitterly. "He'll go straight inland to avoid our men at Oban, but he'll be heading south toward the Lowlands . . . and that English dog, Danvers."

"We have the fourth attacker in the tower room above Argyll's chamber," Emmet said with a grim smile. "He became very willing to talk to you, after just a glimpse of the torture room the good Earl has set up there."

Colin headed for the building with Emmet at his heels.

"Emmet, I want you to treat the villagers humanely. If possible, we want them on our side when Argyll comes back to reclaim all he's left here. And he will come back."

"M'lord," Emmet said. "When you talk to the folk inside, you'll see they're already on our side."

Celia was sitting sideways in a chair in Argyll's chamber when Colin came through the door on his way to the tower room above. After the Abbot and the clerk had been removed, Dunbar had wrapped her head in bandages, and she rested her head against the back of the chair. When she heard Colin enter, she opened her eyes and smiled weakly.

"Did you get him?" she asked.

"No. He got away." Colin didn't want to burden her with the details of Argyll's escape or of the treason she was already aware of.

"Why aren't you lying down?" he scolded gently, crouching in front of her.

"We tried everything," Alec responded from a bench at the table beside her. "But she'd have nothing to do with lying on Argyll's bed."

"I see we'll have to get you back to Kildalton." Colin smiled, taking hold of her hand.

"Nothing would suit me better," Celia replied gratefully, wincing at the pain in her head. "I'm a bit tired of the Earl of Argyll's hospitality."

"We'll be going as soon as my men arrive to help Emmet hold this castle."

"Colin," she asked. "Have you sent the bodies of the Abbot and his clerk back to the abbey yet?"

"Not yet," he answered with a quizzical look. "But they'll be going over shortly. Why?"

"I want a few leaves of common nightshade from their apothecary and a bowl of warm water," she said. "For Alec."

"For Alec?" Colin smiled. "Are you sick, Macpherson?"

"No, I'm not sick," Alec replied in a huff, flushing red.

"Leave him be, Colin," she put in tiredly. "It's for his seasickness."

"After what you've been through, you're worrying about . . ."

Celia silenced him with a gentle look.

"All right, Celia. If they have any, we'll get some," Colin said with a laugh. "But I'm not sure I want Alec free of his . . . character flaws."

"And, Colin," Celia said, glancing at the priest standing beside her. "This is my friend, the court poet, William Dunbar. He warned me that it might not be healthy for me here."

"A warning"—Colin smiled, patting her hand—"which you took seriously, of course."

He stood up, towering over the sparely built cleric, and held out his hand as the name of the priest registered with some surprise. Father William is William Dunbar, he thought.

"Is this the same Lowland poet," Colin asked, his fierce glare betrayed by the hint of a smile, "the same William Dunbar who devastated the Highland poet Kennedy in a flyting match before the entire court?"

The poetic war of insults between Kennedy and Dunbar had become legendary in Scotland. Only a small portion of the series of competitions had been published in a book, printed with the King's approval in 1508, but the Campbells had a copy at Kildalton, and Colin had laughed heartily at the outrageous exchange of barbs.

"Flyting . . ." Dunbar said, spreading his hands outward, palms up. "It's just a game of words."

"Something Father William has *plenty* of." Alec grinned. "Trust me, I've been listening for the last half hour."

"Well, we could always use a bit of wit to lighten the air at Kildalton Castle," Colin said. "I assume you'll be returning with Celia to my home."

"Aye," said the priest. "I will be traveling with the lass."

"Then we'll see if we can make you a bit more welcome than you were here," Colin said graciously.

"Thank you for that," Dunbar replied. "Though a leper would've been more welcome in this den of iniquity than a priest."

Colin grinned and turned back to Celia, looking down at her. Her gaze locked with his, each lost in the depth of emotions they felt for the other. There was so much that hadn't been said yet, but each knew that the time would come.

"We'll be going home soon," Colin said, leaning over her, kissing her forehead, caressing her cheek, feeling the smoothness with the back of his hand.

Colin turned to see a surprised expression on Alec's face and a shocked one on the priest's as they watched.

As he walked past Dunbar, Colin saw the little man cock an ear dramatically toward the small window of the chamber.

"Well, what do you know?" the priest said wryly. "I just now heard 'pirate alerts' sounding up and down the Irish Sea."

Colin laughed and, with a quick look at the puzzled Celia, gestured for the smiling Alec to follow him out past the two fighters standing guard on the landing.

"Celia told me who she is," Alec said as they went up the stone steps.

"She did?" Colin asked. "How did that come up?"

"When Dunbar was cleaning her wound, Celia and he started recounting all the various times she'd been cut and bruised," Alec went on. "Did you know, Colin, she actually used to dress up as a squire and train with the King's warriors? This one time when they were with the King at Falkland, she came this close to . . ."

"Alec, stop," Colin interrupted. "I don't want to know. Not right now, anyway. You know, these bastards were trying to capture her today."

"What is this all about, Colin?" Alec asked pensively.

"Perhaps a little talk with Argyll's henchman will clear some of that up," he replied forcefully.

As Alec and Colin proceeded up the stairwell, the former paused for a moment and faced his friend.

"Imagine that. John Muir's daughter," Alec said, a twinkle in his eye. "She's quite a woman, Colin."

"Well, you can just forget it, Macpherson," Colin threatened with a pleased smile on his face.

"You're serious?" Alec said with some amazement. "Is it possible that Colin Campbell has met his match?"

Colin looked his friend straight in the eye. "Aye, Alec, I've found my lady."

"Damn it." Alec grinned. "And I was growing so fond of her. She even looks after my welfare. Let me know if she decides to dump you."

"Let's go," Colin said, pushing his friend up the steps. "We've got work to do, and I'm not leaving you alone with her anymore."

The confessions of the Argyll man came without any coercion at all. Ferret Face, the English agent, had, on Danvers's orders, sent men that Argyll had supplied to as many castles in the west as he could. They all had the same directions—to kill the child and capture the lady . . . alive.

When the Argyll man had returned from Kildalton, he had heard the Earl tell the Englishman, who was operating out of the abbey, that he didn't want the child dead. All they had to do was wait, and they all would come to Argyll on their own.

This information matched what Colin had already put together, with the exception of why Danvers wanted Celia. Obviously, Ferret Face had recognized Celia and had planned on taking her back to his master. But why? The English were certainly going to extreme lengths to get her.

When they arrive back at Kildalton, Colin thought, Celia would have to confide the rest in him. It was time.

The troop of Campbell men from Oban had come supplied for a possible siege of Argyll's castle, so Colin gave orders for beginning the reorganization and improvement of the village, the castle, and the farms in the surrounding area.

In the early afternoon, when they were ready to make the short walk down to the harbor for the trip to Kildalton, Celia had to fight off the attentions of all three men. She was improving quickly—even the throbbing in her head was beginning to subside. She certainly didn't need to be carried, and she let them know it in no uncertain terms.

Word had quickly filtered to the people of the Argyll lands, and many had gathered in the village to see the new laird. They all knew what Campbell lordship meant, and many knelt in respect as Colin passed. As Colin and his entourage walked through the village on the way to the ship, Celia could see a marked change in the visages of the people they passed. They were still wearing the rags of Argyll oppression, but they were now also wearing the faces of Campbell optimism.

Once aboard ship Celia applied her decoction of common nightshade to the back of Alec's ear with a patch that was held in place with a leather thong. When he saw her put the patch in place, Colin laughed.

"Are you sure it's not supposed to go over his eye?"

But to Alec's and Colin's amazement, it worked.

The journey back to Kildalton took forever—as far as Colin was concerned. Alec was unaffected by the motion of the ship, and between his attentions and Dunbar's, Celia had no moment alone for Colin. As he stood at the stern of the ship, he looked at the bandaged beauty, still dressed in boy's clothing. He shuddered involuntarily at the thought of what might have happened had he not spotted the track of dragging feet leading to the tapestry on the landing outside Argyll's chamber.

He had lost control when he'd burst through the door and seen the Englishman looming over Celia. His years of discipline had gone out the window, and his primal instincts had taken over. This was his woman, and he was going to protect her.

Now, he just wanted to take her away. To be alone with her. To make her well and keep her safe.

But he'd clearly have to lock up Alec and this priest Dunbar to do it. And the next time they took Macpherson on a boat, Colin was going to suggest she put that patch over Alec's mouth.

There was a torch-carrying crowd at the harbor when the ship dropped anchor at Kildalton Castle. From small boats, Hugh and Edmund scrambled up the sides of the ship like men half their age. Hugh's face lit with pride as he embraced Colin, and Edmund went directly to Celia, hugging her gently and nodding at Dunbar.

The knight stood with his arms around his niece, thinking to himself that he must be getting old and stodgy. Even though he knew what Celia was capable of—indeed, even though he had encouraged her to develop her fighting skills with the fighters of King James's court—he now could hardly bear the thought of her being hurt or even in danger. She was all he had left in the world.

Hugh and Colin, followed by Alec, walked over to Celia and her uncle. Edmund let go of his niece and turned to Colin, grasping his hand in a warm clasp.

"Thank you for bringing her back safely," he said, looking at the young warrior with an expression of his gratitude.

Hugh approached Celia with a fatherly smile and wrapped his burly arms around her.

"Aye, Colin," Lord Hugh boomed, still keeping one arm firmly around Celia's shoulders. "A successful trip all around. But we need to get up to the castle, so you can give us all the details. We need to send a message to Huntly and the other barons about Argyll's treason."

"Aye, Father," Colin said. "But I want to get Celia into Agnes's care first. You can see that she's taken a bit of a beating."

Hugh looked tenderly at Celia's weary face, but noted the clear black eyes flashing in the torchlight. "I don't think she's had more than tough old John Muir's daughter can handle."

Celia flashed a look from Colin to Edmund, wondering who had revealed her secret. Colin looked as surprised as she felt. She looked back at Lord Hugh, suddenly embarrassed at her ruse. If the Campbell lord had known all along her real identity, then the Caithness deception had certainly been ineffective. But then again, even John Muir's daughter could have married Lord Caithness.

"I knew who Edmund's sister had married," Hugh said, smiling benignly, answering her unspoken question. "We go back a long way, you know, lass."

"Did you know my father, m'lord?" Celia asked, recovering.

"Indeed I did." Lord Hugh laughed, exchanging amused glances with the men standing around. "But I think we could put that little discussion off until after Agnes sees to your injuries."

"Lord Hugh," Colin said formally, turning to the priest who was standing quietly beside Edmund. "I have the rare honor of introducing a celebrity to you."

"Celebrity!" Lord Hugh exploded. He knew of the identity of the newcomer from Edmund. "You can't mean this poor excuse of a half-pint priest hiding here. Not this slow-witted, Lowland court parasite who takes every opportunity to slander the good names of every Highland clan in Scotland."

"Aye, Father," Colin replied, watching as the priest's temper was about to boil over. "This is William Dunbar."

"Then welcome to Kildalton Castle," Hugh thundered warmly, taking the shaken cleric by the shoulders.

"Thank you for your well-spoken words of welcome, m'lord," Father William responded, eyeing the huge laird warily. "I can see that the Campbell name will no doubt find immortality in the works of *some* poor poet."

"Are you suggesting, priest," Hugh said threateningly, but with a sidelong wink at Celia. "That we're to be your next victims."

"Aye, m'lord." Dunbar smiled matter-of-factly.

"Good," Hugh said, clapping the priest on the back. "Then we'll have a lively Easter celebration after all. Welcome to our home."

*   *   *

Climbing out of one of the small boats that carried them to the dock, Celia was nearly overwhelmed by the men wishing to help her. She was growing more exhausted by the moment, and her head was again throbbing painfully, but she wearily set her mind to the task of climbing the stone-paved road through the village to the castle.

Seeing the crowds that had filled the dockside and the Marketcross, she was thinking how different things could be now for the people who lived in the shadow of Argyll's castle. Their lives would be so much better if Argyll would stay away and leave them in peace.

The question of him returning could be resolved very shortly, she thought. He clearly doesn't know Danvers very well. Argyll had planned to force Celia to marry him. Danvers is insane. If that marriage had ever taken place, the Earl would have been as good as dead. If Danvers ever gets wind of his plan, he could end up dead anyway.

As thoughts of the evil Danvers started pounding in her brain, her head began to swim, and Celia put out her hand to steady herself on Edmund's arm.

The next thing she knew, Celia was cradled in Colin's arms, and she could see the walls of Kildalton Castle looming ahead of them. He was carrying her without any effort at all. Edmund, Hugh, and the others were fluttering around them, cackling like old hens. She could see concern etched in their faces. But they all seemed relieved at the sight of her regaining consciousness.

"Colin, put me down," she demanded, struggling weakly against him. "I can walk perfectly well myself."

"Is that so?" he said soothingly, holding her tighter against his broad chest. "It must have been someone else who fainted in the Marketcross, then."

"I really didn't faint," she said, knowing that she really had. "I just needed to get my land legs, that's all."

"Oh, land legs," Colin said with a laugh. "And then, I suppose, you just thought you'd take a short nap."

"That's right," she responded, snuggling against his shoulder. "And I feel perfectly well rested now. So you can put me down."

"No."

"Why not?" Celia asked, raising her head and looking into his eyes.

"Because I'm enjoying this," Colin responded. "Put your head back down."

"Why?"

"Because this is the first moment I've had alone with you since we left Argyll. Because I . . . Stop asking so many questions." He glared threateningly.

Celia lifted her arms up around his neck and nestled her face against his skin. "Please put me down," she cooed.

"Forget it," Colin replied, smiling. "The next time you put your feet on the ground will be tomorrow morning."

"You just think you can bully me because I took a few hits in the head," she whispered lazily.

"Bullying you?" Colin laughed softly. "Now that's an idea worth considering."

"You wouldn't dare," she flared, raising her head again and looking into his face.

"I would, too," he said, smiling.

"You would what?" This was getting confusing.

"Bully you into picking up where we left off this morning," Colin whispered softly, nuzzling her face with his own.

"Colin, shush!" she whispered forcefully, taking hold of his jaw with her hand.

Celia raised herself in Colin's arms and glanced around, mildly fearful that someone might have heard his words. But the others had fallen back a few paces, and no one seemed to be in hearing range. Also, the darkness of the night had separated them somewhat from the rest of the group.

As Celia's face returned to Colin, his mouth descended on hers so quickly that she never had a chance to object. He just wanted a taste, but her reaction to his simple kiss drove him wild with desire. Her hands gripped the back of his neck, pulling his head down lower as her mouth reached up more fully under his. Celia's mouth opened under the pressure from Colin's searching tongue. They kissed, deeply, intimately, then they both pulled back. They each knew they had to stop.

"I don't have to bully you," he whispered, gripping her hard against his chest as they walked across the drawbridge into the castle courtyard. "All I have to do is kiss you."

"I do like the way you kiss me," Celia murmured, nestling her head back down on Colin's shoulder. She could feel her heartbeat matching his.

"You'll like the rest, too, my love," he whispered, resting his chin lightly on her bandaged head.

Agnes must had been standing watch for the group, because they hadn't even reached the front stairs when she dashed out to them. If Celia had thought that the men fussed a lot over her injury, she hadn't seen anything yet. Agnes had Colin take Celia straight up to her room, while all along the way scolding him for his selfishness in taking the young woman along on the Argyll trip, exposing her to all that danger. When Celia tried to interrupt in Colin's defense, he just stopped her with a wink and a smile.

Agnes pushed open the door to Celia's room, and Colin carried her directly to her bed and deposited her there.

But as soon as she was placed on the bed, Celia looked over at the open door into Kit's and Ellen's room. Immediately she rolled off the bed and disappeared into the darkened chamber.

Ellen was sitting in the only chair in the room, and Kit was asleep at her breast. Her eyes glowed with happiness at seeing Celia, but looked with concern at the wrapping around her head. Celia went to her and placed a hand on her shoulder, caressing Kit's hair and cheek lightly with her free hand.

"How is he doing?" Celia whispered.

"He's as strong as ever," Ellen replied softly. "I was just going to put him in his cradle."

Celia took the baby out of Ellen's arms and placed him over her shoulder. She had really missed him, in spite of all the excitement. She laid him gently in the cradle and covered him with the soft blanket. She smiled at Ellen and quietly tiptoed to the door.

Ellen followed her into the other room, leaving the door open on the sleeping Kit.

"M'lady," she said, startled at the bloody condition of the bandages around Celia's head. She had not seen them clearly in the darkness of the baby's room. "Are you all right?"

"Of course she is," Colin responded, leaning solidly against the hearth. "She was just looking for a way to avoid walking up from the village."

"Now, Colin," Agnes scolded. "If you aren't going to be nice to her ..."

"Nice?" Colin argued, never taking his eyes off Celia. "I've just carried her up from the harbor. And she squirmed like a fish for more than half of the way."

"Out you go," Agnes ordered, pushing the giant warrior toward the door.

"I'm going under protest, Celia, but I'll be back," Colin said over Agnes's head as she shoved him right out into the hallway.

"Men! Really!" Agnes exclaimed, returning with a smile on her face. "Although it does sound as if you and Colin got some time to speak with each other. Well, never mind. Ellen, help Celia get out of those filthy

clothes. I've got a nice hot bath ready for you, my dear.
And while you're soaking, I'll look at your wounds."

Celia sat up in the bed. Agnes had, indeed, prepared
a bath for her in front of a roaring fire. But that was
not all. While Celia had been away, Agnes had moved
furniture into the room: a table covered with beautifully
embroidered linen and a bowl of assorted fruits to go
with the dinner that was laid out for her, several large
chairs · with silk-covered pillows, and a second large
clothing chest. The chest stood with the other by the
wall to Ellen's room, and they were both open, revealing
an array of clothes that Agnes had selected for her.

Celia also noted with amusement that none of the new
furniture in any way blocked the panel.

"Agnes," she said warmly. "This room is beautiful. It
feels like home."

"I'd so hoped that you would like it."

"Like it? I adore it," Celia said. "But, Agnes, please
don't make such a fuss over me. I'd really much rather
be a help to you somehow."

"Celia, that's what I knew you'd say," Agnes responded with open delight. "My dear, it's high time you
did make yourself at home. And if you feel up to it
tomorrow, we'll start."

Celia looked at Ellen for a hint of what was happening, but Ellen simply blushed and looked away.

"No more talk," Agnes commanded, "until you get
into this bathwater."

With Ellen's help, Celia stripped out of her wet
clothes in a moment and stepped into the tub. The scent
of jasmine greeted her, and she melted into the warm
liquid as Agnes carefully unwrapped the bandages from
her head. Agnes gently soaked the dried blood from
Celia's hair using a separate bowl of liquid that smelled
strongly of herbs. The older woman looked very closely
at the wound at the back of Celia's head as she cleaned
it. She carefully pulled Celia's hair back, inspecting the

sizable lump that was half hidden in the tangle of auburn curls.

"It looks like those blows on the head weren't intended to kill you, but those bruises on your neck certainly show lethal intentions on somebody's part."

"Aye," Celia responded. "An Englishman, and a rough one at that."

"Well, I hope somebody killed the bastard."

"Colin did."

"Aye, that doesn't surprise me at all," Agnes said. "Colin's always been a bit protective of those he cares about."

As Celia drifted off in the warm bath, she thought of Agnes's words. Colin had been so open in showing his affection—his attraction to her—in front of everyone. Celia remembered Father William's shocked expression when they'd been at Argyll. He had been so surprised to see them so taken with each other.

She could see that she would have to talk to him about Colin. Father William had always been highly critical of potential suitors for Celia. He believed that the suitable match for her had not yet been born ... did not exist. And all these years she had somehow agreed with him. But now ... it was all different. Colin was different.

Agnes carefully combed out Celia's clean hair and, when the young woman was ready, helped her into a fresh nightshift and robe. Celia could smell the delicate lavender aroma in the clothes and felt incredibly warm in the glow of attention that Agnes was bestowing on her. She ate a little of the food and wine that had been laid out for her and watched as Agnes directed the servants as they carried out the tub and wet linens.

Ellen had returned to Kit when Agnes sat Celia down to her supper. Celia paused before beginning to eat.

"Agnes, there's something you should know," Celia began slowly. "And I want to be the one to tell you."

"What is it, my dear?" she answered with concern.

"I am not who I've been pretending to be. My real name is Celia Muir, not Lady Caithness. You see, traveling through the Highlands with Kit, we've needed to protect ourselves because Lord Danvers, the English commander, is after me. The intention was that by assuming the Caithness identity, we would attract less attention. But I don't want to keep up that pretense any longer. I'm sorry we deceived you."

"My dear, you don't have anything to be sorry about," Agnes said warmly. "These are troubled times, and a woman has to protect herself and the ones she loves any way she can. We all care for you because of the kind of person you are, not because of any name."

"But there is more to it than just that, Agnes," Celia said. "Danvers is evil, he's a butcher, and I've brought that evil into your lives."

She paused, searching for the right words.

"I was to be his wife, Agnes. Not by my own choice, but by the command of a king."

Agnes put her hand on Celia's.

"What kind of king would command a woman to marry such a demon?" she said softly. "We don't honor such commands out here."

Agnes put her arm around Celia and hugged her affectionately.

"You've been through so much already in your young life, child. Don't take the troubles of the world on your shoulders. It's time to leave those bad memories in the past. It's time to look to the future."

Celia felt the tears well up in her eyes at the older woman's unquestioning acceptance and understanding.

"Agnes . . ." she began.

"Enough of that, Celia," Agnes interrupted. "You're here now, and we're glad for that. Now tell me about your adventures at Argyll's castle."

Celia filled her in on most of what occurred there, and she felt the discomfort of the earlier admission wash away as they spoke. She found herself dwelling at length on Colin's heroic response when her life had been in jeopardy. And Agnes noted with inner delight that the young woman returned again and again to Colin in her narration.

But soon Agnes began to dominate the conversation, telling stories of Colin's youth and young manhood to an enraptured Celia. Agnes had been a mother to him, and her pride in Colin was maternal.

Celia thought about what Colin might have been like as a child. He was so much a man now—tall, muscular, weathered—that it was difficult to picture. And yet, sometimes he'd get that boyish look . . .

"It's too bad his mother didn't get a chance to see him grow into what he is now," Agnes continued, as if reading Celia's mind. "She'd be so proud of what he's become."

Agnes's eyes misted over a bit, and Celia reached over and squeezed her hand.

"Do you miss her very much?" Celia asked.

"Less and less since you've arrived," Agnes replied, giving Celia's hand a return squeeze before releasing it. "Although, when Colin was growing, I often missed her dreadfully."

"It must have been very difficult for you."

"There were times in the beginning when I was ready to go back to France," Agnes said with a laugh. "Hugh can be a difficult man, you know."

"Is this a case of like father, like son?" Celia grinned.

"Probably so." Agnes laughed. "But really, my dear, Colin has so much of his mother in him."

"She must have been a wonderful woman."

"Constance was a fine woman," Agnes began. "She had a very sharp mind, and she was a thoughtful and generous friend."

"I'm sure she must have felt the same about you," Celia replied.

As they talked, Agnes realized that it had been a long, long while since she had felt so comfortable talking with another woman. Perhaps since Colin's mother had passed away. She had been Agnes's friend, but this had a feeling of friendship and something more. Agnes felt a bond forming with Celia that she had only felt with Colin. As she sat with the young woman, Agnes knew in her heart why everyone at Kildalton was so drawn to Celia. From all she had heard and all she had seen, she knew this young woman's heart was pure and accepting, strong and courageous, open and giving. Constance Campbell would have loved to have her as a daughter.

Agnes was tucking her into bed when Celia laid her hand on Agnes's arm.

"Agnes, I want to ask you something woman to woman," she began, hesitating as she struggled with the words. "Why hasn't Colin married?"

"He was waiting for someone like you, Celia."

"Seriously," Celia persisted, blushing at her own lack of subtlety. "Certainly he must have been the object of more than a few young women's fancies."

"And more than a few fathers' fancies," Agnes responded. Many a laird had seen Colin Campbell as a way to move his own family up socially and financially. Agnes had seen many a pretty young thing thrown in Colin's path. She could still feel pride in how Colin had always managed to thwart the fathers' attempts while still preserving the young women's reputations and futures. "The Campbell fortune and position have always been a temptation for some, but Colin has always waited for love."

Agnes smiled benignly down on Celia and squeezed her hand gently before leaving the room.

But Celia felt a pain in her heart. A gnawing, empty sadness that undermined in an instant all of the happiness that had been growing there. Suddenly all of the exhausting trials of the day seemed to crush her with weariness.

She had nothing to offer Colin Campbell but love.

How could she even think for a moment that Colin would want her in marriage? Truthfully, he'd never even mentioned it, and Celia had never given him any hint that marriage was what she wanted.

But Celia loved Colin. She loved him with a fervor that burned in her veins. She loved him more than her own life, and he was the only man she had ever wanted. She knew that she would give her body and soul to him for as long as he wanted her, for as long as they had left.

There was something else, though. Celia knew her love for Colin could be construed by others as something less than the passion it truly was. But for Celia, the love she felt for him was too strong, too pure. She could not allow that love to be tainted by anyone's suspicion of it being anything as despicable as opportunism. She was no fortune-seeker. No, she would stay with him as long as she could, but Celia would never allow herself to hope for marriage to Colin.

Celia drifted into a deep, sound, dreamless sleep just moments after Agnes left. When Colin knocked softly at her door, she barely lifted her head from her pillow.

"Who is it?" she called quietly.

Colin pushed the door open and peered into the darkness.

"Have you given up bolting your door?" he whispered.

"Come in, Colin," she said, laying her head back down.

By the time the warrior had traveled the few steps to her bedside, Celia was nearly asleep again. Colin sat beside her and gazed at her face, softly illuminated by the light of the flickering fireglow. Her eyes opened briefly, and she smiled at him. She reached out and took his hand, holding it to her lips.

"Have you sent your messages off?" she asked lazily, dozing off with the last word.

"Aye," Colin replied, stroking the side of her sleeping face. "But I didn't come here to talk about that."

"Hmm?" she responded, not quite able to force her eyes open.

"I came to talk about you and me."

Pausing between each word, Celia murmured without waking, "You? Me? Love me? I love you."

Colin gripped her hands firmly in his. He knew these words came from her heart. And her angelic face reflected the comfortable security she must be feeling beside him.

"Celia," he said softly.

"Hmmm?"

"I love you."

"Hmmm." The satisfaction in her sigh told Colin all he wanted to know. All his life, Colin had had opportunities for marriage. Young, sometimes infantile, daughters of Lowland lairds, Highland chiefs, even French noblemen. For the most part, they were women who offered the homely training of wife and possible mother. These were good things, Colin knew, but they were not enough for him. He wanted a friend, a lover, a companion, with intelligence that she was not afraid to exercise. He wanted an equal who would share in and add to the dreams he had for his people and his land.

As he sat thinking of these things, he knew that he'd begun to doubt that such a woman existed . . . until now. Looking down at her, Colin knew that if he'd ever expected to find such a woman, he never imagined she'd be the beauty who was lying before him.

From the first moment he saw her, Celia had kept him off balance, had even knocked him flat at times. It was not Alec who had been upended, it was Colin. Alec might have felt her sword at his throat, but it was Colin who felt her passion, her desire, her love, pierce his heart.

Colin sat in the fading firelight for a while, thinking of the course of a life that had brought him to this moment, to this woman. Suddenly he couldn't imagine changing any step of the way that had led him here. Suddenly he couldn't imagine a future without her.

This was the woman he had searched for. He would never let her go.

"I've been waiting for you for a long time," Colin whispered to the sleeping Celia, caressing her hair, her smooth face. He leaned over and kissed her lightly.

His words were soft, but they were clear.

"Marry me."

Chapter 11

It is an unholy marriage of demons. These shifty-eyed Scots have arrived with their haggard-faced Earl, and we see him with Danvers. With this disreputable lot, we are thousands strong now, an army on the hunt, and the countryside is our prey. The word is that this land that we scour and pillage, loot and burn, belongs to this Scot, Argyll. But still the killing goes on. And as I watch Danvers, he watches with a sneer as Argyll turns his face.

We make our choices . . . we choose our demons.

"Well, I'm glad you're not thinking of marrying, Celia," Dunbar said. "After all, you're over twenty, and way past the age of being molded into a good wife."

"Good wife? Molded?" Celia exploded. "First of all, don't start in with your old-fashioned views about how a married woman must act. Second, I've just said that I've no intention of marrying Colin. I didn't come to Kildalton to find a husband, and although a woman couldn't find a better man than Colin Campbell, I haven't forgotten why we are here. And lastly, he hasn't asked me and probably won't."

Celia stood at the window in her room, feeling the warm morning sunlight caressing her shoulders. Edmund and Father William had been at her door early, carrying her breakfast and wanting to talk. She had been so overpowered with sleep the night before that now Celia wondered if Agnes had given her something to make her rest. She only had a vague recollection of Colin coming in and sitting beside her, but it could have been a dream.

"That's a fine thing for a priest," Edmund shot at Dunbar. "A member of the clergy recommending that young people live in sin."

"I'm neither recommending sinful ways," Father William glowered, "nor am I speaking about young people."

"Then I believe I'm entering into dotage at an early age," Edmund returned. "What are you talking ab—"

"I'm talking about your niece, you old fool," the priest responded hotly. "But you probably are getting senile, with all the blows to the head that you've taken in your career."

"If you're talking about Celia, I think she'd make someone a fine wife . . ."

"I've known her since she was fourteen years old," Dunbar interrupted. "And I know her to be braver than half the young men who survived Flodden, and more intelligent than the other half. Do you mean to stand there and say that any self-respecting laird left in Scotland will accept a wife who's his superior in every way? Impossible."

"You don't know Colin Campbell, priest," Edmund stated emphatically.

"No, but I know that the Campbells are one of the wealthiest clans in Scotland. His mother was of royal blood . . . French, I know . . . but still royal. When Colin gets around to choosing a wife, it'll be someone of his own social level."

"She *is* of his social level," Edmund exploded. "She might not have a fortune at hand to give him, but she is descended from kings. She is descended from the Bruce himself. She is—"

"Excuse me," Celia cut in, not really wanting to hear all these things. "But weren't we just discussing Kit's situation?"

"There is nothing more to discuss about Kit's situation," the priest responded. He still felt worked up over Celia's relationship with the young Campbell heir. He'd been Celia's confessor and tutor. He'd watched her agile mind bloom into a garden of ideas and intellectual interests. Dunbar loved this young woman as if she were his own daughter. He would not stand by silently and see her hurt by some short-term fancy on the part of the powerful Colin Campbell. It was just a good thing that he was here now, in time to head off Edmund's blind foolishness regarding Celia and Colin. After all, she had seen plenty of the goings-on at court, but she was still an innocent in matters of her own heart.

"Aye, there is, Father William," Celia scolded gently. "But when it comes to me, you two act like a couple of overly protective mother ducks, squabbling over a single little hatchling."

Celia knew just how much these two men loved her, but right now they all had to concentrate on Kit.

"All right," the priest conceded grudgingly. "But not much to discuss. I've agreed to stay right here until Edmund's message reaches Huntly, but there's no reason for us to reveal Kit's identity to the Campbells."

When Colin and Lord Hugh had sent their message the previous evening to Huntly and the other nobles now gathered at Stirling, Father William and Edmund had sent a message, as well. Colin had cast an inquisitive glance at the two when they had approached him, but he did not question them.

"Are you saying that you don't trust the Campbells?" Edmund asked.

"I don't distrust them," Dunbar replied. "But why should we answer a question that hasn't been asked?"

This was difficult for Celia to argue. How could she explain her need to confide in Colin, to share with him all the matters that were pressing on her? If he knew Kit's identity, surely he would help the boy recover what was rightfully his. She knew deep in her heart that she should tell him, but she would honor Father William's judgment. She would wait until Colin asked, but she could not let her feelings go unsaid.

"Colin can be trusted, Father," Celia said, taking the priest's hand. "I'll stake my life and my vow on it."

As Celia, Ellen, and Kit started down the wide steps to the Great Hall, Celia realized that the homeless refugees were no longer in residence there—in fact, the dogs had reclaimed their places about the hall. By the time they'd reached the ground floor, the black canine form of Bear was awaiting them, his long tail wagging. Celia smiled at the beast, taking his great head in her hands.

"Celia!" Lord Hugh called, changing direction as he spotted the women and the bairn. He had been going outside to supervise the ongoing defensive preparations, but that could all wait. He gestured for the men who were attending him to continue on outside. "How's your head this morning, lass?"

"Agnes has just the right touch, Lord Hugh," she responded with a bright smile. "I nearly slept this beautiful morning away."

The grizzled warlord stopped before them, pinching Ellen's cheek and putting a sausagelike finger into Kit's little fist.

"Did you eat anything?" he said, turning again to Celia and taking her arm. "I'm always hungry after a good fight, and I'm sure we can find something for you to eat in the South Hall."

"Aye, m'lord." Celia laughed. "I ate. We just thought we'd go out into the courtyard and enjoy this sun while we have it."

"Trust me, child, you don't want to go out there," Hugh said, stopping in his tracks. "I was out there earlier, and Colin has the whole place in an uproar. You'd think that lowlife Argyll was knocking on our front gate."

"Oh," Celia said. "I suppose we shouldn't get in the way."

Hugh thought a moment, then brightened abruptly.

"I've an idea, lassie." Hugh smiled, directing Celia toward the far side of the hall. "There's a part of this castle I haven't seen in nearly twenty-five years, but I think it's time I ..."

"The garden with the cherry trees, m'lord?"

Hugh stopped and cast a surprised glance at the young woman.

"The cherry tr ..." he started. "So! Colin showed you his mother's garden."

"Aye, Lord Hugh, he did," Cclia responded uncertainly. "I hope that's all right. I never intended to intrude on ..."

"Intrude? Nonsense!" he boomed, his eyes sparkling. "I didn't know the boy had such good sense. Come on, it's time I saw those trees again."

Hugh led them out through the old corridors of the castle and through the library onto the garden's stone terrace. The shocked look on the guard who jumped aside for Lord Hugh attested to the chief's long absence from this portion of the building grounds.

Celia stood back and watched Hugh's expression as he stood looking out at the garden. The four trees were ablaze with color from the delicate pink and white flowers. His eyes reflected the sparkling brilliance of the sunlight as it danced on the blue waves of the water beyond the garden walls, and Celia knew that memories of a beloved woman were flooding back over years of separation.

"These trees have certainly grown since the last time I looked at them," Lord Hugh rumbled softly. They all stood silently for a moment while he took in the entire scene—the formal design, the fountain in the center, the wildly untended arbors and flower beds. His eyes traveled to the now weed-grown turf bench on the outside wall that had been a favorite of his wife's. She had spent many an afternoon sitting there reading to Colin the fables of Robert Henryson and French tales of knights and their ladies. Meanwhile, around them, the workers had roughed out the garden's design.

"I'm sorry," Celia whispered, putting a hand on Hugh's elbow as Ellen took Kit down the steps into the area protected from the wind by the walls. "I didn't mean to put you through this . . ."

"Hush, Celia," Hugh growled gently. "It was high time I came out here. And I can't think of a better person to come out here with."

"Thank you, m'lord." She blushed. She looked out at the sight before them. "The design of the garden is incredibly beautiful."

"Aye," he replied, "Colin's mother was an amazing woman."

Lord Hugh motioned Celia down the steps and the two walked side by side along the leaf-strewn paths between the clumps of yellowed grass and overgrown tangles of briers that Celia assumed must have been roses.

"When Colin's mother died," the chieftain continued, pausing thoughtfully between his sentences as he recalled the years, "I closed off the garden. For some reason, I couldn't bring myself to come out here, and I couldn't bear the thought of anyone else coming out here. 'For some reason' . . . that's not exactly true. I know the reason. I didn't want anyone else here in this garden that was so much a part of her. Sitting where she had sat. Walking where she had walked."

Hugh walked to the circular fountain in the center and put one foot up on the stone retaining wall.

"This was *her* garden. She loved it. She loved planning it, working in it, enjoying it . . . sharing it. And I loved her . . . love her . . . I still do. I couldn't bear to think of this place changing, growing, becoming different. Oh, I know it had to change—but I didn't want to see it happen." He paused, gazing at Ellen playing with Kit by the terrace steps. "I know Colin continued to come out here ... and I never tried to stop him. It is a kind of refuge for him, I suppose. It is a place of good memories."

Hugh looked at the young woman standing quietly beside him. Celia had the same quiet reserve of strength, the same intelligence, the same sense of her own identity that his own Constance had. Colin would be a fool to let this one get away. But somehow Hugh didn't think that was going to happen.

"There is something you ought to know about the Campbells, lass. We may be tough, miserable brigands, but when we love a woman, it's for ever. If you'll pardon an old man's pride here, it's like finding the woman who's been fated for us ... chosen, I suppose ... destined. And when we find her, we know that this woman is our match, our chosen, our anointed ... for life."

Celia's gaze rested on the colors of the tree in the far corner of the garden. How wonderful it must be, she thought, to love ... and be loved ... so much. Unconsciously her hand went to the medallion that hung outside her gown, to the only physical reminder she had of the loving relationship her parents had. Celia had often thought of their love in terms such as those that Lord Hugh had spoken of. Even after so many years had passed, her father had called for Celia's mother before he died. He had cherished her memory, and had always told Celia of her goodness, of her strength, of her beauty.

"I know your father felt that way about your mother," Hugh said.

"You mentioned last night that you knew my father," Celia questioned.

"Aye, I did," Hugh responded wryly. "We had some
. . . business . . . dealings together."

"Did you?" Celia replied with surprise. "I don't ever
remember coming to Kildalton Castle. That must have
been before I traveled with him."

"Probably so," Hugh went on. "Edmund brought us
together about fifteen years ago, I'd guess."

"I *was* traveling with him then."

"A mere bairn?" Hugh laughed. "Traveling with a
bunch of pirates? John Muir must have really distrusted
that York family of his."

"Why do you say 'pirates'?" Celia shot indignantly.
"They were fine sailors."

"Aye, lass," Hugh agreed, eyeing her searchingly.
"Aside from my men, John Muir had assembled the finest sailors a pirate chief could hope for."

"No," she began. "My father was a fine man, a respected merchant. He was no . . ."

Celia stared at the calm face of the giant, and suddenly things started to make sense. In all the years she
had sailed with her father, his ships had never been attacked, even when they had sailed in what the sailors
had called "dangerous waters." But they had always
smiled at each other over her head when they said things
like that. They had never seemed frightened, even when
they heard, as they so often did, the guns of sea battles
in the distance, and later found unmanned, disabled
Spanish ships, their cargo holds full of booty her father
told her the Spaniards had stolen in the New World.

How blind can a child be? she thought. We were simply picking up the loot that his other ships had captured.
Now she knew why her father's name was so well
known. He was no merchant. He was a thief. Respected?
He was feared.

". . . a thief," she finished in shock. "My father was
. . . a common thief."

"No thief he was, lass," Hugh rumbled, taking her

hand in his. "Nor was he common, either. He was an honorable man. A pirate? Aye. And for a long while he served with a nod from old King Henry VII. But in those days, the line between pirate and what the lawyers are now calling 'privateer' was fairly indistinct. There were just a few of us in that business then ... Alec Macpherson's father was my partner in it. We kept the Irish Sea clear and took profits from those whom our kings disliked at the time. But you were so young. It's only natural that your father never told you anything about that side of his life. You shouldn't think ill of him for protecting you as well as he could."

Celia paused before answering him.

"I loved my father, and I know he loved me. We were as close as any father and child could be. But that side of his life ... I was a part of it, and I never saw it. Never suspected it. Suddenly I feel like there's so much I don't know about my family ... about my life."

Hugh sat down on the fountain wall and pulled Celia down beside him.

"Let me tell you how it all started. You probably do know a lot of this, but let me clear up your perception of your father. Let me tell you the truth about your family . . . what the world knows . . . what you should know . . ."

"Your father was the second son in a branch of the York family that was beaten, reconciled, and then beaten again when Henry Tudor took the English crown from old, hunchbacked Yorkist King Richard. When Henry became king, he had no money, and the York family continued to be a thorn in his side. To make matters worse, the Spaniards and the French were harrying the English coastline mercilessly.

"Being the second son in a family who were now political outsiders, John Muir had very little interest in just sitting back and living off the wealth of his ancestors.

So, your father went to the new king and offered his services keeping the Spaniards and the French out of English waters, and King Henry gladly gave him a license to do it. It made sense. Henry got one of the Yorks fighting for him rather than against him. And it gave your father a chance to make his own way in the world.

"In a very short time, his success at sea became a profitable business for everyone. Henry's treasury began to fill up with Spanish bullion, and your father took his share of the booty and established a legitimate shipping business. Needless to say, his trading ships were the best protected on the high seas. But he also continued to raid foreign ships that he came across in English waters. And his fearlessness was legendary.

"By now, your father's extensive wealth was no secret to anyone. He had lands in England and a fleet of ships that exceeded King Henry's. So when he met and decided to marry your mother, the daughter of a Scottish knight and a descendant of Robert the Bruce, his family objected, and later on so did King Henry. It wasn't enough that he'd filled all their pockets—they all wanted a hand in choosing his wife. Marriage is business to a lot of families, in England and in Scotland.

"They were all upset about him marrying a Scottish woman. His haughty York family saw it as a union that was beneath them because it was with a Scot, however noble, and Henry saw it as a threat to his control of Muir's loyalties. They all wanted to be sure that they could control the heir . . . and the fortune.

"But your father fought them all. He married your mother, and he never forgot the way they snubbed her.

"And he loved her. Legend has it that before they married, he went to the Sultan of the Ottomans and bought the largest sapphires in the world for her. They say she wore them in a pendant around her neck.

"Later, when Edmund brought us together, John Muir

was in control of his own destiny. He was powerful enough to ignore Henry's directions when it suited him—he felt no loyalties to either his king or his own family. Your mother had passed away by then, but your father still trusted none of them. I suppose that's why he kept you with him for all those years. I'm sure he feared for your life, and how they would use you for their own purposes if they ever got their hands on you.

"And you should know this, Celia—your father was an honorable man. We met and divided the Irish Sea because he felt that fighting the Scottish was like fighting the only kin that he still cared for. Henry had been right—your father's loyalties were divided because of his love for your mother . . . and for you.

"Your father and I liked each other immediately and kept track of each other until his death. He was an honest man, and he never broke our agreement, even though his power on the west coast grew with every passing year."

Lord Hugh looked at Celia with affection in his eyes. He knew that if John were alive today, he would be very proud of his daughter and the woman she had become.

"Your father died in England," Hugh said. "How is it you came to be a member of the Scottish court?"

"Things were too quiet for her in England," a voice growled from the other side of the fountain.

Colin had come up from the village where he'd been directing preparations for defending the town. When Runt had approached him in the South Hall with word of Lord Hugh's whereabouts, Colin's eyes had widened in disbelief. This was a sight he'd never imagined he'd see again in his lifetime, and something warmed in him at the thought of it.

Entering the garden, Colin had walked past Ellen and Kit to where Celia and Hugh sat talking as comfortably as old friends. His father seemed so at ease there that Colin was hesitant to interrupt.

Lord Hugh started at the sound of Colin's voice. Celia had seen him come into the garden and sit quietly as his father spoke. She had a feeling that Colin knew all that Hugh had related.

"After my father died," Celia answered, loud enough for Colin to hear. "The English king claimed me as ward of the court so that he could seize my father's ships and lands to use to his own profit until I married. When I went to that dreary court, I had nobody."

"Where was Edmund?" Colin asked.

"He went to King James for me because he knew, before I did, that my fate had been decided."

Celia gazed into the empty fountain.

"That court was a dismal place. Everyone knew that the old king was dying. He had spent years trying to secure his crown and build up his treasury. By the time I got there, he was a sick old miser, and the court reflected it.

"I had grown up in the fresh air, with men of action for my companions. Now, I was stuck in drawing rooms with women who treated me like a freak. They tortured me with empty-headed tasks that they said I needed to learn to be a good wife. They were intent on teaching me things I had no interest in learning.

"Then, one day, I was introduced to my intended husband, a soldier that the King intended to reward with a wife and her fortune . . ."

Celia looked across the fountain at Colin.

"Lord Danvers," she said distinctly. "He was a cruel, rude, repulsive man even then. I hated him from the moment I met him. I knew I had to get away, so I went to the only people I had at court. The Yorks.

"I still remember their harshness. They told me that I had to return and marry Danvers. That I was lucky the King was giving me to someone as highly placed as

Danvers was. That I should feel privileged that he would even want a tomboy who was 'half Scotch' besides. They sent me back to my keepers, but at least I finally knew for myself why my father hated them.

"I returned to court, but I was miserable, and I made life miserable for everyone I came in contact with. For six long months I was at that court.

"Then Edmund came back. He had asked King James to make some kind of a deal for me. King Henry's daughter, Margaret, had been the Queen of Scotland for five years, and I was to join her entourage for a year before my marriage to Danvers."

Celia smiled grimly at the memory. "They were so glad to get rid of me. I suppose they thought a year in a 'wild' place like Scotland would make me appreciate the English court more. Edmund said that King Henry agreed only because he got to keep reaping the rewards of my father's wealth for another year."

"Weren't they afraid that you wouldn't return?" Hugh asked.

"Danvers was. But he was the only one. They were sure that I would return, since everything I owned was in King Henry's hands until I married Danvers.

"During that first year that I was with Queen Margaret in Scotland, King Henry died and his son, the new King Henry, succeeded. And as you know, he and King James never agreed on anything till the day James died at Flodden. So I never went back.

"Even though Queen Margaret's ready to send me to England to be married now, my understanding is that her brother, King Henry, doesn't really care if I go back or not. He has everything my father intended for me, and is in no great hurry to part with any of it. Danvers, however, has been pursuing my fortune for six years. He even came to Edinburgh two years ago as a special envoy for his king, but he was really there for me."

Celia turned to Colin.

"That ferret-faced Englishman at Argyll's castle. He was Danvers's right-hand man when he came to the Stuart court."

Celia looked back at Lord Hugh.

"I never found out, though, why King James went out of his way to take me in. He had nothing to gain by it."

Hugh smiled knowingly at her. "Take my word for it, lass. James had a reason for everything. And I'm sure that when the time is right, Edmund will tell you."

Hugh stood and took in once more the neglected sight around him.

"Colin," he thundered, "is this what you call a garden? You need a woman's hand in your life, my boy."

"Celia thinks a woman's hand belongs on the hilt of a sword," Colin answered. "Can you imagine the damage she'd do?"

"Anything she would do would be an improvement, I'd say," Hugh responded, putting his arm around her.

"Well, I'm trying to hire her on as a full-time gardener, but we're just now working out the terms."

"The terms?" Hugh said, laughing. "By God, man, give her what she wants."

Colin turned to Celia. "Well, what do you say to that?"

"I don't have any idea what you two are talking about . . . as usual."

"The garden," the two Campbells responded simultaneously.

Celia looked from one smiling face to the other, knowing full well that Lord Hugh was matchmaking. It was Colin's true meaning that she was unsure of. Better not to acknowledge the double meanings, she thought.

"If you're serious, I'd love to begin putting this garden in order . . . for as long as we're able to stay."

"Colin, you'll have to work that into the terms," Hugh said. "And as an added enticement, Celia, I think I might even volunteer my services for the heavy work."

"That means he'll sit on one of these benches and order you around," Colin said with a smile at Celia.

"I haven't heard too many complaints about the orders I've been giving around here for the last forty some odd years."

"Of course you haven't. Anyone who's complained has been put out to sea in a rudderless boat."

"Aye," Hugh scolded. "And I should have put you out there while I still had the chance."

"If you had, no woman as beautiful as this one would be coming around here."

"You think I came to Kildalton to see you?" Celia asked accusingly, looking up into Colin's laughing eyes.

"Tell him, Celia. You came to Kildalton to see me," Hugh said, drawing Celia protectively toward him.

But Colin's reaction was quick and sure, pulling Celia from his father's protective grip. "One morning in a garden, and you think you can charm my woman away from me."

Something in Celia responded to Colin's words. He was joking with his father, but he'd called her "his woman." That didn't sound like part of the joke. Celia looked up at the younger warrior who was watching her every expression.

"Aren't you my woman?" Colin asked, pulling her affectionately to his side.

"I thought I was the gardener," she said, trying to lighten the suddenly serious turn in the conversation, and turning to Lord Hugh. "Didn't he just say I'm the gardener?"

"The way I remember it, the two jobs have always gone together," Hugh answered, smiling. "But I think it's time I took Ellen and Kit in, so that you two can work out the details of 'employment.'"

Without another word, the Campbell chief turned and walked around the fountain in the direction of the terrace. Celia started to take a step after him, but Colin stopped her with a gentle hand.

"Wait a moment," Colin whispered.

Ellen cast a look over at Celia as Lord Hugh gathered them up. Celia nodded to her, and as Ellen, carrying Kit, and Hugh went up onto the terrace, Celia could see the young woman and the laird chatting amicably.

The spring sun spread a shimmering blanket of diamonds over the rolling blue sea beyond the garden walls. Sheltered from the wind by the protecting walls, Celia sat beside Colin and basked momentarily in a warmth that came from more than the golden orb above. Her eyes scanned the section of flower beds that lay before her, and suddenly were arrested by a glimpse of color beneath a brushy covering of grass and leaves.

Leaving Colin's side for a moment, she moved to the bed and crouched down, sweeping the leaves and debris away with her hand.

"Are you starting your work as gardener already?" Colin asked, coming up beside her and bending on one knee.

"Colin, look," Celia exclaimed, pointing to the white, purple, and blue mass of flowers that had been hidden beneath. "Crocuses! The new season really has begun."

"Aye, you've brought the earliest spring I can remember," Colin responded.

"I'll wager there's a lot of beauty hidden here beneath all this," she sighed, standing and waving her hand toward the untended beds.

"All the beauty out here isn't hidden, Celia," he said, moving behind her and encircling her with his arms. Gently he pulled her to him, burying his face in the mass of curls on her head.

Colin felt the tremor go through Celia as the contours of their bodies fitted together in the embrace.

"How is your head?" he asked, holding her, satisfying

a need he'd been feeling all morning to be in physical contact with her.

"Mmm . . . good . . . my head's much better." She loved the way he held her, the way he enclosed her in his arms.

"You didn't give me an answer about being my woman," he said, whispering in her ear as she rolled her head back against his chest.

"The answer is yes, Colin," Celia answered softly. "I've never been anyone else's."

Colin hugged her fiercely to him, feeling desire for her igniting in his loins. One of his huge hands found its way inside her cloak, and Celia's circular pendant brushed against his hand.

"What's this?" Colin asked, pulling the medallion from her cloak and inspecting it. "Legendary jewels of the Ottomans?"

"Just a memory of my mother," Celia responded, looking down at the keepsake. "It's the only thing I have of hers now."

"The only black sapphires I've ever seen so large or so dark," Colin said in a low voice, "are your eyes."

Colin laid the pendant back against her chest and gathered her tightly to him, cupping her firm breast through the fabric of her soft wool dress. Her body arched outward to his touch, melting into his close embrace.

"I came to your room last night," he rumbled affectionately.

"I thought you did, but I didn't know if that was real or a dream," she responded, caressing the backs of his hands as he held her.

"You were so beautiful, lying there in your thin nightshift," Colin whispered, lowering his head and planting gentle kisses against the skin of her neck.

"You watched me while I was sleeping?" Celia asked in surprise.

"The firelight was reflected on the beautiful curves of your body . . ."

"Wasn't I wearing a blanket?" Celia turned in his arms and faced him, looking into his captivating gray eyes.

"Your smooth, ivory skin was too alluring for me to keep my hands off." Colin pulled her against him, his hands tightening around her waist, her back.

"You touched me? While I was sleeping?" she asked, putting both hands on his shoulders, looking for some hint that he was teasing.

"The ties that held the front of the nightshift pulled apart so easily." While one hand held her waist tightly, the other moved inside the opening of her cloak—exploring, caressing her back, her side, her breast.

"You . . . you untied my nightshift?" she asked, taking his hand and holding it still.

"Starting at the top, one fell away . . ."

"You didn't." This was too much.

"Then the next . . ."

"Did you have Agnes give me something in my wine?"

"Then the last tie fell away . . . revealing . . . revealing . . ." Colin closed his eyes as if remembering.

"Aye? Revealing what?"

"I couldn't hold back. I took you in my arms . . ."

"I had passed out!"

"I held your silky body against me . . ."

"You wouldn't. You didn't." Celia was sure that he wouldn't have. Well, fairly sure.

"You raised your lips to mine . . ." Colin said, lowering his lips toward hers slightly.

"I was asleep!"

"You whispered for me to take you . . ."

"I didn't! I would remember that," she exclaimed.

"To ravish you . . ." His lips were a breath away, threatening to devour her at any moment.

"I wouldn't!"

"To take you to heights of passion that you'd never experienced before ..."

"That wouldn't be difficult." She shrugged, a smile beginning to play on her lips.

"And I did," he concluded, his face transfixed in his rapturous moment.

"Was it satisfying for you, m'lord?"

"It was until I woke up," Colin reported in a casual tone that was completely devoid of the sensuous pretense of the previous moments.

"Then you never were in my room last night," she challenged.

"No?" Colin asked, his smirk taunting her.

"You were the one dreaming last night," she said matter-of-factly.

"Was I?" he continued seductively.

"Absolutely."

"Then how could I know how many ties you have on your nightshift?"

Celia looked down, still standing in his tight embrace, trying to remember the number of ties. Abruptly she looked up, crimson red, suddenly embarrassed. Three ties.

Colin's laughter, though, as he released her, erased her doubts.

"I came to your room last night, but you fell asleep on me," he said, pulling her two steps to a bench and drawing her onto his lap.

"You're a beast, Colin Campbell."

"And you're very talkative in your sleep."

"I'm not," Celia denied hopefully. "What did I say?"

"You really don't remember?"

"Of course I do, you tease, but remind me."

"Do you remember this?" he said, catching her chin with his fingers and guiding her upturned lips to his own.

Colin's kiss began with a slow deliberateness that excited Celia with its promise. She wrapped her arms around his neck and pulled him even closer to her.

Celia opened her lips and received the pressure of his mouth as he caressed her lower lip with his tongue, his teeth, his lips. She moved her head slightly to accommodate him as his mouth brushed her cheek and nibbled gently at the smooth flesh beneath her ear. She shuddered at the erotic sensation that suddenly raged in her veins.

"Do you remember telling me you love me?" he whispered, and her chest heaved as his breath caressed her ear. He tenderly kissed the bruise above her temple.

Celia took his face in her hands and brought his lips to hers.

He suckled her lip momentarily before sweeping into her with his thrusting, tasting tongue. She felt him explore deeply the recesses of her mouth, their tongues entwining with increasing sensual pleasure. She delved into his mouth with her own tongue, feeling the textures, loving the taste of him. She felt his strong hands grip her shoulders and lift her away from him.

"You *do* love me," he growled, pausing to look intimately into the ebon depths of her eyes.

"Aye, Colin. I love you."

Celia wanted to melt into him completely. To lie within the protective shelter of his arms. To be loved by him. She rested her forehead against his full lips.

"Celia, look at me," Colin began. She lifted her gaze to take in his serious expression. "Celia, I love you. I want to marry you. I want you to marry me."

Celia was paralyzed by the words that she'd never expected to hear. Emotions surged within her. A joyful shudder wracked her frame as she gazed into the face that had become a whole world for her.

He loved her. Because of that he wanted to join their lives, a union of bodies, of souls, of futures. Tears suddenly welled into her eyes, overflowing in streams of joy that rolled unchecked down her face.

"Oh, Colin." She wept, smiling through her tears.

Colin brought her face to his, kissing the salty tracks and pressing her eyelids closed with his smooth lips. He gathered her tightly in his arms, as Celia buried her face in the hollow of his neck.

"Before you came here, I was like that shoreline beyond the wall," he began. "My life was rough, unrefined—but solid, supportive of the life above. When you came, it was like the shimmering sea that dashes up against those rock walls, surprising, exciting, powerful— but somehow rhythmic, thoughtful, and secure. Yours is a shaping force, sure, defining and yet nurturing."

Colin felt her soft frame resting snugly against him as she listened.

"Celia, I love everything about you. From the first moment I laid eyes on you, something was branded on my heart, on my soul. I still recall that vision in the moonlit room, so wild and mystical, so beautiful and so utterly fearless. The way you looked at me, the fires glowing in your eyes."

Celia looked up at him, smiling, remembering the scornful way she'd appraised him while all along thinking that he was like a huge, raven-haired Adonis sent down to her.

"And I thought you were ready to put me out that first night," she said, her voice brimming with laughter. "Admit it. You were."

"Would I put out an angel?"

"You didn't look at me as if I were an angel, Colin Campbell."

"I was surprised to see you without your wings and your halo."

"If you're going to speak flippantly about heavenly beings, then you'd better watch out for bolts of lightning."

"The sky is a beautiful shade of blue, Celia," Colin said, looking up at the azure color marked only by the few white patches that were scudding by. "But if you're concerned about the weather, we can go up to my room and finish this discussion."

Celia inwardly thrilled at the thought, but shook her head with a smile.

"I thought you were having a busy day."

"As a matter of fact, my day came to a complete halt the moment I stepped into this garden."

"I'm distracting you from what you should be doing," she said, trying to edge off his lap.

"Would you come down to the village with me?" Colin asked, restraining her for a moment.

"Wouldn't I be in the way?"

"Probably," he said with a smile. "Just where I want you. And speaking of wanting you . . ."

"Aye?" she responded primly, coyly pretending not to understand.

"Tonight," Colin continued suggestively.

"Tonight?" Celia blushed.

"Tonight we'll announce our intentions to the clan at dinner . . ."

"Colin, not at dinner. First, I . . . need to . . ." Celia stumbled over the words she could not say. There was still Kit. Dunbar's words echoed in her head. And, suddenly, thoughts of all the things she lacked came rushing in on her. She couldn't help but wonder if Colin was proposing to her now because of what he had heard. To protect her from the butcher Danvers. Aye, she knew that he loved her . . . but marriage? Was he just trying to do what he thought best for her?

"Celia, I've waited a long time for you," Colin said softly. "I can wait another day."

She reached up to him and kissed his mouth with a fiery passion. Colin answered with his own burning desire. Their passions rekindled in the heat of their embrace, and their feelings for each other poured out in the mingling communion of the kiss.

Colin abruptly pulled away, his eyes riveted on hers.

"Do you want to wait until our wedding night?" Colin whispered in a hoarse growl. He had to ask, while he still had the discipline to honor her wishes. And he didn't know how much more of this pleasurable torture he could take. The wedding would be today, if he had his way.

Celia looked up at him. Every part of her body ached with the need for his touch. She forced herself to try to think this through, to be sensible. But her mind and her body told her only one thing. Celia shook her head slowly.

"When?"

"Very soon," she whispered.

Colin closed his eyes at her words and opened them again immediately.

"It's going to be very difficult to let you out of my sight, you know."

Colin wasn't going to let Celia out of his sight, but neither was Dunbar. Father William had been a bit concerned when Celia, Ellen, and Kit had disappeared during the morning, and Edmund's apparent lack of concern made him even more nervous. When Celia had finally appeared in the South Hall beside the black-haired giant, the priest's suspicions blossomed.

So when Celia said she was going down into the village with the young warrior, Father William had volunteered to chaperon.

"Chaperon!" Celia blurted out in disbelief. "Father, you aren't serious."

"Aye," the priest retorted. "I think . . ."

"It's a fine idea," Colin interrupted, finishing the priest's sentence.

Celia and Father William both turned incredulous eyes on the figure looming above them.

"It'll give us a chance to get to know one another better." Colin shrugged, continuing with a slight smile at Celia. "And we don't want anyone thinking there's anything improper going on up here, now, do we?"

Celia blushed in spite of herself, and quickly turned her face toward Agnes, who was hurrying toward them across the hall.

"Celia, my dear," she began, coming directly to her and taking hold of Celia's two hands. She looked up at the area where Celia's wounds were. "Has your head started throbbing at all?"

"No, Agnes," the young woman answered. "I'm fine today. Honestly."

"Are you sure you're not a little light-headed?" Colin added in a serious tone.

"She's never been light-headed in her entire life," the little priest snapped pugnaciously.

"Now, you two!" Agnes scolded dismissively. "You really shouldn't overdo it today, child. You need to rest a bit. You don't want to miss any of the excitement later."

"That's true," Colin said, taking hold of Celia's elbow.

Celia turned away, trying to ignore his remark, trying to hide the color in her face. She already felt light-headed, as Colin put it, about all that had just occurred and about all that was to come. And his remarks had succeeded in making her inner feelings rush with full color into her face, a face that she tried so desperately to keep calm and reserved. "What excitement, Agnes?"

"Why, Colin didn't tell you?" Agnes responded. "The men are working right now down at the harbor fitting the new cannons into our ships. Hugh says they'll be trying them out before sunset."

"I'd like to see that," Celia said. "And I promise, Agnes. If I begin to tire, I'll come back and rest."

"All right, dear," she acquiesced with a smile of motherly concern before turning sternly to Colin. "But you watch out for her, and do a better job of it than you did at that disgusting . . . place . . . of Argyll's."

Colin's raised eyebrows at Agnes's admonition was all he had time to muster.

"I'm glad someone around here shows good sense," Father William grumbled.

"Then I simply won't let her out of my sight," asserted Colin happily.

With a last half smile at Celia, Agnes turned to the small crowd of servants who were awaiting her directions by the door of the hall.

"It's a mistake teaching girls anything beyond what they need to know to be good wives and mothers," Dunbar pontificated in response to Colin's description of his plans for the village school.

Taken aback, Celia looked at the priest wide-eyed, having heard on a number of occasions Father William argue the exact *opposite* of what he was now saying. Smiling inwardly, she guessed what he was doing and what his motives were. He was testing Colin, and she was the reason.

Together, the three were nearing the village, and Bear was weaving a path before them. Colin had been walking at a considerable pace, until he began to talk about the changes in the village and about the school. Then his pace slowed as he spoke, and Celia and Father William were able to walk comfortably beside him in the afternoon sun.

"A mistake educating girls?" Colin repeated, puzzled at first by the priest's words. "Father, you are an educated man. I assume that you did a bit of tutoring at court."

"Aye, lad," Dunbar replied. "I even tutored Alexander, the King's son, before he went off to Rotterdam to study under Erasmus."

"Did you ever tutor any girls at the court?" Colin continued, giving Celia's arm a light squeeze. He knew full well that the priest had taught Celia.

"Aye, a few girls," Dunbar answered warily.

"Then what did you teach these girls?" Colin persisted. "What makes up a good education for those future 'wives and mothers'?"

"This is a foolish discussion," Dunbar said pompously—and vaguely. "Traditional things."

Celia turned directly toward the priest, her face showing her amusement at his outrageous comments.

"Oh, I see," Colin said. "These girls came to you to learn how to run a household."

"Certainly not," Dunbar retorted. "These were children of quality. I taught them to read—in English and in French. And I taught them religion."

"Nothing else, Father?"

Celia thought about all the things she had learned from Father William: how to be pigheaded to the extreme, how to curse more creatively than any of her father's sailors could, and how to be supremely aloof when it came to the shallow young men at court.

"A few other things, I suppose," the priest answered. "Why, what else should they be taught?"

"No Latin or Greek?" Colin asked.

Aye, Celia reminisced. Father William had drilled her in Latin, Greek, and Gaelic, as well as French, until she could speak, read, and write fluently in any of them.

"What do girls need Latin or Greek for?" Dunbar asked uneasily. "The romances that girls can read ... and they should be carefully controlled ... are in French. But too much reading can lead a young woman into dangerous yearnings."

"Yearnings? Come, Father, no mathematics? Nor

logic?" Colin continued, not letting the priest off the hook. "No philosophy of the ancients? No history?"

Aye, all those, too. Reading Boethius had taught Celia to accept that even the most boring of lessons must have a purpose.

"What use would a girl have for all this?" Father William blurted out. "I'm telling you, lad. Tradition has declared that these subjects can ruin a girl's morals—make her think she's as intellectually capable as a man."

"*Can't* a woman be as intellectually capable as a man?" Colin asked.

Celia shot the priest a threatening look.

"Perhaps," Dunbar responded, ignoring her glare. "But what will she gain by it? There's still her future to consider."

"Future? How?"

"By becoming undesirable as a wife. No husband would accept that in a wife."

Celia had already heard this from Father William. Now she wanted to hear Colin's response.

"I have to disagree. I think you have a misconception about what men need in their wives."

"Do I, lad? Then why don't you correct me on that."

Colin looked at Celia as he chose his words.

"Men need their wives to be soulmates," he said softly, never shifting his gaze from Celia's face. "They need them to share their lives as well as their beds. To bear their dreams as well as their children."

This young heir is certainly a charmer, Dunbar thought, noting the exchange of tender glances. And the things he says certainly show promise.

"Then why would a woman need an education for that?"

"For the same reason that a man needs an education," Colin answered, turning his attention back to the curmudgeonly cleric. "We all need the languages that give us access to Socrates, Plato, Horace, Virgil, and even

Ovid. We all need the history and the logic and the mathematics that give us a sense of where we come from and who we are. These are the elements of education that produce knowledge of our human worth, that produce self-esteem."

The three had reached the harbor's edge, and Dunbar stepped in front of the other two, placing his hand on Colin's arm. He had to admit, Edmund had been right about Colin Campbell. *This is a man whose values are not of the common order. This is a man whose vision extends beyond the end of his own table. This is a man whose intelligence seems to match his obvious strength. If there be any man worthy of Celia, this could be the man.*

"Wouldn't you be intimidated by that?" the priest questioned. "By a wife who has as much intelligence, as much learning, as much discipline as any man?"

Colin now understood clearly that Father William's baiting comments had all been leading to this. The warrior looked down at this combative priest and knew why Celia cared so much for him. He was clearly devoted to protecting her.

"No," Colin answered, gazing steadily into the little man's steel-blue eyes. "She's the woman I've been waiting for."

Colin reached down and took Celia's hand in his, holding it tightly against his side.

"Then I suppose I don't need to tell you, lad," Dunbar concluded. "Women like that are very hard to come by."

"That's true," Colin responded, looking at the woman beside him. "You don't need to tell me."

Father William reached down and clasped their entwined hands in his.

"Well, Celia, this journey's not over yet, but we've certainly come a long way since leaving Linlithgow Castle."

*   *   *

"Lady Celia," Ellen whispered through the adjoining doorway. "May I come in?"

"Of course, Ellen," answered Celia from the window where she stood watching the four Campbell ships sailing along the shoreline in the glowing sunset. Colin had told her that they would be firing the guns at the craggy bluffs south of the castle. She could see the castle's inhabitants gathered on the curtain wall overlooking the sea.

Ellen's fair-skinned face was somewhat paler, Celia thought, noting that as the woman stopped in the middle of the room, she was wringing her hands. Clearly, something was bothering her.

"What's the matter, Ellen?" Celia asked gently, taking her companion by the hand and leading her to the chairs beside the window.

"I was wondering . . . I didn't know . . ." Ellen paused, stumbling over her words. Embarrassed, she avoided Celia's eyes and stared steadily at her lap. "M'lady, will we be staying much longer at Kildalton?"

"Why, Ellen?" Celia asked quickly. "Is there something wrong?"

"No, m'lady," Ellen answered, looking up instantly. "Just the opposite."

Celia smiled into the face of the young widow as the meaning of Ellen's consternation sank in.

"Would this have anything to do with Runt, Ellen?" she asked softly.

"I don't want you to think I'm going to fail in the oath that I've taken, m'lady . . ."

"So it *is* Runt," Celia interrupted with a smile.

"Aye, Lady Celia," Ellen admitted, lowering her eyes again. "Since we came here, he's been watching over us, and . . . we've spent time together . . . then . . . he was hurt . . ."

"But all is well now," Celia said gently. "We should be thankful that he's feeling better, Ellen."

"Aye, m'lady, I was so worried about him," Ellen gushed. "No man ever took a sword wound for me the way he did. He truly cares for me, m'lady."

"Has he made his intentions known to you?"

"Aye, he asked me this afternoon," Ellen whispered. The delight of the thought lit her face.

"What was your answer to him?" Celia asked gently, taking Ellen's ice-cold hands in her own.

"I told him that I couldn't answer him," she responded, her disappointment apparent in her eyes.

"Do you love him, Ellen?"

The young woman answered slowly. "Aye, m'lady. I never thought that I'd be able to love again after my bairn died. But caring for Kit each day, feeling the wee one's need for me. And then, being here at Kildalton ... the object of Runt's attentions ... Lady Celia, I do have a life again. It's almost like I've found a home for the first time ... here, at a place I'd never been before."

Celia leaned forward out of her chair and hugged Ellen. She knew exactly what Ellen was feeling.

"Ellen, I promise you. If Runt is the man you've set your heart on, I'll see to it that you are able to be with him. I don't know what the future holds for us. I don't know how long we'll be staying. But I'll make sure that you don't lose this chance for happiness."

Celia had not finished her words when Ellen began to cry. The two women stood and held each other tightly, and Celia felt her own tears well up and overflow.

Celia had been anxious, fretful, waiting for the sounds of Colin's return.

She was sitting before the fireplace in the near darkness of her room, listening to the crackle of the dying embers of her fire and the occasional sounds from the South Hall. There was the edge of a chill in the room that the fire could not dispel for Celia. Tucking her bare feet under her, she gathered the white robe closer about her, lost in the glowing coals of the fading fire.

After Colin had walked Celia and Father William up from the village, he'd returned to the ships in the harbor to direct the final preparations. Lord Hugh and Alec and Edmund were all aboard the vessels when they sailed down the coastline, and all of them, including Colin, were still on the water when Celia, Ellen, Kit, and Father William had joined Agnes in the South Hall.

As they had entered the hall, Celia had taken the baby, giving Ellen a chance to eat her dinner with Runt, who was making rapid progress in his recovery. As soon as Ellen had turned toward the table where he sat with several others, Runt had quickly cleared a place beside him for the fair-haired beauty. Watching them together had confirmed in Celia's eyes everything Ellen had told her earlier.

After she'd returned to her room, Jean had come with a load of wood and turf for her fire, and his familiar friendliness reminded Celia of how much her position had changed at Kildalton. Somehow Agnes had managed to convey to the household Celia's true identity. Jean no longer treated her like a guest—his patter about the excitement of the household and the villagers had the tone of a longtime confidant. It made her consider the openness of the villagers that they had passed today. They had all saluted her by her real name, and none seemed surprised to see her at Colin's side.

Like Ellen, Celia felt an acceptance of her that made her feel at home. It was not simply hospitality—it was a real sense of approval that she felt from everyone, especially from Lord Hugh and Agnes.

And she owed all that to Colin. Not only had he saved her from a horrible fate at Argyll's castle, he had offered her all of the things that she longed for in her life. And he had accepted her unconditionally, making certain that everyone knew it.

But what had she given in return?

When the booming sounds of the guns had commenced, Celia had been drawn back into a time in her past when she had heard that same far-off thunder. It was that time of childhood when she had put her faith in her father. That faith, that special trust, had been forged from the love that father and daughter had shared. It was a trust that had never diminished to the day he died.

But this afternoon, in her conversation with Lord Hugh, Celia had been hurt by the unknown reality of her childhood. There was a part of her father that she had never known. It was a part of his life that he had not shared with her.

Celia thought of Edmund, who had been beside her all these years, caring for her, watching over her, and yet all the time knowing the truth about her father. He had never even allowed her a suspicion of anything that might diminish her cherished memories. But the memory of the love and trust that she had thought boundless had been abruptly tempered by the words she had heard. Her father had not truly trusted her.

But thinking about that now, Celia knew that her father simply could not. After all, she had been a mere child. He had done what he had to do, and he had done the best he could. She could not fault him in that. But she knew it was time to learn the whole truth from Edmund.

As Colin's ships hammered away at the shoreline, testing the range and accuracy of the new cannons, Celia realized that she was doing to Colin what her father had done to her, with the exception that Colin was no child, and he would not forgive.

Celia knew deep within her what she could give in

return—what she must give in return. She had so little to give him; she had only her heart ... and her trust. She had already given him her heart. It was now time to give him her trust.

The only truth that Celia still withheld from Colin had to be shared. Then Colin would know everything about her. He would be a part of her life, and share in the task that lay upon her shoulders.

It was time. She had to see him.

The men all returned from the ships and the harbor long after dark. In the South Hall during the boisterous meal following the success of the sail, Colin gleaned from his discussion with Agnes and Father William that Celia had retired much earlier. Agnes assured him that Celia was fine, but that the hectic nature of the day had not helped her recovery along. Celia needed to rest, Agnes admonished.

Colin stood drying before the roaring fire in his room. Jean and the others had just finished carrying out the tub of water that he had bathed in, and the huge warrior wrapped the linen drying cloth around his hips. Crouching before the hearth, Colin absently fed pieces of turf and wood into the fire, thinking, instead, of Celia's face when he had asked her to marry him. How he loved the flights of expression that passed across her face. Never had a woman filled him with such a raw mixture of conflicting passions. He wanted to hold her safely in his arms, comfort her, soothe her, protect her, but at the same time he wanted to take her, drive her to a fever of desire, to a wildness that he knew existed within her. He wanted to feel her smooth body under his own, feel the rhythmic dance of love build within her, encompassing them both, taking them both to the zenith of ecstasy.

Colin felt the sharp stirring sensation in his loins at

the thought of Celia. He knew that this was going to be a long night without her.

Colin's head snapped around as the panel to the left of the fireplace opened.

As Celia pulled the panel door open, she could see from the firelight that the room appeared empty. Looking across the room at the huge, curtained bed against the far wall, she could not see whether Colin had retired.

Celia began to call his name softly as she stepped into the room, but the word evaporated on her lips when she saw him.

The sight of him standing beside the fire obliterated any rational thought in Celia's head. His shining black hair hung in tangled disarray around his handsome, chiseled features. The sinewy muscles that enveloped his broad shoulders and chest rippled in the flashing light of the fire. His upper body tapered to a flat, hard abdomen before disappearing into the clinging, white linen that ended abruptly at the brawny swell of his massive thighs.

He was truly magnificent.

Celia heard rather than felt the involuntary intake of air that swept into her lungs. It sounded so sharply in the silence that it seemed to fill the room. Suddenly she could think of nothing else but what those great arms would be like around her right now.

Colin took only a moment to recognize the look of need in her that matched his own. The realization that Celia had come to his bedroom, that they were finally alone, washed any inclination to hesitate from his thoughts. He took the few quick steps and swept her into his embrace.

"Celia, you are here," he whispered, holding her fiercely against his skin. It was as though he wanted to be assured that she was no dream, that she was actual flesh and blood.

The light, fresh scent of her ignited in him a passion so dizzying, so overwhelming, that Colin felt like a man intoxicated. Bending his face over hers, their lips met in a conflagration of desire. Her lips parted slightly, and he penetrated her mouth with his tongue, searching for the taste that might somehow relieve his insatiable need to know her.

Celia thrilled at the feel of Colin's strength around her. Her arms strained to pull him closer. The hunger for him swept through her body, through her every action. Her hands were all over him—feeling, touching, tracing the powerful muscles of his back, of his arms. She arched her body, pressing her hips against him. Suddenly his lips drew away from hers, and she felt his powerful hands grip her wrists, placing them at her sides.

"Celia, I have dreamt of this moment," he whispered as his hands slid under the folds of the robe, and Celia felt it drop off her shoulders to the floor about her feet.

Celia wanted to tell him how she too felt, about her dreams, but instead she could only close her eyes and shudder as she felt his fingers gently undo the tie at the top of her nightshift. He tenderly slid his hands across the skin of her collarbone and took her face in his hands for a light, glancing kiss.

Colin's hands again glided down the front of her shift to the second tie. As he unknotted the string, Celia felt him spread the material slightly, the backs of his fingers caressing the soft curves between her breasts.

The third tie was hardly open when Celia felt his full lips lightly upon hers. His low voice rumbled as he took her chin in his hand.

"Look at me, woman."

She opened her eyes and gazed into the gray expanse of his eyes. They were so full of passion, so full of desire, so full of what she knew to be love for her.

"We belong to each other, now," he said.

Colin slid his hands under the soft collar of the

nightshift. He lightly lifted the linen across the silky skin of Celia's shoulders, and the white cloth was gone.

Colin stepped back to fully appreciate the radiant beauty that stood revealed before him.

"You are a goddess," he whispered raggedly.

Even in the light of the fire, he could see the florid heat that was coloring her cheeks. Her slim body was so perfectly formed, her skin so smooth and so golden in the reflective glow. His eyes took in the incredible beauty of the woman who was his completely. She stood with her hands at her sides. She made no attempt to hide her body from him. She made no attempt to hide her heart.

"Colin," she whispered. "I'm real . . . and I'm yours."

The giant warrior moved back to her, sweeping her up and carrying her effortlessly across the room to his bed. From the moment he touched her, a frenzied passion eclipsed all reason. Her mouth was all over his face, suckling, tasting, caressing with lip and tongue.

Colin placed her gently upon the deep billows of his bed and lay down beside her. His mouth captured hers, and the soft touch of his hands moving slowly across her body made Celia quiver with anticipation. He raised his face and looked down at her with affection and tenderness.

The heat of his chest against her skin scorched her. She reached up to push back the tendril of hair that had fallen across his face. Her hand traced delicately the line of his jaw, the musculature of his shoulder, his arm.

Colin shuddered involuntarily at the erotic sensation her touch produced in him, and he kissed her again— her lips, her chin, the tip of his tongue drawing a line along her throat down into the valley between her breasts. He heard her gasp as his mouth encircled one breast, finally taking her nipple firmly between his lips.

Celia took hold of the bedding on either side of her as Colin's hand slid down along her belly to the junction of her thighs. Her body arched against his hand as his fingers entered the warm opening, softly stoking the raging fire within her. Celia felt a white-hot bolt surging from his lips at her breast to the touch of his fingers within her flesh. A wave of pulsating heat began to take over her body as his fingers expertly massaged the sensitive nub within her.

Colin listened to the soft whimpers of pleasure that were escaping her lips. He felt her hands fly to his hair, gripping his streaming locks with a swelling ambivalence as she intermittently pulled his face away and back again tightly to her. He concentrated on her rising pitch, the short panting breaths, in an effort to control his own mounting excitement.

With one swift movement, Colin swept away the towel that covered him and lifted himself onto her body. Her legs instinctively opened to accept him. He penetrated her gently until his throbbing manhood reached the membrane of her virginity. He stopped and looked into her passion-clouded eyes.

"Celia, hold me," he murmured, sliding his hands under her backside.

Colin felt her hands grip his back, and he could wait no longer. He thrust himself deep within her.

Pinned beneath him, Celia cried out as the sharp pain of his entry exploded in her body. His full weight upon her arrested any movement.

"Hold still, my love," he said through clenched teeth, trying to control his overwhelming urge to withdraw and plunge again and again in the incredible tightness. "I'm sorry for the pain. Wait, it will pass."

Celia felt briefly outside the sudden reality of the moment. As if standing beside the experience, she felt no pain, only a shock that seemed to erase the rending sensation. But then, feelings of a different sort began to stir in her body. Celia felt as if an entirely different force were taking over her being. An urgent need to move was creeping into her.

Colin, too, felt a swelling need growing within him. He kissed her hungrily as her hips began to move rhythmically against him. The tightness of her was wondrously agonizing as she rose to him, drawing him ever deeper until she had taken in all of him.

Waves of white, pulsing heat were consuming Celia. She was not even conscious of the wild, surging dance of her body's pounding drive. Her nails clawed at his back, his shoulders, while her mouth devoured him.

Colin shook with the effort of his restraint. Slowly he withdrew from the depths of her, only to feel her rise up to take him deep within her. He thrust into her again and again, their bodies rocking together, soaring together to a frenzied crescendo of love and release.

Their climax erupted with volcanic force, and they clung to each other, united in a crystal sphere of body and spirit.

Transfixed, they seemed to pass an age in that moment, until Colin gently withdrew from her and rolled to his side, taking her with him.

As his breaths subsided, he caressed her face, lifting her chin and kissing her lightly on the forehead, eyelids, cheeks, chin, lips.

"I love you, Celia. I'm sorry that I had to hurt you."

"Don't be sorry, Colin," she murmured softly, her black eyes clouded with passion. "I'm not."

"It won't hurt like that again," he said in return, stroking her soft hair, her shoulder, her back. "It'll just get better."

"I'll die if it gets any better," she answered, a laugh rippling through the love-scented air. She looked across at him, touching his chest, his shoulder, his upper arm, her face growing serious. "Colin, I hope that next time I can please you as you've pleased me."

Colin laughed aloud at the thought of her not pleasing

him. Pulling her tightly against him, he crushed her lips with a searing kiss.

"Please me?" he growled with a smile. "Never before have I felt what we shared tonight. I felt as if I came out of a dark tunnel into a light I'd never known. You released in me a passion that I could not control. Please me? My God, love, you've pleased me . . . intoxicated me . . . enslaved me."

Celia pushed him onto his back and smiled down into his gray eyes.

"Oh, Colin," she thrilled. "I love you so much. I came here tonight to talk and . . . and one look at you . . . standing there . . . so handsome . . . naked . . ." Celia's hand roamed the muscles in his chest, in his hard stomach, traveling lower to his naval, even lower. "I want to learn everything. And everything about you."

As Celia's fingers reached his manhood, she heard Colin take a sharp breath. Her mouth was on him now, kissing his lips, tasting his neck, his chest. Thinking back on the pleasure that he had given her, she encircled his nipples with her tongue. Colin groaned as her hand lightly grasped his throbbing arousal. Abruptly Celia's face was above his, her eyes mischievous and her expression impish.

"Colin," she began. "I'm ready to talk now."

The giant took her auburn curls in his two great fists and rolled her over onto her back.

"Tomorrow . . . We'll talk tomorrow."

As the first light of dawn crept through Colin's window, the warrior rolled onto the still warm space beside him. As his consciousness emerged through the gray haze of slumber, Colin realized that Celia was no longer there.

Sitting bolt upright, he pushed open the heavy curtains that blocked his view of the panel. The entry was closed, and she was gone.

For a moment Colin wondered whether the night before had really happened. Whether she had come to him. Whether they had shared the incredible passion that seemed almost dreamlike in his memory. But glancing at the bedding, he knew that she had shared with him a cherished moment of her life.

Lying back in the billowy comfort of the bed, Colin felt a gnawing ache begin to grow in him. There was a vacant place inside of him that he knew was intimately connected with the vacant place beside him. He felt almost foolish—like a pubescent schoolboy—knowing that the longing he was feeling was for a woman in the very next room. He smiled into the tentlike darkness above his bed and closed his eyes. He missed her.

Bear was waiting for Celia as she came down the stairway into the Great Hall, his tail wagging fiercely in a now customary morning greeting. Grabbing him by the ears and kissing him in the middle of his square forehead, Celia turned toward the South Hall with a mixture of feelings that were combining to color her cheeks with a rising heat. Her excitement at seeing Colin was combined with a bit of nervousness; her desire to be with those whom she knew cared for her was mixed with a bit of shyness at the thought that they might discern some change in her.

Celia was pleased to see the sun streaming in the open doors of the Entry Hall. Another beautiful day.

Entering the South Hall, Celia paused in the doorway as she noticed a stranger sitting with Lord Hugh, Colin, Edmund, and Alec. Immediately Colin looked up to see her and leapt to his feet. Crossing the hall, they met in the center, and as Colin took her hands, she blushed furiously, noting that all eyes in the hall were upon them.

"You're certainly in good color this morning," he whispered as they turned toward the head table. "Difficult night sleeping?"

Celia could not answer, her face glowing crimson, but she dug her nails deeply into the flesh of his palm. Colin responded immediately, hiding a wince and sandwiching her hand firmly in his.

"I'll be good," he surrendered. "Besides, we have a visitor."

Exchanging looks with the man now standing by his place at the table, Celia thought there was something familiar in his face, though she was sure that she'd never seen him before. The handsome, boyish features were marred by the bright red scar crossing his forehead from just above his right eye and disappearing into the shock of brown hair. His eyes seemed to register recognition as she approached, and that recognition was closely followed by surprise and admiration.

"Lady Celia," Colin said, taking her arm possessively. "I'd like to introduce you to Alec's brother, Ambrose Macpherson."

Celia glanced from one brother's smiling face to the other, realizing now why Ambrose's looks had seemed so familiar. He was just a slightly shorter, scarred version of Alec. But while Celia knew that Alec's brothers had been at court, she was sure she had never met them.

"I know Lady Muir," Ambrose replied heartily.

"You do?" Celia blurted out, perplexed at his response. "I'm sure that we've never met, m'lord."

"Aye, m'lady," Ambrose continued. "I was among the crowd who were following in your wake during the celebration last summer. I'd seen you many times before, but you were never one to cast an eye in an admirer's direction. But pardon my surprise at seeing you here, the word at court was that Queen Margaret had sent you to England."

"There was a change of plans, m'lord," Celia responded evasively.

Colin led Celia to his place at the table and sat beside her. Sitting, Ambrose leaned forward to address Celia.

"M'lady, I was just telling these good gentlemen news of someone you have had some unpleasant dealings with, I believe."

"You've met Danvers, Celia?" Alec asked, craning his neck to see her face.

"Aye, Alec," she said quietly. "Unfortunately, I have."

"Indeed, she has," Ambrose said with admiration. "I was a witness to one meeting they had."

Ambrose turned to Lord Hugh. "M'lord, if I may. During one of the King's tournaments at Stirling—two years ago, I think it was—this English devil Danvers came to our court, supposedly representing the new English king at the festivities."

Celia's back stiffened at the words. She knew this story all too well, and was not entirely happy about hearing it again here and now. She would be happy if she never heard Danvers's name again. She smiled gratefully at Colin as he reached onto her lap and took her hand.

"During the competition," Ambrose continued, "Danvers beat the Earl of Huntly's younger brother."

"Aye," Lord Hugh interrupted. "I recall hearing about this. Instead of accepting the unarmed lad's word of yield, the English dog beat him badly with his truncheon. He almost died of his injuries, didn't he?"

"Aye, Hugh," Edmund said. "But he recovered, and he's a much better fighter now that he's grown . . . and experienced."

"After the beating," Ambrose went on, "the pig Danvers yanked the steel-mesh glove off the bleeding and unconscious warrior and gave him a vicious, unmanly kick. Then he mounted and rode to the grandstand where Queen Margaret was sitting with the King and with her entourage. He went directly before the Queen and asked if he could present the token to his own 'lady.' "

Colin felt Celia quiver with what appeared to be rage as she stared directly at the place before her.

"The spectators were all quiet, disgusted and ashamed at his conduct on the field, and curious to know who his lady might be. Receiving a nod from the Queen, Danvers dismounted and climbed into the seats, stopping in front of Lady Muir, offering the glove as token."

Ambrose stopped his tale a moment, just long enough to drink from the cup by his plate. The South Hall was in total silence, as everyone awaited his next word.

"Danvers stood there for what seemed like an eternity. The crowd's attention was riveted on them. Then Lady Muir stood up, took the glove from his hand, and whipped him across the face so hard that blood ran down his cheek and dripped from his chin like rain from a gargoyle. She spat into his stunned face and turned on her heel, leaving Danvers before a chuckling king and a wildly cheering crowd."

From the hushed onlookers in the hall at Kildalton there suddenly erupted a great cheer for the woman sitting red-faced beside their young laird. Before the noise subsided, Celia was surrounded by the Campbell fighters and the household members, all congratulating her as though the event had just occurred.

Celia looked up at Colin, stunned at the spontaneous response from his people. The gaze that he met her with was one of intense pride, and a sense of relief and joy washed over her.

A short time later the hall began to empty, the fighters still animated at the story Ambrose had told. Several groups of the clan council entered the hall, and as tables were being cleared, Celia and the others stood in clusters in the open space between the tables.

"Colin," Celia said quietly, taking him aside. "Would you mind if I worked out in your garden this morning?"

"It's our garden, now, Celia," Colin answered in a low voice.

"Will you be able to join me there for a few moments?" Celia still wanted to talk to Colin. She still needed to share her last secret with him.

"Join you? What did you have in mind for me, Lady Muir?" Colin asked suggestively.

"Stop it," she responded, blushing. "Really, you *do* have a one-track mind."

"And it hasn't crossed *your* mind this morning?" Colin asked, raising an eyebrow.

"Aye, Colin, it has," Celia replied, gazing steadily into his eyes.

Colin felt a pang of desire for this woman stir in his loins. He knew in his heart that he could get lost in the crystalline blackness of Celia's eyes. He wanted her, now and forever.

"If you're not in too big a hurry to get outside," Colin began mischievously. "I think we have a few moments to . . . discuss gardening plans . . . in my room."

Before Celia could answer, Ambrose and Alec came up beside her.

"Lady Celia," the younger Macpherson said. "You don't know how delighted I am finally to have gotten the opportunity to meet you. Along with the rest of your admirers, I was heartily saddened when I heard that you left court for Engl—"

"Ahem . . ." Alec interrupted, in an attempt to save his brother's good standing with the Campbells. "Not to slight your good opinion of Lady Muir, Ambrose, but I'm sure I've heard you proclaim your admiration for other . . ."

"But none like Lady Celia, Alec," Ambrose protested. "I've always . . ."

Ambrose stopped short as Colin moved closer to Celia and took her hand in his. The fierce scowl that he saw in the giant warrior's face spoke volumes, and the younger Macpherson realized that he was treading on very dangerous ground.

"... I've always ... thought Lady Muir the finest sailor I've ever lost to."

Celia glanced up at Colin's face and nearly laughed aloud.

"She's not only a great sailor, Ambrose," Alec continued, trying to steer the conversation. "She's also incredibly knowledgeable about healing. She could probably cure leprosy. She's cured my motion sickness!"

"You aren't serious, Alec?" Ambrose asked uncertainly.

"Aye," Colin confirmed. "Since Celia gave him the remedy, Alec's been out on my boats more than he's been on land."

"If you gentlemen will excuse me, I've heard enough about my good deeds for one day, thank you."

Colin walked toward the doorway with her.

"I'll join you after I meet with the clan council and Ambrose," he promised. "I clearly can't leave you alone too long with all these new rivals appearing."

"In the whole world, Colin," Celia answered softly, "you have no rival."

Colin squeezed her hand gently, and she turned toward the door.

The dew on the plants sparkled like jewels in the brilliant sunlight. As Celia explored the garden, looking more carefully at the overgrown plants and general neglect, she thought that a great deal could be accomplished with a sharp pruning knife and some hard work. It was just what she needed.

Ellen and Kit stayed with her for a short while, and Runt even joined them there, moving back and forth between helping Celia with the brush she was clearing and chatting affectionately with Ellen.

As Celia worked in one quadrant, she noticed that Runt was piling the brush by a hedgelike growth about halfway down the garden wall. Pulling back the hedge, she saw a small oaken door, heavily barred and moss-covered from disuse.

"I thought we could take the brush out into the training grounds through there, m'lady," Runt said, coming up behind Celia.

"That's a good idea, Runt. I should have figured there'd be another entrance. Why don't we just clear this away and take it all out now?"

"We need to ask Lord Hugh before unbarring the door, m'lady."

"Why, Runt? What's beyond the door?" Celia asked.

"The small garden around the family crypt, m'lady," he responded. "That's where Lord Colin's mother is buried."

Celia hadn't even thought up to now about the final resting place of Lady Campbell. Thinking about her now, Celia wished that she knew more about the woman. She was clearly venerated even now, twenty-five years after her death. And why shouldn't she be, Celia thought; she'd produced a family that was both strong and loving. In Colin, Celia saw Hugh's strength and courage, but there was also compassion, understanding, trust, and love.

The sun was getting high overhead, and Celia could hear Kit beginning to fuss. Returning to Ellen, she asked Runt if he wouldn't mind accompanying them up to Ellen's room. Runt brightened visibly at the prospect.

"I'll be along shortly," Celia teased benignly.

More than an hour later Celia was still hard at work. The sun and the effort had warmed her considerably, and she had rolled up her sleeves in a futile attempt to keep her dress clean. Her hands were scratched and filthy from the briers and the cold, wet soil. And her face and dress were mere reflections of her hands.

But the garden was a different place. Straightening up and stretching her back, Celia looked proudly at the huge pile of brush that she had pruned from the rose-bushes and the hedges. The flower beds in the quadrant where Ellen and Kit had played were also considerably neater. Even the small section of herbs that had once formed an intricate knot garden was beginning to take shape. But there was still so much more to do, and Celia was excited about doing it.

Celia was looking at the cherry tree by the terrace, still brilliant in its vernal raiment of pink and white, when she saw Colin step out onto the terrace. She smiled brightly, taking a step toward him, but her smile froze on her lips when she saw the anger that clouded his features.

She just stood there watching as he approached her. All the fears, all the insecurities that she had overcome since arriving here at Kildalton, all were revived in an instant. The look in Colin's eyes brought back the bleak, empty feeling that she'd lived with for so long.

"You didn't tell me," he growled accusingly. "Why didn't you tell me?"

"Colin, I . . ." she began helplessly.

Chapter 12

He only told us because of the discontent. This is planting time, and still we are moving north. The grumbling is getting louder, and there are even whispers of mutiny. So the devil tells us. Get the baby, he tells us. Or get the woman. She will bring us the baby in exchange. And then we will go home. By the King's order, we will go home.

But he will say anything, the devil.

Ambrose had brought them news. Not only news of Danvers's and Argyll's combined efforts in the Highlands, but also news of a missing bairn. Ambrose had told them how the Queen had been unable to produce the Crown Prince, a concern since no one outside of her household had even seen the bairn for over two months. Ambrose related that there were even rumors that the Queen had sent the Prince to her brother in England. But there was no news from England that intimated in any way that the Prince was there.

All anyone knew for certain was that Huntly and the other nobles were negotiating a peace with the English king that would assure the Stuart prince's safety and sovereignty. But still, the actual whereabouts of the little prince was uncertain.

But as soon as Colin heard Ambrose speak, he'd known where the bairn was. It hadn't been too difficult to piece together the events.

*   *   *

"He's the Crown Prince," Colin rasped through clenched teeth. "Isn't he?"

His face was black with the fury raging just below the surface. Celia felt a squeezing pain in her heart as she watched the muscles in his jaw contracting over and over.

"Aye, Colin," Celia said steadily. "He is."

"Why didn't you tell me?" he shouted, taking her by the wrists.

"I tried to tell you," she pleaded. His grip was hurting her, but she was determined not to fight him. She had intended to tell him. He had every right to be angry.

"Obviously, not hard enough," Colin spat out, releasing her and turning from her. "Why did you bring him here, anyway?"

"That wasn't what we planned . . . originally. Colin, let me . . ."

"Then how did I become part of your scheme?" Colin interrupted, turning back to her, his anger only barely covering the pain in his eyes.

"There was never any . . . scheme . . . when it came to you, Colin," she said in a quiet voice. His look hurt her.

"You expect me to believe that after all the lies?" he responded with scorn in his voice. "From the moment you arrived here, you've been hiding things. Everything about you has been a mystery or a lie."

"You must believe what your heart tells you to believe," she said, knowing her pain and disbelief were evident in her face.

"You talk about my heart," Colin shot back furiously. "You used me. You used my family and my people for your own mercenary ends."

So, this is what it comes down to, Celia thought. Mercenary. Like father, like daughter. This is what he thinks of her. Of her father.

"I never have," Celia answered, her voice steely. "But I assure you, I'll not risk using you again."

Celia stormed past the furious laird, but was stopped and whipped around by his fierce grip on her arm.

"You aren't going anywhere until I know who's paying for your ... services," he sneered.

The violence of Colin's words stunned her, and Celia's face took a moment to register the impact of his insinuation. Then rage colored her face as it surged through her. Celia's free hand shot out, and she slapped him hard across the face.

"You pig!" she spat, tears streaming from her eyes. "And I thought you were different. I'm not for sale, and I'm no mercenary. And I did not abduct the Prince for any ransom."

Celia wrenched her arm from Colin's grip and started for the terrace. Before she reached the steps, though, Colin overtook her and spun her around to face him.

This time, however, Celia's knife flashed menacingly in the space between them and Colin quickly released her arm. Then, pretending to ignore the weapon, he looked directly into her tear-stained face.

"If you're no mercenary, then who's behind this?" he asked, suddenly feeling unsure about what he'd done, about what he'd said. But she hadn't trusted him. Why? What was this game she was playing?

"Who's behind this? The Earl of Huntly and every one of your damned nobles who's remained loyal to the Scottish Crown," she snapped. Her body was shaking with anger.

It was Colin's turn to be stunned. Watching him, Celia wanted to run, to get away from his cold gray eyes. But her body would not move from the spot. Celia knew if she ran now, that would be the end. There would be no other time for explaining. The hate, the hurt, would replace everything else. She couldn't let that happen. She loved him.

"You mean, Huntly had you steal the Prince from his mother the Queen?" The magnitude of the action was difficult to fathom. Was this treason? Or was this patriotism?

"We didn't steal Kit, we saved him. Queen Margaret was planning to send him to England for a 'proper education' in the hands of her brother, King Henry."

Celia paused for a moment, looking into the face looming above her. It was not the same angry face she had confronted just a few moments earlier. She did not resist when Colin reached down and gently took the knife from her hand. Her body still shook with the anger and hurt that was running through her.

"You know what that means . . . proper education . . ." she continued. "He'd be imprisoned for his whole life . . . however long that might be. And I was being sent along to accompany him . . . Kit to prison . . . me to Danvers."

Celia stared straight ahead, a keen sense of loss tormenting her soul. Inwardly, she mourned. Colin's words rang in her ears. She'd betrayed him. He would not forgive.

Two gulls wheeled in the sun beyond the walls, diving at each other in a dance of airy circles.

Colin, too, stood steeped in misery. Why had he been such a fool? Why did he have to think the worst? After hearing of all her admirers, of her fame, of her independence as a woman, an insecurity had crept in, driving his thinking, his emotions. When he'd heard the news from Ambrose, he had made a snap judgment. He'd been searching for a reason why this beautiful woman had chosen him over all others. And then, foolishly, Ambrose's words had brought that reason to him. Aye, she'd just looked for his protection, his name, until her ends were served.

But how wrong he'd been. She was willing to gamble everything—her life, her happiness, her future—to secure the future of the Crown, to secure the future of Scotland.

She was willing to die to save the life of a bairn men were bent on destroying.

Colin reached out and took her hand in his. She did not resist his touch.

"Celia," he began gently. "Why didn't you trust me?"

"Colin, I have trusted you from the first day I met you. But I was not able to reveal the truth. I was under oath, but I knew that Kit was safe here. I just never thought they would find us here. I never intended for Runt or anyone else to be hurt."

"You couldn't know that Danvers's spies were everywhere. And Runt will heal. But don't you think I should have known that the Crown Prince of Scotland was here in my home? Under my protection?"

"Colin, it wouldn't matter," Celia replied, looking up into his concerned gray eyes. "I know you better than you think. If Kit were the last-born bairn of the lowliest peasant in Scotland, you would have protected him as a king . . . as your own."

Colin smiled at Celia and wrapped her tightly into his arms.

"You do know me, Celia," he said, gathering her even closer against him.

"Aye, Colin Campbell," she responded. "And now I know another side of you, as well."

"We never stop growing, love," Colin said thoughtfully. "We never stop learning."

"You were cruel to me, Colin," Celia whispered, her face against his chest.

"You wouldn't confide in me," he countered painfully, knowing that his words had really hurt her.

"That's true, and it crushed me inside, knowing that you'd see that as a betrayal of you," she answered, her eyes again welling up at the thought of it all.

"It wasn't a betrayal," Colin said, defending her

against her own charges. "You had taken an oath to protect the Crown Prince. But I was so insecure about you. About your independence, even about Ambrose's attentions."

"You aren't to blame for that," Celia answered, looking up into his face. "It was I who created that insecurity by not confiding in you."

"No," Colin replied shortly, shaking his head in response. He gazed down at the woman in his arms. "In spite of all the advantages I've had in my life, I still have much to learn. Maybe *because* of those advantages. I get angry when things don't go as I think they should."

"You mean you're spoiled?" Celia teased, smiling tentatively at him.

"Aye, my love," Colin admitted slowly. "And I don't share very well."

"But I thought the Campbells were the most sharing of the Scottish lairds," she said, moving her hands from his chest and encircling his waist with them.

"I'm very possessive of what's mine," he growled affectionately.

"Are you?" she asked in mock disbelief.

"Aye, Celia, you are one thing I won't share," Colin said seriously. "Not now, not ever."

"Do you still want me, Colin?" she asked, her eyes glistening in the noon sun.

"I've never stopped wanting you, Celia," he answered. "I love you."

"Colin, I love y . . ." she began, but did not finish as he stopped her mouth with a kiss.

They clung to one another, each cherishing the sudden knowledge that their love had taken them past an abyss that had threatened to swallow their happiness.

Resting his chin on the top of her head, Colin's gaze finally took in the garden before him. He had not even noticed the changes that Celia had wrought in a single morning.

Drawing his head back to comment to her about the huge brush pile, Colin realized that Celia's hair was tangled with brush. He smiled as he stepped back, examining her disheveled condition.

Celia's face was a blotchy smear of dirt, sweat, and tears. Taking her hands and spreading them to look at her dress, he saw that the evident scratches and dirt were proof of the hard work she'd put into the garden.

"You've been busy, this morning," he said, chuckling.

"Do you like it?" she asked, turning with a sweeping gesture of one hand. "It's just a start, but . . ."

"It's beautiful," he said, hardly looking at the grounds. His eyes were appraising this woman, whose beauty was not one whit diminished by the effects of her labor. Her face was an open expression of one at peace with herself. Colin sensed that he was seeing the Celia who was, for the first time, free of the burdensome secret of her cares and worries. She was radiant.

Glancing around at him, she realized that he wasn't even looking at her work. Whirling on him, she planted her hands on her hips and glared affectionately.

"You're not even looking, Colin," she scolded.

"Oh, aye. That I am," he responded. "And I'm seeing just what I want to see."

Celia's face became contemplative for a moment. Then, taking him by the hand, she led him to a newly cleared turf bench beneath the blossoms of the cherry tree.

"Colin, I want you to see me exactly as I am," she said, holding his hand in her lap. "And I want you to know everything I know."

Celia took a deep breath, thinking back over the past two years, wondering where to begin. She knew that there was so much he wanted to know about her—there was so much she had to tell.

Colin sat patiently, secure in this new level their relationship had reached.

"My life at court was a lonely life," Celia said. "Before the incident that Ambrose spoke of this morning, I had been a member of Queen Margaret's household, but in name only. My relationship with the Queen has never exactly been friendly. She made no secret of the fact that she didn't want me around her. She said often enough I should be married in England to the man her father had picked out ... just as she had to be in Scotland with the man her father had chosen for her. For Margaret, marriages are arranged, and love is a romantic illusion.

"I was in her entourage, but the Queen seemed powerless in matters regarding me, as if I were under the protection of the King himself. Her obvious dislike of me made me an outsider among the other women. Not even one of the Queen's ladies cared to know me. But that, in a way, was a blessing because I was able to spend time studying with Father William or in disguise, training with Edmund's soldiers. But it was borrowed time, and I knew it. Every day I felt as though the future would come crashing down on me.

"And then, two years ago, the King had the tournament that Danvers attended. I thought the time had come when I'd have to go to England with him. God knows, I tried to resign myself to my fate. But when I saw how he acted—so boorishly, so cruelly, so devoid of chivalry or even common decency—all the revulsion that I had for him flooded back into me. I struck him there not to bring any kind of acclaim upon myself, but rather to vent my hatred, my fury, and my disgust for him.

"For some reason, though, Danvers was not allowed to take me out of Scotland after the tournament, and he left soon after.

"But after that, my life at court changed. People noticed me who had never noticed me before. People spoke to me who had never spoken to me before. That was how I met the Earl of Huntly. After the tournament, he took pains to see that I was accepted at court. I realized that I had found a patron."

"Was he trying to arrange a marriage for you in his own family?" Colin asked, curious about Huntly's motives for helping this precious jewel.

"No, everyone knew that I was as good as promised to Danvers. And besides that, I had nothing to bring to his family."

"Celia," Colin responded, taking both her hands in his. "All the riches in the world cannot outweigh what you hold within you."

"Colin, not everyone values me as I know you do."

"You're wrong about that, my love," Colin smiled. "But I interrupted your story."

"Huntly's influence made me feel as if I'd found a country to call my own. I began to know that Scotland's history and mine were connected. I saw the struggle against English oppression as my own struggle. They were both struggles for independence. And during that time I learned about my heritage, about the history of Scotland, and about the Stuarts. I saw the goal of the Stuarts was to make Scotland a single country, one where everyone would have the ability to build a life that is good and wholesome, a life of his or her own choosing."

"What you say is true, Celia," Colin put in. "James's father and grandfather and great-grandfather all had that dream. And the Highlanders have fought them all. But under this James, the Western Isles and the Highlands were finally won over. He was a strong king, and with very few exceptions, the Highland chiefs grew devoted to him."

"But as you know," Celia continued. "Everything changed when the King fell at Flodden. Edinburgh had been struck with the plague at the end of last summer, so the court moved to the palace at Linlithgow. The Queen had been opposed to the King's decision to move against her brother, so before he went back to gather his forces at Edinburgh, the Queen left Kit and took just her inner circle of friends to the castle at Stirling. The Earl of Huntly was left in charge of the forces at Linlithgow, and Edmund and I were left there as well.

"For as long as I live, I'll never forget the days that followed the news of Flodden. The few men who straggled back gave out their news of the dead ... of their friends and neighbors and fathers and brothers ... and then the shrieking and the keening of the women and the old people and the children ... my God, Colin, it was horrible. The sight of the widows wandering ... wretched ... their children clinging to their dresses, their bairns wailing in their arms ..."

Celia paused as the horror of the memory ran its course once again in her mind.

Colin, too, recalled the past October. King James had sent him to aid the King's cousin, the Duke of Albany, in his fight against the English invaders in France. At first, he heard of an overwhelming victory by the Scottish over the English. But then, three days later, the truth had come to them about the devastating loss of the King, the majority of the Scottish nobility, and the thousands upon thousands of Scotland's finest young warriors, all destroyed in a single, bloody afternoon.

Colin's guilt and anguish had torn at him then—as it was tearing at him now. His unseeing gaze swept over the garden walls and out to the watery horizon. If only he had been there. If only he could have ...

"We received word from Argyll," Celia continued, drawing Colin's attention again. "He was one of the few earls to survive the slaughter, and he was going back to his holdings in the Highlands. He said that the King had been wounded and spirited toward Edinburgh.

"But no one knew for certain what had happened to the King. In fact, stories kept arriving at court that the King had been seen riding away from the blood-soaked field, or that he'd been captured and was en route to London. No one knew.

"The Earl of Huntly took only two days to ready his forces for a move to the southeast. He knew he had to fortify Edinburgh Castle in case the English followed up their butchery with an invasion of Scotland. And if the King's life were in jeopardy, he wanted to be near him. By the time Huntly reached Edinburgh, the town had been burned, but the English withdrew as he approached.

"But the night before his army left Linlithgow Palace, a detachment came from the Queen with a message expressing her safety concerns and demanding that the Crown Prince be sent west to Stirling. Huntly called Edmund in and told him that the Queen had commanded that I was to accompany the armed guard, as well, to Stirling in the morning.

"But it didn't make sense. The Queen had never wanted me near her. And there was no reason for her to be suddenly worried about my safety. Suspicious, Edmund went to the captain of the guard, a drinking man who owed Edmund for saving his skin a number of times. Well, Edmund found out that the captain's verbal orders were to take the 'Muir woman' and the Prince not to Stirling but only as far west as Falkirk, where they would be met by another escort.

"Edmund knew exactly what that meant, and so did Huntly. The Queen was turning her own bairn over to the English. Later, I heard that it was Lord Danvers who was waiting to ambush the escort at Falkirk.

"Huntly needed to act quickly. He couldn't defy the Queen publicly, and he had to march southeast to defend Edinburgh. He made a decision and had Edmund summon me and Father William.

"We were to take the Prince and go to Caithness Hall in the Western Lowlands for the time being. Edmund knew that Lady Caithness and her bairn had been in

England for months, and we had received word that Lord Caithness was among the dead. So Huntly decided we were to wait there at Caithness until Argyll arrived with a force to protect us. Until it was safe to return. We were to pretend that Kit was my own. With so many of our nobles dead at Flodden, a widow with a bairn would be, sadly, a common sight.

"Father William was the one who brought Ellen to us. We took the Prince and fled west, making a wide sweep around Falkirk and Stirling Castle. Our first weeks at Caithness Hall were uneventful, and I spent so much time with Kit that I grew to think of him as mine.

"But soon we heard stories of Danvers's bloody massacres. I know that he started his rampage after no one showed up at Falkirk. We also received word from Huntly that the King was dead, and that the Queen indeed had not made public that the Prince was missing. She seemed to be stalling—perhaps she was maneuvering for power, perhaps she had some other reason. Or maybe she was hoping that Danvers would find the child. I don't know. But Huntly's message made it clear that no one knew where we were—with the exception of Kit's uncle, the Earl of Argyll. If we needed anything, we were to send a message to Argyll."

"Argyll fooled a lot of people," Colin remarked, the sharp edge in his voice betraying the violence he was feeling. "He must have sent word to Danvers that you were at Caithness Hall."

"Aye," Celia responded, making the connection. "But at the time, we just thought it was part of Danvers's destructive sweep."

"So when you fled Caithness, you intended to go to Argyll?" Colin asked.

"Aye, the only thing that stopped us from going directly to Argyll's winter castle was that we had heard he was in the Northern Highlands at a gathering of the clan chieftains. When Kit became ill on the journey, it was

Edmund's suggestion that we come to Kildalton, sending
Father William on to the abbey near Argyll's holding.
He was to get word to us of the Earl's return.''

"I think I know the rest," Colin said, putting his arm
around her and pulling her against him.

"Not everything," Celia answered, sitting up straight.
"While we were at Argyll's castle, I heard from a bragging servant girl that he was planning to forcibly marry
me. For money, she said, which doesn't make any
sense.''

"Well, that was a plan that was doomed to fail," Colin
replied firmly. "You're mine, Celia."

Celia glanced up into his warm face. His eyes showed
so much of his character, his self-assurance, his emotions.
She looked across the garden, at the ivy that blanketed
the wall of the South Hall. She looked at that green
covering that had probably been planted by a single pair
of hands on a day perhaps much like this one.

"Colin, what happened last night was incredibly wonderful . . ."

"Aye," he interrupted. "We'll have a lifetime of nights
like that, my sweet."

"Please," she faltered, flustered at what she wanted—
and didn't want—to say. "You are not bound to me by
anything that happened last night. I came to your room
. . . You don't . . . I wouldn't . . ."

Colin lifted her chin gently until Celia was looking
into his eyes. Tenderly he placed his full lips upon hers.
Drawing only a whisper away, his words carried the
depth of his feeling for her.

"I love you, Celia," he said softly, stroking the side of
her face with his fingers. "That is what binds me to you."

Celia took Colin's hand and looked at him steadily.

"Colin, I have nothing to bring to this marriage. I
have no money, no name, no training as a wife . . ."

"Celia, you have everything that I need," he responded, answering her gaze. "You are all that I have ever wanted."

"But ... but ... you know I can't marry you," she said, looking away from him, trying to focus on the reality, the danger still threatening Kit, still awaiting all of them.

"I know you can," he responded, taking her chin again and bringing her gaze back to his own. "I know you want it the same as I."

"Oh, Colin," Celia blurted in frustration, leaping to her feet. Taking a couple of steps, she stood with her back to him, her arms wound tightly around her middle. "It has nothing to do with what I want. I still ... I have a mission that I must accomplish. I have Kit, and I can't think of ... I just don't know what will happen ..."

Colin moved up behind her and wrapped his arms around her. Pulling her tightly against him, he rubbed his cheek against her silky hair. Turning her around, he took both her hands in his.

"Celia," he began. "He is my king, as well. When the Prince was anointed at birth, I took an oath of fealty to serve and to protect him. Our oaths make us allies, but our love makes us invincible. Your mission is to keep him safe until Huntly secures his life and his throne. We are meant to be together. And like everything else we will face in our lives, we will overcome any obstacle and accomplish this mission together."

"But there is still Danvers," she said with frustration. "By now, he knows where we are. I know him, Colin. He might give up the search for Kit by Henry's order, but he'll never give up on me. He hates me. I wounded his pride. He'll not stop until he finds me."

Colin paused, weighing his answer carefully. He would not let her run for the rest of her life from the evil that had been haunting her. She would never have to run again.

"Then we let him find you ... here," Colin said firmly.

"I want him to come here, Celia. It is time he paid for the crimes he has committed across this land. It is time he and I met."

"Colin, he is evil," Celia responded quickly. This was the last thing she wanted—to bring the wrath of Danvers down on these innocent people . . . and on Colin. "He does not fight fair. He uses trickery. He uses spies . . ."

"Celia, trust me," he said reassuringly. "We will be ready for him. Kildalton is the strongest fortress in the Western Isles. We'll know when he's within a day's march or within a day's sail, and we'll let him put his own head in the noose."

A glimmer of hope lightened her soul—but only for a moment. The dangers were still so frightening. But Celia knew what Colin said was true. The only way to stop Danvers was to face him . . . and to kill him.

"Celia, we can't know for certain what the future brings. We can only prepare ourselves as best we can. We can only live today."

Celia nodded. "I know that, Colin. But when the time comes, you must remember that it is my fight, as well."

"Aye. I'll remember." Colin looked at the slender frame of the woman before him. Only when Danvers lay dead at his feet would Colin let Celia near her enemy. He smiled at her again.

"You're a liar, Colin Campbell"—she smiled back—"but a winning one."

"Then you'll marry me?" he asked.

"Aye, Colin," Celia whispered, moving into his embracing arms and tilting her face up against his chest.

"Together, my love," he growled softly, "nothing can stop us."

"Together, my love," she replied, lifting her slightly parted lips to his.

With a gesture as ageless as the love that bound them, the union of their lips sealed the covenant. Each feeling the warmth of the other, they stood pressed together—two bodies, two minds, two hearts ... one future.

The news of their intended marriage broke over the household that afternoon with the power of a tidal wave. The happiness and the excitement of the announcement were only surmounted by the disarray that resulted from Colin's insistence that the ceremony be held on Easter Monday. Agnes and Ellen wept, while Alec jokingly tried to talk "sense" into Celia. Lord Hugh simply smothered her with a hug tight enough to crack her ribs. Celia and Colin both laughed at Father William's threat of continued chaperoning in the days ahead. But the most important person of all still needed to be told. Edmund had gone down into the village with Alec's brother, and Celia and Colin awaited her uncle's return.

Edmund's response was extreme for a man of his reserve. His misty eyes and shaking hands betrayed the sheer joy he was inwardly experiencing. His congratulations were effusive and warm when they sat him down in the South Hall.

"Celia," he said seriously after the first excited moments. "Your father would have been thrilled by this match."

He paused for a moment to consider his next words.

"There are some things we need to discuss. Things about your father. And about his legacy for you."

"I'll leave you two, then," Colin said, excusing himself. He knew that Edmund had been like a father to Celia. They deserved some time alone together.

Celia could not let him go, however. She held tightly to his arm.

"Edmund, I'd like Colin to be present for this," she said softly, awaiting Edmund's nod before continuing. "Lord Hugh has already told me a great deal about my father. I know what he did and what he was."

"Then you know he was a great man," Edmund responded.

"All I really know is that he was a pirate, a merchant . . . and a loving father."

"Then you should also know that there were a great many needy people who benefited from your father's strength and openhandedness," Edmund continued. "He kept order on the western coasts of England and Wales. Peace-loving coastal villagers could live and prosper for the first time in generations, no longer fearing the raiding Spaniards and French.

"But it was not only his countrymen that he aided. Everywhere in the world that his trading business took us, he made an impression. It was routine for John Muir to transport food and water to islands and famine-struck areas from Ireland to the west coast of Africa. He took no profit from any of those goodwill missions, though. He always spent his own money."

Edmund looked at Colin. "In many ways, your father and Celia's had much in common." Colin nodded in affirmation.

"As much as Lord Hugh's interest focused on Colin, John's interest focused on you, Celia," Edmund continued. "One great difference was that Colin's father had Kildalton and Scotland. John Muir was in many ways a man without a country. He saw that as a liberating strength in many ways—he made his decisions free of the restraints of self-serving governments. But it also gave him concerns about where you could be safely raised. That was why he always kept you with him . . . after your mother passed away.

"Your father knew that after he died, all his possessions . . . and you . . . would probably be at King Henry's disposal. So he hid away as much of a fortune as he could for you. It's all tucked away safely in an abbey in Ireland. That treasure far exceeds the value of the fleet of ships that Henry confiscated for his own use—the ships that Danvers still lusts after. He didn't want you to know about this, though, until you were at a point in your life where you could control your own destiny. When it came to your future, he was afraid of everyone—King Henry, his own family, and every fortune hunter who might come seeking your hand in marriage. On his deathbed, he asked me to protect you as well as I could, and to try to get you to Scotland. He had more faith in James's sense of justice than in Henry's.

"So when Henry brought you into his web of an English court, I went to James and told him the truth. He had heard the rumors of John Muir's treasure. James was a good man, but he was also a shrewd businessman. He wanted that wealth in Scotland rather than in England, so he arranged to take you in. He never intended to send you back, and when old King Henry died, James simply ignored the agreement that he'd made concerning you. But he didn't want to do what Henry had done, trying to force you into marrying one of his favorites. He knew that you would eventually find a match for yourself."

Edmund looked across at the entwined hands of the two young people.

"And he was right, you have."

Dinner was far more exuberant than usual for the week before Easter, but the excitement was undeniable. The entire Campbell clan, it seemed, came out of the woodwork to wish their young laird well—and to cast approving looks at the bride. Colin was away from Celia for much of the evening, taking the customary comical advice and needling reserved for bridegrooms. At the center of the circle of clan women, Agnes had shown Celia off as if she were her own daughter. When they had spare moments, Agnes and Celia put their heads together, planning the wedding. With less than a week to put together a feast that might have been months in preparation, the flurry of activity would be dizzying.

Celia was nearly asleep when she heard the panel door open. Opening her eyes, Celia watched the warrior cross the room to her bed. She was so glad to see him, for she had not even had a chance to say good night to him in the crowded hall below. First putting a finger to her lips, though, Colin scooped up his smiling betrothed and started back for the open panel. Celia snuggled her head against his shoulder.

"If you're not careful," she whispered. "I'll get used to being transported like this."

"It's an old Highland custom to carry the bride over the threshold," he replied suavely.

Reaching the wall, the muscular giant turned to edge his way through the opening, but the narrowness of the aperture prevented him from slipping through smoothly. Cursing to the accompaniment of her giggling, Colin pushed and bumped at the sides of the entryway.

"Ouch!" Celia cried, giggling as she exaggerated the effect of a scrape against the door.

"Quiet!" he growled. "We're going over this threshold . . . if I have to take this damned wall down."

"Custom or no custom," she scolded, comically imitating his growl, "do you need to tear my arms off to do it?"

With a final heave, Colin actually managed to work them through the door and into the passageway. Pulling the panel closed with an awkward effort, Colin turned toward the light coming from the open panel into his room.

Seeing the narrowed corridor between the two fireplace walls, Celia glanced with disbelief at the look of devilish determination in Colin's eyes.

"Colin, *no!*" she gasped out, laughing out loud as the

warrior charged down the passageway, wedging them firmly between the walls.

"Oh, well," he sighed with a deadpan expression. "Another custom shot to hell."

Soon thereafter, however, a contented, albeit mildly bruised Celia lay in Colin's arms in his great bed. Her silky skin lay smooth against his warm body, and her eyes half closed in an attitude of satisfied tranquillity. Her fingers unconsciously caressed the sinewy contours of his chest.

"Celia?" Colin said softly.

"Aye?" she responded, propping herself up on his chest with one elbow.

His black hair lay in disarray upon the pillow, and his face was relaxed. His gray eyes peered lovingly up at her in the dim light as he reached up to play with the dark ringlets that hung about her face.

"Father William said tonight that he wants to talk to the two of us tomorrow," he said.

"About what?" she murmured, leaning down and kissing his skin. Laying her ear to his chest, she could hear his great heart beating. Sliding her hand across the taut skin of his belly, she smiled, listening to the pounding accelerate. Colin took a deep breath before continuing.

"I think he wants to have a little prenuptial talk about our . . . husbandly and wifely duties. Not that I think it's necessary, but it'll be either Father William or the Archbishop."

"The Archbishop?" she asked hesitantly.

"Aye, my love. He should arrive early on Easter Monday. And, trust me, his speech will be a wee bit sterner than Dunbar's."

"You don't think Father William suspects anything?" she asked quickly, her head shooting up to look him in the face.

"Aye, no question about it," Colin answered teasingly.

"Suspects? Definitely. Approves? Hmm . . . I'll ask him tomorrow."

"Colin! You won't!" she exploded. "You'd better not bring it up!"

The warrior laughed and lifted her bodily, rolling her onto her back. Laying his head on *her* chest, he listened to her heartbeat race as his hand traveled across the quivering velvet of her abdomen. Lifting his head, he looked smilingly into her eyes.

"Turnabout is not just fair play . . . it's fun, too," he growled. "Don't you think?"

Celia took his face in her hands and lifted her lips to his. The long, slow kiss was as tantalizing as it was satisfying. Laying her head back on the pillow, Colin's hand smoothed back the curls from her forehead, caressing the side of her face, the line of her chin. And all along, his eyes spoke the language of love.

"Celia," he whispered in a low voice. "Do you still want me . . . now that you're a wealthy woman?"

"Aye, Colin Campbell," she said tenderly. "My love is for life. Our wealth, our power, and our position have nothing to do with my love for you."

"I hope you know that I fell in love with the woman that you are," he responded. "Before I ever had any idea who you were, I knew I wanted to marry you. I knew I wanted to spend the rest of my life with you."

"I know that, Colin," Celia whispered. "Nothing outside of ourselves could ever change that."

Colin sealed her lips with a kiss. A hungry, searching, devouring kiss that was met with a fervor that equaled his own, and once ignited, their passion continued to mount, rising and soaring to an uncontrollable moment of ecstasy. Leaving them clinging to each other, breathless and awash in the warm waves of blissful love.

Chapter 13

What king sent us here? I'm so tired of these High-lands. There is nothing for us here. These Scots do not seem to feel the misery we inflict upon them. We even use them as our spies.

But I think I will never see England again. To-night I ride to the west with my company and a shifty-eyed scoundrel of this turncoat Gregor clan. I will probably die in the west, looking for the woman they say is there.

"God created sex."

Beneath the blossoming cherry tree, the old priest paced back and forth before the betrothed couple.

"My job today is to counsel you on the Church's posi-tion regarding the subject," he continued. "Though from my own study, it appears that Christ Himself had pre-cious little to say on the ... well, perhaps my own opin-ion is not particularly relevant at this moment."

Father William paused. He never thought he'd hear himself delivering this sermon to Celia and her future husband. All this silly interference in the natural re-sponse of a man and a woman to each other. Ridiculous.

Ah, well, he thought.

"The only purpose God created ... sex ... for was for the continuation of His people on earth."

"Then why, Father William," Colin interrupted, "does He allow pagans and infidels to make babies?"

"Colin, I like you," Dunbar grouched happily. This may turn out all right after all. "But if you keep on this track, we're going to have trouble. I don't want you trying to put me off the subject with theological quibbling. But ... well ... to answer your question—it's to keep the missionaries busy. Now, where was I?"

"Sex, Father," Colin said helpfully, receiving a white-knuckled·squeeze from Celia, who sat beside him on the turf bench beneath the cherry tree.

"Aye," the priest continued, picking up his train of thought. "Now, St. Paul had a great deal to say on the matter, far too much for the old bachelor he was, I'd say. But regardless of that, I've put together a little list for you concerning when, where, how you should feel free to enjoy ... er ... participate in the ... er ... act."

"A list, Father?" Celia asked incredulously, eyeing the rather long scroll of paper that her spiritual advisor was unrolling before them. She was certain Father William was, to some extent, teasing them, but the size of the scroll was certainly formidable.

"Celia, you surprise me!" Dunbar scolded, suppressing a smile. "Here you are, not even married yet, and you're already questioning my authority on these matters."

"Excuse me, Father William. You're an authority on sex?" Colin asked innocently. Celia tried to hide her laugh behind a pretended cough.

"Aye, of course! I've read volumes on the subject," Father William exploded, crooking a finger at the two. "You are not taking this matter seriously enough."

"Sorry, Father," Celia said, staring into her lap in an attempt to control her mirth.

"Aye, Father," Colin added. "I'll not interrupt again. Please go on."

"Well, that's better," the priest grumbled, smoothing out his paper and preparing to read. They were going to love this part. "Now, after you've been married for three days ... and *no* sex before then ... there are a number of conditions that must be met, every time, before ... er ... well ... before the act takes place."

Father William paused to look at the two young people sitting hand in hand before him. He had their attention for the moment, at least.

"Now," he continued. "Under pain of sin, you cannot have sex on *any* feast day. You cannot have sex on *any* fast day. You cannot have sex during Whitsun week. Nor during Advent. And certainly you wouldn't dream of having sex at any time during Lent."

He stopped for breath and to give the wide-eyed couple as stern a look as he could muster at the moment. Interesting, the color that Celia can turn, Dunbar thought, suppressing a smile.

"It is, of course, also a sin to have sex during Easter week, which I hope you two will bear in mind next week," he went on. "And you will not be having sex on Wednesdays, nor on Fridays, nor on Saturdays or Sundays."

"What day is today?" Colin whispered under his breath to Celia, drawing a threatening glare from the priest.

"You also cannot have sex at any time during daylight hours. You cannot have sex unless you're fully clothed. And, for heaven's sake, try to remember that you cannot have sex in church. And did I mention that the purpose of sex is to have a child?"

"Aye," Celia and Colin answered in unison.

"Very good." Father William grinned. "You must both *want* to have a child at the time of the act. Think of nothing else!"

He paused and stood squarely in front of the two with his hands on his hips, the rolled parchment in one fist.

"Once all these conditions are met, you may proceed ... *but*," he said, staging his most ominous look, "no lascivious kisses! No fondling of any kind!"

Celia playfully tried to pull her hand from Colin's grip, but the warrior held on tightly.

"And no ... er ... oral ... sex. No strange positions ... the natural order must be observed, you know ... males on top. We are very clear on that. And you may only perform the act once. And, for God's sake, clean up afterward."

"But most important of all, my children," he concluded emphatically, "don't enjoy it!"

The penitential guidebooks that he'd used to cull this list from had been serious business in the old days. But times were changing, and the worldly priest could see great changes ahead. And that would be fine, he thought. After all, some of these rules were due for a good dusting ... "natural order," indeed!

"Well, that behind us," Father William exclaimed, his voice becoming gentler, "I want you to know that in spite of all I've just told you, I know you both to be thoughtful, intelligent people, educated in the ways of reason and the world. What you have found in each other is to be cherished, nurtured, and passed on to the generations that will follow. You have discovered, and will continue to discover, your own unique way of expressing your love for one another, and that in itself is an expression of God's love. Celia, Colin, don't let anyone tell you differently."

Visitors soon began arriving at Kildalton from the neighboring areas. News of the wedding had quickly spread, and Lord and Lady Macpherson arrived on Wednesday with their entire family and bringing their Easter feast. To Colin's utter dismay, Agnes gave up her apartment to the guests and moved in with Celia. With all the attention and activity, the two lovers could not find even a moment alone until Lord Hugh's long anticipated Easter hunt, when good fortune caused Celia's horse to throw a shoe.

Over Alec's exaggeratedly courteous offers to escort Celia back to Kildalton, Colin swept his bride up onto the saddle before him and rode off, leaving the high-spirited party behind. A few stolen kisses were all they could enjoy, though, due to the groups of trailing revelers whom they passed at intervals on their return to the castle.

Later, as the festive hunters returned, they heard in great detail how remarkably well the falcons had performed.

The Easter feast that evening was celebrated with customary revelry, but everyone knew that the day's jubilation was only a precursor to the gala week that would follow.

Discussion at dinner quite naturally dwelt on the following day's wedding. While Agnes and Celia worked out final details, Father William scurried around, busily taking various members of the party aside to tell them what their parts would be in the pageantlike masque that would be performed during the wedding dinner.

"Well, my dear, I believe we're all ready for tomorrow," Agnes said, closing the door after the seamstresses who had just completed the finishing touches on the wedding dress.

Celia drew on her robe and cast a glance over at the gown hanging by Ellen's door. On the small bed that had been brought in for Agnes, the bride could see the seemingly endless accessories and undergarments.

"You've really gone to so much trouble, Agnes," Celia said, smiling at her companion.

"Nonsense, child." Agnes shrugged. She went over and sat down beside Celia on the great bed. "Did you get that certain ... item ... back from the metal smith in the village?"

"Aye," Celia replied, her eyes sparkling. "Would you like to see it?"

"Of course," she responded, watching as the young woman sprang from the bed and ran to the chest by the windows.

A knock at the door stopped Celia from opening the chest, and she turned an inquisitive eye toward the sound.

"It's Colin," came the reply to Agnes's question.

"Just wait, you scoundrel," Agnes called, smiling at Celia and motioning for her to sit by the fire. Quickly she scooped up the dress and carried it into Ellen's room. Returning in a moment, she crossed the room and opened the door.

The young warrior entered, moving just inside the door. Colin's eyes locked on his bride immediately. My God, she was a vision of beauty. He had missed her so much. For the past four days they had hardly had a moment alone together. For the past four nights Colin had lain in his big, empty bed—just a passage away from her—thinking of her, longing for her. And now, her bright smile, so warm, so inviting, tantalized and made Colin's heart race. If this was how life would be from now on, he would never leave Kildalton—he might never even leave their room.

As Colin entered, Celia stood up, took a step toward him, and then, remembering the presence of Agnes, stopped. She wanted to rush right to him, to throw her arms around him and crush herself in his embrace. If she'd known that the wedding preparations and the arrival of guests would have kept them apart as much as it had, she would have run away with him instead.

"Hello, Colin," Celia said shyly.

"What do you want, you rascal?" Agnes teased gently.

"Agnes," he said, not taking his eyes off the beauty before the fire. "I'd like a few moments alone with Celia."

"Colin Campbell," she scolded. "If you think I'm

going to leave you alone with a defenseless young woman . . . I can see the way you're looking at her."

"Agnes, I promise I'll behave," Colin countered, smiling. "If you like, I'll leave the door open."

"All right," she conceded. "I'll just look in on Ellen and Kit. But no funny business."

Casting a warning look at Colin, Agnes turned and winked warmly at Celia before moving across the room, closing Ellen's door behind her. As soon as she disappeared, Celia rushed into Colin's outstretched arms.

They held each other in a clasp so tight, so warm, that Celia thought she could mold herself to him, as if they were two soft wax figurines. Colin, too, could not absorb enough of her—his hands tunneled through the soft auburn tresses, skimmed along her shoulders and her back. Celia's sweet jasmine fragrance filled his senses with a headiness that was dizzying. And now, as if they had not kissed for years, they devoured each other, unable to satiate the driving hunger that ached within them.

"I've missed you so much," he breathed into her ear. "If my love for you grows any greater, I may just lose my mind."

"You've been on my mind every moment that we've been apart," Celia whispered in return. "Even when you were just a moment out of my sight, I found myself straining to catch a glimpse of you."

"Well, we're together now," Colin responded, his mouth closing on hers, driving and feeding their need.

"Agnes tells me that I've been calling you in my sleep," she purred, drawing back and placing her forehead against his scorching lips.

"Then you've been having the same dream I've been having," he replied, his hands running down over the firm curve of her backside.

"Colin," she cried softly, a wistful look in her eyes. "How long do we really have to wait before . . before . . . ?"

"About five minutes after the ceremony tomorrow," Colin growled. "That's how long it will take us to get out of the church. Father William did say that we can't make love in a church, I think."

"Colin, you're a devil," she murmured, her hands caressing the small of his back. "We're not going to ignore Father William's advice."

"Ignore it? Absolutely not, my love," he answered, running his lips over the silky skin beneath her ear. "Think of all the things we'd be missing."

"Like what?" she whispered innocently.

In his mind Colin ran through just a few of the things they would experience together, and felt the hot, piercing sensation emanate from his loins. He pulled away from her with a deep breath and a supreme attempt to master his rapidly crumbling self-discipline.

"Don't get me started now, my sweet," he rumbled gently. "I'm having a hard enough time restraining myself as it is ... Tomorrow, love."

Colin took Celia's hand and led her to the two chairs beside the fire. Seating her on one of them, he removed a satchel from his shoulder and placed it on the floor beside his chair.

"As usual, you've completely distracted me from what I came in here for."

"I'm sorry, Colin," she answered, smiling coyly.

"Don't be sorry," he replied. "I'm looking forward to a lifetime of being distracted by you."

Taking her hand again, he gazed lovingly into the lustrous blackness of her eyes.

"I have something for you, Celia," he said softly.

Without another word, he reached down and opened the satchel at his feet. From it he removed a small bundle of blue velvet, tied with two white silk ribbons. Looking tenderly into her face, he laid the gift in her hands.

"Colin, there is nothing that you need to give me. You've already given me everything."

"Open it, my love."

Celia carefully pulled at the bows securing the velvet wrapping and opened the soft folds of cloth.

Within it lay a gleaming circlet of gold.

Lifting the precious gift, Celia looked with awe at the coronet of the Campbell clan. Beautifully wrought to resemble a weave of golden cords, the circlet was embedded with alternating emeralds and rubies ... the Campbell colors.

"Colin," she gasped. "This is magnificent! I can't ..."

"This is only a part of all that is yours, now. You are Lady Campbell."

Celia threw her arms around his neck, and Colin pulled her onto his lap. Taking the coronet from her hand, he started to place it gently on her head, but Celia stopped him with her upraised hand.

"Tomorrow, my love," she whispered. "I can't wear it until tomorrow."

"Why not?" Colin exclaimed.

"Agnes tells me that it's very bad luck for the bridegroom to see the bride wearing any part of her bridal outfit before the wedding ceremony."

"She certainly is enjoying this." The groom laughed. "I've never seen her so elated."

"Colin," Celia whispered, laying a finger softly on his lips. "Of course she's elated. You are a son to her—the only child she'll ever have. But wait here a moment."

Taking the crown back from him, Celia bound from his lap and crossed the room to the great chest. Returning to the fire, she carried only a soft lambskin packet. Colin welcomed her back into his lap with a laugh.

"Oh, I shouldn't have gifts for you, but you have gifts for me?" he growled affectionately.

"I hope you like this, Colin," Celia said, offering him the packet.

Colin pulled the leather thong and opened the flap of leather. Reaching in, he brought out a long dagger housed in a gold-trimmed ebony sheath. The handle was steel and ebony and the steel hilt was fashioned like a scroll embedded with gold chain. At the ends of the hilt, two sapphires gleamed, matching the single larger sapphire set in the heel of the weapon.

Colin looked from the gift to Celia's neck and reached for the pendant that she wore. It wasn't there, and he knew that he was holding it in his hand.

"Celia, that pendant was the only remembrance you had of your mother," he said in a ragged whisper.

"And I'll think of her whenever you wear it," she replied, her eyes misty.

"I'll wear it always, my love," he said hoarsely. "Nothing will make me part with it."

"I had them inscribe it, Colin," she said.

Colin drew the dagger from the sheath and inspected the two entwined C's that had been etched into the blade just above the hilt. His eyes showed the emotion that was overflowing in his heart, and he drew her tightly to him in an embrace that conveyed the feelings that he hardly dared entrust to his constricted throat.

"We, too, are entwined, my sweet, like a thistle and a rose," Colin whispered raggedly. "I am that thistle, and you the rose. We, too, are entwined, and it is the embrace of love ... indivisible, invincible, eternal."

Celia fought down the mad desire to weep for joy.

"I love you, Colin," she whispered.

Chapter 14

The Scottish dawn broke with the fresh blue brilliance of spring, and the morning was filled with the busy preparations of the day.

But just before midday, Celia climbed onto a magnificent bay horse, its harness gleaming with silver and gold. Riding between Edmund and Agnes, the bride began the short journey to the village church at the Marketcross by the harbor. Her two companions were dressed in the finest of clothes, and Edmund was wearing the golden medallion of the Knights of St. Andrew.

Although neither Agnes nor Edmund had ever married, or had ever had a child of their own, both looked on the young woman between them with the pride of natural parents. Agnes had been moved to tears when Celia had asked her to accompany her to the church, and she now more than ever believed that destiny had brought Colin and Celia together. Celia had found a niche in Agnes's heart that only Colin had occupied before. Edmund glowed happily, as well, thinking of the years and the miles that had brought them to this place, to the fulfillment of such cherished dreams.

Emmet and five of Colin's lead warriors, all adorned in Campbell tartans, met them inside the castle's gaily bannered gates, and a hundred mounted fighters awaited as an escort just outside. Trumpets sounded as they left the castle, and a brigade of pipers led the procession noisily toward the town.

This was to be a wedding for all, and the whole village

teemed with the folk of the clan and the Campbell holdings. As soon as the bride entered the village, a great
shout went up, and laughing children ran alongside the
entourage. Everywhere Celia looked, the newly painted
houses and gates sparkled with brilliant greens and reds
and blues. Banners and tartans, flags and tapestries, hung
from every window. And the folk themselves, dressed in
their finest holiday clothes, gathered all along the village
streets to cheer for their new lady and to join in the
growing procession to the church. Festivity and hospitality were the watchwords of the day.

When Celia reached the filled Marketcross, she could
see that even the boats in the harbor had been decked
out for the occasion. In the square itself, pipers and minstrels joined in the chorus of musicians that had led her
cavalcade, and the air was filled with euphonic sounds
of joyous music. From the church belfry and from the
ships in the harbor, the sound of bells ringing out completed the symphonic reception.

The crowds parted for the gaily decorated troop of
warhorses, and Celia was brought before the raised
stone platform at the center of the Marketcross. There,
a misty-eyed Lord Hugh, the entire clan council, and a
delegation of leaders from the village stood in smiling
appreciation of the sight before them.

When Lord Hugh raised his two hands, the bells
ceased to ring, and a sudden and complete hush fell over
the crowd. Celia turned to Agnes who, with a reassuring
smile, reached over and squeezed her hand.

"Sir Edmund Bruce," the Campbell chieftain thundered in a voice all could hear. "Do you deliver this
bride, Lady Celia Muir, freely and without reservation,
to be joined with Colin Campbell, heir to the lordship
of the Campbell lands and the Western Isles?"

"Lord Hugh Campbell," Edmund proclaimed in return. "With the wholehearted consent of the lady her-

self, I deliver her to you as the bride of Lord Colin Campbell!"

Immediately a cacophony of cheers and music erupted from the crowds all around Celia, who was helped from her horse and introduced by Lord Hugh individually to the entire leadership assembled there. The formalities completed, Agnes, Edmund, and the rest of the dignitaries filed quickly into the church. Then, with great pomp and a wave at the crowd, Hugh led Celia across the square to the church.

Colin stood between Father William and the Archbishop by the altar in the packed church. As the last of the wedding guests filed in, the spring sunlight streamed through the stained-glass windows and glittered on stone-carved figures of saints and angels. Alec, standing beside his family at the front of the assembly, nodded at his friend. He had been a constant thorn in Colin's side all morning, "helping" the groom with jokes, bad advice, and even offers to stand in for the Campbell heir ... should Colin have second thoughts.

A hush fell over the congregation as the grand and courtly sound of a lone bagpipe commenced. Colin's eyes strained at the brilliant light of the open doorway for a first glimpse of his bride, and he did not have long to wait.

Lord Hugh and Celia entered the church, and Colin froze, aware of the drumming of his own heart within his chest.

Celia's auburn ringlets hung loose beneath the Campbell coronet. Her black eyes flashed as they focused on Colin, and her gown of white, ornately embroidered with threads of gold, glittered as she crossed the threshold on the arm of Lord Hugh. Colin felt the heat of a thousand suns rush into his face as he gazed upon the ravishing beauty who was advancing toward him.

Walking toward the altar, Celia saw nothing but Colin. Magnificent, dashing, handsome, and more.

Richly arrayed in his finest kilt, a black velvet cape hanging loosely over one shoulder and the Campbell tartan across his broad chest, Colin was every bit the Highland laird. But Celia's eye was caught by the ebony-handled dagger that hung conspicuously from the velvet sash about his waist and by the loving gaze that was riveted upon her.

Lord Hugh, dressed similarly to Colin, with the addition of the gold chain of the Peerage, delivered Celia's steady hand into his son's and, beaming proudly, took his place beside Agnes and Edmund. Indeed, his son had done well, he thought. There had been looks approaching awe as they'd walked to the altar. Celia had the bearing of a queen and the beauty of an angel, but the heart of a saint. And Hugh could sense that others knew that, too. Constance would have been very proud of her son's choice.

The Archbishop, a stern-faced and lighthearted cleric, stood with Father William and listened as Celia and Colin exchanged their vows of love and fidelity, before God and their community. What the Lord hath joined, let no man put asunder.

One by one, the leading members of the Campbell clan approached the altar and the newly wedded couple. One by one, the Campbell knights and fighters knelt before their new lady and pledged their lives and their service to her. The solemnity of their vows, adding to the emotionally charged moment of the wedding event, wracked Celia . . . body and soul. She fought back tears as Emmet and Runt placed their hands over their hearts and delivered their oaths.

As Colin and Celia worked their way out of the church, their ears were greeted once again with the melodious sounds of pealing bells and bagpipes. Outside, the crowds of well-wishers surged against the church steps. The wedded couple stopped at the top, and the crowd quieted immediately.

"Good people of the Campbell clan," Colin proclaimed loudly, holding Celia's hand tightly. "I give you . . . Lady Campbell."

The tumultuous shouts and cheers that followed overwhelmed Celia, and her tears were streaming down her cheeks as Colin swept her up in his arms and kissed her before the entire village. From the ships in the harbor, cannons fired an ongoing salute to the delight of the crowd, and Celia felt as if she were walking on a cloud as they began their procession back up through village festivities to the castle looming benevolently above.

The wedding dinner in the Great Hall was a sumptuous feast accompanied by dancers, musicians, and minstrels. Colin and Celia were inseparable, in spite of all efforts to include them in the ongoing entertainment. Colin held her hand tightly and glared menacingly at any who approached to kiss the bride with anything but the most respectful attitude. And he was particularly threatening when Alec Macpherson took momentary possession of Celia's hand.

"Celia," Alec said in a confidential tone, ignoring Colin's ominous presence. "I was just having an interesting conversation with the Archbishop about annulments."

"Macpherson . . ." Colin growled over ‑Celia's laughter.

"Everyone! Please come into the South Hall!" Dunbar called out. "We have a wee bit of entertainment for you."

The priest looked over at Alec and Colin, each holding one of Celia's hands, and shook his head questioningly. "Lord and Lady Campbell? Would you and Lord Alec care to join us?"

Without any attempt to hide the action Colin detached

Alec's hand from Celia's and put himself between the two as they started for the South Hall entrance.

Everyone filed through the double doors and took places along the wall beneath the windows as Runt disappeared through the entrance and returned in a moment, giving Father William a nod. All was ready.

"Lord Colin, if you would be so kind as to play the part of the Lover," the poet priest requested, beckoning Colin to a place a bit more than halfway down the hall from the entrance. Colin stood undecided for a long moment, to the obvious enjoyment of those looking on.

"And if I could borrow your lovely bride . . . just for a short while . . . to play the part of the Lady Beloved," Dunbar continued.

Runt took Celia's arm, and Colin stopped him with a look. "If anything happens to her, Runt . . ." the giant warned.

"It's a happy ending, Lord Colin." Runt smiled weakly. "I won't take my eyes off her."

With a grunt of grudging resignation, Colin let go of her hand, and Runt led her from the hall.

"Lord Hugh, Lady Agnes, Lord Alec?" Father William continued. "If you would kindly accompany the exquisite Lady Campbell . . . or, rather, the Lady Beloved . . . to your preordained position."

As Celia passed Colin, her smile was enough to warm the entire hall, and everyone in attendance felt it—but none more than the bridegroom. Colin found himself wishing this day to be over, and all the guests either gone or safely tucked in—especially Alec. As his eyes followed the beauty . . . the Beloved . . . through the entrance, Colin found himself wishing . . .

"Ladies, lords, gentlefolk of the Campbell lands!" Dunbar called out from his place at the center of the hall, drawing the guests' attention. "This evening, through the gracious generosity of Lord Hugh Campbell, to help celebrate the union of two loved ones, we present to you a masque ... a pageant ... a play."

Father William paused for effect, then swept his arms like a magician conjuring up a new world ... a world of imagination. The guests were so quiet that the only sound was the crackle of the fires in the great hearths. Then the music of lyres, oboes, and trumpets floated harmoniously in the air.

"Just as the star of day began to shine," the poet began, taking Colin's hand and leading him in a small circle and ending where he began. "The Lover rose up and by a rosebush sat down to rest, for no sleep had he for many days or nights.

"When up sprang the golden candle of Dawn, with clear, crystalline beams of light. And before Phoebus had risen and shed his cloak of purple, the lark, heaven's minstrel, in joy called out to the Morn.

"Then, angellike, the birds sang in the green, green bowers, and the fields were a blanket of colors. Enameled with dew, the meadow gleamed red and white with the May flowers so bright and new. The sun shone on the young rosebuds, the dewdrops burning like ruby sparks. And the birds skipped in the branches in the glory of the spring."

Dunbar took a few steps toward the entrance and turned once again to face the enraptured guests.

"Beside the spot where the Lover lay," he proclaimed, gesturing with his hands toward the entrance end of the hall. "A blue and glittering loch washed the green banks of the meadow.

"There, suddenly," Dunbar called out dramatically in a loud voice, "the Lover saw, as if in a fantastic dream, a sail as white as a blossom upon a green spray, and a ship of gold sped as quickly as a falcon to the shore."

To the surprise of all the guests, what appeared to be

a small, golden boat glided halfway into the open double doors of the hall entrance, a white sail fluttering above.

"And to the Lover's amazed eyes, a hundred fair maidens in clothes of purest white, their glittering hair whipped with golden threads, tripped gaily from the ship and, like dancing lilies, frolicked in the meadow green. Homer and Cicero, with tongues sweet, could not describe the beauty of this paradise."

Two servants quickly placed a plank on the low railing of the boat, and stood by to lend a hand as a dozen or more girls and young women from the village skipped down from the ship and out into the hall, to the appreciative applause of the surprised onlookers.

"And then entered Cupid the King and love's queen, Venus, on his arm," the poet continued, directing the audience's attention back to the ship, where Lord Hugh and Agnes were walking in majesty down the plank and toward three chairs that had been placed at the end of the hall. "And with the company came the lusty knight, Duty, who carries with him the magnificent Golden Targe of the gods."

With great pomp, Alec, as Duty, strode from the boat and stood at his place behind the third chair between "King Cupid" and "Queen Venus." On his arm he bore a brilliant, round shield, the Golden Targe, which he held aloft to the crowd's murmurs of approval.

"And then the Lover spied the Lady who, with her handmaiden, Beauty, entered the meadow to do homage to the spring."

Colin hardly heard the loud cheers as Celia entered the hall. Like a glorious queen, she glowed with a majesty that literally stopped the breath within him. She was like some divinity sent from above. And Celia's eyes never left him as she and a village girl made their way to where Hugh and Agnes awaited them. The young maiden, as Beauty, sat demurely before her Lady.

"As these lovely ladies danced and played, the Lover

hid himself among the green leaves, content to watch the merriment . . . and the Lady. But then, Venus herself spied the spectator and called on her party to arrest the Lover."

As Agnes stood and pointed at Colin, the maidens formed a line to attack him.

"But then the warrior Duty, in armor of plate and mail, with shield of gold, came to the aid of the Lover and defended the noble knight," Dunbar continued, and Alec crossed the room with the gilded shield held high.

"Into the press pursued Youth, Green Innocence, and Obedience. On followed Nurture, Patience, and Stead-fastness. A cloud of arrows fell like a shower of hail."

When the warrior reached Colin, he held the targe up, fending off the invisible arrows that the attacking maid-ens were launching in pantomime at the Lover. The white-clad ladies encircled the Lover and Duty, his de-fender. Again and again they pretended to press forward and then fall back as if repulsed in their efforts.

"Alas, their efforts were rebuffed—the Golden Targe allowed none to find their mark. To Venus and the King they retreated."

Like trained dancers responding to the sound of the music, the village women flew across the floor to Venus and the others. The village maid, as Beauty, rose to her feet at Agnes's beckoning.

"Then Venus the Queen called out for the damsel Beauty to lead her troops once more into the fray."

Crossing to Duty and the Lover, at the head of her legion, Beauty held her fist up in the air, as if holding something in it, and, on the poet priest's word, pre-tended to throw it at Alec.

"Then Beauty cast a powder into Duty's eyes, and he staggered unseeing as a drunken man. Alas, when he was blind, they played the fool with him and led him away."

With a shout of cheerful merriment, some of the ladies

spun the "blind" Duty around and led him playfully away.

"And Beauty took the defenseless Lover as her prisoner," Dunbar went on as the young girl took Colin by the hand directly to Celia, who was now standing between Lord Hugh and Agnes.

"She led him to his Beloved, where he pledged his life and his love to her service."

Great cheers went up as Colin took the blushing Celia by the hand and kissed her soundly before the entire assembly.

Father William approached the couple and whispered a word to them. Then, leading Lord Hugh and Agnes and the entire group of performers, the wedded couple paraded hand in hand before the guests and stopped in the center of the hall.

As they came to a halt before the assembled host, Runt and Ellen entered with Kit and delivered the infant to Celia, who in turn handed the smiling baby to Colin. Colin carefully held the child aloft for all to see, and then gave the infant back to Celia. The crowd applauded happily.

Calling for silence with an upraised hand, Dunbar addressed the audience once more, directing their attention to Edmund, who was marching solemnly across the hall between the performers and the guests.

"And then . . . And then . . . Behold! All at once, Aeolus the Wind enters and spreads his airy blessing. And the Lover and the Beloved and all of that happy legion fled once again to the ship." Celia and Colin led the others across the floor to the ship at the entrance, where all quickly disappeared from sight. The plank was removed, and the ship began to back out the doorway. "In a twinkling of an eye, the ship departed, and out over the flood they flew. And the cannons roared in joyful celebration . . . until it seemed the heavens had opened."

As Dunbar concluded his final words, all of Kildalton's cannons came booming to life in a thunderous chorus of tribute.

Amid the wild cheering of the guests, the performers filed back into the hall, with Lord Hugh and Agnes in the lead.

The last to enter, Alec paused at the door. And with a broad smile on his face, he held up his hand.

"Lord Campbell and Lady Campbell have retired for the night!" he shouted to the boisterous revelers.

Once the assembly had returned to the South Hall, Alec heartily shook Colin's hand and kissed Celia on the forehead and pushed the two of them toward the steps.

Hand in hand, the newlyweds ran all the way to the top of the great stairs. Once there, Colin reached down and swept the blushing Celia into his arms, carrying her the remainder of the way to his room. As they reached his closed door, Celia took his chin in one hand and looked directly into his eyes.

"My bruises have barely healed from the last time we worked on this tradition," she said coolly, her efforts to hide her smile proving inadequate. "I don't recall anything in the ceremony about having to serve as a battering ram."

With a wry smile, Colin kicked open the heavy oak door and carried her straight through into the room.

Going to the bed, he deposited her gently on the edge and kissed her slowly, his mouth lingering on hers with a tangible promise of what was to come.

"Don't go anywhere," he said with a smile, crossing the room to the door and barring it shut.

The room was adorned in a style befitting a royal couple. Everywhere Celia looked in the candlelit room, there were signs of Agnes's thoughtfulness and taste. Every table held stoneware vases of daffodils and tulips and greenery. A multitude of dishes held every imaginable food, prepared with care and presented with artistic flourish. Bottles of ale and French wines sat amid a sparkling collection of crystal goblets, and a small fire crackled cozily on the stone hearth.

"Colin," Celia said, surveying the spread in the room. "We have enough food here to last us a week!"

"That's the plan, my love," he responded with a grin as he moved back to the bed. "It's the custom for the bride to stay in the apartment until the fourth day. We wouldn't want you to starve."

"What do you mean, 'you'?" Celia asked. "Where are you going to be?"

"Well, customarily, the groom participates in the festivities that have been planned for the next week while the bride ... rests." Colin paused. "But I thought we'd change that."

"You mean"—Celia smiled—"that you're going to rest with me?"

"I thought we might rest a little ... play a little ... play a little ... maybe play a little more ..." As Colin spoke the words, he stood in front of Celia and removed her crown, placing it on a small table beside the bed. Then, taking both of her forearms in his hands, he lifted her to him. Running his hands into her auburn locks, he pulled her head back and stared into her beautiful face, her loving eyes.

Celia felt his strength as he pulled her up from the bed. And then, his lips were on hers. Suddenly she wanted to bury herself in him, lose herself, drown in him. Her body arched as she pressed against him, her breasts hurting inside the tight wedding garments, hurting as she pushed against his hard chest, hurting for his touch.

As their mouths caressed searchingly, Colin's hands traveled across the tight bodice of the gown, finding their way to the back, to the thousand and one buttons that imprisoned the body that he longed to feel.

Celia knew that her warrior husband's patience was

growing thin as he fumbled with the first few buttons. He was looking over her shoulder and muttering strange curses when Celia drew Colin's new dagger from the sheath at his waist.

"Colin?" she said, pulling away from him and holding the weapon up.

"Hmm." He nodded with a smile, taking it from her and pulling her back tightly to him.

The whirring sound of pearl buttons being shaved from the thick material was one of the most liberating Celia had ever experienced. Reaching up, she undid the gold clasp that held the black cape on his shoulder. With one motion, Colin ducked out of the leather strap and the scarf of Campbell plaid that crisscrossed his white shirt.

A sense of urgency was building between them as they felt a growing need to remove each other's clothing. As Celia began to slide the gown forward off her shoulders, Colin reached over to place the dagger on the table with the coronet.

"Don't disarm too quickly, love," Celia said enigmatically.

Colin turned to see his bride confined in a corset that revealed more than it hid. The ivory skin of her neck and shoulders, the swells of the bound-up breasts, the long, smooth arms that reached out to him. He took her into his arms and kissed her deeply, longingly, passionately.

"Colin?" she whispered breathlessly into his ear. "Would you help me out of this?"

Colin turned her around and, with a single pass, cut the crisscross of laces that fastened the garment so tightly. Celia shook the corset to the floor and stepped out of the multitude of slips. When she turned around she was dressed only in a silk shift, and Colin was wearing only his kilt, the white shirt tossed carelessly aside.

Celia was drawn into Colin's embrace as the morning dew is drawn to the sun.

The hours that followed were filled with discovery and passion. It seemed to Celia as if one satisfying moment led into the next. As if one fulfilled desire evoked another. Finally, basking in the warm glow of their love, they lay wrapped in each other's arms, watching the colors outside the window lighten with the encroaching dawn.

"That busy old fool of a sun will be peering in at us in no time." Colin smiled, covering Celia's shoulders.

"Colin," she breathed, dozing snugly in the warmth of his embrace. "I think I know why brides get four days to rest."

"Celia," he responded teasingly. "Do you want four days to rest?"

Celia snuggled even closer to him. "I'm getting all the rest I need, right now, thank you."

Those four days were the happiest of Celia's life.

Everyone respected the newlyweds' time together, and Celia and Colin made the most of it. Between the hours of leisurely lovemaking in which Celia learned so much about what a man and a woman can be to each other, they spent time with Kit, giving Ellen and Runt time to share as well. Colin genuinely enjoyed the attentions of the baby and the antics that Kit seemed to save only for him. Once, while watching them playing together, Celia grew misty-eyed, thinking that the day would soon come when she would have to part with Kit.

When Colin noticed the emotion in her face, he casually mentioned that Father William had very clearly stipulated that making babies was a top priority for lovers. The suggestive tilt of his eyebrows made Celia both blush and ardently wish for Ellen's speedy return.

On the day after the wedding, following lunch, Colin took Celia to the garden. To her amazement and delight, the garden had been transformed. It appeared that an army of gardeners had been at work, and Colin admitted that there had been a few members of the castle staff employed in the clean-up.

The walls had been cleared of old, dead vines, and a fresh coat of whitewash had been applied. All of the beds and paths had been emptied of debris. Even the fountain had been cleaned, and Celia dipped her fingers into the cold, clear water flowing within it. The turf bench seats had all been trimmed and large pots of soil had been placed at a number of spots, awaiting Celia's choice of plantings. New trellises replaced the old ones and climbing roses had been pruned and arranged upon them.

"It's all ready for you, my love," Colin whispered, looking over her shoulder and wrapping his arms around her. "It's all yours to do with as you please. I just couldn't see you getting scratched up anymore, correcting twenty-five years of neglect."

"Oh, Colin," she said, overtaken with emotion. "I hope I can make this garden as happy a place as it was when your mother was alive."

"You already have, love," he said. "You've brought my father back out here. He even had the door into the chapel yard opened." Colin pointed at the narrow door in the wall.

"Could we go in there, Colin?" she asked. "I don't want to intrude on your own memories, I just . . ."

"She would have loved you, Celia," he interrupted. "And this castle is your new home now, just as it was once her new home. We are already making our own memories."

Taking her hand, Colin opened the door and led her through the wall into the chapel yard. Cool, green, and walled, the small area was quartered by two crossing paths. To her left, Celia saw an entrance into the castle's small chapel. To her right, she saw a crypt. Walking side by side down the path, they entered the crypt, and Celia saw the reclining sculpture of a young woman. Beside his wife's resting place, Lord Hugh had readied his own, though no sculpture adorned the marble slab that awaited him.

Celia knelt respectfully beside the grave, and after whispering a quiet prayer, she stood and turned to Colin, who stood pensively behind her.

"Thank you, Colin," she said.

Colin smiled lovingly and nodded, and the two went back into the garden.

There, in the friendly surroundings of their little paradise, they sat beneath one of the cherry trees and talked. The pinkish-white flowers of the cherry blossoms were just beginning to fall, and they laughed at the snowlike petals that were floating into their hair.

Celia told him about one of her travels with her father. About the Festival of the Cherry Blossom that she'd witnessed in the Orient. Colin told her about eating so many cherries one day when he was around six years old that he hadn't been able to even look at a cherry for the rest of that summer. He'd been sick to his stomach, but he didn't want to tell Agnes or Hugh what he'd done for fear of admitting that he'd gone into the garden.

They talked of the future, and Celia spoke of her inheritance as belonging to both of them. Of wanting to use it the way that Colin was using the Campbell resources ... for the good of the people who depended on them.

The sun was warm in the protected privacy of the garden. Hidden from everyone, they walked and she talked of herbs and flowers and of the pleasure that they would have seeing them grow. Halting in the most protected corner, Colin sat on a bench behind an enclosing fence of latticework. Pulling her to his lap, he laughingly mentioned other pleasures that the garden might produce.

He lifted Celia's chin and brushed his lips across hers.

"Do you think Father William would consider making love while sitting on my lap 'unnatural'?"

Celia moved her body slightly, aware of the arousal beneath Colin's kilt. The white dress that she was wearing was not so thick as to hinder the sensations she was feeling.

"If you show me," she answered coyly. "We'll be able to make a better decision later."

This was all the encouragement Colin needed, and his mouth took possession of hers. Then, like a great rolling wave, their passion swept them to another level of desire. Colin stood Celia up before him, his knees steadying her as he ran his hands over her body.

Celia felt the laces of her dress pulled and fall away. She felt Colin's hot mouth leaving a trail of kisses from her neck to her breast, and a moan formed in the back of her throat as he took one nipple in his suckling lips. His hand caressed her other breast, his fingers teasing the nipple into an erectness that drew his mouth to it, as well. His tongue flicked at the hardness for a moment before tracing the soft fleshy curve beneath her breast. She felt the dress slide down off her shoulders and past her hips. She stood naked in his embrace, exhilarated by the feel of the sun on her back . . . and his lips on her body.

Reaching over his back, Celia pulled at the shirt that covered his huge upper body. She wanted to feel his skin against hers. Want soon became need as the magic of Colin's tongue wandered over her quivering middle. A near-frantic surge swept over her, and Colin raised his head, stripping his shirt off.

Unwrapping the kilt, he drew Celia gently onto his rock-hard legs. Supporting her weight, he caressed her with his lips, easing her onto the crown of his arousal.

Celia gasped as she lowered herself against it, and Colin groaned with pleasure. Then, pulsing gently, Celia took him into her—deeply, fully, completely.

Colin held her hips as they rocked, and Celia gripped his back, his shoulders, his hair. Together they moved, two bodies as one, giving without a thought of giving, sharing without a thought of sharing, but loving with every fiber of their existence. As their bodies moved to the throbbing measure of the love dance, Celia found herself rising, peeling away the constraints of ten million years.

She was aware—and yet not aware—of the increasing tempo that was carrying her, lifting her, driving her to another dimension. A dimension where time and space are a single, bright, pounding expanse . . . formless, indefinable, eternal.

And Colin was there with her, rising with her, a part of her. Together they reached that momentous release, that shuddering ecstasy, and Celia surrendered herself to that enveloping light, to that illuminating sense of being alight, aloft, alive.

One day melted into the next, and Celia and Colin were nearly inseparable. Rather than simply keeping to her room, as tradition dictated, Celia went out with Colin every day. The Macpherson family, as well as most of the guests who had traveled to Kildalton for the wedding, departed for home. Alec promised to return when they received some word at Kildalton from the Earl of Huntly. He had added, with a somewhat wistful look at Celia and Colin together, that suddenly the bachelor's life was not as attractive as it used to be.

But even with the castle emptying out, the celebrations were continuing without a moment's hesitation, and the townsfolk were delighted when the young laird and their new lady joined in the festivities. Glad for the opportunity to be near the women and the men who were now her kin, Celia soon found herself being included as one of them.

One afternoon Celia spent laughing and singing with the children of the village, learning the songs and the local dance steps. The next morning she taught the same children new ways of trapping the crabs and lobsters that lived amid the rocky inlets. Before she was aware of it, she had drawn an audience of adults who wanted to share in the activity.

Another gray morning found Celia and Colin sitting together by the Marketcross, listening to the village storyteller reciting tales of the Celtic heroes of old, and drinking from the bowl of ale that was being passed around. That same day saw them bringing necessities to the refugees who were being settled in hastily erected cottages on Campbell lands. Seeing them brought back the threatening reality that Danvers still represented while at large in Scotland.

But Colin eased her worries and her fears with his quiet confidence. Showing her the strength and the stability of the Campbell clan life, he convinced her that the prosperity of their own people would one day be the prosperity of all Scottish people. Invaders would be repelled, and murderers would be destroyed.

In those glorious days the newlyweds rode together on the rocky bluffs overlooking the sea, with the black hound Bear ranging alongside. Together, they walked hand in hand along the beach stretching along the harbor. As they laughed and talked, they often expressed the same thoughts simultaneously, like two old partners with many years of shared experience. At times, their knowledge of the world seemed to complement each other's perfectly, and one's ideas would build on the other's in productive exchanges regarding Scotland and the Campbell lands.

On the evening before the Archbishop was to leave, Father William scurried to Celia's side as she entered the South Hall on Colin's arm. His eyes were flashing with excitement as he took Celia's free hand. When the warrior saw the priest, he nodded in friendly greeting.

"I see you two have something to discuss," Colin said, casting a smiling look at the priest and disengaging himself from his bride.

"Aye, lad," Dunbar answered elatedly. "It'll be only a moment."

Practically dragging her back into the Great Hall, the wiry priest sat down with Celia on one of the wooden settles beside a great fireplace.

"Well, lass, the King couldn't do it, but my good friend Lord Hugh and your fine husband certainly could," he began, rubbing his hands together in high glee. Celia thought for a moment that Father William was about to get up and dance a Highland reel.

"What are you talking about?" she asked, smiling at her friend's excitement.

"They've done it, Celia," he said, grabbing her hand. "That young priest they have here ... the Archbishop is taking him into his own service. And they've offered me the benefice here on the island."

Father William paused, waiting for the news to register on her face. "I'll be the priest here and teach the bairns in the new school!" he nearly shouted with delight. "Finally, finally, finally! I'll have my own flock, Celia, and real work to do!"

Celia laughed aloud as Dunbar leapt up and capered about for a moment, before stopping abruptly and coming back to her side.

"Wait just a wee bit," he said accusingly. "You knew all this, didn't you? Don't lie to your confessor, now, lass. You're behind all this, aren't you?"

"No, Father," Celia said with a laugh. "It was Colin's doing."

Celia had been present during the discussion between Colin and the Archbishop, but this arrangement had been Colin's idea completely. She knew that this was all part of Colin's desire to make her feel at home and surrounded by the people who were dear to her. Celia smiled at the thought that Colin would build a new wing onto the castle for Edmund, if he thought that would convince him to stay as well.

"But it was probably your idea, I'm sure," he said, affectionately squeezing her hand. "You're a fine young woman, Celia Muir ... or, rather, Lady Campbell. And I've matched you up with a fine young man."

Regarding his original position on her relationship with Colin, Celia thought with a smile, Father William was certainly developing a selective memory.

The following morning, after insisting that she bring her cloak, Colin took Celia on a tour of the labyrinth of secret passages that honeycombed the castle. Teaching her the secrets of the hidden portals, Celia soon understood both the pattern of construction and the key to moving between one section of passageways and another. It was a fascinating tour that concluded in the caverns at sea level.

"What would you say to going for a sail?" Colin asked, waving his torch at the number of boats resting on the sloping stone quay. They had been sailing a number of times using larger craft from the harbor, but this was the first she knew of these smaller boats, so much like the ones she had sailed in her days at court, after her freedom had been restored by the patronage of the Earl of Huntly.

Colin placed the torch in a holder in one of the great stone pillars as Celia untied one of the boats and made a futile attempt to push the vessel down the slope.

Coming up from behind and giving her no opportunity to object, Colin wordlessly lifted her up bodily and placed her in the boat. Then, with ease, he pushed the boat down the stone slope and jumped in. It occurred to Celia with pride that three strong men were generally needed to put these boats in the water—Colin had done it barely flexing a muscle.

As she worked her way to the stern past the mast and sail stretching most of the boat's length, Celia glanced around at their subterranean surroundings. It appeared in the flashing torchlight that there were high-water marks far up on the rock walls.

"How much time do we have to sail?" she asked.

"The cave entry becomes inaccessible about an hour before high tide," he told her. "Then the bluffs are sheer rock. You wouldn't even know there was a cave here. But even if you try to come in at low tide, getting through the narrows is treacherous."

"Could I try?" she asked, her eyes sparkling at the challenge.

Colin looked across at the low opening and back at Celia. He'd heard from enough people about her considerable skills on the water, and he'd seen some of those skills in the last week of sailing together. But the cross-currents and the wind that hit you at the aperture of the cave took practice to master. Well, no better time to start than now, he thought to himself. The water's not *all* that cold.

"Aye," he responded. "But first let me tell you what the difficulties are."

Celia nodded, taking the tiller and listening patiently. As Colin propelled them toward the low opening, he catalogued a list of possible problems she could face, illustrating them with an amusing history of his own wrecks and minor mishaps.

Colin watched her as she steered carefully, comfortable at the boat's helm. Her beautiful face was intent on her task as they glided across the cave. Then, inexplicably, she broke out into a wide grin.

"You'd better duck, Lord Campbell." She laughed, and Colin did just that, narrowly avoiding bumping his head on the overhanging stone of the cavern entrance. Celia, too, stooped quickly as a swell lifted the boat as it moved out into the open water, and they both laughed heartily.

As they slid smoothly through the center of the opening, Colin sat in the bow, chuckling to himself at his own underestimation of her skills.

Once through the rocky aperture, Colin stepped the mast and with amazing speed attached the lines. Celia moved forward slightly and began to haul the sail up when the mast was supported, and Colin met her with a kiss, taking the line and sending her back to the tiller.

"You certainly handled that with ease," Colin said, admiration in his voice. "Now I know why Ambrose was so impressed with your sailing."

"You know that Ambrose was just playing the courtly gentleman."

"I can just see it—you must have left them far behind." Colin beamed proudly, watching Celia flush with embarrassment at his praise.

"I've always loved the water," she said, changing the topic. She was never very comfortable handling compliments. "I've always been more at home on the sea than anywhere else."

"I know what you mean," Colin said, pausing to look back affectionately at his bride. "We say out here that the sea is our mother . . . perhaps that's even more true for you . . . and me . . . than for most folks."

They sped along the base of the rocky bluffs, and Celia could see the orange line of the tide left by the brightly colored seaweed. And all along the cliffs, seabirds wheeled in great circles or hung motionless in the air, as if suspended by invisible strings from the deep blue vault of sky above.

As they moved away from the shoreline, Celia felt the rush of sense and emotion that she always felt on the water. That feeling of being in control of the sea force, and yet under her control at the same time. Of being free and alone in a single moment in time, and yet still a part of something else—something greater, deeper, inclusive, and everlasting.

And she looked forward at the man she loved. They were alone now—totally. Their sail was the only one in sight—their privacy was complete and shared. This sea and this sky were theirs and theirs alone.

The boat was comfortable and fast, and Celia loved the feel of the tiller in her hand as they skimmed over the open water. Her hair whipped about her, and the cold saltwater droplets stung her happy face. But looking at her magnificent raven-haired warrior setting the lines to her specifications, Celia felt a stirring that she'd never known while sailing. And when Colin came back to the stern to sit beside her, wrapping his arms around her waist, she felt her pulse rise. When his hands began to explore and his mouth began to press warmly against her neck, Celia felt her concentration beginning to lapse.

"Need some help back here?" he whispered, his hand caressing her waist, her breasts, brushing the silky skin of her neck.

"Colin," she admonished weakly, making no attempt to stop his hand as it wandered to her hip, to the outside of her leg, to the inside of her thigh. "I'm trying to steer."

"Aye, Celia," he responded, his breath warm on her ear.

"Trying to keep our course in the wind," she sighed as his hand pulled up the material of the dress that draped to the deck.

"Aye, Celia," he breathed, suckling her earlobe as his fingers tenderly reached the junction of her thighs—feeling her, caressing her.

"Just a moment, Colin Campbell," she gasped, an exhilarated shudder coursing through her entire being.

Reaching forward, she looped two lines over the tiller

to hold their course, and then Celia turned her full attention to the man she loved.

Like a bolt from a crossbow, the boat rocketed toward the rocky bluff. Timing her approach carefully, Celia caught a swelling wave as it rolled toward the shore. Colin paused momentarily at the mast, wondering how she would contról the boat's speed and direction. Well, he thought, it's too late to worry about that now.

"Now, Colin," she shouted, and the giant heaved the mast from its step, lowering it easily into the belly of the boat.

We're not going to make it, he thought, his hands gripping the gunwale of the boat. This roller is going to take us into the side wall of the opening. We're not going to . . .

But his thoughts were interrupted by Celia's slight change of angle on the rudder. Colin felt the boat dip slightly, and suddenly the wave was sweeping them directly toward the mouth of the cave. Looking back at Celia in raw admiration, he saw her return his gaze with a loving smile before turning her attention back to her task. His wife was incredible.

In the wink of an eye, the cliffs were upon them. And without any change of speed at all, the boat slid into the cavern like a dagger into its sheath, skimming across the short distance of water before smoothly climbing the slight incline to its berth between two other boats.

"You are amazing," Colin said warmly, sitting momentarily in appreciation of the impressive economy and mastery of the performance.

"Beginner's luck." Celia laughed, blushing at his words. "But that *was* fun."

"All of it," Colin said, gazing at the scarlet cheeks of his smiling bride.

Suddenly, from the passages leading down from the kitchens, Runt ran toward them, torch in hand.

"M'lord," he panted. "Lord Alec's cousin John has arrived with a message from the Macphersons. He's with Lord Hugh. It's trouble, I think."

"Well," Colin said gravely to Celia as they climbed out of the boat. "We knew it would be coming sooner or later."

Turning back to Runt, he ordered, "You go ahead. Find Celia's uncle and Emmet, then have them all go to the library. Celia and I will meet you there."

As Runt ran off, Celia felt a freezing fire at the base of her spine that spread through her like the onset of plague. She turned to Colin, unsure of what to say, but found words to be unnecessary as the giant wrapped her in his arms.

"Come on, my love," he growled, taking her hand. "We've got a vermin problem that needs attending to."

When they entered the library, Lord Hugh and Edmund were already seated at a great round table before the open shutters of a small window. The messenger, a young knight, stood restlessly pacing the room. The men immediately rose when they saw Celia, and Lord Hugh moved forward to greet her. Emmet hurried through the door as the group settled around the table.

"Well, John," Colin said with concern. "What news do you have for us?"

As Celia listened to the young fighter repeat his message from Alec, Lord Hugh put his pawlike hand over hers on the table.

Refugees were fleeing northward, arriving every day in greater numbers at Benmore Castle, the Macpherson fortress in the Highlands. These unfortunate people were just ahead of a large force of English soldiers under Danvers and Scottish renegades under Argyll, and they were ravaging Argyll's own lands to the south of the Macpherson holdings.

But they were clearly heading north. Alec's message

exuded confidence that the Macphersons would be able to stop the farther advance of the invaders, but he wanted the Campbells to be forewarned in case the marauders turned west toward the coastal countryside and the Campbell lands.

When John was finished, Colin stood and went to a large cabinet by the wall. Opening the front, he revealed a crisscross of pigeonholes filled with scrolls. Selecting one of them, he brought it back to the table, unrolled it before Celia and the others.

Looking at the colors, the symbols, and the lines on the parchment, Celia recalled her own father's coveted maps. Once, their ship had lain at anchor in the gray harbor of a once thriving Danish seaport, now smoldering and desolate in the wake of a Swedish invasion. She had stood at her father's elbow as he explained that the red circle on the map represented the ruined city before them. Celia remembered his grim look and the way he had taken her in his arms when she had so seriously asked why there was no smoke on the map.

Celia smelled that foul smoke now. She felt it stinging her eyes and hindering her breathing. There was no smoke depicted on this map, either. Nor was there any indication of the death and the suffering that one man can inflict on another. No sign of the agony of losing someone that you love—one that you depend on . . . for strength . . . for sustenance.

There was no blanket of gray smoke pictured over the men, the women, and the children scratching out their meager lives in the lands to the south of Benmore Castle. But Celia knew that smoke was there. And she felt the cold grip of it on her own aching heart.

"We need to reinforce them," Colin said. "At the very least."

"Aye, lad," Hugh agreed fervently. "We owe it to the Macphersons. But even if we didn't, it would be a crime to allow the butcher and the traitor to traipse unopposed through the Highlands. We need to stop them."

Colin placed his hand on Celia's shoulder and pointed out Kildalton Castle. Running his finger to the northeast, he indicated Benmore Castle. To the south of the Macphersons' holding, Celia could see the Grampian Mountains stretching to the east. Between the mountains and the Campbell lands along the western coastline, Colin placed his index finger.

"This is where Alec figures Danvers and Argyll to be," he said. "If we don't reinforce the Macphersons, and Benmore Castle falls, then there is nothing to stop the invaders from either knocking off the clans one by one to the north or from driving directly west to Kildalton Castle."

"Why haven't they done that already?" Celia asked. "Marched to the west, I mean?"

"Because they don't want the Macphersons at their back," Edmund put in.

"Aye," Lord Hugh agreed. "But if they're able to hurt the Macphersons, then the entire Western Isles are far more vulnerable."

"But it's Kildalton and everything we have here that Danvers and Argyll want," Colin added.

He leaned forward on the table and scanned the attentive faces around him. "This is what we'll do. Emmet and I will take a force from Oban by boat up Loch Linnhe to the River Spean, and march overland to join Alec's forces at Benmore Castle. That way we can cut off Danvers and Argyll from pushing any farther north . . . or west."

"Aye," Edmund put in. "The English will need to travel south or east through the Grampian Mountain passes to avoid a major battle."

"Nothing would make me happier than to send a force south to cut off those mountain passes," Colin said pensively, looking down at the map. "With the Macphersons to the north, and Campbell fighters to the west and to the south, we could close off the raiders' retreat and engage them where they stand."

Celia watched as Colin weighed the possible outcomes of such an action in his mind.

"But we can't," he decided after a pause. "The risks are too great. We've got to protect Kildalton Castle, and a force large enough to trap the butchers would leave the castle and the western lands far too vulnerable."

"There may be something else," Celia said quietly. "They may be trying to lure us out."

"That's very true," Colin considered, looking thoughtfully at her. "Though I don't think they'd try to attack Kildalton from the sea—even with a smaller number of defenders here."

"Maybe they just don't want to fight us at Kildalton at all," Emmet suggested.

"We'll charge that to cowardice on their part rather than wisdom," Lord Hugh responded. "Argyll's capable of treachery when he thinks you're not looking, but he hasn't the guts to take you on face-to-face."

Lord Hugh squeezed her bloodless hand, but Celia's heart was pounding in her chest. The thought of Colin going out to face these vile and desperate marauders was terrifying. She wanted to cry out against the plan, but she knew that she couldn't—Colin's plan was sound and his friendship with Alec inviolate. With supreme self-control, she tried to fight back the overwhelming fear that was lodged in her throat like some great stone, that clogged her lungs like thick, gray ash.

Looking at Colin and trying to hide the worry that she was feeling, Celia saw the determination on his face soften into a look of reassurance as he returned her glance.

"Then it's settled," Colin said. "We'll bring back all but a handful of fighters from Argyll's castle. And the day after tomorrow, Emmet and I will take a thousand or so men from Oban."

He looked around at those at the table.

"And Celia and Edmund and the rest of us," Hugh rumbled, with a look of tenderness at his new daughter, "we'll guard the loved ones here at Kildalton."

The next day was gray and threatening. As Celia sat with Colin in the garden, the cold, wet wind chilled her to the bone in spite of the heavy cloak and the giant's arm around her.

The cherry blossoms all lay plastered to the ground from the night's rain, and the dark green of the tree's young leaves was a poor substitute against the shiny black bark of the wet branches.

"When the King left for his fight with the English," Celia said, her voice calm and controlled. "The people of Scotland lined the streets, cheering and celebrating a victory before the battle was even fought. The men marched out, handsome and dashing in their armor, the long spears flashing in the sun."

Celia paused as she recalled the vision, a tear running down her cheek.

"The women were weeping as they cheered. I remember thinking that they must be so proud, even in the thought that danger lay ahead for their men. I remember thinking then that I could see their emotions, but I couldn't feel what they were feeling. All I could feel was hope that everyone would return with their honor and their lives. But I never dreamed that Flodden would mean the end of the world as the Scottish people knew it. As these women knew it."

"Nobody could have known what it would mean," Colin agreed, holding her close. "Nobody could have known that the number of deaths would be so high."

"Colin, those deaths caused misery that should never again be repeated. I saw those women . . . I heard them

... shrieking in agony. Wandering the streets, their eyes blind with anguish, their faces the same dead color as the corpses they once called ... husband ... brother ... father."

"Celia, we are not going to our Flodden," Colin said in a low voice. "This is not the same. What happened on those wet fields last fall is not going to happen here."

Colin looked out into the mist that lay like a shroud over the cliffs beyond the wall.

"We have to use what we have learned," he said firmly. "All of his life, James fought for a Scotland that would stand together. He used his charm, his guile, and his strength to achieve that goal. A unified Scotland is what you and I believe in, as well, but we will not make the same mistakes that he made.

"When the battle began, James gave up his role as commander of the forces under his control. It was his fatal error. Without his leadership as king, as the ... symbol ... of strength and authority, the army broke into the factions that it was comprised of. Like Scotland itself, without a central power to hold it together, they fell away ... clan by clan, village by village, man by man. And when traitors like Argyll and the others should have engaged the English, they lay back and watched the King fall as well. James died at Flodden because he fought like a common soldier rather than as a leader, as a commander, as a king.

"But James never had the woman that I have now. I have fought these battles many times before, but I have never had so much to come back to. I am the commander of these men and a leader of the people of these lands. They depend on me to live and to bring them prosperity. I will not die a soldier's death in the hills around Benmore Castle. I will come back to you, the woman I love."

Chapter 15

Kildalton Castle was a solemn place in the first days following the fighters' departure.

Celia, Lord Hugh, and the others waited anxiously for news of Colin and his men, but when it came, by way of a daily messenger, there was never anything of importance. Although a speedy messenger could reach the Macpherson holding in less than a day, the Campbell troops were progressing slowly and carefully toward Benmore Castle. The only signs of the enemy were the constant streams of refugees limping into the northern hills.

Finally, the message arrived that Colin had reached Benmore Castle, only to find it under siege by a combination of English troops fighting alongside Gregor clan and Macleod clan warriors.

The outrage at the Highlanders' treachery was expressed strongly and openly by Lord Hugh. Torquil Macleod was vying for power, just as Argyll was. The Gregors were in it simply for the money.

Hugh's greatest concern, however, a concern that he tried to hide from Celia, regarded the sheer numbers that Colin might be facing there. The message gave no information about that.

That afternoon Celia walked with Bear in the courtyard of the castle, all the time thinking of Colin, fearing for him. These past days he'd been all she thought of. In the long hours of night he had been all she dreamed of. She had found herself praying as she'd never prayed before. Walking by the open drawbridge of the fortress, she found herself praying now. Praying for his success. Praying for his safe return.

But Celia's meditations were interrupted when, from the castle gates, a child hesitantly approached her. She recognized him immediately as the nephew of Eustace, the woman who had saved Celia from her husband's Gregor clan kinsmen.

"M'lady," the lad mumbled nervously. "My aunt . . . My aunt's been hurt. I was sent to ask for your help . . . to bring you."

"What happened?" Celia asked, crouching before him and peering into his face. "Is she badly injured?"

"I can't say, m'lady," he responded. "They just said to come and get you."

Without another word, the boy broke away from Celia and ran out the great castle gates.

"Shall I get your horse, m'lady," Runt said from behind, startling Celia with his presence.

"I can get it, Runt, thank you," she said quickly.

"It may not be a good idea going out alone, m'lady."

"Runt, I'm just going to the cottages outside the village," she said reassuringly. "I'll be back in an hour."

"I don't know if Lord Hugh will . . ."

"Besides, I'm always armed," she said, patting a sheathed dagger that she was wearing inside the waist of her belt. "But if it will make you feel better, I'll wear a short sword as well."

"Let me go with you, m'lady," he suggested.

"Runt, I really prefer that you check in on Ellen and Kit for me."

"Aye, m'lady!" he responded cheerfully. "If that's your wish, I'll be going up there right away."

A few moments later Celia was riding toward the village. Since Eustace's arrival at Kildalton, Celia had visited with her a number of times and had been happy to see her settling into her younger sister's home. Her sister was a widow who was now sustaining herself by working at the clothworks in the village. Celia knew that Eustace hoped to do the same.

But as she rode to the cottage, something in the boy's face bothered Celia. There had been a hint of something—fear, perhaps—in his eyes.

The cottage sat on a knoll overlooking a quiet inlet away from the village. When Celia called at the door, the timber plank swung inward. Going into the semi-darkness, her eyes took a moment to focus on those within. Across the room beneath a shuttered window, the boy sat huddled with his mother, their eyes openly displaying terror. On the floor beside them lay a battered heap that Celia recognized as Eustace.

With a cry, she stepped into the room, suddenly aware of the shapes that were surrounding her from the dark corners. Turning back as the door slammed shut, Celia looked into the ugly face of Eustace's husband.

Leaping back toward the frightened group, Celia whipped out the short sword, facing the five thugs who were approaching carefully.

"You promised to let my mamma go!" the boy sobbed behind her.

"Shut your trap," Eustace's husband sneered. "You think we would let any of you live to tell what you've seen?"

"Laddie," Celia ordered. "Open the shutter behind you, and you and your mother go out . . . NOW!"

The boy scrambled into action, and as light flooded the room from the opening shutter, the assailants stepped forward, only to scurry backward before the slashing arc of Celia's sword blade.

The ugly sneer turned to concern on the leader's face as the mother and son clambered through the window. "Get her, before they come back with help," he shouted, lunging at Celia.

With a short stroke, Celia drove the point of her sword into the hollow at the base of his throat. Before Eustace's husband hit the floor, however, Celia had spun sharply, slashing another attacker beneath the ear.

But this was to be her final act of self-defense before the crashing blow from the right exploded in her head a shower of yellows and reds, shutting down the conscious functions of her brain. And then, all was in darkness.

Celia knew she was in a boat before her senses fully cleared. The throbbing in her head was aggravated by a loud roaring noise that gradually settled into the sound of three arguing voices. Listening to the voices, she slowly began to piece together what had happened.

"Are you sure this is Loch Etive?" one voice growled in English.

"No, I'm not sure," another responded in the same English accent. "The bitch killed that thieving Gregor scum, and he was the only one that knew the way, for certain."

"That dirty Scot surely enjoyed beating his woman," a third English voice chipped in, his voice betraying an attitude of loathing.

"We should have killed her anyway. She'll live to tell a tale or two," the first one answered.

"We're here to do a job," the third replied with disgust. "Although some of us have forgotten, we're not here to kill women and children."

The other two laughed the inhuman laugh of the monsters they were.

"What have you been doing the last six months?" the second soldier spat out.

"I wouldn't mind putting my hands on this fine lady," the first man said lecherously.

Celia heard the sound of a sword being drawn.

"You lay one finger on her, and Lord Danvers will

have you impaled and left for the crows," the third soldier warned. "She's the hostage that we'll use to get the baby king."

The two others laughed again. "Where do you get your information from, Sergeant High and Mighty?"

"Aren't we still under orders of King Henry?" he snapped.

While the other two cursed under their breaths, Celia shot a glance at the third soldier. It was good to know that at least all English soldiers were not like Danvers and the other two. With this man aboard, she had a chance of surviving this trip, at least.

"Is this Loch Etive or *not*?" the first voice asked angrily again.

"We'll know by nightfall ... if the wind holds," the second man growled in response as the three lapsed into silence.

Celia knew that Loch Etive was a long, watery wedge snaking far into the mainland in the area south of Benmore Castle. If these pigs were taking her into that area, then the marauders had obviously divided their forces. Some were attacking Benmore, and the rest, under Danvers it seemed, were waiting farther to the south.

Lying in the belly of the boat, Celia became acutely aware of one of the craft's ribs pressing against her shoulder. She tried to move ever so slightly, so as not to draw the attention of the soldiers. Realizing that her hands were tied in front of her, Celia carefully felt the material of her dress beneath the cloak. Her dagger was still in its sheath. They had not thought to see if she was carrying another weapon.

It seemed as if an eternity passed before the boat bumped ashore. The sun had set a good hour earlier, and Celia had been surprised that the soldiers continued to sail in the dark. But the darkness had covered Celia's movements, and she'd been able to shift her position from time to time, even feeling the lump and the drying blood on her face.

Why do these louts always go for my aching head? she thought to herself. Well, when Colin gets hold of them, they'll prefer Danvers's impaling.

As they reached the stony shoreline, Celia realized why they'd been able to sail the past hour. The blazing light of a bonfire atop a nearby hill and the torches that the troop of waiting soldiers held must have provided quite a beacon for her captors, she thought. There was no longer any reason to pretend unconsciousness, and Celia pulled herself to her feet before rough hands dragged her out of the boat and across the strand to a waiting horse.

After a few hours of hard riding, it began to rain on the dozen or so soldiers who were taking her to Danvers. Celia was nearing exhaustion, and her head felt as if it were going to split in half, but she was determined to remain strong in the eyes of the soldiers and to be ready for her chance.

When they reached a gushing river only to find the timber bridge swept away by the swollen waters, the leader, amid a string of curses, called for the troop to stop for the night. They would have to wait until daylight to find another crossing.

Celia huddled under her cloak beneath a tree, soldiers posted all around her. She had decided to remain awake through the night, but her eyes closed within moments of dismounting. She awoke as the dawn broke gray and steely, only to find the soldiers being roused for the days' ride.

A few moments later, as Celia was pushed up onto her horse, she wondered if by now Colin could have been notified of her abduction. But would he know where she was being taken?

*　　*　　*

Lord Danvers and the Earl of Argyll hunched over the map in Danvers's tent. The rain had been pounding down for most of the morning, but was just letting up as the dripping messenger standing by the entrance slipped out into the muddy camp.

"It would figure that Macleod couldn't take a single fortress," Danvers sneered. The two allies had just received word that the Macleod and Gregor forces had been smashed the previous day. The word was that Torquil Macleod had been captured and was locked up in Benmore Castle's dungeons.

"You don't know what the Campbells and the Macphersons are like when they fight together," Argyll responded, walking nervously away from the table.

"They were only fighting other Scots, and cowardly turncoats at that," Danvers spat, his insinuation stinging Argyll. "I've carved and burned my way across this miserable country of yours, and there's no Scot alive who can stop me."

"Then why are you looking for a way to retreat through the Grampians?" Argyll muttered tensely.

"Once I have my . . . bride . . . you can all rot to hell in this stinking perch you call the Highlands."

"You can't just take her and go." Argyll responded, his voice rising in surprise at Danvers's intention. "You can't back out on our deal. Henry wants the Crown Prince in our hands, and I want him, too."

Danvers strode arrogantly to a chest and drew out a parchment, tossing it carelessly at Argyll. "If you can read this message I received a while ago, it appears that your Earl of Huntly has come to an agreement with King Henry. That half-breed brat will be King of Scotland after all, and you, my dear Argyll, will have nothing."

"You bastard," Argyll paled, reading the document. "This is weeks old. You've known this and said nothing. This says for you to return to England. You've been killing and looting not in your king's name, but just to satisfy your own twisted desires."

"You'd better be careful how you speak to me, Scot." Danvers laughed, the evil in his voice showing in his face. "Because I am the only one keeping you alive. So make sure you remain useful to me."

The pounding of hooves outside broke into the conflict within as a dozen soldiers and their captive splashed up to the commander's tent.

When Celia entered the tent, Danvers and Argyll were glaring at each other across the table at the center. For the fifth time since dismounting outside a soldier tried to take Celia's arm, and for the fifth time she yanked her arm out of his grasp. Her hands were numb and her wrists bleeding from the chafing cords that bound her hands before her, but she held herself erect.

Looking from Argyll's bloodless face to Danvers's ugly sneer, Celia knew that they'd come in the middle of an argument, an argument that Danvers was clearly winning.

Danvers turned his hulking body toward Celia, and the sight of her bloody, rain-soaked figure brought a gleam into his eye.

"Lady Muir," he said with a malicious smirk. "How nice of you to finally come to me ... to your rightful husband."

He held his hand out to her as if expecting her to walk to him. At Celia's failure to respond, she felt the soldier shove her from behind. But she only moved the half step that she was pushed, looking steadily and meaningfully into the butcher's pig eyes. That look was a look of sheer hate, the result of all the long years of pain, intimidation, and suffering—not just Celia's, but that of the innocent men, women, and children of Scotland who had felt the scourge of Danvers's barbaric cruelty.

And Danvers saw it. He had expected fear; however,

there was none in her eyes. But he would enjoy watching fear replace all other emotions in Celia Muir. At last, she was at his mercy. At last, she would feel the lash of his supreme mastery over her. Before he was finished with her, she would crawl to him on her knees.

"You will come to me ... NOW!" he shouted, his face flushed with rage.

Celia stood coolly before him. She knew what she had to do.

Turning away from Danvers, she strode across the tent to Argyll. Argyll's shocked expression quickly turned to a look of satisfaction as Celia stopped in front of him.

"I'm so glad you're here, m'lord," she said calmly, her voice the embodiment of sincerity and control. "I've been looking forward to meeting with you for months now. As you know, I was given the task of delivering your nephew into the safety of your hands. But the vile activity of ... the scum in this room ... has gotten between us."

Argyll nearly laughed aloud at this woman's audacity. No wonder Huntly had entrusted her with the future of Scotland. No wonder so many men wanted her. No wonder Danvers wanted to crush her.

Looking at the raw flesh of her wrists, Argyll drew the dagger from his belt. At his action, Celia held her bonds up to be cut and was soon freed from the cords that held her.

"It's a pleasure to finally meet you, as well, Lady ... Campbell," Argyll said as the two of them shared a conspiring look.

"She's NOT Lady Campbell," Danvers screamed, smashing his fist on the table. "She'll never be Lady anything ... because she's mine."

"I'm not yours," Celia shouted back, her eyes ablaze as she wheeled to face him. "I'm not now. I never have been. And I never will be."

"Your king has commanded your rightful place," Danvers spat. "And you will abide by that."

"That king is dead," she replied. "But Henry was never my king."

"You crossbreed traitor," he sneered. "You think that because you've slept with some cowering Highland oaf, you now have a country that will claim you? A home that will accept you? You have nothing! You are nothing!"

"What I have, you will never understand," Celia answered disdainfully. "What I am . . . will never be yours. I am Scottish, proud and free. I have a king that I fight to protect. I have a home that I honor and will serve. I have a husband and a family that I love. These are things that you will never have nor ever know."

"Husband," he jeered. "Where is your husband now? Where will he be when you are begging me for mercy? Begging me to kill you rather than take any more of what I have planned for you."

"Long before I beg you for anything, my husband Colin Campbell will cut out your heart," Celia vowed.

Danvers laughed, but there was something hollow in the sound and Celia knew that her words had struck home.

A horse galloped to a halt outside the tent, and a soldier entered with the breathless rider.

"M'lord," the horseman cried, waiting for permission to address his commander.

"SPEAK!" Danvers shouted angrily.

"M'lord, they're coming," he panted. "Only hours away. A force from the west, and Campbells and Macphersons from the north."

"How many?" Danvers demanded.

"We can't tell. They're spread across the hills, moving slowly and combing the countryside."

Danvers shouted for his subordinates outside. "Break

camp now," he shouted. "We're going through the mountain pass to the south."

"We can't go south now," Argyll bellowed, moving to the table. "We can't outrun Campbell. Our only chance is to cut a deal with him while we have his wife."

"And give up what I've waited so long for?" Danvers retorted. "There won't be any deals. I'm leaving with my troops, and I'm taking her with me."

"She's not yours to take," Argyll replied, turning back toward Celia. "She is a woman of great value. She will never be an object for your sadistic pleasures. I'll not order my men south, and I'm keeping Lady Campbell here. You can run all the way to England . . . or to hell if you please."

As he strode back to Celia, his broad, gaunt frame blocked Danvers from her vision momentarily. But that was all that was required for Danvers to follow from behind. Argyll smirked and gave Celia a wink as he came up to her, but then his expression abruptly changed. Shock registered on his face as his opponent's sword blade slid between the ribs in his back and cut a path through the vital organs before protruding from his chest.

As Argyll sank to the floor in the agonies of his final moments, Danvers braced his foot against the bloody back and withdrew his sword. The look of blood lust was in his face as he eyed Celia over the twitching body.

"This is what happens to any that defy me," he sneered, his lecherous eyes raking her body. "And now I'll take you as I please."

Celia stepped back, her eyes quickly scanning the surroundings as she assessed the situation. Not too promising, she thought. Two soldiers stood at the entrance, observing the spectacle. Danvers stood leering, enjoying his moment of murderous power and intimidation, waiting for the total impact of Celia's powerlessness to descend upon her. Judging from the shouts and movement

outside, the camp was already a mad rush of activity.
Her hand edged closer to the dagger hidden inside her
dress belt.

She might possibly kill Danvers, but she would not be
able to escape the two guards. I will turn this knife on
myself, she vowed silently, before I let this pig touch me.

Suddenly bedlam broke out in the camp. The sound
of hooves and the uproar of voices drew Danvers's attention to the entry of the tent.

"What's going on out there?" he shouted at the
guards. Before either could move, though, one of the
captains entered.

"M'lord, they're here," he rasped hoarsely, his face
ashen at the prospect of being the bearer of the news.

"Who's here?" Danvers screamed, moving back to his
subordinate, his dripping sword still in his hand.

"An army of Scots, m'lord. To the south," he replied,
his eyes riveted to the body lying on the ground.

"No, you idiot," Danvers hissed, taking hold of the
captain's throat. "They're coming from the *north! We're*
going south!"

"I know, m'lord," the captain choked out. "But the
vanguard of our troops met a force under the Earl of
Huntly's banner not two miles to the south. They've cut
off our escape, m'lord!"

Danvers went to the map on the table, but before he
could look at it, the sound of fighting broke out in the
camp. Another soldier ran breathlessly into the tent.

"Lord Danvers, the Scots are attacking from the
north!" he cried. "And there's another army coming
over the hills from the west. They're in the camp,
m'lord! They're fighting in the camp!"

As soon as Celia saw Danvers move to the captain,
she edged backward to the corner of the tent. Ignored
in the sudden furor that ensued, she drew her dagger
and quickly cut a slit in the thick cloth wall.

As she slipped through the opening, she heard Danvers bellow after her.

"Get her," the giant butcher shrieked, fiendlike in his fury. "I want her!"

Without turning back, Celia ran toward the battle roar of shouts, horses, and clashing steel. It had to be Colin coming from the north. But who would have followed her from the west? Edmund, she thought, coming from Kildalton.

But there was not much time for thinking. Danvers and his men were in close pursuit. As she rounded a grove of trees into a cluster of lean-to huts of earth and sticks, she caught a glimpse of Danvers and the others pounding ever closer behind her.

In a hilly clearing beyond the huts, Celia saw a battle being waged. Hundreds of men fighting in close and bloody combat were throwing themselves at one another. As she ran down a small knoll to the right between two huts, a sudden roar came from behind. A hand grabbed her hair and yanked her off balance.

As Celia fell to the side, she managed to turn and slash at her attacker's face. As she rolled clear, she saw Danvers's hand clutch his cheek as blood streamed through his fingers. As they faced each other breathlessly, Danvers's malignant sneer fixed itself on his prey. He shouted to the others at his back.

"Join the fighting," he barked, never taking his eyes off of Celia. "I'll be there in a moment."

The sound of the fighting was moving away. And as the soldiers ran off, he spoke directly to her. "I can see that we are not going to have a long ... honeymoon," he leered malevolently. "But at least I'll have the pleasure of gutting you here and now."

"Then you made a mistake sending away your helpers," Celia taunted, putting as much courage as she could muster in her voice as she whipped off her heavy cloak, holding it in her outstretched hand.

"Ha! Ha!" came Danvers's surprised and admiring response as he moved a step toward her. "Still the fearless and haughty young woman. Still Celia Muir!"

Celia saw Danvers raise his sword, and prepared herself to jump, duck, or roll and to strike back with her dagger if she could. If she still lived.

Suddenly the devil's eyes looked up, and Celia saw irritation turn to recognition, and then a flash of fear.

"That's Celia *Campbell* now, you cowardly swine," the voice behind her growled. "You may address her as Lady Campbell . . . once . . . before you die."

Celia had to restrain herself from turning and facing Colin. He had come for her. He was here.

She didn't dare avert her eyes from Danvers. She knew it would be a mistake, a fatal mistake, to allow him even an instant to strike.

Suddenly he moved, lunging toward her, sword upraised, hand outstretched.

But Celia was too quick for him. Leaping backward with the agility of a cat, she was beside Colin in a flash. Her hero moved forward to meet the onrushing madman, shielding her with his arm and then his body.

The clang of steel rang out in the mist-enshrouded camp. The two men swung their heavy swords at each other with matched ferocity, and sparks flew from their weapons as they struck over and over again with sheer might and deadly determination. Watching them, Celia saw the wild look in Danvers's eyes, which was so different from the cold fury of Colin's glare.

Slowly Colin began to drive the Englishman up the hill, and Danvers's blows started coming more and more quickly. The demon was now lashing out at the Highlander frantically. Celia knew that her enemy was losing control.

Driving his body back into Colin, though, Danvers was able to gain a momentary respite, and he was breathing heavily as the two giants clinched. Then, with a mighty heave, Colin sent his adversary crashing through the side of the hut, losing his sword, though, in the fierce explosiveness of the action.

Never taking his eyes from the dark shape that was Danvers, Colin drew his dagger and plunged after him into the murky and narrow structure. Celia picked up the sword from the tall grass beside the lean-to and ran around the hut in time to see the two great men struggling hand to hand in the shadowy interior of the hovel.

She watched in a cold sweat as Colin and Danvers fought, the two warriors holding nothing back in this fight to the death.

And suddenly they stopped. Celia watched as Danvers backed slowly out the front of the hut. She raised the sword to cut him down—a fury coursing through her that she had never before felt—when his arm reached up to steady himself on the post by the entry. Then, with a half turn, the Scourge of Scotland fell lifeless to the ground, the ebony handle of Colin's dagger protruding from the base of his throat. The black sapphires set in the hilt flashed in silent testimony that justice had been finally, at long last, served.

Colin came to the opening of the hut and looked out at his beloved. Celia rushed to him, and tears of relief washed her cheeks. The two lovers embraced each other, and Colin anointed her forehead with a kiss. Feeling his lips pressed against her skin, Celia felt a great chain slip away—the chain of oppression and intimidation that she had unwillingly carried from the moment of her father's death in England. And as they both turned to look at the body of the madman, a speech that Edmund had once taught her came into her mind ... "As long as a hundred of us remain alive, we will never be subject to the English; because it is not for riches, or honors, or glory that we fight, but for liberty alone!"

Standing in the gray mist on the rain-soaked hill, Celia wrapped her arms tightly about the man she loved. And looking down into Danvers's unseeing eyes, Celia knew she had found her liberty. Finally, she was free of the evil that lay in the mud at her feet. Finally, after so long, after so much, Celia was completely and truly free . . . to love . . . to live.

Chapter 16

Finally the spring planting is done. As I watch the children herding the cow back toward the shed, I can hear them singing. By the cottage, my wife is standing with her hands on her hips, and I know she can hear them singing, as well. She turns her head and smiles at me across the newly turned field.

This is a season of great promise.

The June sun was shining down on the huge crowd that had gathered to celebrate the coronation of Kit as King James V of Scotland. Foreign dignitaries, archbishops from Rome, clan chieftains, burghers, and peasants all rubbed shoulders in the grand festival that had descended on what had once been the thriving city surrounding Edinburgh Castle. Everywhere the signs of rebuilding were visible, and the coronation reinforced that sense of renewal. Once inside, invited guests admired a Great Hall festooned with the tartans of every clan in Scotland.

Made regent by the deal stuck between her brother Henry VIII and the Scottish nobles led by Huntly, Queen Margaret, arrayed in a gown of English cloth of gold, sat beside the infant Kit, who was propped on pillows on the ancient throne of the Scottish kings. The Earl of Huntly stood nearby with two other earls, each holding a velvet pillow. A crown, a scepter, and a sword rested on the pillows, and the line of Scotland's elite stretched into the Outer Hall and beyond.

Gripping Colin's arm as they made their way to the dais, Celia fought back the tears that were welling up in her eyes. For nearly eight months, Kit had been hers— to love and care for. Now he was the King of Scotland, and safe at last.

Queen Margaret and Celia had made their peace in the weeks following the defeat of Lord Danvers. Celia and Margaret had talked of the child and about the ways each had tried to preserve the Crown Prince's safety in the days following Flodden. To Margaret, the English court had always been home, and the safest place she knew. That was why she had arranged to have Kit taken there.

But after the Prince's disappearance, the Queen had heard reports of the horrifying activities of the man to whom she had tried to deliver her child. It was only then that she realized the magnitude of the error she had nearly committed. After that, Margaret had pressed for a speedy settlement to the negotiations insuring her son's safety, and her gratitude to Celia was evident in the words she had spoken when they met.

Colin placed his hand over hers, gently stroking it as they stepped closer to the front. As they reached the dais, the Earl of Angus looked at the couple and introduced them.

"Lord and Lady Campbell ... The Earl of Argyll."

In recognition of Colin's success in defense of Scotland against the barbaric invader, Lord Danvers, and Celia's heroic protection of the Crown Prince, the nobles of Scotland, with the full support of Queen Margaret, had made Lord and Lady Campbell Peers of the Realm, bestowing on them the Earldom of Argyll.

As Colin recited his oath of loyalty to the new king, Kit raised his arms to the two kneeling before him. With a laugh the Queen stood and picked up the child, placing

him in Celia's arms. Celia wept, no longer able to restrain the emotions that were overflowing within her,
and Colin gathered the two in his arms, whispering his
words of love. After the momentary embrace, Celia
stood and placed the smiling Kit back in his mother's
arms.

"You are expected to remain close to us," the Queen
whispered quietly.

Walking back past the nods of approval from the rest
of the Scottish nobility, Celia thought with a smile of
how wonderful it would be to watch the young king grow
up healthy and strong.

"How do you feel?" Colin asked in a low voice.

"I'm fine, my love," she responded, looking up into
his loving eyes. Her hand gently patted her waistline.
"Do you think our son will be as good a bairn as Kit is?"

"Son or daughter"—Colin smiled—"With you for a
mother, ours will be the smartest, the most beautiful,
and the best bairn in all the world."

"You don't think he'll be a wild little terror?" Celia
laughed.

"If she's lucky enough to be like her mother," Colin
quipped, "she'll conquer the world."

Celia thought of how full the coming Christmas would
be with the birth of their first child. The thought of having a bairn was downright scary, but Agnes's and Lord
Hugh's excitement at hearing the news assured her that
she'd have more help than she could possibly imagine.

Indeed, everyone was delighted at their happiness. Father William, settling in comfortably with his flock to
tend and his pupils to teach, said cantankerously that he
had learned from his mistakes. He was going to go to
extra lengths to see that the bairn would turn out better
than his disrespectful parents. Although Edmund was
returning home to begin a renovation of the ancient
Bruce holdings, he was going with the promise of returning to the Western Isles before Christmas. Ellen and

Runt had also found marital bliss, and before Colin and Celia had left for the coronation, Ellen had mentioned happily that Celia's bairn might just have a companion growing up.

Everyone was delighted. Celia cast a loving glance up at the rugged face looking at her with such warmth and affection.

"I'm ready to go home," she whispered, hugging his arm close to her. "I don't want to miss a moment of this summer at Kildalton."

"Aye," he returned. "We can travel tomorrow; you've had enough excitement today."

"The roses will be in full bloom by the time we get back," she said cheerfully.

"And that garden will be the perfect place for you to spend the summer," Colin responded.

"Of course! For part of the day," she exclaimed. "And there's so much to do before the bairn comes ... the people in the Argyll lands need so much ... and those poor unfortunates who haven't a home to go back to. We need to help them rebuild. And the ..."

"Celia, you're not going to exhaust yourself this summer," Colin growled, his threatening look belied by the sparkle in his eyes. "You're going to rest, and stay strong while our bairn grows inside you."

"Of course, Colin," she said, pretending to ignore him. "And we need to build schools in the larger villages, so that all the children will have the chance to ..."

"Well, that's just typical," a familiar voice rang out from behind them. "The culmination of all you two have worked at, in your own ways, since last autumn, and you have to talk about the work you need to be doing."

"Alec," Celia scolded, smiling. "Life is not just one big festival, you know."

"Aye," Colin added with a wink at Celia. "A couple of decisive victories, a few more acres of land added to the family fortune, and Alec thinks he can rest on his laurels for the rest of his life."

Actually, Alec's and Colin's military exploits had earned them both fame and rank. And at every gathering, Alec was enjoying his role as the object of attention of every unmarried Scottish woman in attendance.

"Now, if you two . . . or rather, you three . . . are going to gang up on me . . ." Alec grinned, his face becoming sober for a moment. "Truly, though, after you left last night, I had a serious moment thinking of you and all the wonderful things that marriage might hold."

"Really," Celia exclaimed. "I'm surprised. And was there a particular woman in any of these . . . wonderful thoughts?"

"As a matter of fact, there wasn't," Alec responded seriously, his face breaking into a broad smile again. "No wonder I was able to get over it so quickly!"

"You'd best not even try to match Alec up in marriage, Celia." Colin laughed. "He just doesn't have the good sense of some of his friends . . . or the good luck."

"You know," Alec said, his tone becoming humorously contentious. "I've been meaning to talk to you about the fact that I saw Celia first . . ."

"Aye," Colin retorted. "Over the blade of her knife . . ."

"Now, boys," Celia interjected with a smile. "I believe there are laws about fighting on Coronation Day."

"Aye," Colin responded. "It's a required activity late in the afternoon."

"Depending on how quickly and how much a person can consume this good Edinburgh ale," Alec added as they all laughed.

"Well, I'll not be drinking any ale until Christmas," Celia declared with a firm nod of her head.

"You don't think a little ale will hurt *my* godson, do you?" Alec asked.

"In the Orient, they say the unborn child should get

no alcoholic beverages," she informed him. "And you, above all people, the man who can now enjoy sailing, should appreciate their medical knowledge."

"Aye," Alec agreed seriously. "In fact, I may just give it up myself until the bairn comes."

Seeing the scoffing looks of his two friends, Alec beamed broadly. "Well, perhaps until dinner, anyway." He laughed.

Outside the castle walls, Celia and Colin walked in the sun among the revelers in the carnival atmosphere that had taken hold of Edinburgh. As they wound their way from the castle along the Royal Mile to the Abbey of Holyrood, they admired the new buildings, so brightly painted and decorated for the grand occasion. The main street and the closes running off of it were alive with jugglers, minstrels, clowns, and dancers; and the air was filled with music and laughter, with shouts and cheers.

Life, indeed, was beginning again, and with her arm linked in Colin's, Celia walked among her people with joy in her heart.

Epilogue

In 1566 Mary, Queen of Scots, daughter of James V, gave birth to another James. And in 1603 this James VI of Scotland succeeded Henry VIII's daughter Elizabeth, last of the Tudor monarchs, and became King of England and Scotland, thereby uniting British rule under the banner of the Stuart kings.

Gareth said slowly, "I believe I might be able to provide an alternative for you, Lady Althea."

Althea looked at him. There was mingled surprise and disappointment in her expression. Her voice grew noticeably cooler as she asked, "Yes?"

Gareth was startled by Lady Althea's swift change in demeanor until he suddenly recalled what she had said about being wise to the ploys of gentlemen. He realized with almost a sense of horror that she thought that he meant to offer her an indelicate proposition. Quietly he said, "I would not insult you so, my lady."

For the second time, color flared in Althea's face. However, her eyes did not waver from his own steady gaze. Very carefully she asked, "If it is not carte blanche that you offer, then what?"

Lady Althea had spoken with a fair amount of composure, but Gareth could see that she was holding herself very stiffly. He had seen just such tension among his battle-scarred companions and had felt it himself many, many times. Always the feeling of being wound up tight as a screw struck just minutes before a battle was opened.

Gareth began divulging slowly what he had in mind. "As you might not know, before Lynley was killed last year he had affianced himself to an unexceptional girl. They planned to wed when he had completed his tour of duty. Lynley was killed before he was able to make the girl his wife." He stopped, frowning into the middle distance. "I am now heir to Chard and must take upon myself all the duties and obligations that have fallen upon my shoulders."

"Of course," said Althea. She fully appreciated the situation that he had explained, but what she did not understand was what any of this family history had to do with her own circumstances.

Gareth turned his dark gaze back to her. His eyes held an indefinable expression. "My father, the earl, is anxious to see the succession secured. Lynley died before he could accomplish that. My father does not wish me to return to the war, fearing that I, too, will be killed, thus erasing all chance of another generation of Marshalls to succeed him."

"But you are returning to the army," said Althea.

"Yes, I am. I swore an oath before God and for my king. I cannot in all conscience turn my back upon that. Until Bonaparte is completely defeated, I cannot take up my position here in England." Gareth smiled wryly then. "My father was not best pleased at my decision."

"Yes, I understand his lordship's concern," said Althea. She hesitated a moment. "Gareth, forgive me. But what has this to do with me?"

Gareth's expression sombered. There was a sudden intentness in his eyes that could not be ignored or escaped. His keen gaze pinned her to her chair. "What I propose is simply this, Lady Althea. You need an escape from an intolerable position. I could do with a wife, one who could perhaps produce an heir for Chard if I do not return from the war. As I see it, we are each in the position to help the other."

He stated it baldly, without fancy dressing or false declarations. Somehow he knew that otherwise she would not even consider his outrageous suggestion.

Althea stared at her companion, shocked.

It was indeed outrageous. Gareth could see from her

wide-eyed expression how startling his bold proposal was. But as he watched the varying emotions that began to flit over her face, he thought that he could not have hit upon a solution that would so well benefit both of them.

Althea looked at Major Gareth Marshall, Lord Lynley, for a long moment. Never in her life had she expected to be offered a stark marriage of convenience.

If she had ever given a thought to accepting such an arrangement at all, she would have dismissed it out of hand. She had seen the effects of a convenient loveless marriage that had not even had mutual respect to grace it. She did not want that for herself. She had seen the results of just such a marriage, the one that had produced herself, and the extreme disillusionment that had affected the Earl and Countess of Hawthorne.

But as Althea reflected on Lord Lynley's extraordinary proposal, she realized that the contract that he offered would not be the same as that which her parents had entered into. Her mother had told Althea more than once how fortunate she had thought herself to be chosen to become Lady Hawthorne; how excited she had been at the preparations for the social wedding; how she had enjoyed being feted as the new countess. Althea's mother had gone to the altar a dreamy-eyed romantic with scarcely a thought given to the kind of gentleman she was to wed.

Althea was not a romantic. She knew herself to be irrevocably marked by her upbringing. She was too cynical, too wise, to be caught up in the intrigues of the heart. She had meant on her come-out to identify a like-minded gentleman who shared her tastes and thus one with whom she could be comfortable. It would be a marriage of convenience, yes, but one built upon respect that would with time deepen into affection.

Love in the romantic sense was arrant nonsense. How often she had observed her father's pursuits and conquests. The prize had been pleasing for a time; then his interest had inevitably waned. Love had no place in a sensible marriage, but neither did the hatred and bitterness that had plagued her parents.

Lord Lynley's direct gaze held hers while he awaited her answer. Althea liked that. He was not pressuring her or attempting to persuade her in any way. He was merely waiting.

She considered him thoughtfully with new eyes. She had known him when they had been children. Gareth Marshall had never been a cruel or a bullying boy. It was doubtful that his basic character had changed to any degree. The very fact that he was allowing her time to reflect without interruption was proof of that.

Lord Lynley was handsome of face. The hawkish set of his features was pleasing to her eyes, while his deep voice was pleasant to her ear. He was well set up. There were few gentlemen who would equal him in physical attractions, she felt. Yet he did not appear to be puffed up in his own esteem. Not once had he glanced toward the mirror or reached up to assure himself of the set of his cravat.

She knew him to be an active man. His choice of career indicated that as much as did his lean, fit physique. That suited her very well, for she had never been a die-away miss. If she accepted him, there would be horses and holidays into the wilds of Scotland. She would be freer than she had ever been in her life.

Althea almost regretted that Lord Lynley meant to take up his obligations as heir to Chard. She rather thought that she would have enjoyed following the drum as a soldier's wife.

Lastly, she considered the fact that they were social equals. According to the world's wisdom it would not be a misalliance for either of them. If they were agreed on what the marriage was to mean to each partner, then Althea thought that they might go along very well.

The terms of the contract between them had already been established. His obligation would be to provide for and to protect her. Hers, to produce the much needed heir for Chard.

It was a simple enough bargain and better than she might have hoped for. She had always liked Gareth Marshall, and her former feelings had only taken firmer root upon being in his company for the hour past.

As for how he viewed her, she had already seen that he had a strong sense of chivalry. He had realized that she was in some sort of difficulty and had offered his help to her before even knowing the circumstances. A gentleman with a chivalric streak automatically offered respect to his lady.

She could not ask for more.

Done with her reflections, Althea did not hesitate. She said, simply, "Yes."

Gareth was unaware of the flow of dispassionate logic that had concluded in that one syllable. He mistakenly thought, with compassion, that Lady Althea had been engaged in a wavering conflict between fear and hope. In a gesture of reassurance he took her hand and lifted her fingers to his lips. "You will not regret it, I promise," he said quietly.

"I know that I shall not," she said with equal quiet.

Gareth was struck once more by her calm. His admiration for her poise under stress was strengthened. Whatever the fears she might harbor, she had placed her trust and her life in his hands and had done so in a fashion that spoke of generations of breeding. It humbled him to realize the enormity of the responsibility that he was taking on. He would not fail her.

"We must make proper arrangements. I am due back with my regiment in little more than a fortnight, so we shall have to be wed by special license," he said.

"I am underage, Gareth," said Althea softly. "And I do not know whether my mother will grant her consent."

He was surprised, not by the reminder of her age but by her uncertainty over her mother's agreement to the match. "Surely you do not believe that Lady Haw— Lady Bottlesby will object to having me for a son-in-law. Why, she has known me since I was in short coats," he said.

"Left to herself, my mother would willingly grant her blessing, I think. However, she is easily overridden. What I fear is that Sir Bartholomew will persuade her to withhold her consent," said Althea.

"Left him in a towering rage, did you?" asked Gareth, at once fully comprehending and appreciating the difficulty.

"Sir Bartholomew is known for his genial nature rather than his strength of character. He is like many such weak men. He will go to great lengths to punish those who defy him," said Althea. She smiled a little. "His choice of husband for me was to be of that nature. I was to pay for my lifetime for the sin of upsetting his applecart."

Gareth sat frowning for a moment, then asked, "Your maid has agreed to remain with you?"

"Yes. I would not otherwise have been able to travel in a respectable fashion." Althea's eyes glinted with laughter. "Though I do not care overmuch for such things, I suspected that my great-aunt would refuse to admit me if I did not present the proper appearance."

Gareth cast a keen glance at the tall, thin female with a lantern jaw in black who was sitting quietly at a discreet distance from them. "She looks the sort able and willing to throw a man into a mud pond just on the basis of a familiar glance."

"Yes, that is Darcy. She is loyal to me to a fault," said Althea.

Gareth understood what he thought was the underlying message in her words. "Then you trust her implicitly. Good, that simplifies matters, for we shall have to present a tale to the world to explain the suddenness of our marriage. The less talk there is, the better it will be."

"How do you mean?" asked Althea, her winged brows drawing together in a faint frown of puzzlement.

He smiled at her, amused that as worldly as she was in some ways, she was as yet such a babe. "Any time there is a hole-in-the-wall affair, speculation runs riot. Ours will be to all intents and purposes a runaway match. I do not think that you would like it to become known that you were forced to flee from your stepfather's advances. Nor would I like it whispered that my heir must surely have been conceived before our vows were ever exchanged."

Althea flushed, feeling abruptly far less worldly than she had supposed. "No, I should not like that," she agreed. "What tale shall we put about, then?"

"That the agreement between us was of long standing and that due to the deaths in each of our families— your father and my brother—it was felt best to make the ceremony a quiet one. Thus the reason behind my leave from the army and your traveling here to Berkshire to meet me. We shall have to be wed at Gretna, but no one need know of that. My parents will endorse our tale that we were married privately at Chard. I am certain that your mother and stepfather will be anxious to avoid scandal, and they will repeat the same story," said Gareth.

"I do not care for the notion of Gretna Green," said Althea, frowning a little. Though her upbringing had been unusual in one facet, she nevertheless knew what was considered to be beyond the pale. She had lived in the shadow of scandal all of her life. She did not want to be tainted by whispers for the remainder of her days as well.

"It is reprehensible," agreed Gareth. "But I do not see what other choice we have."

"Perhaps there is a way to secure my mother's permission," said Althea thoughtfully. She looked up to meet his eyes and smiled. "My great-aunt, Lady Aurelia, is a forceful character. Prodded properly, she might very well use her influence on our behalf. That is why I decided to seek out her protection in the first place. I had hoped that she would stand for me when Mama would not."

Gareth kept an impassive expression on his face, though anger surged through him that she had had to resort to such a forlorn hope. What fear and bitterness she must have endured when she was confronted with her own mother's betrayal. "Could you persuade her to such effort? I had gathered that the lady was rather crotchety and intractable," he said.

"Oh, she is indeed all of that. However, she is also very proud. I do not think that the match proposed by Sir Bartholomew will meet with her approval, while your suit must surely prove unexceptional," said Althea.

"My thanks," said Gareth dryly. "How do you propose to enlist the lady's help?"

"I shall continue on to my great-aunt's abode. I believe that when I have put her in possession of the facts, she will at once write to my mother. My mother has always stood in great awe of my great-aunt. I am certain that under those circumstances, she will give her consent that I may be wed," said Althea. Her eyes glinted. "And I do not think that Sir Bartholomew will be able to counter Lady Aurelia's wishes."

"It sounds a plausible enough plan." Gareth made up his mind quickly. "Very well, then; that is how we shall go about it. I shall go up to London to the Commons for the purpose of securing a special license. I shall return with it to your great-aunt's home and we shall be married from there. I take it that Lady Aurelia has a chaplain or that there is a parish church?"

"Yes."

"I shall write a letter that you can carry to her, introducing myself and the reasoning behind our actions. It would be churlish to expect the lady to aid me without appealing to her good nature first," said Gareth.

He left Althea then to go out and see about her chaise.

Althea's dresser approached her mistress. Darcy's sharp eyes had missed nothing, so that even though she had not been able to hear what had been said she knew something of moment had transpired. "My lady, what are you up to now?" she asked sharply.

"I am to be married, Darcy. To Lord Lynley. He will join us at Lady Aurelia's with a special license in hand," said Althea. She laughed at her dresser's shocked expression. "Yes, that is precisely how I felt when his lordship first broached his offer to me. But the more I thought about it, the more strongly I felt that this is just the solution that I need."

"From the skillet into the fire," muttered Darcy, shaking her head. She said nothing more because the gentleman was returning, but her lips were pressed together in firm disapproval over the swift turn of events.

Althea and her dresser were accompanied outside to the waiting carriage. The dresser ducked into the vehicle, carrying the portmanteaus and bandbox.

When Gareth handed Althea up into the chaise, he stayed her a moment by keeping hold of her hand. Looking up at her, he asked softly, "Have you thought what should be done if we fail in this?"

"It will be Gretna," said Althea calmly.

"You do not falter at the thought?"

"My father taught me to take all my fences, but not until I was properly set," said Althea, a faint smile touching her face.

He laughed. Releasing her and closing the door, he stepped back and waved a hand as the chaise set off.

From *Lady Althea's Bargain*
by Gayle Buck

Have you read a Regency lately?

Available at your local bookstore
or call 1-800-253-6476
to order directly with
Visa or Mastercard.